D0175232

A
MAGIC
STEEPED
IN
POISON

A MAGIC STEEPED IN POISON

JUDY I. LIN

FEIWEL AND FRIENDS
New York

WITHDRAWN

A Feiwel and Friends Book
An imprint of Macmillan Publishing Group, LLC
120 Broadway, New York, NY 10271 • fiercereads.com

Copyright © 2022 by Judy I. Lin. All rights reserved.

Our books may be purchased in bulk for promotional, educational, or business use. Please
contact your local bookseller or the Macmillan Corporate and Premium Sales Department at
(800) 221-7945 ext. 5442 or by email at MacmillanSpecialMarkets@macmillan.com.

Library of Congress Cataloging-in-Publication Data

Names: Lin, Judy I., author.
Title: A magic steeped in poison / Judy I. Lin.
Description: First edition. | New York : Feiwel and Friends, 2022. | Series: The book
of tea ; 1 | Audience: Ages 13–18. | Audience: Grades 10–12. | Summary: Ning enters
a cutthroat magical competition to find the kingdom's greatest master of the art of
brewing tea, but political schemes and secrets make her goal of gaining access to royal
physicians to cure her dying sister far more dangerous than she imagined.
Identifiers: LCCN 2021019249 | ISBN 9781250767080 (hardcover) |
ISBN 9781250767097 (ebook)
Subjects: CYAC: Tea—Fiction. | Contests—Fiction. | Princesses—Fiction. |
Magic—Fiction. | LCGFT: Novels.
Classification: LCC PZ7.1.L554 Mag 2022 | DDC [Fic]—dc23
LC record available at https://lccn.loc.gov/2021019249

First edition, 2022
Book design by Michelle Gengaro-Kokmen
Feiwel and Friends logo designed by Filomena Tuosto
Printed in the United States of America

3 5 7 9 10 8 6 4 2

FOR LYRA.
YOU ARE THE BEGINNING OF EVERYTHING.

CHAPTER ONE

THEY SAY YOU CAN SPOT A TRUE SHÉNNÓNG-SHĪ BY THEIR hands—palms colored by the stain of the earth, fingertips scarred from thorns, a permanent crust of soil and blood darkening the crescents of their nails.

I used to look at my hands with pride.

Now, all I can think is, *These are the hands that buried my mother.*

Our house is dim and quiet as I move through the rooms like a thief. Rifling through boxes and drawers, fumbling with things my father kept hidden, so as not to be reminded of his grief. I weave between chairs and baskets, drying racks and jars, my footsteps careful. I can hear Shu coughing softly through the walls, tossing in her bed. She has gotten worse in these past few days.

Soon the poison will take her, as it did our mother.

Which is why I must leave tonight, before my father tries to stop me and I'm bound here by guilt and fear until it is too late. I touch the scroll hidden in the folds of my tunic, to reassure myself it is still there.

I find what I'm looking for in the back of the storeroom: my mother's shénnóng-shī box, hidden from view in a corner cupboard. Memories slip from beneath the opened lid with a sigh, as if they've been waiting for me there in the tea-scented dark. I run my fingers over each groove in the wood, touching every compartment, remembering how we repeated the names of the stored items over and over again. This box is a map of her. Her teachings, her stories, her magic.

But the sight brings back other memories.

A broken teacup. A dark stain on our floor.

I shut the lid quickly.

In the back of the same cupboard, I find other jars, labeled in Mother's meticulous writing. My hands tremble slightly when I open the jar of last summer's tea leaves. The final harvest I helped her with, walking along the garden paths, plucking the leaves from willing branches.

As I inhale the scent of the roasted leaves, the fragrance turns to bitterness on the back of my tongue. I'm reminded of how my last attempts at wielding the magic resulted in tears and failure, and I swore I would not touch these tools again. But that was before the scroll appeared on our doorstep. Failure is no longer an option.

People who don't know any better often reduce the shénnóng-shī to the role of the skilled entertainer, able to artfully pour and present the common drink. Trained shénnóng-shī are proficient at the basics, of course—the flavors appropriate for different occasions, the correct shape and make of the cup to match the tea being served. But the true wielders of Shénnóng magic have their unique specialties. Some brew teas for emotions—compassion, hope, love. Others are able to imbue the body with energy or encourage the drinker to remember something long thought lost. They move past the walls of the body and into the soul itself.

Using the flickering light of the brazier to guide me, I pull out the tray and the accompanying pots, one for steeping and one for resting. Over the sound of the bubbling water, I hear a creak in the next room. I freeze, afraid of a long, dark shadow against the wall, and my father's accompanying wrath.

But it's only the rumbling of Father's snores. I let out a quiet breath and return to my tools. Using the wooden tongs, I pick up the balls of tea leaves and place them in the vessel. With a careful turn of the wrist, the hot water flows over the leaves. They uncurl slowly, releasing their secrets.

The greatest shénnóng-shī can see the future unfolding, wavering in the steam over a well-brewed cup. Once, Mother brewed fù pén zǐ, dried from the leaves of the raspberry bush, for a pregnant woman in the village. The steam burned blue in the morning air, taking the form of four shining needles. From this, she discerned correctly that the child would be stillborn.

I hear her voice as the leaves expand in the water. How she used to tell us the evening fog follows the white wingtips of the Mountain Guardian, the goddess who turns into a bird at dusk. She is the Lady of the South, who dropped a single leaf from her beak into the cup of the First Emperor, and gifted humans the pleasure of tea.

When I was little, Shu and I would trail behind our parents through the gardens and the orchards, baskets at our hips. I often thought I felt the brush of those wingtips against my skin. Sometimes we'd stop to listen as the goddess guided us to the place where a nest of hatchlings chirped, or warned us of heavy rains that could cause rot in the roots if we weren't diligent in turning the land.

I empty the golden liquid from the steeping pot into the one for resting. Mother never allowed us to forget the old, old ways, from before the conquered clans, before the rise and fall of empires. It was in every cup of tea she brewed, a ritual carried out with reverence. It was in the way she knew every single component that entered her tea—the origin of the water, the aroma of the wood that stoked the fire, the vessel the water was heated in. All the way to the leaves plucked by her fingers, steeped in a cup shaped by her own hands and fired in her own kiln. Distilled into liquid contained in the palms of two hands, offered as a blessing.

Here I am. Drink, and be well.

I lean forward and breathe in the sweet scent of apples. I hear the drowsy drone of bees among the wildflower blooms. A feeling of comfort envelops me, wrapping me in warmth. My eyelids start to droop, but the moment dissipates when something darts across my vision.

My entire body prickles with awareness.

A flutter of black wings to my right. A crow, gliding through the smoky dark before disappearing.

It takes a lifetime of training to learn how to read tea like a master, and I had already resigned myself to becoming a physician's apprentice. A year ago, it was decided. For my sister could not stomach the sight of blood, and my father required another pair of steady hands.

Doubt crawls across my skin as my fingers return to clutch the scroll once more. An invitation meant for someone else—my mother's true apprentice.

But Mother is dead. And only one of us is strong enough to travel now.

I force myself to focus. Deep breath in, let it go. The steam wavers in the path of my exhaled breath. No more visions. A trickle of tea is transferred to the small cup for drinking, just a mouthful. The drink goes down my throat with the honey taste of optimism, the promise that summer will last forever . . .

Courage burns bright and strong in my chest, hot as a sunbaked river rock.

Confidence ripples down my limbs. My shoulders pull back, and I feel poised, like a cat ready to leap. The tightness at the bottom of my stomach uncurls slightly. The magic is still there. The gods have not taken it away as punishment for my neglect.

The sound of violent coughing disrupts my concentration. I knock over one of the pots, tea spilling onto the tray as I run into the next room.

My sister struggles to hold herself up with shaking arms, the coughs racking her slender frame. She fumbles for the basin we keep beside her bed, and I pass it to her. Blood splatters against the wood, too much of it, again and again. After an eternity, the heaving finally relents, and she shivers against me.

"Cold," she whispers.

I climb into bed beside her and pull the blankets around us. She clutches at my tunic and draws a rattling breath. I hold her as her breathing eases, and the strained lines beside her mouth smooth away.

We have tried our best, my father and I, to treat Shu in the absence of my mother's knowledge. Me, struggling to recall those childhood lessons, and my father, himself a trained physician, educated at the imperial college. He knows how to set bones and mend cuts, how to treat the external ailments. Although he's familiar with some of the internal medicines, he always deferred to Mother's art for the more complex problems. It was what made their partnership work so well.

My father has used every drop of knowledge he possesses, even swallowed his pride to send a letter to the college for aid. All possible antidotes within his reach, he's tried. But I know the dark truth we circle around.

My sister is dying.

The tonics and tinctures act as a dam to keep the poison at bay, but one day it will spill over. There is nothing we can do to stop it.

And I'm the one who failed her.

In the dark, I wrestle with my thoughts and my worry. I do not want to leave her behind, but there is no other way forward. The scroll is the only answer. Delivered by royal procession to the household of every shénnóng-shī in Dàxī. Shu was the only one at home when we received it. I was in the village with Father, tending to one of his patients. She unfurled it for me to see in the privacy of our bedroom later that evening. The fabric glimmered then, threaded with gold. The dragon rippled from its back, the embroidery so fine it seemed it could come alive and dance around us, leaving flames trailing in its wake.

"This came for us today," she told me with an intensity I've rarely seen from my mild-mannered sister. "An imperial convoy carrying a decree from the princess."

The words I have almost learned by heart: *By Imperial Decree, Princess Li Ying-Zhen welcomes you to a celebration and remembrance of the dowager empress, to be honored through a festival to seek a rising star. All shénnóng-tú are invited to the challenge, and the next shénnóng-shī to serve in the court will be decided. The winner of the competition will be granted a favor from the princess herself.*

The words sing to me, beckoning.

There has not been a shénnóng-shī admitted to court this generation, and to be the one selected would be the highest honor. It would allow a shénnóng-tú to bypass the trials and become a master. Riches would be bestowed on their household, their village celebrated. But it is the hope of the favor that calls out to me the most. I could demand that my sister be attended by the best physicians in the realm, those who have read the pulse of the emperor himself.

My throat clenches as I look down at my sister now, sleeping soundly beside me. If I could take the poison inside of her and ingest it myself, I would do so gladly. I would do anything to ease her suffering.

I brewed that fated cup of tea for Mother and for Shu, from the brick of tea typically distributed to all the emperor's subjects for the Mid-Autumn Festival. For a moment, when the scalding water seeped into the block of leaves, I thought I saw a snake, white and shimmering, writhing in the air. When I waved away the steam, it vanished. I should have known better than to dismiss it.

But not long after, my mother's lips turned black. The snake had been an omen, a warning from the goddess. I didn't listen. Even while she must have been in immense pain, even as the poison ripped through her body, Mother made a tonic that forced my sister to empty her stomach and saved her life.

At least for the time being.

I climb out of bed, careful not to disturb my sister's rest. It doesn't take long to pack the rest of my belongings. The clothes I stuff into a sack, along with the only possession I own of any value: a necklace I was gifted on my tenth birthday. One I will sell to fetch some coin to travel to the capital.

"Ning!" Shu's whisper cuts through the night. I guess she wasn't asleep after all. My heart aches at the sight of her face, pale as milk. She looks like a feral creature from one of Mother's tales—eyes glimmering wild, hair a tangle around her head, a deer wearing human skin.

I kneel at her side while her hands find mine, holding out something small wrapped in cloth. The sharp end of a pin pricks my palm. Unwrapping the handkerchief, I raise the object to the moonlight and see a jeweled hairpin from one of Mother's grateful patrons, a precious memory of the capital. This treasure she had intended for Shu, like the necklace Mother gave to me.

"Take this with you," my sister says, "so you can feel beautiful in the palace. As beautiful as she was."

I open my mouth to speak, but she quiets my protests with a shake of her head.

"You must leave tonight." Her voice takes on a stern tone, sounding like she is the older sister, and me, the younger. "Don't stuff yourself with too many chestnut tarts."

I laugh too loud and swallow it down, gulping back tears in the same breath. What if I come back, and she's gone?

"I believe in you," she says, echoing last night's ferocity, when she told me I had to go to the capital and leave her behind. "I'll tell Father in the morning you are visiting our aunt. That will give you some time before he notices you are gone."

I squeeze her hand tightly, not sure if I can speak. Not sure what I would even say.

"Don't let the Banished Prince catch you in the dark," she whispers.

A childhood tale, a bedtime story we've all grown up on. The Banished Prince and his isle of criminals and brigands. What she means is, *Be safe*.

I press my lips to my sister's forehead and slip out the door.

Chapter Two

With the courage tea still unfurling through my body, I move quicker than usual through the misty night. The moon is a pale disc that lights my way, leading me toward the main road.

Mother used to say there is a beautiful woman who lives on the moon, stolen away by her celestial husband, who coveted her beauty on earth. He built her a crystal palace and gave her a rabbit as a companion, with the hope that the solitude would make her crave his presence. But she was clever and stole the elixir of immortality he had brewed for himself. The gods offered her a place among them, but she chose to remain in her palace, having grown accustomed to the quiet.

They gave her the title of Moon Goddess and named her Ning, for tranquility. I can still remember Mother's soft voice, telling me stories as she stroked my hair. The feeling of love that enveloped me when she told me the origin of my name.

With her voice guiding me, my feet lead me to a small grove of pomelo trees at the outer edge of our orchards. Here, I touch the waxy leaves. These trees were painstakingly raised by my mother from seed. She picked me and Shu up and spun us around when they finally blossomed and bore fruit, her joy encircling us and making us laugh. She's buried here, among the trees. My breath catches when I notice a shimmer of white among the green buds. The first blossom of the season, barely opening in bloom.

Her favorite flower. A sign her soul still lingers here, watching over us.

A sudden wind picks up and rustles the trees. The leaves brush against my hair, as if they sense the sadness inside and wish to offer me comfort.

I run my thumb over the necklace I wear at the base of my throat—the bumps and crevices of the symbol signifying eternity, the cosmic balance. Three souls contained within each of us, separated from our bodies when we die. One returning to the earth, one to the air, and the final soul descending into the wheel of life. I press my lips against the hard, smooth bead at the knot's center.

Grief has a taste, bitter and lingering, but so soft it sometimes disguises itself as sweetness.

Mother, it is here I miss you the most.

I whisper a promise to her, to return with a cure for Shu's illness.

With my hands clasped over my heart, I bow, a promise to the dead and the living, and leave my childhood home behind.

I reach the main road, which leads me close to the slumbering village. I turn back only once, to glance at the night softening around our gardens. Even in the darkness, fog curls around the top of the tea trees, muting their color. A sea of swaying green and white.

That's when I hear something—a curious rustling, birdlike. I pause. There's movement across the tiled roof of a nearby building, down the sloped ridges. I recognize the shape of the rafters—it's the tea warehouse at the edge of town. Holding my breath, I listen. That is no bird. It's the whisper of shoes sliding across the rooftop.

A shadow appears in the dirt before me, cast from above—crouched and furtive. An intruder.

There is no good reason to skulk about the governor's warehouse. Unless you want to be pulled into pieces by four horses, spurred in opposing directions. Or . . . if you have the power to defy him with the strength of three men, the ability to leap up to the rooftop in a single bound, and can cut your way out of a crowd of soldiers with the swiftness of your sword.

The Shadow.

People have spread warnings about the Shadow—the strange figure said to be behind the rash of tea poisonings throughout the land. It is known that bandits lurk near the borders of Dàxī, robbing caravans and hurting anyone who gets in their way. But there is a certain outlaw who does not associate with the list of gangs known to the Ministry of Justice. One outlaw who is able to find hidden treasures and expose secrets, leaving a trail of bodies behind them.

The flash of a crow's wing I saw in the steam above the teacup . . . it was an omen, after all.

Something flies past my head and falls at my feet with a thud. A curse rings above me and the footsteps quicken, scurrying away. It's the curse that piques my interest: If it is the famed Shadow, then they sound terribly human. Curiosity strikes against the suspicion within me, so quick—spark to flame.

I pick up the fallen object and my nail pierces the thin paper covering. Underneath, I feel something familiar—slender strands compacted into a solid block, emitting an earthy smell. A tea brick. I flip over the package, and the red seal leaps up at me in warning.

The governor promised us that all the poisoned bricks have been seized, marked to be destroyed.

I follow the sound of the footsteps on the roof, the dread in my stomach growing tighter with each step, turning from fear to anger. Anger at my mother's death, at Shu's constant pain.

Rolling my shoulders back, a growl rises in my throat as the power of the courage tea moves through my body, encouraging my boldness. I shrug off my belongings and set them against the side of the warehouse. The tea brick, I crush in my hands. The pieces crumble to powder and scatter in a trail behind me as I push myself into a run. The anger feels good. It feels real, a welcome reprieve from my usual helplessness. My mind narrows down to a single point of focus: I cannot let them escape with the poison. Not when it means another girl might have to bury her mother.

I fly around the corner, discarding all pretense at stealth. Only speed matters now.

My eyes catch the dark blur moving through the air, landing in front of me not twenty steps away. Their back is to me and I don't think; I close the distance in the span of two breaths and throw myself at them with all my fury.

We fall to the ground, their balance thrown off by my weight. My hands grab for anything I can find, tightening around fabric, even as the impact of landing sends a wave of pain through my shoulder. They're already moving, twisting under my grasp. I jab the thief under the ribs with my elbow, forcing a breath out in a whoosh. Knowledge gained from assisting my father in holding down grown men as he resets their bones.

Too bad the thief is not one of Father's patients, usually weak from illness or delirious from pain.

They react swiftly, grabbing my right wrist and thrusting it in a direction it's not meant to go. I howl and loosen my grasp. In one fluid motion, they're up on two feet before I can even brush the hair from my eyes.

I scramble less gracefully to my feet, too, and we assess one another. The moon shines bright above our heads, illuminating us both. Their body is lean, a head taller than me. Darkness obscures their features, a figure from a nightmare—a piece of wood covers the upper half of their face. Horns curve out from slashed, angry brows. They appear as the God of Demons, able to slice off the head of troublesome ghosts with one swipe of a broadsword.

A mask, hiding the face of the terror stalking Dàxī.

They pick up a sack that was dropped in our tussle and secure it over their shoulder with a knot. Their gaze burns from behind the mask, mouth settling into a hard line.

Behind me is freedom, down to the docks where the warehouse workers receive their deliveries. They can steal one of the boats or disappear down the alleyway. The other way leads to the center of the village, with a greater likelihood of being caught by the patrols.

They run at me and try to use brute force to knock me aside. But I duck down and barrel toward their legs, trying to throw them off-balance. They sidestep and push me out of the way, but I grab onto the sack as they pass, causing them to stumble.

They whirl around and kick my knee. My leg crumples and I fall onto my arm, sending a searing pain down my left side. Another kick thrusts me down to the dirt. This thief knows exactly where to strike. I am no match.

They try to leave again, but I flop onto my stomach and claw at their legs, forcing them to drag me behind. I can't let them get away with the poison. I suck in a deep breath to scream, but before any sound comes out, a swift punch lands at my temple. I fall back, the pain exploding in my head like firecrackers.

I try to stagger after them, but I can't seem to catch my breath. My vision wavers in front of me, the buildings undulating like trees. Catching myself against the wall, I look up just in time to see a dark figure leap off a few stacked barrels and land on the rooftop.

The thief disappears into the night, with no proof anyone was even here at all. Except for the blood seeping through my hair and the ringing, still echoing through my ears.

CHAPTER THREE

I WALK—LIMPING, MY ANKLE AND FACE THROBBING IN pain—until the barest hint of dawn peeks over the horizon, and a farmer passes me in his wagon. He gives me the once-over and offers me a spot in the back. I doze between bags of millet and rice, with a squawking duck for company. The duck remains outraged at the rough ride until we get to the town of Nánjiāng, which sits on the southern bank of the Jade River, several hours from Sù by horse. It would have taken most of the day if I'd had to walk.

I sell my necklace at a pawnshop in order to afford the ferry ride to the capital. Another memory of my mother, gone. But it isn't until I step on the boat that afternoon, jostled by the crowd, that a sudden pang of loneliness strikes me. In my corner of Sù province, I know all the villagers by face and most by name, and they know me. Here, I am no longer Dr. Zhang's willful daughter. It's like I've put on someone else's face.

I retreat to the back of the ferry and sit down, holding my belongings close. Around me, people laugh and mingle with one another. The air is filled with music from wandering musicians, playing for coin. But I remain anxious, afraid that Shu's lies have not worked and I will be discovered before the ferry leaves the dock.

I feel Father's inevitable disapproval like a heaviness around my neck. He never understood me, even though we slept under the same roof. He would not have permitted me to leave for the competition. He would have found reason to discourage me from this foolish endeavor—I'm too young and untrained to travel alone, Shu is too sick to leave in the care of someone else, he would never leave the village because of his duty to his patients ...

A girl starts to dance in front of me, a welcome reprieve from my worries. The elegant sweeping gestures of her arms are accompanied by the sweet sound of her voice. Delighted claps begin in the crowd as they recognize "The Song of the Beggar Girl."

It is a story about mourning. An orphaned girl with no name. A city lost to war. She walks through the streets, hungry and alone.

Emotions fill the faces of my fellow travelers as the strands of music weave around them. The dancer's swaying movements, the gentle rocking of the boat, the longing of her words, all intermingle into a bitter taste at the back of my throat.

My sister has always been the warm one, quick to smile from the moment she was born, whereas I am prickly and restless, more at home with plants than with people. I could tell the villagers tolerated my presence, but they loved Shu. She could have easily left me behind, surrounded by their adoration, yet she never forgot about me. She always shared what they gave her, defended me against their harsh words.

It's my turn to protect her now.

I lower my head to my arms.

The girl's voice rises keenly above the crowd: "*I have wandered so far from home ...*"

"Here." Something is thrust into my hand, and my eyes snap open to see a woman's concerned face. She has a baby tucked contentedly against her, wrapped in thick fabric. The woman's wide, dark eyes are kind.

"If you eat something, your stomach might settle," she says.

I look down at what she gave me. A piece of dried pork, oily and red. When I bring it to my nose, the smell immediately makes my mouth water. I take a tentative bite, and the meat is both sweet and salty, with a great chew. Gnawing on it bit by bit distracts me from the mournful tune, gives me something to focus on until my head feels a little clearer.

"Thank you," I mumble, wiping the grease on my tunic. "It was delicious."

"First time on the ferry?" she asks, patting the baby rhythmically on the back.

Without waiting for my response, she continues, "I remember my first time traveling to Jia. How overwhelming it was. The sheer number of people! I was embarrassed because I was sick over the railing so many times I could barely stand."

"You seem to be a practiced traveler now," I tell her. There is something about her that reminds me of my mother. She, too, would have helped a stranger without hesitation.

The woman smiles. "I was a girl newly married then. And unknown to me, what I thought was seasickness was actually due to being pregnant with this one's brother." Her gaze turns lovingly toward two people standing a few steps away, one tall, one short—a man and a boy, who looks to be around six years of age.

"Now your children will grow up to be practiced travelers, too," I say.

She laughs. "Every spring we journey to Jia to sweep the tombs of my husband's ancestors and visit those who have moved to the capital. But I'm happy my husband was posted to a provincial town, away from the politics of Jia. It is a simpler life. One I dream of for my son and daughter."

The capital city is where my parents met long ago. My mother returned to our village heavily pregnant, with a stranger at her side who will become her husband. Over the years she would mention the capital in passing. A wistful comment about the sound of the zither, an offhand remark on the perfume of the wisteria flowers that climbed the east wall of the palace.

Shu and I used to ask her: *Why can we not go back, Mama?* We would sit on her lap and beg for more stories about the beauty of the capital. She would tell us there was nothing left for her there, not in comparison to our family. But our family crumbled without her holding us together, and I'm leaving now to save what remains.

The woman kisses the wispy hair on the baby's head with a look of contentment. The baby opens her tiny mouth to yawn, then nestles closer to her mother's chest. This woman lives the life my father wants for me: to be satisfied with food on the table and a comfortable home, a husband who provides. Except my parents have seen the wonders of Jia and lived in its bustling depths, wanted nothing more than what waited for them back home, while I have only known our village and the surrounding countryside.

The time on the ferry passes like a peculiar dream. My companion, Lifen, welcomes me as part of her family. I bounce her baby girl on my knee, pull the boy away from leaning too far over the railing. They refuse to accept any payment for the food and drink they share with me, and my heart is humbled by their kindness.

On our route we pass several towns, picking up and depositing passengers. The journey is a boisterous affair, as the musicians continue to play and vendors sell their goods from baskets they carry on their backs or heads.

At night, I lean against the railing and watch the stars swirl overhead. *Don't be deceived*, my mother once told me. *The stars are not as peaceful as they appear. The astronomers are tasked with deciphering their celestial travels, prophecies that predict the rise and ruin of great families and kingdoms. They burn with as much ferocity as our sun.*

"I used to dream of being a stargazer," a voice interrupts my thoughts. Lifen's husband, Official Yao, sits down heavily beside me on the deck and hands me a clay cup of millet wine. I sip it, and the earthy liquid burns through me, warming my chest. "Didn't have the aptitude for it. Then I wanted to be a poet. Wrote soulful scribbles about the Banished Prince and his sequestered isle."

I laugh at this, imagining him younger and more solemn, brush in hand. "And?"

"Life has a way of taking the wind out of our dreams sometimes," he says, gazing not at me but at the flickering reflection of light on the water.

The heat of the wine emboldens me to announce, "I'm not going to let it."

He laughs, full and relaxed, like he doesn't believe me. When Lifen mentioned that her husband works for the government, I was wary of him at first. But even from our brief conversations, I realized quickly he is remarkably different from the governor who is in charge of my village.

I shudder, thinking of Governor Wang. The formidable man whose black cloak always billowed around him like a dark cloud. The governor never asks; he only knows how to take, to demand, to squeeze until every last remnant can be wrung from the people in his jurisdiction. They say he dragged someone's hound into the road and beat it to death, for all to see. They say he laughed as the creature howled, punishment for its owner's inability to pay the month's taxes.

Governor Wang has taken a particular interest in my father

over the years, as if he sees him as his nemesis. Often the villagers rely on my father to appeal to the officials for leniency when times are hard. He has seen for himself how the people have suffered, yet he is still obedient to the governor's whims. Perhaps this is what makes it hard for me to understand my father. It is the most unforgivable kind of loyalty. Especially when, deep down, I know Governor Wang could have done more to stop the poisonings, and even deeper down, I sometimes suspect he is behind them.

I sit there with Official Yao in companionable silence, sharing sips of millet wine, until my hands and cheeks feel warm and tingly.

After the last drop is poured, we clink our cups together and empty them. He lets out a sigh. "The nice thing about getting old is you realize everything circles back on itself," he says, with a dreamy lilt to his voice. "Things change, but they cycle back, too. The stars continue along their course, the cowherd is always reunited with the maiden. It's comforting in a way. Makes it feel less lonely."

He pats my shoulder and stands, leaving me to my own thoughts.

I stare out at the water. I have never thought of it until now, but he's right. I *am* lonely, not just homesick. I've always felt this way, like I don't belong in the village. Sometimes, late at night, when Shu is peacefully resting and sleep refuses to find me, twisted thoughts come for me instead. They take root and refuse to let go. They whisper terrible things—that my father wishes it were me, and not Shu, who had the sickness. That my family would be happier if I were gone.

Father exists in a circle of his own imagining, each of us playing our roles of how a good doctor and his good daughters should behave. He always believed that if I only spoke the right words, acted the proper way, I wouldn't bring trouble on our household again and again.

Even when Mother was alive, even when I was happy in the gardens with my family, I always felt like I was orbiting them, occupying a similar space but charting my own invisible course, with no idea where it would take me.

Maybe I'm about to find out.

Chapter Four

With my mother's shénnóng-shī chest on my back and my legs cramped from restless sleep aboard the ferry, I finally arrive to chaos at the west gate of the palace the next morning. I raced here after disembarking, with only a hurried goodbye to Lifen and her family. There was no time to even take in more than a glimpse or two of the city itself; I have to gain admittance to the palace before the time listed on the scroll, or the gate will be closed to me.

People crowd the street near the gate, craning their necks for a better view. I feel the pulse of anticipation in my throat as the crowd carries me closer to the entrance. The guards wait at the door with a harassed-looking official of lower rank, who seems irritated that he was given this task. He admits only those who have an invitation in hand.

It's clear some of the shénnóng-shī are well-known in the capital: They accompany their apprentices to the gate, and even the official bows to them, allowing them to pass without requiring a look at their scrolls. Some in the crowd call out their names, cheering. My mother never saw this sort of recognition in the village, and it pains me to see how she could have been revered, instead of taken for granted.

Change is slow, she used to say. The dowager empress recognized this. She was the one who elevated the shénnóng-shī in court, established it as a healing art alongside the physician's branch. She encouraged learning from village apothecaries all the way to the highest-ranked imperial physician. The joining of traditions, old and new. But in our province, Shénnóng magic is still regarded with suspicion—especially if practiced by a woman.

The official casts a cursory glance at my scroll before waving me in. Those of us admitted are crowded into a small courtyard. I catch a glimpse of the palace through a door that has been left slightly ajar. A splash of greenery at the entry, ornamental shrubs and decorative trees. The polished sheen of a railing leading down a path. To come this far and be denied entrance . . . I cannot even consider that possibility.

"If I could have your attention!" Another court official climbs onto a makeshift stage in the middle of the courtyard. "There are one hundred and ten shénnóng-shī recognized in the *Book of Tea*. To ensure you are indeed a shénnóng-tú under their tutelage and able to enter the palace, we will have you pass a simple test of your skills."

Murmurs spread through the crowd as we look at each other, uncertain.

"If you will form a line," the official calls out, "we will begin."

It does make sense to test for those who may have gotten the scroll through illicit means—such as myself. My palms grow damp. I try to wipe them on my tunic furtively.

A short girl with a long braid coiled on top of her head bumps into me. She whispers an apology and a question. "What do you think they will be asking of us?"

"I don't know." I stand on my tiptoes and strain to see. The competitors are lined up at a tent beside a second gate, and what happens inside is obscured from view.

"Step aside," one of the young men walking by says with disdain. He wears an umber tunic, with detailed embroidery in blue thread on the collar and sleeves someone must have toiled over for hours. "A pair of tǔ bāo zi."

I stare at him, seething at the insult. At the implication that we're so poor, we must resort to eating dirt to sustain us.

The girl next to me bristles in turn and hisses at him. "What did you say?" she demands.

He only laughs. "The kitten from Yún thinks she has claws."

A quick glance at the guards standing at the perimeter reminds me not to start a fight, even as I would like nothing more than to push him into the mud where he belongs. I shuffle along next to the girl, head down.

"You're from Yún province?" I murmur, making conversation so I do not put my fist through that arrogant face. I know little about Yún, other than that women who are from there usually wear their hair in a long braid, over the shoulder or pinned in a coil on their head.

She shakes her head and rolls her eyes. "I'm actually from the 'dirt-poor' plateaus of Kallah." I notice her warm copper complexion, a sign that she spends more time under the sun than the shade.

"I'm Ning. Of the 'backward' Sù province."

"I'm Lian. Tigress of the North." She snarls, then her ferocity dissolves into giggles. I laugh, too, glad I'm not the only competitor who has traveled from afar to attend the competition.

It isn't long before we find ourselves at the front of the line. I duck under the lifted door of the tent first. Inside, a man in an official-looking robe sits behind a desk, a guard standing on either side. On the wall above his head unfurls the banner of Dàxī and the great length of the imperial dragon.

"Show us your belongings." The official gestures, and the guards advance.

"Wait!" I try to protest, but they lift the box off my back and take the sack that holds the few items I own.

"We must do this to ensure the safety of the royal family," the official continues, with an uninterested flatness to his voice.

"Surely this must be too much." I gather my clump of clothing in my arms while they continue to rummage through my personal garments. My face burns as I hastily shove everything back into the sack. "Is everyone so paranoid in the capital?"

The younger guard gives me a curious look. "Have you not heard the news? There has been an increase in assassination attempts in the past month. Someone even dared to attack the princess in broad daylight at the Spring Festival!"

"You!" the official's voice booms. "We do not speak to the participants."

"Apologies." The guard ducks his head and drops to one knee.

The official mumbles something that does not sound too friendly under his breath and waves at the other guard to open my mother's shénnóng-shī box. My stomach twists at the thought of another person handling this most precious possession, but I cannot refuse a representative of the emperor.

The beautifully carved redwood chest is lacquered to a shine and gleams even in the low light of the tent. The lid is held in place with a leather strap, which opens to reveal nine compartments. Three on either side of the largest compartment in the center, then two long compartments above and below. The long compartments house my mother's porcelain teacups and bamboo utensils, while the smaller compartments contain an assortment of ingredients.

"Where did you learn your art?" the official asks, checking a scroll that must contain details on the names inscribed in the *Book of Tea*.

"I am apprentice to my mother, Wu Yiting. She is the shénnóng-shī of Xīnyì village of Sù province." The only thing that will allow me to pass this test is the distance of my village from Jia, and the fact that my sister is too young to have been named as my mother's official shénnóng-tú.

"We'll see if that's true" is the only thing the official says as he picks up one of the teacups and examines it with a critical eye. "We have already sent a few impostors to the city dungeons for impersonating a shénnóng-tú. A serious crime."

I wring my hands, waiting for my ruse to be discovered.

He opens one of the jars and peers at the substance, pinching the petals within and smelling the residue on his fingertips. "Tell me what this is."

"Honeysuckle," I reply.

So begins a careful examination of each item in the box. I answer the best I know how, naming each ingredient as a flower or an herb. Sù is an agricultural province, with fertile land suitable for growing rice, but our climate is not ideal for the more valuable types of tea that thrive in the highlands. Instead, my mother sourced different types of flowers to accent the tea and provide flavor, and used their medicinal natures to treat seasonal illnesses.

The official furrows his brow when he pulls out something green, rolling it between his fingers. A fresh bloom. White buds in clusters. I almost gasp, and bite my tongue in order to keep still.

"And this?" He holds it up to his eye, analyzing the blossoms.

"That's a pomelo flower." I hope he doesn't hear the quiver in my voice. "Known for its pungent scent."

Just the few buds in his fingers fill the small space with an almost overwhelming floral perfume. I don't know how the bloom I left undisturbed in Sù followed me all the way to the capital, but somehow I think it must be my mother watching over me still.

The official eyes me, then drops the flower back into the box. "I believe you are who you say you are." I let out a sigh of relief as he stamps my invitation with a royal seal.

"Second Guard Chen?" The young man immediately stands to attention. "Mark this case with her name and take it to the competitors' storeroom."

"Yes, sir." He bows and tries to tug the box away from my hands.

I protest again, my fingers unwilling to let go. I would rather wear rags to the competition than have to give the box to a stranger.

"We will keep your items safe," the official says with disinterest. "There is too high of a risk of poison for everyone to bring their possessions into the palace."

"But . . . my teacups . . . ," I say feebly, and let go of the box.

"Follow him before I change my mind," the official warns with a shake of his head. "I have too many people to question today."

I bow and scurry after the guard, my belly seizing.

"Don't worry," the guard carrying my box whispers to me when the tent flap falls closed behind us. "I'll make sure it's kept safe."

And then the gates open before me, and I am ushered through.

The palace is a vision, an incredible sight to behold. I blink several times to make sure it is real. It is even grander than the great houses I glimpsed from the ferry when we approached the capital. Lacquered pillars too large for me to put my arms around hold up sweeping rooftops of purple tile. I can hardly distinguish the feelings of fear, excitement, and awe churning within me as we shuffle behind the guards. They grumble at us if we linger too long in one spot, but there is so much to marvel at.

A rock garden, arranged in perfect symmetry.

A glimmering koi pond, flickers of orange, white, and gold beneath the rippling surface.

Dainty, dark-branched cherry trees covered in shimmering pink and white flowers.

The heady scents of blossoms and incense swirl through the air of the outdoor pavilions we are guided through. We follow the guards through dizzying turns on wooden bridges and stone platforms until we reach our residences. The young women, only eleven of us, are all to be housed in the same place. The majority of the competitors are men, and many of them are older, on the cusp of being able to attend the shénnóng-shī trials at Hánxiá Academy at the age of twenty-six. I'm happy to see that Lian has also been admitted to the palace, and we both quickly choose to room together.

The stern-faced guard instructs us to remain in this wing of the palace for the duration of the competition. No wandering about the halls and getting in the way of palace servants, no cavorting with court officials to gain insight into the preferences of the judges, no sneaking out the back gate to illicitly obtain expensive ingredients.

Within the residence, each wall is lined with art of wondrous detail. Scrolls of calligraphy hang alongside elaborate paintings of serene bamboo forests or ladies posing gracefully beside orchids. Decorative walls of shelves, housing fragile vases or wood carvings. Even the incense burners are works of art—statues of monkeys in various poses.

I touch a woodprint gingerly, marveling at the detail captured in the tiny eye of a hummingbird. Lian shakes out her blankets beside me, and the embroidered flowers that trail from one edge of the silk coverlet to the other catch my eye with their vivid colors. A lump rises in my throat when I am reminded of Shu. She loves to embroider, spending hours carefully tucking each stitch in place to form petals like these. She should be in the bed next to me, talking about everything we've seen and everything we've yet to experience.

We're not given much time to settle before we are called to the hallway in front of our pavilion. When the mid-hour gong strikes, two servant girls lead us to the first part of the competition. After passing through another maze of hallways and courtyards, we arrive at a splendid building with black stone pillars carved with an aquatic motif. Fish leap from underwater palaces and crabs scuttle around and around in patterns dazzling to the eye. The doors are the height of two men, and they open into a large chamber. The walls are covered in wood panels, which must be expensive to maintain in the humidity of the capital.

Raised platforms to the right and left are already lined with tables and occupied by seated guests. Murmurs and whispered names rise around me, speculating on the identity of the judges who have been selected to oversee the competition. At the far end of the room there is a dais, with two men seated in that place of prominence, and an empty seat in the middle waiting for one final occupant.

"Who are those officials?" I whisper to Lian as we are jostled in the crowd. We hook our arms in order not to be separated in the crowd of competitors, who are all pushing their way forward for a better view. Our feet slide on the wood floors, polished to a gleaming shine.

"The one to the left is the Minister of Rites, Song Ling," she says. From the little I know of the court, I'm aware that this is one of the highest-ranked men in the kingdom. The four ministers oversee the Court of Officials, who advise the emperor on the governance of Dàxī.

"The one to the right is the Esteemed Qian." This name I recognize from one of Mother's lessons: He was the shénnóng-shī who the dowager empress recognized when she was the regent. His silver hair and long, flowing beard make him look like one of the philosophers from the classic tales. "The princess must have called him back from the academy to attend the competition. Last I heard from my mentor, he had gone to Yěliǔ to study some ancient texts."

I'd assumed that Lian, because she is from a more distant province like me, would be less attuned to the politics of the court. But it appears my new friend also has connections in the palace. Before I can ask any other questions, the heralds call for quiet, and we kneel.

Minister Song stands to speak. "Greetings to the shénnóng-tú of our great empire. You are part of our celebrations to honor the late Dowager Empress Wuyang and her legacy. The High Lady regarded the art of tea with great respect. It is present in our culture, in our ancestry. It is a gift from the gods themselves."

The minister drones on about the virtues of tea until my legs grow numb from kneeling. Finally, we are told to rise.

"Her Imperial Highness, the Princess Ying-Zhen!" the herald cries out.

The princess walks in through the side door, her posture erect, her movements composed. Her handmaiden follows at her side, hand on the hilt of her sword. I remember the words of the guard, about the assassination attempts that trail this young woman, and I shiver.

Even though the princess's ceremonial robe must be heavy on her shoulders, she does not give any indication of straining under its weight. The robe is colored a shade of purple so dark it is almost black. As she moves, it sways behind her, and the threads shimmer and ripple, revealing mountain peaks and winding rivers in silver thread. She wears the kingdom on her back.

When she turns to face us, I can see how her skin glows like a pearl, even from a distance. Her mouth is a bright spot of red, like a flower petal. She settles into the chair between the minister and the shénnóng-shī and speaks:

"I look forward to what you have to present to us." Even while sitting, the voice of the princess carries over the hall, with the confidence of one who knows she will be listened to. "The competition will commence this evening in the Courtyard of Promising Future. As the Ascending Emperor once said, farmers are the backbone of the country, and our food sustains the soul. Each of you will be assigned a dish from your province. I would like you to brew a tea that is the perfect accompaniment to your dish.

"But—" Those lips curve into a smile. "We endeavor to make each test as fair as possible. All of you will receive three silver yuan and two hours in the market to purchase your teas and additives. Those found to have spent more than the allotted amount or who do not return in time will be disqualified."

Grumbles run through the crowd, no doubt from those with the money to purchase the more expensive teas that could have gained a foothold over others.

"The first test will be open to the public, so all can witness the beauty of the art of Shénnóng." Her keen gaze sweeps over us, and the underlying message is clear: *I trust you will not disappoint me.*

The princess stands to take her leave. She is regal, poised, intimidating, older than her nineteen years.

"Glory to the princess!" one of the heralds calls out, his voice ringing down the length of the hall like a gong.

"Glory to the princess!" Those seated raise their cups in a salute. Those of us who are standing kneel and bow instead, touching our foreheads to the ground, remaining so until she leaves the room.

The competition has begun.

CHAPTER FIVE

WE ARE LED DIRECTLY TO THE KITCHENS TO BEGIN PREPArations at once. Steward Yang is a stern-faced woman, with her dark, gray-threaded hair pulled back into a severe bun. She examines our group with an unimpressed sniffle.

"The imperial kitchens have served princes and high officials from faraway lands." She waves two servants over, each holding a basket filled with red tokens. "Do not embarrass the products of my kitchen."

One after another, tokens are pulled out, each carved with our name and the dish we are to complement. Eager hands dart forward to receive them.

My dish is sticky rice dumpling—a simple peasant's dish and one of my favorites. Glutinous rice stuffed with peanuts, wrapped in bamboo leaves, and steamed. It is something farmers can carry around with them for lunch, tied to their sashes with string.

"Rice cake?" Lian scoffs as she shows me her token. "How typical."

"Do you have an issue with your assignment?" The steward descends on us menacingly, and Lian squeaks out a negative. The two of us scurry away before she can exact her punishment.

Outside the entrance to the kitchens, Lian starts listing an assortment of regional cuisines the kitchens could have picked from Kallah, and it's enough to make my stomach growl. Fish cooked in a spicy and sour sauce, sweet milk batter grilled on a stick, duck with honey rubbed all over its skin and roasted to a golden brown.

She must have sounded passionate enough that even the guard standing by the door chimes in: "I prefer pòsū myself. Fried crispy, filled with ham and sugar." He closes his eyes, like he's savoring the taste of it in his mind. "Sounds like home."

Lian looks delighted. "I thought I'd met all the people from Kallah in the palace."

The young man beams back, flashing white teeth. "I only transferred here a few months ago."

"It's nice to meet you, brother." Lian touches her hand to her chest and bows. The guard bows in turn, mirroring her stance.

The sound of the mid-hour gong ripples through the air, reminding us of the urgency of our task. With a quick goodbye to Lian's new acquaintance, we hurry to catch up with the other competitors.

The city opens to us when we are let out of the palace. Lian navigates through the street confidently, braid swinging, and I follow. We end up in a market when she finally slows her brisk walk.

I take in the lively energy around me, to invigorate myself for the trial ahead. Ladies sashay by with long flowing dresses, their servants following closely behind, carrying their purchases. We pass by fabric shops, with beautiful bolts of silk and cotton lined up for sale. I furtively touch a few of the fabrics, just to experience the luxurious feel of them against my skin, so different from the homespun materials I am used to. Another narrow street seems to contain only small shops with an assortment of inks and brushes for calligraphy and painting. A part of me longs to stare at them for a while, to take in the sweeping curves and assertive strokes on the scrolls or the landscapes with the wisps of cloud on top of sharp peaks, the boats made of bamboo sailing serenely by.

Drinking all this in, I could see Shu everywhere. She would have loved that light green outfit worn by a young noblewoman perusing a brush stall, the color reminiscent of the first buds of spring. Instead of lingering by the calligraphy shop, her interest would have been in the embroidery stretched over frames, depicting cranes perched on top of thick boughs of white pine. She would have marveled over the shimmer of the feathers and the tiny details of the pine needles. I am determined to one day bring her here, so that she can see it for herself.

I turn my head away from a stall selling embroidered flowers and realize I've lost Lian in the crowd, and a sudden panic grips me.

I'm alone, in this massive city.

The silver pieces weigh heavily in the pouch hidden in my skirt. It is the most money I have ever had on me, and I remember Father's lectures about the capital being full of thieves and degenerates, looking to take advantage of young women. But I take in a deep breath and force my racing heart to settle. I got to Jia on my own, and I can prove to those boys and myself I am not some tŭ bāo zi from Sù.

I walk past residences with imposing gates and try not to gawk at the ornate rafters that hold up their rooftops. Passing through a small stone gate, I enter a market consisting of different fruit vendors. Large baskets sit stacked high with mounds of fruit: pink-skinned dragon fruit, golden kumquats, green and purple plums. The scents of the fruits ripening in the warm afternoon sun is intoxicating, and one of them may be the ingredient I'm looking for to complement my dish.

I have a soft plum from a basket in hand when I notice a young boy dart forward and pick up a piece of fruit that has fallen to the ground. He shoves it into his mouth and chews so eagerly that the juices dribble down his chin. I can't help but smile at his exuberance.

"Thief!" A guard grabs the boy by his shoulders and shakes him, attracting the attention of others around us.

"It fell on the ground!" the boy cries. He tries to run, but the guard knees him in the back and he falls in the dirt.

My amusement quickly dissipates. I've seen the sorts of punishments soldiers are capable of. I've seen grown men with their backs reduced to bloody pulp. This is just a child, and my father isn't here to step in. I must help him on my own.

I grab the boy's arm and haul him up to his feet, wanting to make a run for it. The guard's reaction is quicker than I anticipated and he grabs the child's other arm, so the boy is trapped between the two of us.

"Who are you?" the guard demands.

"This is my brother!" In my desperation, the lie rolls easily from my tongue. "What did he do now?"

"He stole fruit from my stand!" The merchant sweeps in, shaking his fist. "He's lucky I don't demand that his hand be chopped off!"

I almost choke at the absurdity of such a claim, imagining the Ministry of Justice jumping at the whim of a common fruit seller. But I compose myself, remembering I have to return to my task for the competition.

"We've been traveling, good sirs, from the Sù countryside. My brother is only tired and hungry, but we can pay!" With my free hand, I dig in my pocket for a coin.

"Is this true?" The guard shakes the boy again, demanding a

response. I tighten my grip and dig my nails in as well, until the boy is forced to meet my eyes.

Follow my lead, I try to say with only my gaze.

He nods in terror, tears spilling from his eyes now.

"Oh, come off him!" one of the more sympathetic men in the crowd calls out. "He's just a child." Other market-goers nod in agreement. The mood of the audience turns from savoring the spectacle to pity for the sobbing boy, and they start throwing coppers at the fruit seller in disgust.

I can't help but smile as the merchant's face turns bright red, but he's not embarrassed enough to counter his greed for the shining coins. He waves the guard off while his fingers reach eagerly for the gleam of coppers in the dirt.

I pull the young boy aside and speak to him quietly, pressing a few of my own coppers into his hand. "Leave the market as fast as you can and don't get into any more trouble." He nods and wipes the tears and snot off his face with his sleeve before running away.

I remind myself I should listen to my own advice and leave here before I make another mistake. As I move to leave the marketplace, I catch another boy—this one older, about my age—smirking at me. He looks wealthy, from the trim on his cloak—a merchant's son, perhaps, or even someone who is noble-born. He smiles at me knowingly, like we are in on the same joke. I feel a twinge of annoyance and turn away. We couldn't be any more different, he and I, yet he pretends like he understands.

The hour gong rings, time slipping away too fast for my liking. I ask one of the vendors for directions to the teahouse district and he points me down a quiet side alley, assuring me it's a shortcut.

The alley has only a handful of shops, then shuttered doorways. I hurry down the street, intent on my destination, until a skittering noise above distracts me. I slow down and look up, squinting past the curve of the high rooftops. But all I notice is the glare of the sun behind the tiles.

A shadow passes over me briefly.

Only a trick of the light, I try to assure myself.

I look up again. Still nothing. But the memory of the tussle with the masked thief flashes in my mind.

It's not until I'm nearly at the end of the alley that I notice a figure watching me from behind a vendor.

Movement. A swath of black.

I take off running, hoping to catch a better glimpse. It's not the thief. It can't be.

When I run into the next street, it takes only a moment, then I catch sight of them again: the back of their head, moving quickly through the crowd. I slip between the passersby, but the figure keeps a few steps ahead of me, until I've forgotten the number of turns I've taken.

The figure is nowhere to be found.

And I'm completely and utterly lost.

Panic drums in my chest again. I shouldn't have let my curiosity interfere. Quickly, I beg another person for new directions, committing them to memory. But as I turn the corner, a shadow falls over me again.

Don't let the Banished Prince catch you in the dark.

I take a step back, retreating into a solid body ... and an arm that encircles me from behind.

CHAPTER SIX

I REACT ON INSTINCT, STOMPING MY HEEL ONTO MY CAP-tor's toes. The grip of my tunic is released, and I dart forward, suddenly free.

"Wait!" a voice calls out behind me. "Just a moment!"

I turn and see the young man from earlier—the rich boy who smiled at me in the marketplace—hopping on one foot.

"Please don't make me run after you," he says with a wincing laugh.

I take him in—his tousled dark hair brushing his shoulders, the golden warmth of his skin complementing the angles of his face, the glimmer in his eyes, that quirk of a grin. My mother would say he was yù shù lín fēng. The confidence of jade trees in the wind. Someone who takes your breath away.

"I doubt it's broken," I retort, not able to offer false sympathy. "Why are you following me?"

He sets his foot down gently and grimaces as he tests his weight. "I was trying to get your attention, but you were in your own world."

"Where I come from, it's customary not to grab girls in back alleys," I tell him.

"Yes, I'm sorry for that." He brushes the hair out of his eyes, looking contrite. "I . . . I saw what you did for the boy."

I gauge his expression. He looks sincere. He looks . . . handsome.

Like one of the boys Shu would flirt with in the village. But as I've learned, pretty faces cannot always be trusted, and the pain is his own fault entirely. "What do you want from me?"

"You lied on the boy's behalf," he says, stepping closer, his expression turning earnest. "It was . . . brave. Unexpected. You're not from around here?"

"How can you tell?"

"You talk in the way of someone from the southern provinces, the words coming from the back of your throat. Somewhere upriver, perhaps? But also, the people of Jia don't usually go out of their way to stand up for thieves. Too jaded for acts of kindness. You must be a new arrival. And, well . . . you seem lost. You've been wandering about for quite a while."

Of course I look like a traveler, like I don't belong. Are all the inhabitants in the city so eager to point out those who do not fit in?

He winces again. "I don't mean it that way."

I realize all my emotions must show on my face. Shu used to make fun of me. *Tuck your chin in*, she would say with a laugh, *you look like an insulted rooster*. She is the only one I would allow to tease me in such a way.

"I only want to offer my help."

I look at him warily. "What could you possibly help me with?"

"I know this city. If you are looking to go somewhere or if you're looking for something, I can lead you to the right place. Jia isn't the safest for lone travelers. Haven't you heard the tales? The Shadow could be on the loose, trying to catch you."

I know he is joking, but a shiver shoots through me at the thought, remembering the secrets behind the mask.

A fleeting suspicion brushes my mind. Why did he follow me from the market?

Could he be the Shadow, who I tussled with all the way back in Sù?

But no, these thoughts are irrational. I take in the fineness of his silk tunic and the sheen of the jewels sewn into his belt. He is no bandit, and he has certainly never spent any time in a place like Sù.

The boy grins, and the sunlight makes his eyes sparkle. Something flutters inside me in response. Something not altogether unpleasant.

I do need help finding my way, and he may be able to help me find the tea I need more quickly than me stumbling around in the city, getting lost.

"Where are you going?" he asks. "Studying for an academic exam? Joining a performing troupe? Terrorizing the city guard?" Each option is more absurd than the last, until I can't help but chuckle. It does remind me of my purpose, though, and my mood becomes somber again.

"I'm here for the competition," I say gruffly.

His eyes widen. "A shénnóng-tú, are you? You don't look like you're old enough to attempt the trials."

"The gift can be seen at any age," I say, offended. It's an assurance many shénnóng-shī give their apprentices. Each shénnóng-tú begins with an affinity for magic, but some are simply naturals at the art. If the talent is innate, it will show itself early, as Mother always said. She loved to tell the story of when she found me sifting through the dirt, no more than three years of age, pointing out the places where it sparkled, knowing what plants would thrive there. But I always brushed her away in embarrassment, believing it to be an exaggeration.

"What do you need to find?" He rubs his hands together. "I know all the best shops in the city."

41

"I need a teahouse," I tell him, deciding to trust this stranger if it will get me closer to my goal. "With the best selection of teas."

"I shouldn't be surprised at such a request by a shénnóng-tú," he says. "That should be to the northwest of here. I can show you some of my favorite places along the way."

I quickly calculate the time I have left to gather the items and return to the palace and find this acceptable. "Is there a name I should call my benefactor?"

"You can call me whatever you want," he says with a bow, which seems charming and mocking, all at once. "Scoundrel? Trickster?"

He's acting the way the boys in the village sometimes do with Shu when they are hoping she will pay them attention. No one ever behaves like this with me.

I find it . . . unsettling.

I shake my head.

"Bo, then. You can call me Bo." He follows that with a grin. A common nickname for boys, unlikely to be his real name. Except I don't mind. It would be better not to know. Remove the temptation of looking up the names of the sons of ministers after we part ways. "And you? Defender of the helpless?"

"You can call me . . . Mei." Two can play at this game. The teasing tone of my voice makes me sound like someone else. Someone confident. Flirtatious, even.

He squints at me and chuckles. "Fair enough."

"Did you grow up here?" I ask, following him for a few turns until we emerge onto a bustling square.

"Ah!" he exclaims, not answering my question. "I haven't seen one of these in years!" His expression transforms to one of genuine, boyish delight, almost unbearable in its sweetness. It's as if the real Bo has burst out from behind his facade, like the sun breaking through clouds for the briefest moment, pouring its warmth over me.

I hurry to follow and catch up to him in front of a stall covered by a white marble counter. The artist lifts a ladle out of a bubbling pot of melted sugar and drizzles the outline of a carp on the plain surface. With a few swirls and tilts, he fills in the details, giving the carp long whiskers and zigzag scales. He affixes a wooden rod to it with more sugar, and with a cooling breath, the whole thing is picked up. His happy customer shrieks in delight and wiggles the candy sculpture in the air, where it appears to bob on top of invisible waves.

"You have to try this!" Bo turns to me, with great exuberance. I notice for the first time that despite the auspicious angles of his jaw and brow, his front teeth have a little gap between them. "I used to hoard my coppers for this every time we were allowed to go to the market."

He is as excited as the other children watching the display, and I don't want to disrupt that with a refusal. The artist bids us each to draw a tightly rolled sheet of paper from a bottle, and that will reveal what sort of wondrous creation he will draw for us next.

We sit on the steps of an apothecary to marvel at the golden sculptures, almost too beautiful to eat. My candy tiger roars in mid-pounce, while the dragon in Bo's hand twines sinuously skyward. The sweetness of the malt sugar tingles as it melts against my tongue.

"I could eat this every day," I tell him, and he chortles in response and agreement.

"When I was a child, I once stuffed as much candy as I could into my mouth, until I was sick," he admits.

"What was it like, growing up in the palace?" I ask him.

"It was—" He then stops himself, looking at me sideways. "Clever indeed. I won't fall for your tricks."

I grin back at him, pleased that I almost got him to slip up. "You did grow up here, in Jia. Within or very close to the palace, and yet you don't like to talk about it."

"I grew up in a soldier's household." He chews on the dragon's tail, sugar making his lips shine. "My father was very disciplined. Candy was a treat only permitted at the New Year Festival."

"My father, too, but my mother loved sweets and would sneak us treats." Snacks from Auntie's household would somehow find their way into our house for me and Shu to furtively devour when Father was away. *The tongue needs a little sweetness*, she'd say. *It teaches the heart how to love.*

Bo brushes his hands on his thighs. "I would have liked to know if my mother loved sweets," he says, looking into the distance. "She died when I was very young."

I look up at him and think about the past few months without my mother. What it would have been like to live without the years of her patient guidance. What it would be like to not only live in a world devoid of her laughter, but to have never heard it at all.

But when he turns to me, his face is open and without sadness. He stands and extends his hand to me, smiling, when I take it.

"Only good things today," he declares.

And with sweetness still lingering on my lips and fingertips, I follow him.

Jia in Bo's eyes is a place that would thrill a small child. He is an attentive guide as we make our way through the city center, on the inevitable path to the teahouse. I find myself walking slowly, wanting to savor the journey, but eventually Bo is true to his word and we enter the district where the teahouses are located.

I wonder how my parents could have ever left this place, so filled with color and light—so much more than what my mother ever told me.

Lanterns hang at the entrances, with the names of the establishments written in calligraphy. Lotus. Peony. Magnolia. Flowers seem to be a common theme.

Beside the entrance to Lotus House, a covered stall is crowded with children. We stop and watch when the curtain flies open, and paper puppets arrive onstage to thunderous applause.

"Once, an emperor in his prime died of a sweating sickness and left two princes, both too young to rule," an unseen narrator begins. "But his mother, now the dowager empress, emerged from her palace and sat behind the elder prince at court. Guided his hand and taught him to be wise and just. When he was twenty two he became worthy of the throne, and when he was thirty-two he threw a great hunt to celebrate his tenth year as ruler."

A white stag flits across the stage, and the emperor on his horse follows. But a stray arrow crosses their path and strikes the emperor in the shoulder. Several children in the audience gasp, and I'm so startled I grab Bo's sleeve.

He laughs. "Steady there. Puppets can be deadly."

I shove him lightly, surprised by how comfortable I feel around him after not long in his company. As if we'd known each other in another life.

"Deep in the forest," the narrator goes on, "an accident such as this could have cost him his life, but the emperor was lucky that a shénnóng-shī lived not far away."

At the mention of the shénnóng-shī, Bo's eyes sweep toward me for a brief second, wanting to see my reaction, then turn back to the puppets.

"The shénnóng-shī mended his wound and drew out the infection and told him his future." The shénnóng-shī puppet has long streaming hair made of strands of silk. Something knots up in my throat as I watch.

The crowd of children joins in—it is a prophecy that every child in Dàxī knows: "Your child will bring you great sorrow and great joy. They will walk a path of starlight, but shadows will follow.

"The emperor scoffed at this, for his empress had not produced any heirs for his line. But a few months later . . . his daughter, the princess, was born."

After the show ends and the crowd begins to disperse, I tell Bo, "The princess is as beautiful as they say. I always thought the poets and artists tended to exaggerate, but she is how they described." Her striking image from earlier today is still fresh in my mind. She's now the regent while the emperor is sequestered in his private quarters due to a serious illness. Could this be the great sorrow the prophecy speaks of?

"Is she? I'm more interested to know if she has truly survived a hundred assassination attempts," Bo says. "Some say the princess has a talisman that can guard her from ill will, or a stone that cures all illness, gifted by the mysterious shénnóng-shī who saved her father's life."

A stone that cures all illness. I stop, causing a girl to stumble into me, but I pay her and her muttered curses no attention. Bo notices that I'm not beside him and looks back at me, puzzled.

"H-have you—" I pause and clear my throat. "Have you seen

this stone?" If the princess really does have such a cure-all, then it's a sign. I have to win this competition.

Bo's expression turns serious. "I should warn you. You should be cautious when you ask questions about Princess Zhen."

"Why is that?"

"She isn't exactly . . . well-liked by everyone. Many blame her for the unrest that is spreading throughout the kingdom. Sickness, poverty, cruel acts committed by the emperor's representatives, and . . . other rumors."

I know the rumors to which he refers—we heard whispers of them even in our rural province. About the clumsy handling of the northern floods. About the princess being too young to act as regent. Questions about who is really the one behind the throne. Words too dangerous to utter in the capital.

"Rumors? You mean . . . the poison?"

Bo furrows his brow. "You ask a lot of questions, don't you?"

"You avoid a lot of answers."

"That I do." He gives me that disarming grin again, the serious moment passing as quickly as it came. "Azalea House is the one we are looking for, and it's across the street."

Lost in thought—about the rumors, the princess, and the favor I'll ask of her—I'm almost run over by a passing carriage. Bo grabs my arm and pulls me out of harm's way, throwing us both against the side of a building. For a moment, my body is tucked against his, and instead of pushing him away, I find myself leaning into his warmth. His hip against mine, his hands on my arms—

"Careful, clever one," he says next to my ear, his breath stirring my hair. I shiver again, now for an entirely different reason.

He's too close. I jump away, putting distance between us.

Reminding myself I will soon return to the palace, and we will never see each other again.

In the shop area of Azalea House, I am quickly swept away by one of the shopkeepers, who guides me to touch, smell, and taste a variety of tea leaves. There are jars and pots and drawers containing different varieties of tea, towering from floor to ceiling. The capable staff answers all my questions with a professional demeanor, and the mistress overseeing the storefront briskly completes my transaction. With my task done, the package wrapped and tucked under my arm, I feel the tension in my shoulders ease slightly.

Before I can thank Bo and take my leave to the palace, he catches my arm. "Let me buy you at least one cup of tea," he insists. "An apology for scaring you today, and to show you the people of Jia are more welcoming than what you've experienced."

Before I can protest, he leads me toward the open part of the teahouse, where patrons can feast on delicacies paired with the assortment of tea available in the shop. Most teahouses are boisterous affairs, with as many round tables as the proprietor can fit into the dining room. The servers have to navigate through narrow pathways, carrying heavy platters overflowing with steaming pots of tea and accompanying dishes. But even in the first few steps into Azalea House, I can tell it serves a different sort of clientele.

The space is separated with beautiful silk screens and potted plants. Music drifts overhead, but within each compartment there's an illusion of privacy. We are led to a table with a view of the Jade River, the pleasure boats of the rich and the ferries of the commoners drifting by.

There are already candied fruits and smoked watermelon seeds on the table for snacking on, and Bo pops a few of each into his mouth immediately when we sit down. My eyes are too full to join him just yet, distracted by the ornate vase next to us crafted from white porcelain, painted with a figure of a woman playing the lute.

A maid dressed in the softest shades of pastel blue with a sash of pink sets a lacquered tray with tools for preparing tea before us—Bo chooses the Golden Key, a tea so rare and valuable, the proceeds from selling only a handful of it could feed my entire family for a year. Once again, a pang of something like anger and sorrow moves through me.

A servant pours hot coals into a brazier to my right, and another maid sets a kettle on top, already steaming.

"Will our capable Ming be serving you today, honored guest?" The first maid curtsies, her eyes flicking to me. Her lips tighten slightly, but I know it signifies disapproval, probably at either my unkempt appearance or my decidedly un-demure behavior. "Or will you be using your own servant?"

"She's not—" Bo starts, but I stand and smile at her.

"I'll assist him from here," I say. "Leave us."

She stares at me, then her eyes move to the "honored guest" beside me, who just shrugs. The maid opens her mouth to protest, but then the servant sets the bowl of Golden Key before us.

Bo looks at the bowl with curiosity, and I do my best not to snatch it greedily away. A few thin black strands sit at the bottom of the green bowl, which is carved in the shape of a leaf. Using the tongs, I place the strands into the next bowl for steeping the tea.

"Is this what you'll be doing at the competition?" Bo asks.

"I don't know." I'm going in without a mentor, without years of training. My hand shakes slightly, and I fight to still it.

"I'll be thinking of you when they make the proclamations," he says with a smile, and I feel another flutter in my stomach. One I try to excuse, and busy myself with pouring the tea. *It's only because of my own loneliness, my first time traveling from home.*

We each reach for our own cups, and lifting our heads, we sip . . . and the world somehow changes. Steam rises from our cups and hovers between us, blurring our faces. The sounds of the teahouse fall away, until it's only the two of us sitting across from each other. Everything around us wavers, dreamlike. The air is scented with camellia, like walking among the tea trees in autumn, amid white blossoms.

I hear my mother's whispered voice. *If you ever travel to the capital, bring me back just a few strands of Golden Key. It is my dream to taste it.*

Judging by the wonder on his face, I almost believe Bo could hear her, too.

Bo stretches his hand before him, as if compelled by something outside himself. I can see the pinprick of black at the center of his pupils, drawing me in. Almost of its own accord, my own hand lifts, reaching out to him.

Our fingers touch, and it feels like my hand has plunged into a warm pool of water, the heat climbing up my arm. Our fingers intertwine, joined hands glowing with a strange light.

"Mei . . . ," he says, with breathless awe.

That's not me, a voice inside me protests, but how can I explain what I've called forth into being?

A burning begins at the center of my chest, memories being drawn out of me, faster and faster. Mother, teaching us how to pour tea with steady hands. Shu on her knees, retching up blood. A sob rises in my throat.

I can feel the subtle tug of the powers of the tea, as if it's pulling us together. Bo shudders, and suddenly I'm aware he can feel the guilt and the grief gnawing inside me, even if he does not understand the reasons why. His other hand reaches out and cups my cheek; the warmth of it makes me shiver.

He brushes my lip with his thumb, the barest of movements, and I feel sparks trailing behind it. It's too intimate a connection, too much of myself peeling away all at once. I recoil, but he only lets his hand fall from my face so he can catch both of my hands within his own.

Stay, he begs soundlessly. *Show me more.*

He doesn't know, though, until it's too late. The Golden Key is a tea of secrets, and I know—even though I can't explain how or why—that it is now trying to show me Bo's secrets, just as it showed him mine. I'm afraid of what it will uncover, but despite my fear, I don't pull away. The longing inside me for the connection, the desire to stay within the enchantment, is too strong.

As Bo and I stare at each other in wonder, hands still grasped tightly, his shirt begins to glow. A breeze sweeps around us, and I gasp as Bo's shirt blows open slightly, exposing part of his chest, where I notice something like a scar . . . no, a circular imprint blooming red, almost the size of my palm. At the center, there is a character I do not recognize, written in the straight lines of the traditional script. I feel the sizzle of hot iron as if it had touched my own chest, smell the stench of the metal burning away skin, and a vision overcomes me that feels like a memory, as I—no, Bo—fights against the men holding him down. The men who did this to him.

It's a brand.

So much loss. So much, torn away from him . . .

What he lost, I don't understand, but the tide has turned. It's reaching out to him, to pull on the strands of his inner self, to unravel him like it did to me.

And then Bo shoves himself away from the table, and just like that, our connection breaks, like a string snapping.

The world returns in a sudden rush, the noises of the teahouse patrons surrounding us again, too loud for my ears. His stool lands on the floor beside him with a clatter. I notice his shirt is no longer spread open; I wonder if it ever was at all.

"You are capable of prying into human minds." His breath comes short and ragged, and there's a new shine to his eyes. Fear. "What do you want from me?"

I force myself to a center of calm, to be as still as frozen trees in winter. Rumors abound about the shénnóng-shī, for they are few in number, and not everyone understands their abilities. There are some who would call them sorcerers and would rather use the services of the physicians. Calling our abilities superstition, mysticism, or worse. I could lose my head. Especially if this boy is affiliated with a powerful family.

"You are the one who came to me," I say to him, mindful that each word could be my last. "You found me. You spoke to me. You sought *me* out, remember? Who are you, Bo? Who are you really?"

He looks behind me, beyond me, anywhere but at my face. I stare at his throat, waiting for an explanation.

"I believe our bargain is done," he says. "Thank you for your company."

With a blink he is gone, and I am left alone again.

CHAPTER SEVEN

I RETURN TO THE PALACE, READY TO LEAVE THE PECULIAR afternoon behind me like a dream best forgotten. Lian greets me at our residence by clasping my hands and apologizing profusely for losing me in the market. I open my mouth to tell her about everything that happened, but then shut it again when the servants arrive to take our ingredients away in preparation for tonight's competition. I don't yet have the words to describe what occurred. Where do I even start?

Evening has settled into deepening violet when we are separated into two rows to march down long, torchlit hallways toward the Courtyard of Promising Future. As we approach the courtyard, we can already hear the noise of the throng of spectators.

Soldiers block our view past the gate. The light from the torches bounces off their red armor and shields, casting an ominous hue on the walls. When they step aside to admit us, there is only a single path for us to walk shoulder to shoulder. We continue along the line of soldiers until we reach a set of stairs leading upward.

When we reach the first platform, we are directed to separate— one line to the right, one to the left. We fill in the spaces between the rows of black tables, each with a cushion for us to kneel on. At the center of each table, there is a wooden box with our name written on the lid.

It is then that I sneak a glance over at the crowd, and suddenly there's a koi in my gut, wiggling and flipping in protest. I almost sway at the size of the gathering before me. It's but a blur of faces, illuminated by the lanterns that dangle above the spectators' heads. They number more than all the people in my village, several times over. Around the perimeter, more soldiers in red stand guard, faces hidden beneath their helmets.

The stage in front of us continues onto another set of stairs, leading to a platform with empty tables, awaiting the judges. Behind that rises the grand hall, a splendor of Dàxī's architecture, built in the days of the Ascended Emperor. A bell is struck, and the crowd quiets, following the cue. A herald dressed in resplendent purple appears at the top of the steps to make the proclamation.

"Welcome all to join in the celebrations honoring Dowager Empress Wuyang, long may her name resound in the heavens. The princess hopes all have enjoyed the feast shared with you today . . ." He pauses for a moment. "The emperor sends his regrets that he is unable to attend. He will be eagerly awaiting the results in his chambers and will personally bless the winner when the time comes."

Stomps and shouts arise from the assembly, demands to see the emperor, for an explanation as to why he will not be making an appearance. The herald raises his arm to quiet the din before speaking again.

"Our competitors and our honorable judges! The Minister of Rites, Song Ling. The Marquis Kuang of Ānhé province, from which our most precious tea originates. Elder Guo of the venerable Hánxiá Academy, and . . . Grand Chancellor Zhou."

As they are named, the judges descend the steps from the balcony of the Great Hall to the upper platform. My gaze rests on the imposing figure of the chancellor, his hair done in a severe topknot, clad in a dark-colored ceremonial robe bereft of embroidery. He is known for his commoner background, as someone who rose through the ranks due to his shrewd intelligence and his high marks in the imperial examinations. He surveys the crowd with keen eyes, his expression betraying nothing.

"Finally, we welcome Her Imperial Highness, the Princess Li Ying-Zhen!" She appears at the balcony to cheers, but there are also a few scattered jeers and hisses. I remember what Bo said to me: that she is not well-liked by all, that the people grow restless.

The princess slowly descends. Her robe, its train cascading down the steps, is even finer than the one she wore at our welcome ceremony. Hundreds of embroidered cranes fly from her shoulders, over a midnight sky gradually lightening to the palest blue. Her hair is swept up atop her head, adorned with jeweled pins shaped like birds that sparkle in the light. She takes her seat at the center of the table, the other judges framing her on either side.

Minister Song stands, voice booming out over the crowd. "What these competitors before you do not know is that our judges have already reviewed their choice ingredients. They have deemed half of the competitors worthy of partaking in the first round."

Startled at this sudden turn, we look at each other in confusion.

"You will lift the lid from your box," the minister continues. "If you see your dish and the tea contained within, then you will continue today. If your box is empty, please leave immediately."

There are gasps and murmurs—from both the stage and the crowd—and I freeze. This could be it. Gone before I've even had a chance to brew a single cup.

I reach out with shaking hands. Around me, people yell in happiness or despair. Some of the younger apprentices are crying as soldiers assist them down the steps. I shut my eyes, terrified of the emptiness I may find within. Taking a deep breath, I lift the lid and look down.

There is a dish inside my box.

Tears spring to my eyes as I take in the two plump rice dumplings, glistening on a carefully cut triangle of banana leaf, a dusting of crushed peanuts on top. The dumplings are smaller in scale, meant to be popped into one's mouth in one bite. Despite the pressure of the moment, all I can think of is how the village aunties would have complained. What a waste of time to make something so small!

I glance around and take in the fact that we've—just like that—gone from over fifty competitors to twenty-some. The way forward will still be steep, but I've made it past the first step.

I catch Lian's eye. She, too, has made it through. The same is not true for many of the girls housed in our residence; I can see a few of them dejectedly leaving the stage.

Now, servants in red livery begin to set up for the next step of the competition on the judges' platform. A small brazier filled with hot coals is placed to the left of the prepared table, a pot filled with water placed on top to boil. And finally, a row of teacups, numbering five—one for each taster. I can't tell the material of the utensils even when I squint. I'll know when it's my turn.

Just like a martial arts fighter, each belief system follows a different style that the shénnóng-shī believes to produce the best cup of tea. But the outcome depends on the practitioner and the rules of the competition. In previous trials to determine whether an apprentice could become worthy of the rank of shénnóng-shī, it was rumored that one session involved identifying a selection of tea leaves, all unlabeled—the apprentices had to discern the teas by scent alone. In another session, all the shénnóng-tú were blindfolded before preparing their tea, to test their steadiness of hand. The trials were all held in secret, the knowledge passed down from teacher to student. Now, we are on display for all to see.

A young shénnóng-tú named Chen Shao goes first, and I recognize him as the one who uttered the slur at us before the gates. With the arrogant confidence of a man who has known his station all his life, he flips his robe behind him with flair before kneeling. When you're told since you came out of the womb that you can do anything, why would you ever hesitate? If you were told at birth that the world is supposed to bow down to you, you would think it natural that you are destined to climb.

The mood from the crowd is expectant, watching his every move.

"What dish do you have for us today?" Elder Guo asks.

Shao bows in a courtly manner before answering. "I am from the Western District of Jia, renowned for our arts, culture, and famous teahouses. My dish for you today is an appetizer of crystal shrimp and chives."

He lifts up a piece with his chopsticks—pink shrimp speckled with green and encased in a thin, translucent skin made of rice. He bites into it, chews and tastes, before proceeding.

Even though Shao seems incredibly arrogant, I have to admit it is indeed magical to watch him prepare a cup of tea. The water reaches a gentle boil, then he uses it to rinse all his vessels. In his tradition, each of the steps of serving tea has a name, following an ancient story of one of the old gods. A story Mother taught to me from the time I could hold a teacup.

As the water flows down the side of the pots, it forms beads that shimmer like silver scales. *Dragon Shakes Off the Morning Dew After Sleeping.*

He carefully scoops a set amount of tea leaves into the first pot, then swishes the water inside, each movement exaggerated for his audience to see. *Dragon Encircles His Royal Residence.*

With a quick turn of the wrist, he swirls the water three times, then pours it out into the tray from a great height, causing the people to gasp. It trickles into the basin below, not a drop wasted. *Rolling Waves Announce His Displeasure.*

He fills the first pot again with hot water, this time allowing the tea to steep.

Head bowed, he waits, and this is when the servants enter, presenting each of the judges with a dish of crystal shrimp.

When the time is up, he rinses the second pot again, and while it's still steaming, he fills it with the steeped tea. Then the tea is carefully poured into each of the five teacups without spilling. *The Dragon Enters the Palace, and the Usurper Is Cast Aside.*

I admire the precision of his movements, and the way the golden tea obeys him.

"Look, look!" Those closest to the stage jostle, calling out as they gaze up at the performance. The steam from all five cups joins to form the brief, rippling outline of a dragon, before dissipating, demonstrating Shao's competence in illusion magic.

Servants quickly step forward to ferry one of the small cups to each of the judges.

The results are unanimous. Each judge throws down a wooden tile on the floor below, to be picked up by an attendant and hung on a hook for all to see. Four purple tiles proclaim him *Excellent.*

"I would expect nothing less from one who apprenticed to the Esteemed Qian." The princess smiles her approval, and I suppress an eye roll. Of course Shao is legacy. Already a front-runner, expected to win because he follows in the footsteps of a renowned mentor. "Tell me, is it true you had to pass tests, each more grueling than the last, in order to gain a spot as his apprentice?"

"I hope the princess will not ask me to divulge my teacher's secrets," Shao says with an edge of flirtation. The audience titters, then gives thunderous applause, scandalized and intrigued by this haughty and good-looking young man.

The competition continues, and I am so dazzled by the sheer variety of teas and techniques that I could almost forget the nausea roiling inside me.

Palate-cleansing white tea to accompany the sweets typical of Yún province, the high mountain streams feeding into tender leaves that provide notes of peppermint. Able to coax droplets of rain from the sky.

Roasted black tea with a rich and earthy flavor to counteract the spice of the broths favored by the people of Huá prefecture, a district to the west of Jia.

The heaviness of a fried taro dumpling is lightened by green tea mildly scented with flowers. Both specialties of a southern city nicknamed the City of Jasmine.

All the different cuisines and people celebrated are given their turn. Each time a region is announced, their people in the audience cheer. I can see then the cleverness of the competition. If the princess is looking to uplift the spirits of the people, as Bo implied, she has surely succeeded, dazzling their eyes and ensuring that every corner of Dàxī is seen and recognized. The public is intent, their reactions pure. They boo those they dislike, and cheer their favored competitors.

When Lian is called, I try to give her an encouraging smile, but her eyes are focused on the task ahead. She has lost her cheerful demeanor. She reaches the table and, head down, begins the ritual.

But her hands shake so hard, the dish she lifts out of the tray slips and clatters against the teapots. I wince.

"Clumsy!" a faceless stranger jeers from within the crowd.

Lian jumps to her feet and bows. "I'm sorry, I'm sorry, Your Excellencies."

"I'm only a minister and not worthy of such a title," Minister Song says dryly, but not unkindly, and the spectators chuckle. "What is your name, child?"

"I'm Lian," she says. "Of the Kallah plateau." She names herself in her people's way, no family name, and the marquis's face twitches in response.

"There is no need to rush." Minister Song gestures lightly. "Please, begin again."

Like most of the others, Lian prepares her tea without speaking. There is only the clinking of the teapot as it is set on the wood, the slight clatter of the dishes against one another, but gentler this time.

The judges pick up the neat white rolls with their chopsticks and take a tentative bite.

"What is your dish?" the elder asks. "I have not tasted something like this before."

"These are rice cakes," Lian replies. "Rolled around brown sugar sauce and peanuts."

"It's quite an . . . acquired taste." Elder Guo sets half her portion back down on the plate, uneaten.

Lian's technique is unique even among the variations of the other provinces. Her choice of tea is in the form of a brick, which is commonly thought to be an inferior variety of tea leaves, a mixture of all the broken bits of stems and discarded leaves. After slicing a piece of compressed tea off, she places it into her pot. To her bowl, she adds an assortment of ingredients I cannot discern from where I am seated.

The princess leans forward, her eyes shining intently in the lantern light, watching Lian's every movement. As the servants approach the judges with the cups, the scent of cinnamon drifts by in the air.

"Tell us about each ingredient." Minister Song lifts his cup and wafts the steam toward his nose.

"Tea, to represent the bitterness of life," Lian says in a small voice, then, clearing her throat, she speaks a little louder. "Red sugar cubes and walnuts for sweetness. Then inside us all, there is a spark. Peppercorns and ginger, to awaken the fire within."

When the bowls are placed in front of the judges, I take note of their expressions. Elder Guo is definitely a traditionalist—she barely touches her mouth to her cup before placing it back down. Minister Song appears to be more receptive, savoring each mouthful carefully. The marquis wrinkles his nose in distaste, sipping at his cup hurriedly as if eager to move on to the next competitor. The chancellor's stoic features say nothing. The princess appears contemplative, considering the remnants in her cup.

I clench my fist in my lap, wanting to protest their dismissal, to tell them there are other ways of representing Shénnóng than with flamboyant ceremony. But even I know I need to keep my head down and remain quiet. Instead, I hold my breath for Lian as the judges cast their verdict.

Two red tokens for *No*, while Minister Song provides a purple token in the affirmative. Surprisingly, the chancellor also provides a purple token, with a nod in Lian's direction.

"Not an altogether unpleasant taste," he comments. "A subtle use of magic to invigorate the mind."

It comes down to the princess. She drains what remains in the cup and smiles.

"It lingers on the palate, a lovely progression," she says, delicately patting her mouth with a handkerchief. She sets down a purple token. "And so you, too, shall linger in the competition."

"Thank you!" Lian bows deeply, her happiness evident. The audience, charmed by her sincerity, claps and cheers for her.

I, too, can't help but break into applause.

Until I realize it's my turn.

Chapter Eight

YOU CANNOT COMMUNE WITH THE GODS IN SILENCE.

This is what my mother always taught us: The art of Shénnóng is a dialogue. For her, it is not one of meditation and quiet or tradition and rigidity. It is a dance between people, a communion between and beyond the body. To understand a patron's ailments or a loved one's needs, you must be close to them.

To pay tribute to Shénnóng is an intimate experience, a bond.

It is not, I realize, something I ever watched her conduct in public with a crowd of passive onlookers. She did not *perform.*

I'm shaking as I walk toward the judges' platform. Not only because I am nervous, but also because I feel like a tree stripped of its leaves, naked and exposed, about to attempt something so personal in front of so many. I remind myself of the moment in the teahouse, when I experienced the connection with Bo. I accomplished it once, and I will again. Mother always told me I had the gift. Raw and uncultivated, but mine to reject and mine to embrace. It will not leave me so easily.

I am still my mother's daughter.

I clear my throat so I can raise my voice for all to hear.

"I am from Sù, Highness." I address the princess directly—only the barest arch of her brow indicates her surprise. My sister would know I speak to stop my whole body from shaking, but I realize too late I may be too forward, not knowing the niceties of the capital. I can only forge ahead, despite my mistake. "The renowned Poet Bai once penned a poem about my province."

There are quiet murmurs from the crowd, but I pay them no mind as I begin by removing the lids from the jars, setting them on the black tray.

"'The figures toil on the distant hills.'" I pluck the curled balls of tea leaves from the tin, sending them rolling to the bottom of the cup one by one. I conjure the image of me and Shu tumbling down the hills past the tea trees at home, laughing even as our baskets of harvested leaves tumble with us, scattering our efforts into our hair and our clothes. Tea for me is home, is joy, is family.

"'Mist, blurring them in the distance.'" The water settles over the tea, steam rising upward and misting my cheeks as I bend over it. For a moment, I feel the tears I only let fall in the privacy of night. In my peripheral vision, I see the princess's face soften. I sense a sorrowful memory, conjured by the power of the tea.

"'The tea is served while I recline.'" I swirl the tea and pour it into the resting pot, the liquid disappearing below as I imagine the poet, reclining, observing my homeland through a window.

"'My fingers, ink-stained.'" Instead of using the tongs, I select three petals of osmanthus with my own fingers and let them fall into each teacup. Elder Guo's hand opens slightly, as if catching the flowers for herself, remembering when she, too, used to dance in the petals as a little girl.

"'No more blessed than the fragrant scent of green.'"

These are merely human hands, another thing my mother often said. When someone brings up one of my blunders, like the fire that once destroyed our fields, or when I got in the way of Governor Wang's temper and made things worse. *Human hands make mistakes, Ning, but they are the hands the gods gave us. We use them to make amends, to do good things.*

And that is what this brew is about. The taste of being human. Of making mistakes. Of being young again. The reminder that sometimes we are the laborer and sometimes we are the one at rest.

The final step is the pour. The tea I chose has barely been treated in the sun, retaining most of the flavor in the leaves. The slightest hint of green remains, caressing the edges of the flower petals. It reminds me of growth, reaching for the light—

"How *dare* she?!"

I do not have time to admire my work before a sharp line of pain cuts across my hand as the teacup nearest me shatters. I'm too stunned to react. Gasps can be heard as Marquis Kuang stands, pointing his finger accusingly in my direction.

The steam dissipates, and the memories I so carefully cultivated scatter into nothing. Chancellor Zhou blinks, confusion furrowing his brow, as if waking from a pleasant daydream. The wonderment on Elder Guo's face smooths back into a careful mask.

"Are you making a mockery of this competition?" the marquis snarls, spittle shooting out of his mouth. "She dares to quote the Revolutionary Bai? Is she calling us indulgent and spoiled?!"

My insides quivering in fear, I stare down at my feet, not wanting my face to so easily reveal my emotions again. My not-so-respectful thoughts on the nobility with their tender hearts and paper-thin skins.

"Honored One," I say carefully. "Poet Bai's words only mean to suggest that tea is a drink for both peasants and poets. It can be enjoyed by the lowest farmer and the highest ranks of the court, as befitting your grand status."

I swallow. The poem had always seemed special to me. It never occurred to me that it was written by a revolutionary. But now I recall the stories of Poet Bai's beheading, and I realize I may have made a grave mistake.

"This...this cup of tea shows my...my joy at serving you today," I stutter. All I can hear is my father's voice, chastising me, telling me I have made yet another error.

There's a rumble in the crowd to my right—voices, overlapping one another.

"Leave her alone!" someone yells out.

Another voice joins theirs. "She speaks the truth!"

The tension in the air rises, like a pot of boiling water about to spill over.

"My dear marquis." It's the grand chancellor who chooses to speak, stepping around the table and putting his hand on the nobleman's arm. He looks calm, amused even. Though Chancellor Zhou bends down, as if the words are intended only for his peer, his voice is loud enough for everyone to hear. "Do you not understand? We must praise the dowager empress. For we can tell the world, even our peasants can quote poetry!"

Laughter ripples through the audience, their agitation subsiding slightly. All eyes are on the marquis and the chancellor. The marquis is clearly still furious, but the chancellor is all smiles, eager to return the competition to a more celebratory mood. But from my perspective, I can see the way his hand is clutched tight on the marquis's arm. A warning for him not to go further.

I'm relieved that Chancellor Zhou seems to be on my side—maybe I will get out of this unscathed.

But no sooner have I let out a breath when a sudden whistle pierces the dark, then a thud.

An arrow quivers in the center of the judges' table.

I stumble backward as gasps and screams fill the air, then there is the sound of boots hitting the ground. A flurry of movement to my right and the brush of fabric against my arm. A purple cloak flutters in the air, and in the distance, the princess's bodyguard leaps over the heads of the crowd with deadly intent. If the person who fired the arrow is still out there, she will find them.

In the blink of an eye, soldiers are everywhere, all around me, a crush of metal and sweat filling my nose.

"Protect the princess!" someone yells.

Bo's casual words return to me: *A hundred assassination attempts...*

A dark shadow flies overhead, leaping from the crowd to the stage in one bound. Then, the flash of a blade.

I duck for cover and see the princess's pale face as she notices the new threat. But the figure who leaped toward her turns his body to face the whistle of several more arrows, a lithe serpent spiraling through a whirlpool, protecting her from the barbed tips.

Whoever he is, he's not the attacker. He's defending her from the unknown threat.

His sword darts like a silver fish in the middle of a swiftly moving stream, and the arrows fall to the ground, harmless.

More chaos erupts around us as the audience reacts, realizing what has happened. Some cheer for the brave savior of the princess, while others attempt to flee. Just before the guards pull the mystery rescuer aside and force him off the platform, his hood falls back and the swinging light of a lantern catches his face.

My heart stutters.

It's Bo.

Behind him, the wind tugs at the robe of the princess as she is rushed up the stairs by her guards, the embroidered cranes fluttering in the air as if flying, sparkling in the light.

The chancellor sways, blood dripping down his shoulder. He shouts something in the commotion, but all I can see is his mouth moving.

Someone shoves me aside. I try to stay small, huddled, out of the way. There's nowhere safe to go. As I cling to the table, I can't help but notice two of my cups turned on their side, their contents spilled, reduced to smears on the wood.

Just like my hopes in the competition. Ruined.

CHAPTER NINE

I DON'T KNOW HOW I RETURN TO THE RESIDENCE. I REMEM-
ber figures casting shadows on the walls of the courtyard, blurs of
bodies and faces, soldiers forming a wall around me and the other
competitors. And then I'm stumbling through our gate.

Lian calls my name, her lips pinched, eyes anxious. "You're
bleeding," she tells me.

I can see the cut on my hand, the thin trickle of blood, but I
don't feel it.

"Do you . . . do you think I failed?" I ask her.

"Don't think about that right now," she says, trying to sound
comforting. "You'll find out in the morning."

I thought it would be impossible to sleep, but I wake up to the
morning light streaming in from the opened shutters, and a servant
setting down a basin of water in front of the dressing table.

"You have been called to the next gathering," she informs me
with a curtsy, before leaving me to make myself presentable. I
can spare only a longing glance at the morning meal set out in the
main room. A warm pot of bubbling congee, small plates of pick-
led cucumber dotted with chilis, shredded chicken glistening with
sesame oil. My stomach growls in protest, but the hunger is chased

away when I see soldiers through the opened front gate of our residence.

We are escorted to meet the other competitors, and there is a somber feeling in the air, in stark contrast to the celebratory atmosphere of the day before. As we are hurried down the long hallways, I notice the fine armor of the guards. In the dim light, the details were obscured, but now in the daylight I can see the finery, the design carved into the back plate. A tiger, the symbol of the Ministry of War.

I recall, uneasily, the nightmares that troubled my sleep last night. I was surrounded by a circle of jeering soldiers, kept at bay only by the long staff I held in my hand. As they approached, menacingly, I swung and my aim struck true, only to realize with horror there was nothing beneath the helmets. They had no heads.

I bump into Lian, not realizing we've stopped before a pavilion. She steadies me and gives me a worried look. I manage a smile back at her, holding up my bandaged hand and mouthing my thanks for her help last night. She gives me a nod in return.

I compose myself and look around to see another well-tended garden, consisting of a collection of miniature trees and stone sculptures. We do not wait too long before the herald announces the entrance of Minister Song, who appears in distinguished white robes. We kneel, the crushed stones of the path digging into our knees. He addresses us with a severe expression, hands clasped behind him.

"I know there has been much speculation about the events of last evening, but the competition must continue. We refuse to be intimidated by those who believe the great emperor will cower before their attempts at disruption and disharmony." His nostrils flare as he continues his speech, as if unable to consider such a distasteful thought. "The Ministry of Justice will be investigating the identity of the assassins who dared to attack the princess, and for her safety, the competition will resume in a few days' time. Until then, all competitors will remain in the palace. I expect your full cooperation with officials of the investigative bureau."

It might be a trick of the light, but I can swear the minister's eyes meet mine with disapproval for a moment.

"For the few of you who have yet to be judged, the princess has mercifully granted you passage to the next round of the competition due to the circumstances. Do not squander this opportunity." There are a few grumbles from a handful of competitors, but they are quickly silenced with a pointed look from the minister.

We bow our heads and murmur our acknowledgment, seventeen voices joined together in one. After we rise, I shuffle alongside the other shénnóng-tú, pondering my good fortune at being able to move on to the next round even with my misstep, but then my arm is caught by one of the guards.

"Your presence is requested." His voice is low, but it still draws the attention of a few of the other competitors, who scurry away as if the guard would start grabbing them, too, if they hesitated for too long. I despise the expression flitting across their faces, a mixture of pity and revulsion.

The hand of the guard is secure at my elbow as he guides me back to the pavilion. My empty stomach clenches in worry when I realize the grand chancellor has replaced Minister Song at the pavilion. I'm pushed up the stone steps to stand before him, uncertain of what I should say or what I should do with my hands.

Chancellor Zhou regards the water beyond the barrier, and I follow his gaze. The water lilies have yet to bloom, but their leaves are spreading on the water's surface. Clusters of purple-red, vibrant green, a sign that nature continues to wake in the progression of the season.

I straighten my posture to match his. If I am to be removed from the competition, I can exit with dignity at least.

"Zhang Ning," he says, voice hard as granite. "You are aware your . . . *choices* last night have consequences?"

Moments fly through my mind like arrows shot into the night. The implication of the poet's words. The shattered teacup.

"I didn't know," I whisper. Regret spreads into my limbs, making me wish I could crumble into ash in front of him. If only I had the courage to look at him, defiant, to name myself as a revolutionary. But I am nothing except cowardice. "I meant no harm."

He sighs and rubs his chin with his thumb. "I will not lie to you, child. Your path forward in this competition will be difficult. You have gained the animosity of the Marquis of Ānhé. If he had his way, you would be out of the competition already."

My hope sinks, heavy as a stone. I am to be sent back to Sù. I am certain of it.

"You are lucky the princess indicated she was interested in seeing more of your skills." He turns to face me, gaze intent. "I also see potential in you."

I lower myself to my knees, legs weak with fear and relief.

"You are too kind to someone as unworthy as me," I murmur.

"Please, stand." He grasps my arm and helps me up, but his next words send a trickle of cold down my spine. "I hesitate to call it a kindness. You will be placed under careful scrutiny. One more misstep, and you will be thrown into the dungeons."

I force myself to look at him. With his neatly trimmed beard, the set of his jaw, he reminds me a little of my grandfather—they both have a commanding presence. I meet his steady gaze, sensing no malice there, only a warning.

"If we uncover any ties between you and the assassins, then you and everyone you care about will be banished to Lùzhou. You and your family will die there, along with any other co-conspirators who are foolish enough to oppose the emperor."

"I understand." I manage to force the words out. Lùzhou is a peninsula and a collection of islands to the east. Also known as the Emerald Isles, it is known to be the most dangerous place in the empire, where ruthless criminals are exiled in service to the kingdom. They are destined for backbreaking work in the salt marshes or the stone quarries. To live there is to await a slow death.

Chancellor Zhou sighs and waves his hand, dismissing me.

I flee, afraid still for my place in the palace. I have drawn attention to myself, and not the kind of attention that will benefit my position. I have to be especially careful of how my actions will affect the way the judges view me. It's clear that if I make the wrong step, my family will suffer. I will not forget again.

What have I gotten myself into?

I return to the residence to find Lian picking away at her bowl of congee.

"You're here!" She shoots up out of her seat, her spoon falling to the table with a clatter. "What happened? What did the minister say?"

I sit down on the stool with a sigh, my face in my hands. "I spoke with the chancellor instead. He wanted to make sure my family are not revolutionaries. I'm permitted to stay in the competition for now, but I've made an enemy of the marquis."

"The marquis." Lian snorts, sitting down again. She pours us both cups of tea. I accept mine with a nod, grateful for the warmth between my hands. "That old toad. So set in his ways."

The familiarity with which she speaks about the ministers and the officials in the palace reminds me to ask, "Lian, how do you know so many officials of the court?"

"You didn't know?" She looks at me, then says with a casual shrug, "I'm the daughter of the diplomat to the western kingdoms, Ambassador Luo."

"That's why you are so familiar with the palace..." I process this revelation slowly. "And why you know everyone from Kallah."

She gives me a wry smile. "We are bound by the sky tenets. My mother believes in knowing your people, that we are all one family."

"In Sù we do not see many people from outside our province," I tell her. "Pardon my ignorance."

Lian laughs. "Don't be so formal with me, Ning. I hate the rigidity of the court. I feel more comfortable on horseback under an open sky."

I nod. I can understand that. Just like my place used to be among the plants of the medicine garden. Someday I will return to the rows of tea trees and call myself a Daughter of Shénnóng.

Lian tells me about her home while we nibble on our now-cold breakfast. Kallah is a small province. Some of its more agriculturally minded people have settled in pockets of fertile areas. Others live a nomadic life, raising animals on the grasslands. They trade mostly with those from Yún province, which is why Shao must have mistaken her for a girl from Yún.

The freedom she describes is alluring. She doesn't have to settle in the same village and see the same faces for the rest of her life. She's free to travel where she wants. She's probably seen more of the world than any of us, traveled farther than I could have ever imagined.

Lian suddenly throws her chopsticks down. "I can't stand this cold congee. It isn't enough to sustain me. Let's go to the kitchens."

I protest, mindful of the rules and my new status as "one to be watched," but Lian ignores me as she purposefully strides through the gardens. I half expect the guards to stop us from entering the servants' area, but they do not pay us any attention. Enticing scents drift by—smoke and roasted meat, the familiar smell of earthy herbs and damp fronds.

Lian strolls into the imperial kitchens as if she owns the place, with a nod at one of the servants hurrying by with an armful of vegetables. I glance about, curiosity overruling caution, as the last time we were only permitted to crowd into the kitchen courtyard. Now, past the stacks of steamers and racks of dried fish, we are in the kitchen proper.

The room is busy with activity. The sounds of chopping, cooking, and fire crackling fill the space. It is a large room, but to my surprise, this is only one wing of the kitchen. I can see moon doors separating one section from another. Servants walk in and out of the round openings, carrying trays piled high with ingredients or baskets filled with goods. Against the far wall, there is a line of wood-burning stoves made of brick. More steamers are stacked up against the wall in the corner. In the center of the room there is a huge table covered with flour. The uniforms of the servants here are dusted with white, their hands working rapidly. The dough is rolled out, filled, then fingers pinch and turn, quickly closing each bundle, before it lands on a tray.

Before I can discern what sort of filling goes into those buns, a rumbling voice greets us.

"It's been a long time!"

Lian is picked up by a giant of a man and spun around, before being placed back down on the floor, both of them laughing.

"Small Wu!" She giggles. "Here, meet my friend, Zhang Ning."

This man looks as big and broad as an ox, contrary to his name, with bronzed skin and fierce eyebrows that match his bushy beard.

"Pleasure." He bows, clasping his massive hands across his chest, before turning again to look at Lian with affection. "I thought once you advanced in the competition you would forget about your people."

She smirks. "Do you think my father would permit it? Or that you would allow me to forget?"

He lets out a round of booming laughter, clapping her on the back.

Lian turns to me and explains, "Small Wu is in charge of the bakery. He's an expert at jiaozi, pastries, buns . . ."

Such food is not common in my province, as we eat mostly rice, but I am ready to experience it all.

"She does not believe you, girl. She thinks I am meant for chopping wood and stoking the fires." Small Wu gives me a wink, then chuckles at my attempts to reassure him.

"I wake the dough." He flexes the muscles in his arm. "I am up before the dawn gong. Not like those lazy workers of the Rice Department." He looks at a woman who is walking by. She gives a snort, not even pausing to respond to his antics.

"Small Wu!" one of the women at the table barks at him. "The dough is not going to work itself!"

"Yes, yes, boss!" He stands up tall and salutes her, before turning to us again with a grin. "Some days I am not sure if I am in charge of the staff or if they are in charge of me. You two should make yourself useful as well."

"Us?" I look at Lian, who smiles.

"When I was little, before I left for my apprenticeship, I used to sneak into the kitchen all the time. They give the best treats." She pulls me to the table. "If we help, there will be food for us, too."

We're set to work on basic tasks. Small Wu pulls out a mound of dough almost the size of his torso from a basket and slams it on the table, releasing a cloud of flour into the air. Lian and I are given—thankfully—much smaller balls of dough to work with. We roll them into logs and then cut them into small pieces to be weighed on the scales. It reminds me of working in my father's storeroom. Rolling, cutting, weighing, the familiarity of each step. I feel the pang of homesickness in my chest once more, but I force myself to swallow it away. Instead, I focus on making the best buns possible.

We cover the bottom of several wicker baskets with these dough balls, sending them down the line to be filled. At the end of the table, a great number of buns are placed on trays to rise, enough for a feast. After Small Wu deems that we've worked enough, we are able to try some for ourselves.

Rolling out our shoulders after having been hunched over for so long, we set up tables in the courtyard for the midday meal. We're given buns with airy pockets inside them, a center of juicy pork, mixed with minced shallots and ginger. They taste even sweeter because we shaped these with our own hands. Small Wu introduces us to his husband, A'bing, who works in the Fish Department. He brings us a soup pot with an entire deep-fried fish head bobbing inside it, surrounded by cabbage, tofu, gold mushrooms, and bean curd. The soup is meant to be eaten with grilled radish cakes, for dipping into the broth.

The conversation flows as freely around the table as the wine that is constantly poured into our cups. I listen to Small Wu and Lian's banter, reminiscing about funny moments they shared long ago. A'bing is subjected to Lian's teasing about enduring Small Wu's bad jokes and how she imagined herself their matchmaker when they first met. I'm content to sit there for a while, letting the sound of their voices wash over me. If I close my eyes, I can pretend I am back home again, listening to the melodic sound of my mother's voice and my father's responses.

"Boss! Boss!" A rapid patter of feet and a slam of a tray on the table. I jump, eyes snapping open. A boy leaps on top of a stool, shaking with excitement. Small Wu pulls him back before he lands face-first in the fish soup. "Have I got news for you!"

Small Wu sits him back down properly on the stool and gives him a small bun to munch on. "What did you hear, Qing'er?"

"Ruwan from the Meat Department has a cousin who is one of the chancellor's maids," Qing'er says through a mouthful of food. "When she came by to pick up the morning's deliveries, she said she found out about the assassins. The princess's handmaiden caught the ones who shot those arrows. Ruwan said they bit through their tongues to avoid interrogation!" I grimace at this grisly knowledge, but the boy doesn't seem to be disturbed. He takes a huge bite of his bun and gulps it down quickly before exclaiming, "But that's not the most exciting part!"

Without pausing for breath, he continues, "They found out who the warrior was. You know, the one who saved the princess last night?"

"Who?" Small Wu arches a brow. My heart starts to race, thinking about Bo. The way he stood in front of the arrows, unafraid, the sword an extension of himself. The echo of my own words ringing in my head: *Who are you, Bo? Who are you really?*

"His full name is..." The boy puffs up, cheeks flushing with pride at his discovery. "Li Kang. Son of Li Yuan, once known as the Prince of Dài."

The attentive expressions of the people around the table change swiftly. Small Wu's face darkens, exchanging an uneasy look with A'bing.

Qing'er doesn't seem to notice and continues on, gleefully announcing, "The son of the Banished Prince himself!"

The big man quickly pulls the boy toward him and slaps his hand over his mouth. Qing'er wiggles under his grasp, but he's not strong enough to break his hold.

"We don't speak of him within these walls," Small Wu whispers harshly, his eyes darting toward the main door. Everyone nods, acknowledging his warning. I can sense his protectiveness, the care he has for the people under his charge.

"We must never speak his true name, you hear?" The big man finally lets go, but he waves his finger sternly at the now contrite-looking child. "Before you were born, the emperor executed all those he suspected to be in alliance with his brother. Although his tolerance of the man's existence has grown over the years, it's still not something we can speak of freely. What do I always tell you?"

"There is always someone listening," Qing'er responds, sullenly scratching his head. "I remember, boss."

"Good." Small Wu returns to his meal.

The conversation resumes, but I'm only half paying attention. I worry over this new knowledge. I knew the Banished Prince was a figure in history, but I thought it was something in the distant past. Scattered bones in a river. Not a person who may still be alive today.

"Once the princess learned of his identity, she pulled him from the dungeons." Qing'er still chatters away, but quieter this time. "The maid said he was seen by the princess in the early hours, then he was moved to the west wing."

Lian's eyes widen at that. "The dignitaries' wing? He isn't an assassin after all?"

Small Wu barks out a laugh. "Deep within the palace? Surrounded by guards? I suspect the princess wants to keep a close eye on him and wait out his true intentions. They will reveal themselves in time . . . They always do."

"True," A'bing chimes in. "His father was a cunning rival for the throne. Perhaps the son hopes to establish himself by following in his father's footsteps."

With that ominous thought in mind, I find myself with more questions. Wondering where Bo's—no, *Kang's*—true intentions lie.

Chapter Ten

EAGER TO THINK ABOUT SOMETHING ELSE BESIDES QING'ER'S gruesome revelations, we busy ourselves with the afternoon's tasks—filling up large baskets wider than my arms with buns. The baskets are stacked, then placed on top of woks filled with bubbling water. The steam rises through the bottoms, allowing the buns to puff up and cook to perfection.

I don't want to think about the role I may have played in the assassination attempt on the princess. Did I somehow provide Bo with access to the palace, or offer some information that helped him with his purpose? I curse myself for being so naive, believing that I could have innocently drawn the attention of a handsome stranger in the market.

In order to stop myself from contemplating all the ways the interrogators in the imperial dungeons could torture me, I ask Small Wu questions. Questions about this vegetable and that grain, about the various names and cooking processes of the humble dumpling. I learn about the varieties of wheat, which are not so common in the southern provinces, but common to Yún and Huá. He doesn't mind my queries, even while he directs the others to their tasks. The errand boys like Qing'er are responsible for chopping wood and feeding the fires that have to constantly run hot in order to keep the steamers running. With all the activity, the temperature of the kitchen rises in the heat of the afternoon. I can feel the sweat dripping under my arms, my damp tunic sticking to my back.

During the brief reprieve when the fires have to be stoked again, one of the bakery women, Qiuyue, gives me a cool cloth to wipe my brow.

"I'm glad we have your help," she says to me. "Steward Yang has been even more . . . particular of late. These are trying times."

"It is not only her, though," a man next to us comments. "This winter has been hard on all of us. The coughing sickness spread through the palace, but the royal physicians have been busy attending to the emperor. We used to have their occasional assistance, but no longer."

"And now with the competition, there are many more mouths to feed," a sour-faced woman across the table says. "We have so much more to do with much less."

"At least they're here, Mingwen," Qiuyue tells her. "They're helping. Not like . . ." Her voice trails off as a commotion arises in the doorway. Our attention is drawn to two maidservants, dressed in sleek finery, like two peacocks strutting in a crowd of plain yellow-tuft chickens. A harried-looking servant points in our direction.

"Like the worthless lumps hovering around the court?" Mingwen sniffs and then grudgingly agrees. "Yes, I suppose you're right."

One of the peacock girls, her robes in a delicate shade of green and her sash a deep azure, comes over with her head raised.

"Where's the tray for the marquis?" she demands. "He grows impatient. He needs to attend to his guests."

Mingwen purses her lips, like she's considering saying something sharp to the girls, but then decides against it.

"The desserts are ready," she finally says after a long, awkward pause. Snapping her fingers, she gestures for the man beside her to bring what is needed. He returns with a beautiful lacquered red basket, gold designs of leaves and flowers winding their way up the handle. The lid has painted red birds perched on black vines curving in beguiling patterns.

The maidservant appears displeased, and she folds her hands in front of her, refusing to take the offered basket. The man stands there, uncertain, looking over at Mingwen.

The older woman lifts a brow. "Is there a problem?"

"We have to examine everything." The maidservant smiles sweetly. "To ensure that it is up to the standards of the marquis."

"Of course," Mingwen says with exaggerated sincerity. She gestures for the man to place the basket on the table and lifts the lid with a flourish, waving him away. "Anything for the marquis."

She pulls out the inner tray and lays it upon the table. Bite-size sesame balls are clustered in blue porcelain bowls. Lotus blossom cookies sit on another plate; each bloom is the size of my palm, fried to golden perfection. There is also a small tray of milky white jellies, sliced into squares and rolled in shredded coconut. The young woman examines the desserts with a critical eye before nodding and returning them to the basket, then tucking it under one arm.

The other maidservant joins us, arms laden with trays. "But where are the pastries? The additional order was placed earlier this morning. He will not be pleased if they are missing."

"Come." Qiuyue grabs my arm and guides me back to the other side of the table. "They'll continue to posture at each other, then we'll be scolded for the work piling up."

I return my attention this time to rolling balls of sweetened red bean paste, destined for the inside of pastries. Beside me, Qiuyue rolls out the thin wrappers that will turn into the flaky topping. With nimble fingers, she tucks the red bean balls into the dough pockets, shapes them into discs, and places the toppers above. They are ready now for the egg wash that gives them a beautiful yellow color.

When the maidservants are finally sent off, Mingwen returns to the table with a huff and attacks the bowl of red bean paste with frenzied energy.

"Who do they think they are?" she mutters, hands moving quickly. "All our departments are busy, but the marquis assumes we have time to cater to his every request."

"I'm sure they are under pressure as well," Qiuyue offers, establishing who has the more positive outlook in this group of servants.

Mingwen snorts, but before she says anything further, a look of panic flits across her face. "She's here," she hisses. "Look busy."

Steward Yang stalks into the bakery, wearing a scowl worthy of a thunderstorm.

"Small Wu!" she barks. The tall man walks over to her and bows. Everyone lowers their gaze and pretends to be attentive to their jobs, but I know we are all straining to hear what she wants. "I heard from Marquis Kuang's household that the pastries they asked for have not yet arrived," the steward says with displeasure. "I don't like hearing complaints about any of our departments."

Small Wu scratches the back of his head. "Uh, we are a bit delayed because of the buns we have to make for tonight's banquet. They sent over the request midmorning and we are still catching up."

"Unacceptable!" Steward Yang claps her hands together, making me and Qiuyue jump. "We treat every guest of the emperor like we are serving his own distinguished presence."

She approaches us, and her gaze scrutinizes us all, just like when she examined the competitors before the first round. I hold my breath, hoping she does not notice me. But the stars do not smile upon me today, for her shadow falls across the table.

She looks down at me. "And who are you?"

My mind goes blank. I must have appeared like a gaping fish, because Small Wu comes to my rescue.

"This is one of the new hires," he says without missing a step, giving her a placid smile. "We needed more help because of the competition."

"If she's one of the new girls, then she won't be as quick at the pastries. Come with me. And where is Qing'er?" She marches away.

I look around, desperate for help. I can see Lian hiding on the other side of the room.

Small Wu shakes his head. "You should follow her," he says.

And so I have no choice but to walk through the moon doors. Steward Yang is speaking with Qing'er, and she points in my direction. He jogs toward me, giving me a wave in greeting.

"Follow me," he says, leading me away from where the steward is in the process of terrorizing another maid, who cowers under the weight of a heavy pot. "I'll get you a more appropriate outfit."

I have never imagined I would be pulling on a servant's uniform outside the imperial kitchens, pretending to be a maid. But pretense seems to be a cloak I've been donning lately, so I tighten the sash around my waist and step out from behind the shed.

Steward Yang scrutinizes me and thrusts a basket into my arms. "Pull yourself together. We're asking you to deliver pastries, not poison." She laughs like she's told a splendid joke, but it reminds me again of Small Wu's warning—*someone is always listening*. It isn't the most reassuring thought.

Qing'er leads me past other wings of the kitchen. One room is filled with people stirring large pots, wafting delicious scents our way. Another room rings with the thud of knives hitting wood, chefs chopping away at huge slabs of meat.

When we are past the kitchens, we walk down a narrow path that meanders through a garden, sidestepping to allow other servants to pass. So many people coming and going. There must be more servants in the palace than there are in the entirety of my village. So many to serve the whims of so few.

Back home, we bend to the wishes of the governor. We break our backs under his yoke, but at least we don't have to live constantly under his scrutiny. Not until the next time his retinue passes through our village and the taxes are due. We are free, in a sense—free to wander outside the walls of our village, yet trapped by the restrictions of family and obligation. Here, the servants are surrounded by the riches of Dàxī, able to wear fine clothes and eat rich palace foods, but they must endure the capricious moods of those they serve.

While we cross various courtyards, Qing'er points out the different features of the palace we walk past. The Hall of Celestial Harmony is one I recognize, with its wide black pillars. We pass the back of the Great Hall, which sits upon a series of stone steps, and I have to crane my neck to even catch a glimpse of the carved wood doors.

"I've never been allowed up here," the boy continues. "But I hear the servants of that hall polish the floors every morning and evening until everything shines."

We walk past a grassy bank lined with weeping willows, long branches skimming the surface of a winding creek. He explains how the residences of the west wing are aired out and opened only when there are guests of state. These could be representatives from other kingdoms or the nobles and officials who do not have their own residences within Jia.

"Your judges also reside there." He nods at an attendant sweeping the walk. "Even though Minister Song and the chancellor have their private homes in the city. It is a great honor."

A man floats by in a small boat. His hair is peppered gray, swept back in a tight topknot. He sweeps his oar through the pond, looking like a figure from an old painting.

"Who is that?" I ask Qing'er, wondering if he is a scholar looking for inspiration in the reflections of the trees and the water.

"Oh, him? That's Lao Huang, the garbageman," Qing'er says. "He cleans the pond every afternoon."

I wince, having to laugh at myself, at how little I know of anything in the capital. What a fool I am.

I tug at the sleeves of my uniform when it snags a passing branch, unused to the feeling of so many layers of fabric. The flowing sleeves are the latest fashion everywhere in the capital, but they are cumbersome despite their beautiful embroidery. I am certain everyone will see how uncomfortable I am. I should have just told Steward Yang who I was and suffered the consequences.

The marquis is set up at the Residence of Autumnal Longing— the area's name is written in calligraphy on a plaque hanging over the gate. The double doors open to a small courtyard with a bamboo grove to the right. One of the household servants is already there, waiting to greet us. She leads us toward the building to the left of the courtyard, making tutting noises of displeasure, huffing, "It's unacceptable for the kitchen to have such a delay."

We're led through a sitting area decorated with water and ink paintings. I long to take a closer look at them, but we're hurried past. Our basket is set by two trays already prepared with bowls and plates crafted of fine porcelain, pale green veined with dark crackle. Qing'er helps me transfer our collection of tidbits carefully, finishing with the round pastries with different colors of dots on top to indicate the flavor hidden within, the edges already crumbling under our touch.

"What is this?" the servant demands, pointing at each pastry in turn. Thankfully, Qing'er is able to answer on my behalf. One is filled with pork floss and mung bean for a sweet and savory treat, while another is stuffed with salted egg custard. The thinner pieces have a layer of winter-melon paste inside or a mixture of dates and crushed nuts.

When the treats are arranged to her satisfaction, she gathers up one of the trays and gestures for me to take the other.

"I can help—" Qing'er reaches for it, but she shakes her head.

"The marquis does not like to be served by boys."

I look at Qing'er, but he steps back, giving me an apologetic look.

"And he does *not* like to be kept waiting," she snaps impatiently, already walking away. "Come along."

I stand there rooted, tray in hand. I'm going to be recognized when I step into the room, and the marquis will banish me from the competition and from the palace.

"You have to go," Qing'er whispers, tugging at my sleeve.

My chest tightens. I will go in and out quickly, and pray my face is plain enough that I will not be recognized. I force myself to take one step forward, then another.

To face the marquis, who threw a teacup at me. Who is certain I am a traitor to Dàxī.

The servant stops me before a wood-screen door. The sound of music streams out, and the voices of men in low conversation.

88

"Follow my lead," she instructs. "Set the tray on the side table to your right. Do not linger."

I nod.

We step through the door into another lovely room. My eyes are drawn to a map of a city mounted on the wall. A collection of vases, of varying sizes and shapes, line another wall. A musician sits on a stool in the center of the room, plucking at the strings of a pipa.

I hold the tray carefully, moving as fast as I dare so I do not draw attention to myself. I set the tray next to where the other has already been placed, then I spare one curious glance around the room to see which honored guests the marquis is entertaining today.

Marquis Kuang himself holds court up front, reclining on one arm, the picture of lazy indulgence. Around the room there are men seated at small tables, the surfaces already littered with plates and cups. My eyes skim over the faces of the guests, then . . . my heart drops. I recognize the face leering at the lovely musician, and the two men with their heads together, clinking cups. Every single one of them in the room looks familiar.

It's Shao, and other shénnóng-tú from the competition. Breaking the rules, cavorting with the judges.

I suddenly know how it feels to be a rabbit thrown into a nest of vipers. But before I can turn and flee, one of the men lifts his head from his cup and his eyes meet my own.

Chapter Eleven

My breathing is suddenly too loud. I pray the stars will shine kindly on me today, instead of banishing me to a life of ruin and disgrace.

The man stands, swaying on his feet, and points at me. "You—" He stumbles toward me, catching himself on a pillar.

I turn quickly toward the door, but he lunges for me, too quick for me to react, and grabs my arm. I struggle to pull my arm out of his grasp, but his grip is too tight. He pulls me closer, and I can smell the rice wine on him, on his clothes and wafting from his open mouth. It's not only tea these men are partaking in.

I try to push him away, but I'm a bird trapped by a hunter, fluttering uselessly in his grasp.

"Even the palace maids are prettier than the rest." He chuckles.

A flash of anger ignites within me. Embarrassment tinged with fury—at being grabbed, at the thought of this buffoon believing I am his plaything.

"Stop!" I lash out at him, kicking at the side of his knee with one foot and thrusting my elbow into the middle of his chest, where I know it will hurt him the most.

He yelps in pain, letting me go, but the musician finishes her performance at precisely that moment, and the sound of our struggle draws everyone's attention.

I back away, out of reach of his grasping fingers, keeping my head down. The door is just behind me, only a few steps away.

"Please," I whisper, trying to disguise my voice. "I must get back, the kitchens are waiting for me to return."

"You!" The man clutches at his chest with one hand, the other raised in a fist. "You will pay for this!"

"Young man!" The commanding voice of the marquis cuts through the other conversations, dripping with disdain. "You'll respect the servants of the palace. You cannot buy their attention like the whores of the entertainment houses you frequent."

"Do you not understand?" I look up to see the Esteemed Qian standing at one of the tables at the end of the room. From his appearance, that of a wise sage with a flowing white beard, I expected a kindly voice filled with warmth and wisdom. But instead, the voice that comes out is sharp, like he has bitten into a sour plum.

A friend of the young man who grabbed me quickly pulls him back down, his face crimson with shame.

"The astronomers all speak of change in the stars," the Esteemed Qian continues. "It is a period of shifting alliances and fickle natures. It is a time for focus, not for chasing after the skirts of any pretty girl who comes across your path. Not to be glutting your stomach on wine and food. You will have this life if you are the court shénnóng-shī. It will all be within your grasp if you win the competition. You will have all the entertainment houses at your disposal, all the coin you need to buy whatever you want."

Faces nod around the room in smug agreement. I feel my face twist with disgust. How could it be possible that my mother used to revere this man, the one who counseled the dowager empress into supporting the role of the shénnóng-shī in society? Was it because he truly believed in the benefits of Shénnóng's magic, or was it because he was hungry for the power it would provide him?

I'm grabbed and pulled toward the door. I react, struggling, but the next words stop me.

"Wipe that look off your face, or we'll both be killed," the servant whispers into my ear.

"You there!" Shao's voice calls out. "Stop!"

With disgust, the maidservant throws my arm down, leaving me to fend for myself.

I turn, slowly. I make myself as small as I possibly can, to play the part of the demure servant they expect. "Yes?"

"Don't you have to thank Marquis Kuang?" His voice still exudes that lazy, indulgent confidence. "Do you not know your place?"

I look up and see the marquis with his eyes narrowed, as if he will recognize me in the next moment—name me as that girl with the rebel poetry that rolled off my tongue, calling out for the blood of nobles to be spilled. But there is no pointed finger, no accusation.

"M-my thanks, Honored One," I stutter with a curtsy, and flee.

No one chases after me through the halls of the Residence of Autumnal Longing. The only sound is that of my own hurried footsteps and the harsh wheezing of my breath. Before we are permitted to leave the residence, Qing'er and I receive a tongue-lashing from the head of the marquis's household.

"What happened in there?" Qing'er whispers to me when we are finally permitted to leave.

I cannot find the words to explain what I saw; I don't trust myself to speak without screaming. At the injustice of it, at the way these people can disregard the rules without fear of punishment. I can only grab his arm and hurry as far away from that place as we are able. Away from those who already have the opportunities and connections of those who reside in Jia. They can seek an audience with the marquis, receive the personal counsel of the Esteemed Qian. I don't know how I will ever get Shu the help she needs.

Returning to the competitors' residence, I pull off the maidservant's clothes, disgusted that I had thought of them as beautiful. The embroidered finery, the lovely flowing sleeves, all of it pretty and useless. Just another rope for them to bind us with. Looking down at my competitor's robes, I remember how I felt when I pulled them on for the first time. The tentative hope, the brief break of sun through the clouds. The longer I reside in the palace, the more I realize that hope is an illusion. They have already selected who is to be the victor and who is to fail.

Lian bursts into the room when I make the final pull of my sash to ensure I appear presentable, even as my insides tremble.

"You're safe," she says with relief.

"You left me there." My words come out sharper than I expected, and the corners of her mouth drag down into a frown.

"I . . . I'm sorry." She shakes her head, looking contrite. "I know I should have said something, but I froze. It was like I was a child again, getting my hands hit with the rod for eating something meant for the banquet."

A part of me wants to snarl at her and tell her I will not be part of her games any longer, like I have done to the village children around my age who made fun of my clothes and my mannerisms. But a part of me did enjoy the time we spent in the kitchens. It was a welcome distraction from the stress of the competition, and she had helped bandage my hand. It wasn't her fault the steward picked me, and she doesn't have to be kind. She could dismiss me easily, like the others already have.

"I understand," I finally mutter. "It's not your fault. I . . . I saw Marquis Kuang again."

Lian sucks in a breath. "What happened? Did he recognize you?"

It all comes out in a rush. What I saw in the residence, the people I recognized, what the Esteemed Qian said. By the time I'm done speaking, Lian is furious, too, pacing back and forth in our small room.

"Those conniving creatures," she growls. "Everything about Jia is political, as you will soon learn. And the shénnóng-tú . . . they are especially so." She shakes her head with disdain.

"Many who are recognized with an affinity to Shénnóng's art come from families who can afford to nurture that talent. These shénnóng-tú become shénnóng-shī, who use their abilities to help their own families, to gain money or influence. Some of the court cannot be seen at each other's households, so they meet in the tea district instead. They partake in the 'proper' entertainment, but then also conduct meetings in the private rooms."

"That is not what my mother taught me," I say. "She says the magic is to be useful, not for your own personal gain."

"To do otherwise would be a waste." She nods solemnly. "When I first learned the tea spoke to me, I thought it meant I was special. But now I know that even with magic, some of us will always have the advantage."

"In coin, in birth." I sigh.

"This is why I wanted to befriend you that first day in the court-yard," Lian says earnestly. "You know what it is like to be on the outside."

94

Like recognizing like. In some ways, Lian also does not belong, even though she is the ambassador's daughter. Because of the way she dresses, because her ways are not the ways common to those of the capital.

"I see you as my friend, Ning," she says, squeezing my fingers and letting go. "I hope one day you will see me as the same."

"I hope to."

I'm not ready to acknowledge her as that. Not yet. I've learned how people can be different from what they first appear. One thing is for certain: My competitors will not hesitate to step over one another on their way to victory, and I had best figure out a way to catch up before I'm left behind for good.

The palace room I share with Lian grows increasingly stifling as I find myself turning in bed, my body as restless as my mind. Back home, when I was not able to sleep at night, I would leave our house and the sound of Father's snores. I would make my way to the orchard beyond the tea garden and find solace in climbing the trees. I liked the feel of the bark in my hands, finding the footholds and handholds, sending me higher and higher. The soothing rustle of the wind through the trees and the sound of the cicadas were music that I understood. I leave the residence in an attempt to find that solace, careful not to disturb the others.

The courtyard is lined with ornamental stones and low trees along the walls. My hands find nooks and crannies, and I easily pull myself up to the roof to sit on the tiles. The moon watches over the palace tonight, a crescent glimmering through the wisps of clouds.

In the night, the palace is finally quiet. Quiet, but not silent. I can hear the sound of the nightly patrols moving in the distance, even though I cannot see them. Voices speak through an open window, one high, one low. The sound of a flute trills nearby. From my vantage point, I can see the rooftops of the other residences, but I am alone up here, with not even a bird for company.

The palace provides an illusion of space, fitting so many, but we are all walled in. I didn't know I could crave the hills of my village so much until now. I miss the sprawling greenery, the mountains ever watchful in the distance. The soldiers who are posted in our area always complain there is so little to do, so they fill their bellies with cheap wine and cause a ruckus in the market. Yet there is a part of me that even misses the sound of their drunken singing as they stumble through the streets.

I pull my knees close to me as I sit there, remembering playing with Shu among the trees, while she imagined us as dancers or fighters, leaping over the roots in our routines and battles. How much like our mother she was, except instead of retelling old stories she created her own. I remember the feel of my mother's hands, smoothing out the waves of my hair. The bitter brews my father forced us to drink to strengthen our bodies against the winter chill. The pear candy Mother used to give us afterward as a treat. All these memories, as precious as any jewel. Things we do not think to miss until they are gone.

My memories are disrupted by a rustle in the distance. A few birds caw, fleeing into the night. The sound of their wings brings up a feeling of foreboding: The last time I found someone on a rooftop, they struck me and left me for dead. But I don't think the Shadow intended to kill me that night. They would have pulled out a weapon for that. I think they meant for me to live, even if the bandit may be as cruel and coldhearted as all the rumors say. There was some semblance of mercy behind the mask.

My eyes watch, disbelieving, as someone drops onto the stone path of the courtyard. The figure moves, slippery, its shadow sliding over the earth. I dare not breathe. I will myself to become one with the roof itself, to channel the solidity of the tiles under my hands and disappear.

The figure creeps along the side of the building, and I think of Lian, and all the other girls sleeping soundly in there. I tuck a broken tile against my palm.

I know what I must do next.

Chapter Twelve

I DROP FROM THE ROOF WITH A YELL, TUMBLING FEETFIRST into the chest of the person below, sending them sprawling. I land half on top of them and roll off, knowing I have to get the attention of the nearby patrols. I stumble to my feet, but then a hand grabs my shoulder, yanking me back. I fall heavily onto the hard stones. They jump on top of me, hand over my mouth, knee against my stomach, looking down at me in the faint light of the moon.

My heart stutters.

Bo. What is he doing here?

And suddenly, the recognition flares in his eyes, too. There's a shout in the distance, and he quickly pulls me to my feet. We shuffle backward into the trees. We're pressed close enough that I can feel him breathing as we watch the door to the courtyard creak open and a guard poke his head in, torch in hand.

I'm aware—*too* aware—of the warmth of him beside me. The tautness of the muscles in his arm, trembling under my hand. The tension held in the long line of his body, ready to react if the guard discovers us. The door eases shut, and we let out a collective sigh. It's then that I remember he shouldn't be here, and I shouldn't be assisting him.

I throw myself away from him, pressing my back against the solidity of the wall. We regard each other warily. I press my hands into my arms, feeling the aches of bruises I know are blooming from my rough landing.

A sudden wind picks up, spinning around my body and rustling his hair, leaving me hollow and cold.

I remember all his lies. His fake name. His fake identity. The way he wore his hair, as if he was someone not used to the fashions of his city. How he appeared on the dais, how he handled the sword, his training apparent. This boy is more than he seems. Not the slightly clumsy, eager-to-please Bo I met in the market, who spoke about his family and growing up in the capital. This boy, crouching on the ground in the dark, is a weapon.

"What are you doing here?" I stand, wielding my words like a blade, jabbing at him in self-defense. It's a feeling I am used to—knowing that if I'm prickly, no one will approach me. I won't have to listen to criticisms about my dirty nails, my mended clothes.

He stands as well, and opens his hands to show me he's unarmed. "I wanted to see you."

"Why? What could you possibly want with me?" Anger is good. Anger is safe. I choke down my confusion, until it remains only as a tremor in my leg, tapping a frantic beat on the ground.

"To apologize." He steps forward, and I move away.

"Why would the cousin to the princess, son of a prince, need to apologize to me?" I snap. "You made a fool of me, pretended you were just a resident of the capital. Pretended to be kind, when it was all a lie."

"Yes, I suppose I did, but ..." He gives me a wry smile. "So did you."

"Only about a name."

"I've learned a name can be everything." The corner of his mouth lifts as he continues, a mocking lilt to his voice. "Kang, son of the Banished Prince, nephew to the emperor, carrier of the family legacy. Betrayer of the throne, capable of killing without a single thought, able to bend darkness to his will—"

"Not funny," I growl. It grates at me that he doesn't know what is at stake, that he has no idea what he disrupted.

He holds up a hand. "Yes, I'm sorry. I've been told I like to make light of things, especially when they bother me." He gestures to the front steps of the residence. "Please, can we sit? Can we ... talk?"

I keep an eye on him, wary of any sudden movements, as I perch myself on the edge of the step. He sits down beside me, more serious now, and clears his throat.

"I ..." He interrupts himself with a sigh, before starting again. "You reminded me of my life before I left the capital."

He stares down at the ground, fingers making meaningless patterns of swirls and loops on the stone. "I wanted to pretend I was a student in the city, not bound by my family history. I was just a boy who met a girl in the market one spring afternoon and wanted to spend time with her."

For a moment, I warm to the sadness in his voice, and I can almost believe him. But then I remember the flash of his sword in the firelight.

"You swooped down from the rooftops." I'm speaking to him but I'm also reminding myself. "You were captured by the guards. Interrogated and locked away. Now you're in front of me again. How am I to believe you have no supernatural origins? Or no evil intent?"

He glances at me, amusement evident. "Nothing that exciting, I'm afraid. My father still has friends in the palace. The officials have long memories, and ten years is nothing to them. They've arranged for me to stay in the Residence of Winter's Dreaming, under heavy guard. I slipped out during the shift change, but they will be looking for me soon."

Soon. The word hangs between us like a sigh.

"Why don't you leave the palace?" I blurt suddenly. "You can escape. Go back home to your father."

He frowns. "It's not that simple. I came here for a reason, a purpose I have to see fulfilled."

I wait for him to elaborate, but he remains quiet. We sit there in silence, each of us brooding over our own thoughts, until he speaks again.

"But I needed to find you." My gaze flicks over to him; he's watching me, his dark eyes catching the light. "To ... I don't know. Explain myself? Make amends? To ensure I do not leave you with a poor memory of me if I'm to be executed by the end of the week?"

I look at him with horror, and he reaches for me, as if to offer some reassurance, but looks crestfallen when I shrink back. "She has no plans to execute me that I know of. Although I'm sure a few of her advisers would love to pin some nefarious deed to my name."

I stare at him, trying to see him fully this time. Even though he may still be lying at this very moment, I know what the Golden Key revealed. I know for a moment we glimpsed each other's deepest, darkest truths. The brand over his heart. The tea that I poured for my mother. The things that irreparably changed us.

"In my cell, I kept on thinking of our afternoon together," he says softly. "It's been a long time since I've had even an hour like that. No expectations. Without worry. It meant a lot to me." He meets my eyes, earnest again. Vulnerable.

Something still hums between us, a dangerous kind of connection.

"I'm not sure how to prove it to you," he continues. "That I'm still the boy from the market. That everything I said was true. I grew up near the palace. My father is a soldier."

"I wouldn't call the General of Kǎiláng a common soldier." I chuckle, despite myself. Discussions about the general had continued in the kitchens, even after Small Wu's warnings. A reminder of the history of Dàxī. The general carving a bloody arc through the kingdom, consolidating the power of the emperor. The rumors that the general was not content with the tiger seal. He wanted more. More power, more soldiers, more wealth, until he coveted even the dragon throne.

"To everyone he was the general, but he is still my father. The one who took me into his household when I was a baby." He shrugs, lips drawing into a thin line. "I don't want to talk about my father."

"I—" I open my mouth to speak, to ask more questions. About how he came to be the adopted son of the Banished Prince. But the voice of the crier pierces the night, announcing the hour.

He's on his feet before I can blink, alert and ready. It reminds me again that he is more than he claims to be. A threat.

"Tomorrow?" He looks down at me, a question in his voice but a promise in his eyes. "I hope you will give me your name."

Footsteps approach. The patrols must be making their way back. He's still waiting for his answer. It's a risk I can't afford to take. I'm in enough trouble as it is. But I also need to see him again.

I nod.

The quick flash of his smile in the night is lightning against a dark sky. And then he's gone before I can even take another breath, vanishing back over the rooftops.

For this one night, in this city inside a city, I find myself feeling a little less alone.

CHAPTER THIRTEEN

THE NEXT MORNING BRINGS WINDS FROM THE EAST AND rain dripping from the rafters. Qing'er is the one who delivers our breakfast, contained in a round pot, while Mingwen holds an umbrella over their heads. She grumbles about the bad weather, balancing a basket tucked under her arm.

Qing'er dances around the table while "helping" Mingwen, gleefully explaining each item they are pulling out when he realizes I am unfamiliar with these northern dishes. Hot soy milk is ladled into bowls, tiny shrimp sprinkled over the surface, then drizzled with soy sauce, vinegar, and red chili oil, and finally dotted with a handful of chives. Another plate is piled high with fried golden dough, meant for dipping.

Lian invites them both to sit down and eat with us, which causes the two other shénnóng-tú in the room to give us odd looks and take their food elsewhere. It's clear from our brief encounters with the other competitors that they believe our mannerisms to be peculiar—particularly our lack of a respectable background and our habit of associating with the servants. Mingwen's mouth tightens at the obvious snub and she turns to leave, but Qing'er convinces her to stay by pushing a stool in her direction.

"I suppose I can rest my feet for a moment," she mutters, accepting one of the steaming bowls and inhaling the scent rising from the top. Qing'er already has his mouth full of the crispy dough, nodding with pleasure as he swirls his spoon into the soup. I do the same and take a tentative slurp. It is rich, savory, salty, and sour. The heat then creeps up as a pleasant burn at the back of my throat, confusing my senses.

The table is quiet for a few moments, but for the slurping and munching as we enjoy our meal. After he makes quick work of his food, Qing'er pushes his dish away, declaring himself full, and looks at Lian slyly. "I heard them talking about the two of you in the kitchens after you left last night."

"Qing'er!" Mingwen scolds.

Lian leans toward him, and even I set my spoon down for a moment with interest.

"Wait, he can tell us." Lian smiles. "What did they say?"

"They said the shénnóng-shī can give people the strength of ten men. Is this true?"

I can tell this boy is trouble, but of the sort where he knows he is more likely to get his hair ruffled than to be beaten for having a smart mouth. A different sort of reality compared to that boy in the market.

"My teacher is able to brew tonics that can make you stronger, for a period of time," Lian tells him. "He can pull out the inner potential placed inside you by the old gods. But not all shénnóng-shī have that capability. Just like some of your uncles demonstrate greater skill at folding dumplings and others have a knack for cooking with the wok, the shénnóng-shī have specializations, too."

"Some shénnóng-shī have healing powers," I add. "They look inside you to see what sickness there is, and help to draw it out. My—" I almost say *mother*, even though those in the capital may not yet know she is dead. "My teacher always taught me Shénnóng chooses each of us for a reason," I mumble, knowing I need to be more careful of my words next time. I pretend to sip at my soy milk so that someone else can speak.

Mingwen nods. "They brew powerful magic. I saw it for myself once, when a cup of tea drew the age out of a person's face. Made him look ten years younger!" She then clears her throat, as if embarrassed to be part of the conversation.

I wonder what sort of recognition my mother would have received if she had remained at the palace and practiced her art here. In our village, she was sometimes mistaken for Father's assistant, or turned away from patients due to their preference for a "properly trained" physician. I know it always hurt her, even though she never stated it out loud.

"Why can't you make everyone strong and young?" Qing'er blurts out with excitement. "Wouldn't that solve all our problems? Wouldn't Dàxī be the most powerful kingdom in all the world? We'd have soldiers who could destroy everything in their path!"

"Good question!" Lian claps him on the back. "The magic is temporary. It takes something out of the shénnóng-shī to use it. Once my teacher needed to send an urgent message across Dàxī. The messenger traveled for three days and three nights without rest, but in turn, my teacher was unable to leave his bed for almost a week. We do not have enough shénnóng-shī in the kingdom specializing in this particular type of magic to keep all our soldiers going for so long."

"The more you ask of the magic," I say, "the more it takes, either from the one who casts or the one who receives."

"What else do they say about us?" Lian asks, still amused.

"That the shénnóng-shī deal in secrets," Mingwen says, her

interest outpacing her suspicion. "Many of you don't accept payment in coin, only in truths."

"They say you will require payment years later because of the poison you put in the tea. It may seize you in the middle of the night and kill you," Qing'er rambles on, before looking at us with worry. "Is it true? You don't seem like murderers."

Lian and I can't help ourselves. I double over, scarcely able to breathe, while Lian laughs so hard she has to wipe tears from her eyes. Qing'er looks at the spectacle of us, bewildered, while Mingwen huffs beside him.

"What sort of demons do you think we are?" I can't help but sputter through my mirth.

Mingwen stands, scowling again. "Forget it," she snaps.

Lian gets to her feet, too, and helps her gather our used bowls and utensils. "We're happy to answer any of your questions. I used to believe so many rumors, but I would have never known what is true and what is a lie until I started my apprenticeship."

Mingwen nods after considering this, slightly appeased. "I suppose you are not all bad."

With the four of us, it takes no time at all before everything is packed away. As Mingwen secures the lid onto the top of the basket, she pauses.

"I . . . probably shouldn't tell you this," she says, glancing at the door to make sure no one else is listening, before looking back at me. "The steward knows you are the one who took the snacks to the marquis. She will be coming to find you soon."

With that cryptic warning, she hurries outside before I have a chance to ask her any questions.

"Oh no," Lian says to me, eyes wide as saucers. "I would make myself scarce if I were you."

"Grandmother!" Qing'er exclaims. Before Lian and I can even move to save ourselves, Steward Yang strolls in through the opened doors.

Dressed in a dark gray robe with a black sash, not a hair out of place, Steward Yang examines the room. Although she is not a particularly tall woman, her presence is commanding. She makes me want to stand up straighter and check my collar to make sure my appearance is as it should be.

"You!" She catches sight of me and stalks over, grabbing my arm. I am rooted in place, not knowing where to turn or where to flee. Lian is no help; she looks as petrified as I am.

"Laughing, the two of you? Think it's all a joke? Pretending to be someone else for a day?" Steward Yang's voice starts out deceptively low, but increases in volume quickly, until her words come out as a yell. "Conspiring to make a fool out of me? Make a fool out of my departments?!"

Her nails dig into the soft skin of my arm, making me wince. "Competitors are to remain to themselves. Not cavort with court officials. Not play with costumes.

"And you!" With her other arm, Steward Yang points an accusing finger at Lian, who puts the table between us as if it would be enough to save her. "I recognize you. I remember you from when you were young. Always getting into trouble. Always underfoot. I was too soft on you, thinking you a child. I had hoped that the Esteemed Lu would have taught you manners.

"But now I discover the two of you are sneaking around *my* kitchens. I'm sure Minister Song would love to hear how competitors like you are pretending to be maids, traipsing around the palace, making a mockery of the competition. He would love to hear what sort of trouble you've gotten yourself into."

Fear gives way to annoyance, then to anger. It brings forth the same feeling of choking helplessness I had standing before the marquis, and those red-faced, drunken fools, who can break the rules without a care. They do not have their reputations and their futures at stake in this competition. Their fortunes are aligned, their futures secure. They will go on to receive the training they need to enter the trials regardless of the outcome. And as for me . . . I will lose my sister like I have already lost my mother.

I snatch my arm out of her grasp and snarl at her, "Some of the other competitors are enjoying private audiences with the marquis himself. How is that fair? I know many of the kitchen staff have been to his residence, so you must have known about these transgressions. Why did you not inform the minister immediately?"

Steward Yang blanches at the mention of the marquis. "How do you know that?" she demands. "What did you see?"

I realize she must have believed I only passed the dishes to the servants of the household. She didn't know I saw who the marquis was entertaining within his private chambers.

Lian pounces to my rescue. "Beloved Auntie Yang—" She links her arm with the older woman, laying on her charm. "We have tried to be helpful, to keep our hands from lying idle, but we failed you in our attempts. You are right; you should indeed inform the minister of all we have seen. Tell him you were the one who provided us with the wisdom and the courage to do the right thing."

Steward Yang now looks like a rabbit in a trap, brushing Lian off and shaking her head. "No . . . I realize now. There is no need for that, I assure you."

"But you taught us such an important lesson!" Lian exclaims with exaggerated sincerity. "We have no choice but to follow—"

"Oh, stop it, foolish girl!" Steward Yang snaps. She closes her eyes and takes a breath, massaging one temple with her fingers. "The longer I remain in the palace, the more it drains the life out of me."

"Come, sit, Auntie," Lian says, gentler now, leading her to a stool.

I catch a whiff of something when she walks past me—the distinct odor of the bark from the chénxiāng tree, and the sharp sweetness of dried tangerine peel. Medicinal smells that were often found in my father's workshop. Peering closer, I can see the sallow tinge of her skin, and the purple shadows under her eyes. This woman is ill, and from the look of the lines pulled taut around her mouth, she is also in pain.

"Are you feeling quite all right, Grandmother?" Qing'er was hovering at the door during our argument, but he now presses closer, tucking himself under her arm.

"Yes, don't worry about me, Qing-qing." She sighs. "It's only a headache that won't go away."

Even though she came in here accusing us of deception, I feel nothing but pity for her at this moment. Father's teachings continue to hold fast in my heart: I cannot stand by while someone is suffering.

"Can I pour you a cup of tea?" I ask. "It might help."

She is already turning away, muttering about other tasks to attend to, but Qing'er starts to massage her shoulders helpfully.

"You always talk about how it's unfair that the shénnóng-shī serve the courtly folk," he says, "but now this is our chance! We can finally see the magic for ourselves. Like the teahouses along the river, with the music and the pretty ladies!"

Color blooms on Steward Yang's pinched face, as if she's embarrassed by the young boy's innocent words.

Lian encourages her with a smile. "Ning's father is a physician. She might be able to help."

Steward Yang looks at Lian, then at me.

"Go! Go!" Qing'er chirps. "Before she changes her mind!"

I head to the cabinet against the wall, where our ingredients are stored. The tea leaves we have in our room are a common loose-leaf variety but are still higher quality than anything we could ever purchase back in the village. And I have some remnants of the osmanthus flowers from my disastrous encounter in the first round of the competition—the tea the judges never tasted.

Displayed in the cabinet are also several tea sets. I pick one that is the color of cream with a brush of blue along the edge, but my eyes also linger on the others: cool white with a hint of green or crackled gray. Back home, my uncle is a merchant who travels the region to sell both tea and pottery from our village. In his study, there is a shelf containing various tea wares he's collected through-out his travels, and he loves to show off his treasures. How one was bestowed by this high official or gifted by that famous ship's captain. I was never permitted to touch them, only to admire them from a distance. But here, even the servants are permitted to use such lovely wares.

It does not take long for the water to boil in the earthen pot. The leaves steep, then I pour the tea into a cup, followed by two tiny osmanthus blooms. They float to the surface of the tea, caressed by bubbles.

Although my mother's favorite flower was the pomelo, it only bloomed in spring for a brief time. In the summer, she preferred the osmanthus, which carries a sweet fragrance. In autumn, the scent of the flower turns, and it is harvested for wine instead. In one of Mother's stories, the first osmanthus tree grew so tall and abundant, it once overshadowed the moon itself. The Sky Emperor, enraged, punished the negligent immortal responsible for pruning the heavenly forest. He was tethered to it forever, living out his eternal life no more than ten steps away from the great tree. On nights when the moon is cast in shadow, it is because the woodcutter has fallen asleep again.

Steward Yang picks up the cup and inhales. "It smells like peaches," she says, surprised.

Even though Qing'er still wants to chatter away, Lian takes him away to the side of the room to show him something, understanding that I require concentration to practice my art.

My mother used her shénnóng-shī skills to coax the truth out of the soul, the problems that worried at the edges of the mind. Like the shadows of the moon, the pruning of branches from a tree. I asked it to reveal the hidden memories of the judges in the competition, and now I want to unveil the cause of the steward's pain.

"Let the tea flow through you and bring you comfort," I whisper. She drinks and I close my eyes. Ready to communicate, ready to receive.

A sharp pain quickly pricks the middle of my forehead, like the point of a needle. Then it snaps outward, fracturing from the center. I hiss from the sharpness of it, then the pain funnels into my mouth, causing a bitterness that spreads from my tongue to my throat.

"What's happening?" I hear her voice, dimly, from a distance. I force myself to inhale, breathe through it. Was this what my mother felt when she opened herself up? Did she take the pain of others into herself? An image spreads in my mind, expanding like watercolor on paper.

I am both inside and outside of myself.

I can feel the firm surface of the table underneath my arm, but I am also somewhere else. Floating above us, watching the steward looking at me. I wish, once again, that Mother was here to show me, to teach me . . .

Did people watch her with luminous eyes, expectant and afraid?

The pain isn't only in my head. It extends like roots, tendrils worming their way through my body—her body. Vines choke my heart, squeezing my organs, until it is difficult to breathe.

It's the worry that is undoing her. The anxiety eating away a hollow in her belly, the thoughts keeping her up late at night.

With a gasp, my eyes snap open.

"Qing'er!" I call out, and the boy is quick to appear at my side. "Go to the storeroom and fetch a few pieces of dānggūi, and five handfuls of dried huáng qí. Try to pick the thinnest strands you can find."

He nods and runs through the door.

Steward Yang sets down her cup. "Why? What did you see?"

Without the rest she needs, her body will only grow weaker. Dryness in the mouth, affecting the way things taste, loss of strength in her limbs, difficulty catching her breath . . . and eventually far graver effects.

"I think there is something you are terribly worried about . . ." I try to untangle the symptoms from the cause, the phantom ache in my head still ringing. "No, not something . . . someone. Someone close to you, as close to you as a part of your body. It's keeping you up at night."

"Like carving out my organs," she whispers.

Mother used to call us her dear ones, her xīn gān bǎo bèi. Her heart and her organs, an irreplaceable part of her. Shu and

I would laugh at her exaggerated affection, but we loved her attention.

It finally dawns on me. I should have seen it sooner. "Your daughter."

She nods. "Chunhua was picked to be the emperor's handmaiden. I was so proud ... she's clever. Even the emperor himself praised her once. She was happy with her position, until the illness came last winter. All the servants of the emperor's personal residences have been shut into the inner court. No one in, no one out. I have not seen her for two seasons!" She trembles, and Lian places a comforting hand on her shoulder.

"We've all heard about the emperor's illness," Lian says. "The news has already reached the border towns."

"Yes, you would know, wouldn't you? The ambassador's daughter." Steward Yang sniffles, but her tone is now resigned. "There have been ... rumors as well. Rumors that the emperor himself has been poisoned by the Shadow, that he is permanently bedridden, which is why he has not shown his face in months."

The thought is troubling, but it would explain the lack of his presence.

"The emperor must need to eat," I say. "Can't you get a message to your daughter somehow through the kitchen deliveries?"

The steward shakes her head. "The inner palace has its own kitchen. When we deliver our goods, we leave them in the courtyard. The staff pick up what they need, then we return to collect the rest. I've tried before to supervise the delivery, but they speak through the gate and ask us to leave. The physicians say it is for our own protection, but ... I fear the worst."

Qing'er runs in with the requested ingredients in hand, disrupting the somber atmosphere. I pour the ingredients into an earthen pot that can withstand the heat of coals, just like the pot that held our breakfast earlier. I pour the hot water over the dried herbs and allow the water to settle. The medicinal musk wafts into the air, tingling my nose.

I always thought it was my father who wanted to help everyone in the village, even if it put the family at risk and attracted the attention of the governor. I never understood why. I resented our threadbare clothes, how some days Mother had to stretch a handful of rice into congee. I wondered why Mother always helped him without question. But now I can see why. If you can feel someone else's suffering, how can you look away?

I convince myself it's only the steam making my eyes water.

The steward suddenly grabs my hands, insistent. "I heard the shénnóng-shī can send messages across distances. That you can whisper a word into the night and it will find the target. Can you do that for me? Can you send a message to my daughter?"

I shake my head. "I wish I could. I don't know how to send messages through walls or speak to someone in dreams. It may be something a truly powerful shénnóng-shī is able to do, but I have never learned it."

Steward Yang pulls back, folding her arms over her chest. "Sometimes I wish I were the Shadow. Able to step through walls and hide in the darkness. I always thought the palace was a refuge from the harsh reality of life, but now I know it is a prison."

I stir the tonic in the pot with a wooden spoon, ensuring that it remains at a simmer and not a boil. The thought of the emperor shut in his grand palace leaves me feeling unsettled, and I remember what the Esteemed Qian hinted at: Change is coming.

When the tonic is done, I strain it using one of the resting pots, then pour it into a bowl. The color of the liquid has darkened considerably, into an unappealing brown. I bring it over to the steward, setting it in front of her.

"You have to sleep," I tell her. "Without sleep, you cannot be ready if she needs you. How can you take care of your heart if your mind is slow?"

She grumbles at the lecture but places her hands around the bowl. "Look at me, listening to a mere child. I'm getting muddled in my old age."

"Grandmother." Qing'er hugs her from behind, sweet as malt sugar. "You are still young."

Steward Yang smiles at that and lowers her head to blow on the surface of the tonic.

"Wait!" I jump up and return to my room to fetch a small bundle from my dressing table. "This will make it easier to drink, if you like."

Yesterday while in the kitchens, I picked up a few pieces of pear-syrup candy from the servant's tray. They are one of the few luxuries from Jia my mother splurged on, the one thing guaranteed to make her light up when we received a delivery. She could pop them into her mouth directly, but they were so sweet they made my teeth ache, so she would always put them into a pot of hot water for me to drink.

Steward Yang regards me with an odd, contemplative look.

"You can put it under your tongue," I tell her, thinking it is not common practice in the capital. "It should ease the bitterness of the tonic."

She ignores the offered candy, but follows my other instructions, sipping at the bowl slowly until all of it is gone. "You see, Qing'er?" She shows the empty bowl to her grandson. "Grandmother drank all her medicine."

He beams at her, adoration for her evident. "Well done!"

Steward Yang picks up my handkerchief from the table and examines the bird stitched on it. I resist the urge to snatch it away; that was Shu's. Now that I have been separated from Mother's shénnóng-shī box, I have so little remaining of home.

"Did you make this?" she asks. "The stitching is quite fine even with the coarse materials."

"No, that is my sister's work." I reach out and take it from her—not caring if it's rude to do so—and tuck it away in my sash, where I can keep it safe.

"Lian, could you take Qing'er outside to play?" the steward says. "I would like to speak to Ning in private."

Lian looks at me, questioning. I give her a small shrug, and she takes the young boy's hand, leading him outside. He's already chattering again.

The steward turns back to me, but when we're alone her shrewd expression reappears, as if there is an abacus working in her head, considering my worth and value.

"You remind me of someone," she says.

Lian told me Steward Yang was the tyrant of her kitchens, able to notice even the smallest thing out of place: a single fruit missing from a display, the count of the evening meal being off by two, or the incorrect order of utensils on a tray. Her memory is impeccable, her attention to detail frightening. It is why she commands both respect and fear.

"With the years passing, my memory isn't quite what it used to be, so it took me a while to recall. But now I can see it. It's in the shape of your eyes and face, the way you speak." She picks up the square of pear candy, holding it up to the light until it glows. "It was this, though, that made me remember."

My pulse quickens in my throat. Mother never mentioned anyone from the capital. She said very little about it, even when we begged to hear more.

"I used to know a woman who worked in the palace. She was a midwife who attended to the servants, and she used to make us drink the bitterest brews." She chuckles at the memory, her fondness for this woman evident. "They would cause your toes to curl and your stomach to roll. She used to give us all squares of pear candy to make them easier to drink, reminding us to hold it under our tongues."

Her eyes meet mine. "You're Yiting's daughter."

The sound of my mother's name rings through the room. She always left an impression. Even now, seventeen years later, someone remembers her.

"I wondered how she fared when she left the palace. There was ... a scandal. For the first few years, I was certain she would return." She smiles. "Yiting got out, like she always said she would. She made a life out there, with a family of her own. I admire her for it."

"You do?" I have so many questions about what she was like when she was young, and why she left the palace. So many questions she brushed off, left forever unanswered.

"Not many are able to adjust to life outside the capital once they've had a taste of palace finery. They usually come back. Some in mere days, others in a few months, but they always find their way back. Her, though ... How is your mother?"

"She's dead," I say without thinking, still overwhelmed by the swell of emotion rising inside me. I slap my hand over my mouth.

"She is?" She reaches out and pats my shoulder. "I'm sorry."

She has clearly mistaken my shock for sorrow. I cover my face with my hand, allowing her to believe it.

117

"How long ago did she pass?" she asks softly, and I find myself telling her. About my mother's death, about the poison, about the unfairness of it all. Because this woman used to know my mother. She knew her brilliance and her generosity, the beauty that lit her up from within.

And she pretends she does not see me dab at my eyes with my handkerchief, giving me space to grieve.

Chapter Fourteen

I POUR STEWARD YANG ANOTHER CUP OF TEA, AND SHE accepts it when she is assured there is no magic infused in the cup.

"Can you . . . can you tell me more about my mother?" I ask hesitantly, desperate for the smallest scrap of information.

"That's a story for another day," she says. "I don't have much time left before I have to return to the kitchens. I should speak to you and Lian about the competition."

When Lian returns with Qing'er, I have already washed my face and tidied my appearance. I feel like I have been emptied inside, wrung out by tears.

Steward Yang gestures for Lian to join us, and I hide my trembling hands under the table. "I heard about what happened the first round, and that your position is uncertain at best."

A rush of embarrassment runs through me. I made a fool of myself in front of not only the judges and the other competitors, but also other citizens of the capital. I have only myself to blame.

"It's not her fault the marquis is an antiquated bag," Lian mumbles.

I can tell Steward Yang is trying to be stern, but the corner of her mouth betrays her.

"You have eased my headache," she says. "Because of your help, because I knew and respected your mother, and because I cannot stand to see the wealthy shénnóng-tú brazenly disregard the rules, I have decided to help you both."

"You will?" I gasp.

Lian claps. "We would be so grateful, Auntie."

"I know the tea they will be using in the next round." She examines her cup, frowning. "But before I tell you its name, I want you to each make me a promise."

Lian and I both wait, expectant.

"I don't want either of you in the kitchens again, understand? I have people to take care of. If any of the judges catch you . . . I can't risk the lives of everyone else." She waits for both of us to agree before nodding. "The name of the tea is Silver Needle. I will obtain a sample for you, if you think it may be useful."

After Steward Yang and Qing'er leave us, Lian and I turn to each other excitedly. Finally, something we can use. A hint to give us a clear focus, instead of the feeling that we are stumbling around in the dark.

"What do you know about Silver Needle?" I ask. It's not a name I remember from Mother's teachings.

"It sounds familiar. I think I've read about it once."

We return to our room, where Lian rummages through her things before coming up with a book in hand. Sitting cross-legged on the bed, she flips through the pages until she finds the section she is looking for.

"'Silver Needle is known for its thin, slender leaves, covered with the lightest layer of silver fuzz,'" she reads aloud. "'Many attempts have been made to cultivate it from the wild, though none have been successful, which makes it highly sought after. In the hands of a master shénnóng-shī, it can coax the truth out of anyone, but even a shénnóng-tú would be able to use it to discern a truth from a lie.'"

"A truth serum?" I ask. "Anyone who drinks it will be forced to tell the truth?" It seems a precious resource, to have such an ability.

Lian laughs. "If it were as easy as that, do you think it would not be worth more than the Golden Key? But the Silver Needle, like all other tea leaves, depends on the wielder. It depends on the severity of the lie, and on how much the other person wants to hide the truth."

When Lian and I return from dinner, we find a small package waiting for us on our table. I open it to find a note from Steward Yang and a few silvery-yellow leaves in a small pouch. We agree to split the amount to prepare for the next round of the competition, hoping it will give us an advantage if we can learn how to wield the tea.

We continue to speculate on what will happen tomorrow until it is time to rest. But I find myself lying there, staring into the dark, listening to Lian's breathing as it slows. My mind is unable to rest, thinking of that boy who is able to traverse the palace walls in the dark. The one who promised to return for my real name.

Lost in my thoughts, the sound of the gong startles me.

"Sān gēng!" The distant sound of the criers reaches my ears, reminding me of the chant every child learned in school:

> Yī gēng rén (First hour for the people, preparing
>   for rest)
> Èr gēng luó (Second hour for the gong, watching
>   over those safe in their beds)

Sān gēng guǐ (Third hour for the ghosts, coming
    out of the dark)
Sì gēng zéi (Fourth hour for the thieves, taking
    advantage of night)
Wǔ gēng jī (The final hour for the rooster, first
    to awake / Dawn arrives to welcome the new
    day)

It's the third hour, the Hour of the Ghost. The darkest time of night, when the spirits are the most active. My feet touch the cold floor. My fingers fumble in the dark until I find my cloak. I wrap it around me before tiptoeing past the screen that separates our room from the foyer, then out the door into the dim courtyard. I remember the other rhyme: *The Banished Prince, Demon Born, who thrives in the dark...*

"I wasn't sure you would remember." Bo steps out from behind the shadow of the willow tree, and I jump back, swallowing a startled cry.

Kang, I remind myself. His other name. His true name.

"Sorry." He comes closer until I can see him in the light of the lantern hanging from the rafters, and he raises his hands to show he is unarmed. My hands clutch the front of my cloak, as if it is armor that can protect me.

"Do you want—" "Come—" We speak over each other, then stop.

Kang walks carefully toward me until he is at the foot of the steps, looking up.

"This is the first time we've met where you haven't attacked me," he states with a slow grin. The one that unsettles me, as if he knows something I do not. I find it insufferable. I find *him* insufferable, and yet ... I like to see it.

"You've deserved it every time," I retort.

"That's fair." His smile stretches even wider, not bothered by my sharpness. "Will you finally tell me your name?"

My name doesn't carry as much weight as his. My family is not renowned, infamous like his. Why does he care so much about my name and about who I am?

I must have stared at him for too long—I can feel the chasm between us widen again, and his face grows serious. He turns and sits down on the steps with a sigh. After a pause, I follow, careful to keep an arm's length between us.

"I thought you wanted me to come back." He sounds disappointed.

"I did!" The moment the words leave my mouth, I wish I could take them back. I hurry to explain, "I still find it difficult to trust you, however. Knowing what I know."

"Why? Who do you believe I am?" he demands. "You still think I'm an assassin?"

It's easier to deal with him when he is prickly and defensive, rather than soft and vulnerable.

"Tell me!" I press. "Are you the Shadow? Are you the one who poisoned the tea bricks?"

I look for any hint of deception—a flicker in the eyes, a certain nervous twitch—to confirm my suspicions. But he looks stunned that I would even believe that of him, sputtering for a moment before regaining his ability to speak. "Why would I poison the tea? What do I possibly have to gain?"

"To create unrest in the empire." I'm repeating back what I've heard in the village, the kitchens, and among the other shénnóng-tú. "To regain the throne for your father. I have seen what people will do for power." I know the extent of the governor's terrible

123

influence within Sù. The taxes that grow higher each year for our protection, while the people suspect the bandits we are "protected" from are his own hired thugs.

I expect Kang to react angrily to my accusations, that I would goad him into leaving and never speaking to me again, but he appears thoughtful instead.

"We feel the burden in all corners of the empire," he says. "That's why I'm here in the capital. I'm here to petition the emperor to help my people. If he will not see me, then a regent must continue to rule if he is ill. While the court continues their political games, the people will slowly starve."

I don't know what to say to that.

"How can I convince you I'm telling the truth?" His hand tightens into a fist at his side. "If I cannot even win over a stranger in the market, how could I possibly sway the court?"

My mouth drops open as it all becomes clear. "Is that why you care so much about what I think of you? I'm the practice target for your oratory skills? That if you can convince an uneducated commoner to join your cause, you would be able to convince the scholars and the nobles?"

"That is not—" He scowls. "That is not what I meant. You're twisting things. Purposely misunderstanding me."

Even with my pride hurt, I remember what Lian said: If the shénnóng-tú from the capital are using all the tools at their disposal to win, so too must we rally our strengths. The Silver Needle can tell the truth from a lie, and what better person to test it on than Kang?

"Prove it to me," I say, standing. It's my turn to look down at him. "Prove to me you are not lying."

He looks up at me, already wary. "What would you have me do?"

"The next round of the competition is a test of honesty," I tell him. "Of untangling truth from lies. I need someone to practice on. If you are telling me the truth, then you have nothing to fear." Perhaps he can even reveal something about the court that can help me advance in the competition.

He accepts without hesitation, which surprises me. Is he so confident in his ability to deceive a mere shénnóng-tú, or does he believe in the truthfulness of every word he utters?

I mull over these possibilities while restoking the fire inside the residence, using the moment to myself to gather my thoughts. I've never been taught this sort of magic, and the doubt continues to worry at me. *You cannot pull the truth from the unwilling, and you cannot tear something out of a mind that is closed off. A give and a take.*

Will he be willing to tell me the truth? Can I handle whatever secrets he's hiding?

I set the tea ware on the stone table in the courtyard, stifling a yawn when he is not looking. The weariness is starting to fray my nerves, since I already exerted myself with the use of my magic earlier on Steward Yang.

My portion of the Silver Needle is only enough for a single cup. I pour the water over the delicate strands. What I've gleaned from my afternoon reviewing books with Lian is this: Silver Needle is a tribute tea, each leaf plucked individually from the tree by hand. The weight is so featherlight, even the slightest movement of the water sends each strand swirling in a vortex, down to a point. That is where it is said to be able to pierce the veil, to draw out the fine thread of truth from the mind.

I take the first sip, then place the cup in front of him. A challenge.

"Do I just drink it?" he asks, picking it up gingerly. I'm reminded of the way he fled after the last time we shared a drink. I nod.

Meeting my eyes, he drinks, draining the cup. The magic flares inside me immediately, remembering him. The light in the courtyard shifts, encircling us once again, until everything appears lit with a silver tinge. I can hear the strumming of the pipa, the sweet sound of the singer's voice drifting over the Jade River . . .

Time for me to ask, and time for him to answer.

Chapter Fifteen

"Are you the Shadow?" The magic works itself into my voice, making it low and breathy, like someone else is speaking through me. As if I am truly calling down the gods.

"No," he whispers in turn. His features waver, obscured by a sudden mist, and the scent of camellia blossoms settles around us once again.

We regard each other, as if on either side of a waterfall. I lift my hand, and his own arm rises, too, parting the mist until we touch. I think of the figure in the darkness I sparred with, face obscured by a black mask.

The Shadow ... The Silver Needle spins in the bottom of the cup, looking for an answer. But it doesn't match. It's not him.

"Do you wish the princess harm?" I ask. "Why are you here, Kang?" His fingers flutter under my hand at the sound of his name. The mist parts, changes. The palace disappears around me, and the mist shows me a vision.

An ornamental bridge. Two children stand above the water, scattering blueberries and wild rice to the koi below. One is Kang and the other is the princess. They laugh, joined in companionship and a warm familiarity.

The mist sweeps in again, obscuring the memory, replacing it with another.

The princess steps forward, her face scrubbed of makeup, her hair devoid of ornamentation. Younger than the regal beauty who presided over the ceremonies.

They're in a garden. Her garden. He remembers. The branches rustle overhead, spring buds only just beginning to emerge. He notices the soldiers standing guard. He is reminded: Someone is always watching.

"Why are you here, Kang?" Her voice is sharp, accusatory.

"I had hoped we would meet again under better circumstances," he says.

"Share a drink with me then, so I can thank the person who saved my life." The corner of her lips quirks up, and he knows she is mocking him. Before her, a tray holds a pot and cups.

"It was simply my duty, Princess."

"Are you refusing an order?" her bodyguard asks brusquely, stepping out from her place under the tree, hand on the hilt of her sword. Her white outfit contrasts with the warmth of her tanned skin, bringing out the golden hue. Even in this private garden, she wears an armored chest plate, ready to defend the princess against any threat.

"No . . ." He sighs. "Hello, Ruyi."

The handmaiden inclines her head in acknowledgment, but her hand still remains on her sword.

"I am simply not worthy." He bows and sits down in front of the princess.

"My guards say it was like you flew down from the skies to protect me from the assassins' arrows." With one hand drawing her sleeve back, the princess places a scoop of tea leaves into a pot. The hot water swells and spills over onto the marble tray. "They were ready to cut you down if you were a threat," she says lightly, as if she was speaking of someone else.

"My loyalty is to the emperor!" he protests. "I owe him my life, cousin."

My stomach constricts for him. She wants him to break.

With a tilt of the wrist, she pours the water. The light catches the stream in a beautiful arc, filling two cups. She nudges one of the cups in his direction.

He does not move.

"You will not drink?" she asks, an edge to her voice. A deadly question.

"I will not drink before you, Highness." He inclines his head, keeping his voice cool.

I am impressed by his restraint, by the way he allows nothing to show, even though I can feel the turmoil inside him. Something I am incapable of hiding myself.

The surface of the cup shimmers before him. No magic, but a different sort of weapon.

"You speak of loyalty to my father." She smiles, but it's more like a baring of teeth. "Do you think I would give you poison?"

"Before I drink, I ask that you hear my own request." He bows his head. "And then, my life will be in your hands."

"How dare you—" Ruyi steps forward, outraged, but the princess waves her back.

"You use words like 'duty' and 'loyalty,'" the princess says, each word intended to wound. "And yet you forget where you come from."

"I remember my place," he concedes. "I only wish to speak with my uncle."

"Anything you wish to say to my father, you can say to me. Cousin." The last word uttered as a distasteful reminder of his family's lineage.

"I only wish to ask him to reconsider our exile." He keeps speaking, *undeterred by her warning.* "And to reassure him of our loyalty. These are dangerous times. With the unrest at the borders, the bandits, the threat of the northern clans . . . He can rely on us, for we are family—"

"Family." *The princess runs her finger over the edge of her cup.* "My own family will not drink something poured by my hand."

With one swift movement, he lifts the cup to his lips and drains it, then salutes her. He sets it down on the stone with a forceful clatter, betraying his impatience.

"Is that enough?" *he asks.* "Now will you allow me to speak with him?"

She leaps across the table, a flash of steel in her hand. The point of a dagger presses against his throat, but he does not flinch. He sits with his hands resting on the table. Waiting.

"I will remind you that you were banished, told never to return to Jia under threat of death." *The knifepoint trails downward, to rest over his heart, where the red seal sits, branding him as traitor.*

"It is a matter of life and death, Princess," *he says, sitting utterly still.*

"Whose life?" *the princess asks.* "And whose death?"

Kang's hand jerks away from mine, the vision dissipating into nothing. The magic releases us from its grasp, loosening the connection between my mind and his. I did not merely listen to their conversation—I'd felt every motion, as if I were inside his body.

He does not mean her any harm. It is his own life that is in danger.

We are back in the twilight of the courtyard, on either side of the stone table. There is anguish in his expression, and I can still feel the pull of his desperation, his need to achieve the task he set out to accomplish. He fights for his people—his mother's people, the woman who took him in as her own.

"Do you believe me now?" he asks.

I nod. I don't trust my voice.

"Lùzhou is not a place where shénnóng-shī care to visit," he goes on to say. "But perhaps one day you will join me there, and you can teach us about your art. It's a beautiful place, even with its reputation."

His offer startles me; I remember the revulsion that caused him to pull away when he found out what I was capable of in Azalea House.

"It's not . . ." He blinks. "It's not for the reason you believe . . ."

He does not finish his thought, for the simple act of remembering draws it back again. The ghostly strains of a flute, floating in the air. The remnants of the Golden Key, shimmering once again into being, forces our connection back together, sharply, until we both gasp at the force of it.

He tries to fall back, to sever the memory, but it's too late.

We return to the garden.

The dagger pointed at his heart. His words that follow: "I wonder what the people of Jia will think of a regent who is hiding the death of an emperor. I wonder if they will accept a princess who sits on a throne of lies."

The princess sinks back in her seat, face devoid of color.

The emperor is dead. I gasp at the revelation.

The mist quickly parts as he closes the distance between us. His hands grab my shoulders.

"Listen, this is important," he hisses. I can feel his whole body trembling. "Did you put something in the tea? Did you put in more Golden Key?"

I start to shake my head. "No . . ." And then I stop, because that would be a lie, and he would be able to sense it. The Silver Needle points both ways. "I don't know. It wasn't the Silver Needle. I think it was from . . . before. Something the Golden Key left behind."

"It's dangerous," he says. "You have to forget what you heard. I didn't understand, I underestimated your power—"

The wind picks up, whistling around us. We are caught in the dizzying space between memory and present.

"They will kill you." He's so close. His expression wild. Afraid. "I do not believe the shénnóng-shī are capable of resurrection."

"You believe it to be true?" I whisper, not wanting to believe the palace able to contain such a large secret.

His hands drop away from me. The connection quivers between us, like the plucked string of a zither. "I have been in the capital for a few weeks," he says, turning away so I can only see the side of his face. "Watching to see what comes in and out of the palace. The last reports said the emperor appeared gravely ill, but now . . . I'm not sure what Zhen is doing. Waiting to see who will reveal themselves as a potential threat? Who will offer an alliance?"

Kang paces in front of me, all composure lost. "They will kill you, do you understand? They will not hesitate."

I hear the sound of thunder in the distance, even though the sky was clear before we entered this dreamscape. The intensity of his emotions having conjured the wind, whipping our hair across our faces. Lifting, spinning us up until our feet are dangling above the ghostly forms of our bodies. My stomach revolts at the sudden movement. I have to hold us both together, before our souls are severed and we are unable to find our way back to our physical forms.

"Kang!" I call out, fighting against the wind to maintain my grip on his shoulder. Reaching up, I dig my fingers into his neck, at the pressure point there. His eyes burn into mine. "My name, you wanted to know my name, right? It's Ning. Zhang Ning."

"Zhang Ning," he repeats softly.

With a rush, we return into our bodies, a dizzying fall. I sag against the stone table for support, uncertain if my legs can hold me up any longer. Across from me, Kang pants as if he's run a great distance.

"I'm just a girl from Sù," I say to him. "Who will believe me, even if I try to tell them?"

A peculiar expression crosses his face. "Ning," he sighs, and a shiver runs through me. "You . . . you have power. More than you know. More power than those foolish nobles in their grand residences, protected from the hardships of the world. You know what it's like out there, living each day wondering if you will survive the next. You have *hungered.*"

He says this with an edge to his voice, reminding me he could have been a prince, if his father had succeeded in taking over the throne. He would be the one residing in the inner palace instead, dressed in silk. In Mother's stories, princes never had a happy ending. They were exchanged for skinned cats, stolen away in the dark of night. They were killed in their beds while another power ascended.

It is dangerous, to be a prince.

"When she comes into power, her advisers will suggest she rid herself of her opponents. I left without my father's knowledge, hoping she could at least spare the lives of my mother's people." He looks into the distance. "I hoped I could offer myself as . . . a hostage? An assurance? That the people of Lùzhou will swear fealty as long as she does not do us harm. Lùzhou has suffered enough because of my family."

"What will you do then, if she does not agree?" I ask.

His jaw clenches. "We hope she will be different, or else we will fight to defend what is ours. She—"

"Don't," I warn. "The effects of Silver Needle are still active. Don't say anything you don't want to tell me."

Kang hesitates, then nods. "I hope she will walk a peaceful path."

He is a well-trained swordsman, and if the people of the Emerald Isles are the same . . . He speaks of rebellion.

An empire on the precipice of change. Alliances shifting at the whims of those in power. Just like the Ascended Emperor cut a swath through the provinces to secure the throne, just like his sons fought for control. One rules, one is banished.

Anything is possible now that the emperor is dead.

We all have people we care about, those we would give our lives for. It puts us in danger, or makes us dangerous. In a way, I resent the village I come from. I resent the ties that bind me there, because the people there remember my mother returning to the village, unwed and pregnant. They know my awkward ways, my ineptitude for social niceties, my many mistakes. But they are also a part of me. The dirt under my nails, the blood in my veins. I belong with those tea trees, the rice fields, the clay of the riverbanks, the fire in the kilns.

I am selfish, and I know now that I will no longer apologize for it. Let the world burn, if Shu can live.

The gong sounds. The Hour of the Thief.

"I have to go," Kang says, yet he makes no effort to move.

"You should," I say, yearning for him to stay.

"I'll see you again." It sounds like a promise. He bows, a courtly gesture wasted on someone like me. Yet I can feel the phantom pull of the thread still humming between us.

I can feel it long after he disappears into the night. Long after it feels like he was never there at all.

Chapter Sixteen

We gather to meet the judges at midday, the sun beating high above our heads as we cross the grand courtyard. Without the crowds, without the soldiers, I feel like a tiny ant crawling across the large space. Minister Song greets us at the top of the marble steps, Marquis Kuang standing beside him. I take care to keep myself at the back of the group, to hide my face so he does not suddenly recall that I am the maid responsible for the commotion in his residence two days before.

The roof of the covered balcony shields us from the sun, and we can look over the Courtyard of Promising Future to the rooftops of the palace and then the city beyond. The view is spectacular, too much to take in all at once. A black pagoda stands in the distance, the watchful tower looking over the city's red-tiled rooftops.

"You stand before the Hall of Eternal Light." Minister Song's voice brings us back to the challenge at hand. "This is where the next round will be held. The competition will no longer be open to the public."

This is not a surprise, but the competitors still murmur at each other before the minister holds up one hand to silence us.

"Still, it is a great honor to be received in this hall. It was built for the Ascended Emperor, to both honor and humble him. From this vantage point, he will remember his purpose: to protect the people of Dàxī, and to remember that even the sun can be shot down from the sky."

I remember the legend of the archer who once rose to the greatest heights. He shot down nine of the arrogant sons of the Sky Emperor when the earth was on fire beneath them.

Just like the archers who attempted to kill the princess. But no one dares say that aloud.

Minister Song gestures to the man beside him. "Marquis Kuang?"

The nobleman steps forward, spreading his arms with a jovial grin. "I present to you a simple enough task." A servant comes forward and bows, holding a tray on which five cups are balanced. "You will have five cups to choose from. One cup is safe. The other four cups contain poison." He waves and the servant backs away.

"Poison!" he declares again, delighted at this challenge. But I know the truth: This competition is rigged in his favor, ensuring that his preferred competitors will have his assistance and the guidance of the Esteemed Qian. Two old men playing at courtly games, confident they will still be in power when a new dawn rises over Dàxī.

Does he know the emperor is dead? Do they all know?

"What sort of poison will you face?" he continues theatrically. "Will it be one that will rack your body with unspeakable pain? Make you bleed from every orifice? Cause you to fall asleep . . . forever?"

The other shénnóng-tú fret at this, but no one seems particularly afraid. It's the most basic training of a shénnóng-tú, the discernment of common poisons. They're expected to be able to identify them by scent, taste, and appearance. But I know that today's challenge will involve the use of the Silver Needle; it cannot merely be a simple test of skill.

"I have arranged for the assistance of the finest entertainers in Jia." His smile is slippery as an eel. A bell rings, and five figures walk in from the side of the hall. Five beautiful women, dressed in white skirts and white bodices, their sashes containing the faintest hint of color, their shoulders wrapped in wisps of shimmering gauze. They tuck their hands beside their hips, gracefully arch their wrists, and curtsy in unison to the marquis, ethereal in their beauty. Like they have stepped directly from a painting depicting the star goddesses of the celestial palace.

I'm sure my own mouth is open in awe, as are many of my fellow competitors'.

The marquis claps, round cheeks flushed. "Some of the greatest beauties of Jia, from Azalea, Peony, Lotus, Orchid, and Chrysanthemum—five of the oldest teahouses in the capital. They are apprentices like you, seeking to make a name for themselves."

The competitors whisper among themselves; some of the men look as if they wished they could swallow the young women whole.

"These ladies are trained in the intricacies of the tea ceremony," the marquis continues. "You will prepare a cup for them to drink, and they will prepare you five cups in turn. You will be permitted to select only one cup out of the five, and that is the one you will drink from."

"How is that fair?" one of my fellow shénnóng-tú protests. "How are we supposed to discern the poison?"

"That is an excellent question." The marquis smirks. "The emperor requires a shénnóng-shī who will be able to assist him in court, who will be able to assess danger from delegates and tributes by reading a room."

"This is not a challenge at all." Another young man speaks, stepping forward from the group with a bow. With fierce brows and a sharp nose, he is striking in appearance, his shaved head indicating he may have been dedicated to a monastery of one of the gods. "Beg pardon, Honored One. It is simple enough to determine whether a person is lying without the use of tea." I suspect he may be from Yún province due to his heavy accent.

"In the venerable competition on Wǔlín Mountain, do you demonstrate your skills only by fighting to the death?" the marquis snaps, his displeasure clear. He does not like to be questioned. "Last year the finale of that competition was a Tower Rite. The competitors ascended a bamboo tower and sparred with their bare hands, without any weapons, in order to determine who would be the victor.

"Green Snake and Frozen Snow..." He names two of the most revered martial arts warriors who have come out of Wǔlín Academy. "Their weapons are spear and sword, but Green Snake won the competition against Frozen Snow without her spear, in direct hand-to-hand combat. It was a test of their balance, intelligence, and endurance, not only a test of brute strength."

Marquis Kuang's expression turns cold. "It is not a matter of who is able to use tea like a trained dog. We are not looking for those who can pour tea with the greatest flourish. We are looking for someone who is capable of fitting in with the court, providing sound counsel. And I have not mentioned the last and final rule of this competition."

We all wait expectantly. Standing beside him, the entertainers offer bland, pretty smiles, unaffected by this demonstration of temper from a powerful man.

"You will be given enough tea leaves for a single cup, enough for you to tell truth from lie... without a word being uttered."

Confused mutters sweep through the gathered shénnóng-tú.

The competitor from Yún bows deeply in acquiescence to the difficulty of the challenge, and retreats back into the line. Now we understand this is a true test of our skill: a single cup of tea to read the mind of a stranger, to operate in silence, with only the magic to speak for us.

"Any other questions?" the marquis asks mockingly, his slippery smile returning.

We all cast our eyes to the ground. No one else dares to say anything.

"Good," he says. "I will see you back in the Hall of Eternal Light when the next gong rings." With a sweep of his sleeve, he exits the balcony, the entertainers following behind him.

We return to our residences to be made presentable for the judges. The shénnóng-tú of our residence are escorted to the bathhouse, where we bathe in great tubs scented with flowers. Servants swarm around us, pinning and pulling our hair and dotting makeup on our freshly scrubbed faces.

"I feel like I'm about to be roasted for a feast," I grumble as two maids pull hard on my sash. Lian rolls her eyes and selects a jeweled pin from the offered tray.

Shu would have loved to be made a fuss of. She would have spent all her time in the Embroidery Department, learning new techniques from the seamstresses. But for me, the robes feel restrictive at my throat and my back, making it difficult to breathe. Strangling me with continuous thoughts of my own inferiority and doubt.

The Hall of Eternal Light is constructed of wood panels, the ones I briefly glimpsed before with Qing'er. The windows are opened to the views all around, the greatest vantage point of Jia. A gold statue of a horse with its saddle glittering with gems rears against the wall beside the statue of an archer on one knee, arms straining from pulling at a bow aimed high for the sky.

There is enough room to entertain hundreds in this hall, so the seventeen tables—one for each competitor—barely fill the space.

"Her Royal Highness, Princess Ying-Zhen!" the herald announces, and we all sink to our knees.

"Please, stand." The princess dismisses the formality immediately, and we rise awkwardly again to our feet to watch her stride across the room. She is still a sight to behold, cloaked in a robe embroidered to look like peacock feathers, the fabric moving from side to side like the blinking of a thousand eyes. Under that glorious robe she wears a slim sheath of dark blue, a sash of glimmering gold at her waist. She settles herself in a carved chair at the front of the room, the wings of a phoenix expanding behind her.

"Will you risk your life for the chance to serve Dàxī?" Marquis Kuang asks. "You can walk away now if you are afraid of picking the wrong cup."

We lose five in number immediately. They hurry out the door after bowing to the princess, mumbling their apologies and their thanks for no one to hear.

Kang's memory returns to me. The princess poured him two cups and bade him drink. Even though he is a skilled martial artist, he had only his words to spar with, and only his words saved him. Yet still he drank. He took the risk, on behalf of his people. Now I face a similar test.

Those of us remaining are told to approach the long table on the other side of the hall and pick up the tray labeled with our name. I pick up my tray with reverent hands, always mindful to treat my tools with respect. The tea ware is even more beautiful than the sets in the residence. The porcelain is so thin, it feels like it could shatter with a breath. At the bottom of the bowl lie loose strands of slender, bare leaves.

I stare at the tea leaves, not understanding. My face turns hot, blood rushing to my head.

My vision blurs, then refocuses as I blink. The leaves are missing the fine silver fuzz that gives the tea its name.

This is not Silver Needle.

Someone put a different tea in my cup.

"Is everything all right?" There is a graceful hand on my arm. My nose fills with the delicate perfume of lilies. I stare up at the entertainer assigned to me, waiting for me to walk with her to our table.

The marquis crosses the room, drawing attention to my hesitation. "If you are afraid, there is no need to proceed further in this competition."

Should I call out the error? But it would be no use if *he* was the one to place the wrong tea leaves on my tray, and it would reveal that I had assistance from someone in the kitchens.

He gets closer and closer, and I know what I must do.

I turn and allow the entertainer to lead me to our table, and I catch my foot on an empty stool.

I let myself fall.

Chapter Seventeen

The tray strikes the floor with a *crack* and the cup bounces out and shatters. I land sprawled on the floor in a heap. My dignity is wounded, but better that than the alternative.

The girl from the teahouse looks shocked, her mouth open in an O, before taking a moment to regain her composure. It's a true accomplishment to disturb a teahouse apprentice so.

"Clumsy girl!" The marquis hurries to my side and looks down at me in disgust. "That tea costs more than a year's wages for even a palace servant. How dare you waste such a precious resource!"

I do my best to appear chastised, while inside I recite a litany of curses at the man.

"The girl from Sù," he drawls. "I didn't recognize you until now. But you wouldn't know anything about how valuable this tea is, being from such a place."

The hate boils in my veins as I stare at the marquis's treacherous smirk. He relishes my humiliation.

"Come, let me help you." My entertainer assists me off the floor. The servants step in quickly to sweep up the broken pieces of the tea ware.

A part of me wants to throw myself at the marquis and wipe that smug look off his face, to show him I am not someone he can torment, but the grip on my arm holds fast. A warning. I look down, focusing on the embroidery on her sleeve, fighting to stay in control. I recognize the flowers. She is from Peony House.

I take a deep breath.

"I apologize, Your Eminence," I murmur. "My hands are not accustomed to handling such fine wares, and I embarrassed myself."

I can feel the entertainer's relief, as her hands release me.

The marquis's cheek twitches as he contemplates his next move. He would love to dismiss me from the competition outright, but even he would need proper cause to do so.

The girl from Peony House curtsies low, her tone low and deferent. "Please, allow me to bring forth another tray belonging to a competitor who has forfeited the competition. Do not let this trouble Your Eminence. It is only a cup, nothing more."

"Fine." Marquis Kuang reluctantly waves us away. "Help the girl."

I sit and wait for the young woman to bring over another tray to the table. I realize how close I was to snapping, and how she pulled me back. I am grateful for that, but I cannot acknowledge her at this moment without risking both of us further.

She sits in front of me, her features now smooth and devoid of emotion, a pleasant mask. In the capital I feel exposed—my accent, my walk, my clothes, everything betraying me. But I had a lifetime of freedom where I could do what I pleased, my mother who never asked me to be anything other than who I am, flaws and all. What would it be like to always have to wear this careful face?

I check the leaves one more time, half expecting the bowl to contain the same falsehood, but I recognize the characteristic fuzz. Letting out a shaky sigh, I focus now on steadying my hands, on the pour of the hot water, the rise and fall in a sparkling stream. The spinning vortex shows the truth. The tea leaves are pointing to the center. The lid is carefully placed on top, the tea allowed to steep.

Someone tried to disqualify me, leaving me vulnerable to poison, and I would not have known if Steward Yang had not helped me. Am I absolutely certain it was the marquis? I force myself to focus on the steam, instead of turning around to see who else could be watching me, eager to see if their plot has succeeded.

I pour the tea into the cup and gesture for the entertainer to take her sip. She does so with delicate movements, covering her face with the sleeve of her other arm, part of her performance.

Something heavy hits the floor behind me with a loud thud, making me jump. I turn to see one of the shénnóng-tú lying on the ground. Two soldiers come in without prompting to carry the prone body out of the room.

Despite the rule of silence, whispers ripple among the other competitors, questions of "Is he dead?" and "What will happen to him?"

"I would advise you to focus on your own fate, competitors," the marquis announces, his enjoyment at our discomfort apparent.

I turn back to the entertainer, who has already begun her ceremony, unaffected by all the disturbances around her. The rinsing of the cups, the preparation of the pot, the wait during the steep. The light fragrance of a bright spring green tea wafts toward me, a perfect selection for an afternoon drink.

I return my attention to the five cups before me. All identical in color, the same painted design of peach blossoms running along the outer curve, all appearing to be empty. She pours the tea into each, steam curling gently above the surface. I stare at them, willing them to speak to me.

How does one become an apprentice of Shénnóng? A question rises unbidden in my mind, one of Mother's basic lessons. *The magic sounds like ringing to my ears. You may sense it differently. Is it a taste? A brush against the skin?* Mother had sat us both down in front of her while she poured the tea for us. Shu gasped, said she could see it—colorful lines being pulled from her hands, like fabric from a loom. But I smelled it, distinctly.

It smelled like pomelo flowers.

I had banished that memory when I thought I would never pour another cup of magic again. But it returns to me now, waiting for direction.

I am aware from last night that the Silver Needle does not need long to take effect. But was it only because of Kang's previous connection with me, wrenched into place by the Golden Key?

Slowly, so as not to startle her, I reach for the entertainer's hand, resting my palm on top of her knuckles. She tenses but does not pull away. The magic spills over to her, making the connection. I learn at this moment that I do not need to also drink the tea in order to wield the magic. If the receiver ingests it, then it is sufficient.

The fingers of my other hand hover over the first cup. My eyelids flutter, and I am suddenly overwhelmed by a luxurious heaviness of the limbs, the lull in the thoughts before sleep overtakes me . . . I snatch my hand back, and the feeling dissipates.

The next cup sparks a sensation of rolling within my stomach, like the unsteadiness of being on the ferry. This one causes vomiting.

The third, nothing. Empty.

I move to the fourth, to test whether the magic is true, and a sharp pain strikes my temple, like someone has stabbed a dagger into my skull. I quickly snatch the third cup, swallowing its contents in one gulp, and place it back on the table.

My breath quickens as my gaze flashes upward to meet the eyes of the girl from Peony House. I can see the barest, almost imperceptible curve at the corners of her eyes. I already know from that almost smile—I picked the right cup. Her eyes flick downward briefly, and I realize I'm still holding her hand. I let go and return my hands to my lap, suddenly feeling awkward.

My senses still remain my own. Sleep does not overtake me. Pain does not wash over me. Looking around, I see the number of shénnóng-tú continues to diminish, until the ones who remain are told to rise and approach the marquis.

"You have survived the round," he says, the golden hooves of the horse statue rearing above his head. "From fifty-some to seventeen to eight." His eyes land on me, still standing before him, and a scowl crosses his face.

I wish a sudden strong wind would topple the statue onto his head, but the heavens do not comply.

"The next round will commence in three days' time, at the start of summer. We welcome the longer days, a time for everything to begin anew. You will be given further instructions tomorrow morning in preparation. After that, you can take a much-deserved rest. Congratulations."

Even though his words are celebratory, something about them makes my blood run cold. We leave the Month of Lengthening, when daylight begins to stretch later into the evening. We approach the start of summer, but where the season is supposed to promise warmth and growth, it seems to have brought forth continued unrest.

The questions uttered by the princess in her own garden echo in my mind as we leave the Hall of Eternal Light: *Whose life? Whose death?*

Only time will tell.

I'm determined to find the steward this afternoon. It's possible she was the one who was tasked by the marquis to change out my tea leaves. Perhaps her clue was also a warning. She said she was the one who sourced the tea for the competition, so she is the most likely person to give me the answer I'm looking for.

Lian and I promised we would not return to the kitchens again, but I set forth with only one purpose. I will not involve anyone else in my plans. I want to find Qing'er but encounter Small Wu instead. He's busy twisting and pulling more dough, sweat dripping off his forehead at the strenuous work.

"Do you know where I can find Steward Yang?" I ask.

He stops and wipes his face with a cloth before answering. "At this time, she is usually reviewing the kitchen accounts in her room. Go past the Fish Department and through the far gate to the women's quarters. Give them my name or find A'bing if you run into any trouble."

I duck my head in thanks and hurry through the twisting corridors past the kitchens, keeping to myself. No one stops me, everyone busy attending to their own tasks.

Steward Yang is my only connection here to my mother, my hope of finding out more about her past. I don't want her to be the one who betrayed me, but I know her loyalty is to her immediate family first and then to her staff in the kitchens. I'm only a disruption to her, a potential threat.

I enter the women's quarters and walk down the open-air

hallway, checking each door. The ranks of those who reside within are hung on plaques beside each doorway, but no names are recorded. Her room is near the end of the quarters, only one plaque beside the doorway—with her position as supervisor of the kitchens, she is afforded her own private room. The door is open, and through it, I see her sitting at a table, brush in hand.

I raise my fist and rap on the door twice.

She starts, turning her head to look at me. Then she frowns. "I thought I told you not to come to the kitchens again."

A part of me shrivels, wanting to apologize. But another part of me is ready for answers, and ready to tear things apart to find them.

I cross her threshold without invitation and stand in front of her with my arms crossed. She tosses her brush to the table, prepared to throw me out for intruding in her space.

"Did you switch out the Silver Needle on my tray?" I ask her, imagining my words like fists, striking the first blow. "Was that why you warned me, because you had already been tasked by the Marquis of Ānhé to sabotage me?"

Her expression changes from anger to confusion. "The marquis? Why would I help him?" She curls her lip, then, as she ponders this, the reason I am standing there seems to dawn on her. "Close the door. We can't be seen together by the others."

Even though I bristle at her forceful tone, I still obey.

"Now, sit down." She points at the bamboo chair across from her when I return. "Tell me everything."

Chapter Eighteen

I TELL HER WHAT HAPPENED DURING THE SECOND ROUND of the competition—the rules, what we were tasked to do, and my discovery that it was the wrong tea in my cup. Her face grows pale as I recount the events, her finger tapping a frantic beat on the table.

"You are certain it was not Silver Needle?" she asks.

I nod.

"But how?" she ponders, deep lines forming on her brow. "One of the royal physicians handed me the tea leaves, and I prepared all the trays . . . It must have been one of the servants." She looks perturbed at this realization.

"It seems like the stars have different plans for you. Your mother fled this place and told me she would never return. Now you are here in her stead." She shakes her head. "Ah, Yiting . . . how could fate have been so cruel to you?"

It seems like she genuinely cared for my mother. I think they must have been friends.

"You said she left because of a scandal. What was the reason?" Memories are all I have left of her, and I'm desperate for any other knowledge.

"It was a bitter cold winter, and the empress was pregnant with the princess . . . ," she tells me. "The empress fell ill, as did the midwife who was in charge of her care. Same with many of the royal physicians. Your mother used magic from Shénnóng to save her, and she found favor in the eyes of the emperor and the empress."

My uncle—my mother's brother—had always bragged about how he could have attended the imperial college but chose to remain with the family business instead. He always looked down on my mother's profession, even though the process to become a shénnóng-shī was similarly selective, if not more so. Why did my mother never mention that she attended to the empress herself?

"The emperor had arranged for a suitable match for Yiting, for all who serve at the palace may leave at the age of twenty-five to start their own families. But during that winter she fell in love with your father, an up-and-coming imperial physician, and he with her. And to refuse the emperor's blessing means a death sentence."

I envision in my mind this younger version of my mother and father, with their own dreams, their imagined futures lit up in front of them like lanterns glowing in the sky. The tenderness in my father's face as he watches her while she shapes pottery for the kiln. The way she laughs when they prepare herbs to dry in the storeroom.

"With the permission of the empress, your mother began to secretly study for her shénnóng-shī trials. She managed to win the attention of the Esteemed Xu when he visited the palace, and gained a token for admittance to the next trials at Hánxiá. She returned from the academy with her name inscribed in the *Book of Tea*, and she asked for an audience with the emperor and the empress. She requested that they honor the boon they offered when she saved the life of the empress and the princess, asking to be freed from the engagement the emperor had arranged for her. The emperor was furious, but the empress was understanding. She helped your mother flee the palace in one of her own carriages when Yiting admitted she was with child."

"And she returned to her family in Sù," I say to myself softly. "She gave birth to me a few months later."

This is why Father's mouth turns into a hard line when I ask about his family. Why Mother's face always smoothed into a blank mask when Shu would wonder aloud why some children had two sets of grandparents, while we had only one. I'm not even sure where Father's family is. All I know is they are in one of the prefectures west of Jia, but we have never met them. His name must have been stricken from their family books in disgrace.

The implication of this knowledge stabs me in the chest. If Mother hadn't gotten pregnant, she could have continued her comfortable life in the palace. As a favorite of the empress, she would have served her as shénnóng-shī and adviser. She would never have needed to toil in the fields. She would have walked among the nobles and the court officials.

"You are halfway through the competition, girl," the steward scoffs. "You are just as intelligent as your mother. She risked everything to keep you. You know that, right? She fought for you and you are here, following her legacy. You are the symbol of her strength. Be careful. Don't get yourself killed in the process."

I stand and mumble my thanks. I stumble over my feet in my haste to get out of that suddenly suffocating room, heavy with the burden of my new knowledge.

To my relief when I return, I find our room empty. I sit down heavily on my bed, narrowly missing crushing the note Lian left for me.

Dear Ning, I have been called to be plucked like a chicken and

paraded in front of musty old officials as part of Father's diplomacy
obligations. I will see you tomorrow.

Even though I am choking on tears, I still chuckle. Lian's brashness, her carefree demeanor, feel so similar to my mother, forging
her own destiny. I should follow their examples, instead of wal-
lowing in my own self-pity. I pick up Mother's pendant, wrap it in
Shu's handkerchief, and tuck it away in my sash. For them, I will be
strong.

Without Lian's company, I debate whether I should still join the
other competitors for the evening meal. In the end, hunger wins
out. I promised Steward Yang I would not associate with the
kitchen staff any longer, and I'm not as confident as Lian, able to
request extra portions from the serving staff without hesitation.

Each night, our meals are presented at the Garden of Fragrant
Reflection, under the cover of the cluster of pavilions that sit in the
middle of an ornamental garden paved with white stones. As our
numbers grow fewer, we now eat under the central pavilion, separated by two stone tables. Lanterns sway in the breeze, lighting up
the paths, and the air is scented by gardenia flower blooms.

Shao holds court at one table with those who remain of his
friends, whose faces I have committed to memory. One of the loud-
est and most boorish among them is Guoming, who was present
in the residence of the marquis. Even though the drunken buffoon
who grabbed me was eliminated in the second round of the competition, I see all of them as complicit in the scheming. I've taken
to avoiding them at every turn, casting my eyes down and continuing to behave as the quiet girl from the countryside who poses no
threat.

Today we feast on sweet-and-sour fish, the carp cut into beautiful flower patterns and then fried, curling into petals. It's bathed in a vividly red sauce cooked with vinegar. Giant lion's head meatballs, bigger than my fist, have been cooked in their own juices, then ladled into bowls to be accompanied by greens and a light broth sweetened by mushrooms. Even something as simple as carrots and cucumbers have been turned into flowers as accompaniments, so that the platter appears to be a garden in bloom.

My head is still in turmoil from the revelations shared by the steward. What she told me explains why my parents were always so careful to keep Shu and me within the village. Why they rarely traveled, and why they never wanted to be in attendance when the emperor visited a nearby town on one of his summer tours. Why Father was so angry whenever I drew the attention of the soldiers.

I'm so focused on my food, I don't notice I'm no longer alone until two fists strike the table in front of me. I jump, my spoon dropping out of my hand and hitting my bowl with a clatter. I look up, my mouth full of rice, only to see Shao looking down at me with a disapproving glare.

"You lost me money today, girl," he drawls, his capital accent even more pronounced then usual. I can see over his shoulder the young men at the other table, elbowing each other and looking over at us, laughing.

I swallow, confused. "I don't know what you mean."

"He put down an entire coin purse betting you would fail this round," one of his friends calls out, chortling. "I'm glad you proved him wrong."

Heat flares in my face, and there's a tightness in my chest. They're ... betting on who will win or lose?

"It was pure luck that she passed." Shao turns back to me, regaining his composure. The lazy smile returns to his face. He dangles a small pouch in front of me, shaking it until I can hear the coins clink within. "Why don't we make it more of a challenge for the rest of us? Take these coins, then you can leave. Return to the poor village you came from. Save yourself the embarrassment of defeat."

The pouch lands on the table with a clatter, the silver contained within spilling out. I stand up, knocking my stool down behind me, arms trembling at my sides.

I look at the faces of the rest of the competitors at my table. All of them looked shocked, surprised, some amused, but no one speaks up for me.

Slowly, I pick up the pouch, putting each coin back inside carefully. Weighing the pouch in my hand, I can tell there is more than enough in here to stock the entirety of my father's store. Ingredients to treat the villagers, to fill our kitchen shelves for months . . .

I meet Shao's eyes, and he looks at me with growing amusement. "There is no shame in—"

Pulling my arm back, I throw the pouch at Shao as hard as I can. It hits him in the chest and lands on the stone floor below. Coins roll in every direction.

"Keep betting against me," I say to him, voice shaking only very slightly. "I'd love to see what else you'll lose."

Shao's eyes bulge as he steps forward, but even quicker, the shénnóng-tú from Yún blocks his path with his arm.

"Move out of my way, Wenyi," Shao hisses.

"Careful, Shao," the monk drawls. "You wouldn't want us to think you are feeling threatened by her . . . Right?"

Shao sputters at the absurdity of that thought, and I turn, flee-ing. Away from their mocking gazes. Away from their ridicule.

Shao's jeers remind me of my family's history, my disgraceful lin-eage. How I keep embarrassing my family at each turn. Like the time before the autumn rains, years ago, when the soldiers came to collect the harvest taxes, and my family grumbled about how they could not wait for them to leave.

That night, I had searched for the corpse lilies in bloom, flow-ers that blossom only once every six years. I gathered as many of them as I could carry and placed them around the campsite, hop-ing their scent would repel the soldiers. In the morning I woke to the sound of screams and smoke rolling down the hills. The soldiers had burned the fields, believing that the flowers had bloomed in the middle of the night, a bad omen. Our orchards were destroyed, along with half of our family's tea garden. The blackened sky, the smell of charred trees . . .

I wake in the dark, thrashing. There is a heavy weight on my body, a shadow crouched at my legs. I swing my arms wildly at my attacker, but my reward is a heavy pressure on my chest. A hand closes over my throat, and another over my mouth, smothering me.

I consider, fleetingly, if it could be Kang, but the face above me is not the one who visits me in the night. She's a girl. Her hair is pulled up high above her head, kept back from her face with a band. But the rest of her hair spills over one shoulder, black waves brushing my face as she breathes.

I know her now: the one who stands beside the princess.

"My name is Gao Ruyi." Her whisper confirms her identity.

"I am handmaiden to the princess. If I take my hand from your mouth, will you scream?"

I shake my head no, and the weight is lifted from my chest and throat when she rolls off me. I wheeze a little as my lungs protest the rough treatment.

I can feel her watching me with intensity, looking for weaknesses. I know she has calculated how to silence me if I make the wrong move. The lantern light from the courtyard streams through the carved shutters, leaving patterns of light and shadow across her skin.

"The princess requests your presence," she says. Not a question. An order.

"Let me get dressed," I tell her, a slight tremble in my voice. "I cannot see her in my current state."

"It won't be long," she says, dismissing my concerns. "Throw on a cloak. That will be sufficient."

I step behind the dressing screen, fumbling with the ties of my cloak, questions tumbling inside my head. Wondering how much the princess knows. If this is about my time in the kitchens, the accusations of the marquis ... Or is it about my nightly conversations with Kang?

I trudge behind the handmaiden, my feet feeling heavier with each step. She does not speak when we make our way through the corridors of the palace, past unfamiliar gates with soldiers standing guard. They bow their heads and allow us to pass without question, until we reach an alcove with a sad-looking tree. I place my hand against the bark and sense that the life is being choked out of it, the leaves brown and crumbling. At the foot of the tree there is a stone carving of a lion, a snarl on its face, one paw extended with claws out.

Ruyi steps around the tree and touches the wall. In front of my eyes, a door opens, revealing a dark tunnel behind it. I gawk at it, marveling at how such a mechanism is possible, but she quickly pulls me through, shutting the opening behind me. We're enclosed in darkness. I reach out and touch the wall. Stone.

With a strike of a match and the smell of sulfur tingling in my nose, Ruyi's face is illuminated by an ignited torch. We make our way deeper through the dark tunnel, me hurrying after her confident strides. She seems like someone who has passed through these passages many times before, navigating the turns until we reach a wall with an iron ring hanging from the nose of a stone boar, sharp tusks curving from its mouth.

She pulls the ring and a door opens, revealing a moonlit garden. A figure, dressed in white, waits for us under the trees.

CHAPTER NINETEEN

THE GARDEN LOOKS EXACTLY LIKE IT DID IN KANG'S MEM-
ory: the weeping willow trailing leaves on the ground, the graceful dwarf pines in their round pots, and white decorative boulders
placed around the perimeter in auspicious locations. The princess,
seated at the stone table, the branches of the plum tree behind her
in full bloom.

"Approach," Ruyi says with a hand at my back.

I take a step forward and kneel, touching my forehead to the
cold stones. I could never have imagined this moment, even in Shu's
most fanciful tales, that I would be standing before the princess,
carrying a secret I am certain she does not want me to know.

"Rise," her voice instructs me. I stand to look into the face of
the regent of Dàxī, the heir to the throne.

Her hair is missing the pins and combs that usually adorn it,
falling loose around her face instead. She's dressed in a gown of
pale purple, in a shade so light I had mistaken it initially as white.
She appears to be the ethereal embodiment of the Moon Goddess,
and I am the unworthy peasant.

"The girl from Sù," she says with a wry smile. Does it mean
amusement or distaste? I cannot tell. "You are the shénnóng-tú
who has created a stir in this competition."

I hide my hands behind my back, suddenly aware of my dirty nails and calloused skin.

"You have captured the attention of Marquis Kuang and also of Chancellor Zhou. The two of them have been in multiple debates about whether you should be permitted to remain in the competition. Whether your presence is too … disruptive in these times."

Fierce anger flashes within me. Familiar names, familiar accusations. *Troublemaker.*

"I see something burning within you," she remarks. "Tell me the truth: Why are you here? Do you dream of toppling the empire?"

I feign ignorance, believing it to be safer than the words of protest that I want to utter. "I … I am not sure of what you speak, Highness," I say.

"If your purpose is to create unrest, then you have succeeded in your mission," the princess muses. "But if you had so simple a goal, you would have left when given the opportunity."

"I want to win the competition," I tell her, recognizing that now is the time I need to defend myself, walking this precarious path between two people of ambition—the princess and the marquis. "I am not working for anyone but myself."

Her eyes bore into mine. "Why?"

How much have they looked into the backgrounds of those who are present in the competition? I know with certainty that my mother's name is in the *Book of Tea*, but I still don't know if anyone else in the capital other than Steward Yang knows of her death.

"I am only here for myself. My mother passed away this past winter, Highness." I have to offer enough of the truth, and I have already given up this information to the steward. "My sister is ill. Without both of them, my family is struggling. Winning this competition, this position, will mean a better life for my family."

But there is so much I want to ask *her*. About the poison, the Shadow, how it all ties to my mother's death. How I want to find the person responsible and tear them apart with my bare hands.

She contemplates this, searching my face as if she wants to carve the truth out of me.

"Do you understand the empire the Ascended Emperor wanted to build? A vision my grandmother upheld, a legacy my father continued to believe in? A better life for the people."

Your people are starving, I think *They're angry. While you're deluding yourself with dreams of a grandiose empire.*

The princess laughs, a brittle sound. "I see you do not believe me, and I should send you to the dungeons for that."

I should drop to my knees, beg for her forgiveness. Ensure my survival another day in this competition, yet . . . yet that is not who I am. It seems to go against my very nature. Even if it dooms me.

She senses my struggle and seems amused by it. "Perhaps you are not lying. I should do as the marquis suggests and have you whipped for your insolence."

"All of you are the same," I say. "Afraid of the truth."

Ruyi is immediately beside me, wrenching my arms behind my back, forcing me to drop to the ground.

"Do you understand my dilemma?" Princess Ying-Zhen looks down at me. "I cannot have people like you creating unrest. I have to maintain order until my father's illness improves." Her pulse twitches at her throat. A beautiful lie.

But then she pauses. "What truth are you speaking of?"

"Every season, taxes are expected of us," I say through gritted teeth, ignoring the painful twisting of my shoulder in Ruyi's grip. "Even when the harvest is poor, even when there is nothing in our stores and our granaries."

"Do you think I am unaware of the reports?" the princess snaps at me. "Do you think it pleases me to know my people are suffering?"

"Send me home, and others will take my place," I tell her. "We will demand to be heard."

"Watch yourself!" Ruyi warns, and wrenches my arm so hard that I cry out.

"Beg pardon, Your Highness." I pant, trying to breathe through the pain. "There is a difference between living the suffering and reading about it."

She stares down at me for a long moment, contemplating this, then turns away. "Let her go."

Ruyi drops me and I clutch my arm to my body, cradling it. The pain throbs to the beat of my heart.

"Keep your spirited nature," the princess says with cold amusement. "You will need it for what I require of you."

I do not understand.

"It surprised me when I realized you had caught the eye of another in the palace," she continues. "I had my cousin followed when he was moved to the residences. My guards report to me that each night he leaves at the Hour of the Ghost and returns at the Hour of the Thief. To visit . . . you."

There's a sour taste in my mouth. I swallow. This *is* about Kang. Threads tying me to him, and him to her. The threads of fate, pulsing between us.

The princess approaches, her shadow falling over me. "Tell me, Ning. Are you working with him? What is he planning?"

"I don't know." I shake my head. "I met him in the market, the day of the start of the competition."

She grabs my chin, twisting it until my neck is bent back, forcing me to look up at her. "If you are lying to me," she says calmly, "I will have your family killed."

The only threat that will undo me. "He . . . he told me he knows the emperor is dead."

The princess regards me without emotion, as if considering all the splendid ways in which she could silence me.

I force myself to hold her gaze, to speak slowly and carefully. "You know I am telling you the truth."

She lets me go, and I close my eyes.

"Tell no one of his lies," she says quietly. "You will get close to him, discover what he has planned and report back to me. If you provide me with useful information, then I will reward you after the competition and provide what you need for your family. If you provide me with nothing useful, then . . ."

The threat is clear. She wants me to be her spy. She wants me to use Kang in order to find out his father's plans. I have little choice but to agree.

I have everything to gain, and everything to lose.

I nod. "I'll do it."

"Then you should leave soon. The Hour of the Ghost approaches." The princess reaches up and breaks a branch from the plum tree. Some of the blossoms are already wilting. Nothing beautiful lasts forever.

"How will I find you if I have information to share?" I ask.

"Ruyi will show you how to reach me." She waves her hand, dismissing me.

Ruyi approaches me again and gestures for me to follow. A woman of few words. She leads me to a gate on the other side of the garden. Another stone tunnel, but considerably shorter than the previous one.

We emerge in a back corridor, and I recognize from the white walls that we are behind the palace library. There is a shaded path, stone pebbles forming a walkway for scholars to shed their shoes and walk upon for mental clarity and acuity, following the patterns of the gods. Stone lions border the path, wearing the same fierce snarl as the one previous.

"Count two from the southern end," Ruyi says, pointing at the lion in question. She gives me an embroidered pendant made of yellow string, a similar design to my mother's mourning knot. Easy to spot from a distance. "Tie this to its paw before the first gong of the evening. I will meet you here at the Hour of the Thief. If the princess needs to speak with you, I will put the same pendant on the lion in front of your courtyard. Meet me at the same time."

Ruyi bows to me then, touching her hand to her shoulder. "Good hunting, Ning of Sù."

With barely a rustle, she departs into the shadows, leaving me to find my way back to the residences alone.

CHAPTER TWENTY

I FALL ASLEEP SOMETIME AFTER THE FOURTH GONG, AFTER realizing that Kang is not going to appear tonight. I suppose that makes me already a failure at spy work, but I am thankful for this reprieve. My nerves are frayed after my meeting with the princess, and I am not sure I could manage the pretense it would require to face him tonight.

In the morning, Lian and I tuck into a breakfast of fluffy baozi, fresh from the bamboo steamers of Small Wu's kitchen. We pull the dough apart to reveal the filling within—ground pork mixed with chopped chives and drizzled with sesame oil—and blow to cool the steaming insides. I should be grateful to even be here, but the unease continues to crawl up the back of my throat, until I lose my appetite.

I wonder how long the princess hopes to keep up her lie about the emperor's health. How furious the people will be if they realize they have been deceived. The many facets of her mask I have glimpsed—on the stage, through Kang's eyes, and witnessed first-hand. The look of someone slowly being forced to the edge.

"Ning!" Lian waves her hand in front of my face. "You've been so quiet!"

"I'm . . ." I turn back to her, take a large bite out of the bun, and almost choke. "I'm . . . I'm only worried about the next round."

I'll need to get better at lying, and fast, or else all my secrets will unravel around me.

She nods. "Understandable. It will only get harder from here. Especially if we need two days to prepare for this next challenge."

Lian tries to offer a distraction by regaling me with stories of last night's banquet. How she had to sit next to some of the lower officials, who have a penchant for talking too much when the wine flows freely. How everyone was abuzz with speculation about whether the emperor would grace them with his presence, even a glimpse. But he did not appear.

How did the Banished Prince manage to find out about the emperor's death even while the princess has been able to keep it from the court? The rumors worm their way back into my thoughts again, how his spies have ears and eyes everywhere . . . snatching children to become residents of his dark kingdom . . .

"Can you tell me more about the princess?" I ask. If I can use Lian as a resource, perhaps she can help me navigate all I have seen in the past few days.

"When I used to spend the winters here, all the children spent time together," she says. "Zhen was . . . serious. Quiet, focused on her studies. Not surprising, considering her grandmother was the dowager empress." She grimaces.

I nod, remembering my own grandmother, who ruled over the Wu household with an iron fist. Only Grandfather could get her to calm if someone managed to anger her.

"We used to call her hǔ gū pó." Lian chuckles at the memory. Grandmother Tiger, the legendary tigress who roams the forest, who has a taste for evil men and likes to clean her teeth with their bones. Myths reflected in life.

"Hǔ gū pó was the scariest thing to roam these halls," she goes on. "And all her attention was on Zhen, to make sure she lived up to the Li name. She had lessons from the moment she woke up and late into the night."

"That sounds . . . lonely."

Lian nods. "If your closest companion is someone who your grandmother picked to be your shadow from a young age . . . it's not a life I would want to live."

"You mean her bodyguard?" *Ruyi.* The girl who launched herself into the air with a single jump, like a bird taking flight, defending the life of the princess.

"Her family has served the royal family for generations, and when the dowager empress married the Ascended Emperor, she was permitted to bring some of her own people with her. Ruyi was one of them. She was trained in a secret fighting art that is passed down only to those in her family."

One born to rule. One born to serve.

"I suppose it is easy to ensure a person's loyalty if the lives of their entire family depend on it," I mumble.

"Or they could care for them," Lian says, unaware of the turmoil in my mind, countering my bitterness. "From what I remember, Zhen was always kind to Ruyi. She was kind to everyone, actually. Never behaved like I thought a princess should."

I remember the chill in her gaze, the casual threat of her words. Something happened to that kind girl Lian remembers in the years since.

Mingwen walks in and bows. Her demeanor has been warmer to us since our encounter in the kitchens. She has taken over the care of our residence as the senior maidservant, and even though we are no longer permitted to associate with the rest of the kitchen staff, it is still nice to see a familiar face. "Competitors, your presence has been requested by the judges in the Hall of Reflection."

"So soon?" Lian downs her cup of tea with a hurried slurp, and I regret not eating more to settle my stomach. If I am sick in front of the judges, it will simply add another mark to my already long list of misdeeds.

The few of us who remain file into the Hall of Reflection, a small indoor pavilion located in the Scholar's Gardens surrounding the library. The floors are a pale white marble, swirls and patterns like clouds contained within. The walls are a gleaming blue-black stone, shiny enough to show our reflections when we stand before them. Above our heads, the roof ascends in a dizzying pattern. At first it appears to be a spiral, leading upward. Peering closer, I realize it is an illusion. Instead, tablets are inset into the shelves. Carved with names, memorials to the dead.

Melodic trills fill the air, redirecting my attention. There are golden cages positioned on stands, each containing a single bird, talking to each other in a series of calls and song. They are a beautiful addition to the room, living adornments for an emperor to admire. The coexistence of life and death.

Elder Guo stands among them, regarding us with a stern expression. Even with her plain gray robes devoid of any adornment, she exudes a serene confidence.

"Welcome to those who remain, as a testament to Shénnóng's legacy." She raises her arms in greeting.

The scholars and the monks commit their lives to the study of pursuits worthy of the respective gods they honor. Just like Hánxiá is dedicated to the Blue Carp, Wǔlín is devoted to the Black Tiger, renowned for its study of martial arts and military techniques. Yěliŭ Academy is where one would attend for the study of philosophy and history. The shénnóng-tú who spoke up for me against Shao, the one named Wenyi, wears a pendant that shows he is pledged to the Emerald Tortoise of Yěliŭ, I've noticed. Only the Lady of the South has no monastery or academy. She is found in the trees and fields.

"At Hánxiá, we are dedicated to the service of Shénnóng. We study his teachings, all he has passed on regarding agriculture and animal husbandry, and of course, the art of tea."

What I know of Hánxiá is that it is located west of the Jade River, on the border of the mountain range that separates Yún and Ānhé, overlooking the most fertile valley of Dàxī. Mother always mentioned the name with reverence; the most renowned shénnóng-shī have passed through those hallowed halls, where she obtained her rank. The rarest of tea leaves are grown at that elevation, some of which have been tasted only by the royal family and the court officials.

Elder Guo's expression turns somber. "By now you must have all heard about the rot that is attempting to infiltrate the empire through poisoned tea bricks. Treacherous attempts to undermine the rule of the great emperor."

A rush fills my ears. The tea responsible for my mother's death. So far, we have been told nothing about its origins, about who may be behind the poisonings. The governor and his people have many excuses, offering only a promise that the threat has been contained.

"Your third challenge honors the virtue of wisdom. You will continue to the next round in pairs," she states. "Choose your partner."

I'm surprised she would permit us to form our own alliances. Lian and I step closer to one another without hesitation. The others do the same, having already formed their own bonds.

"We will—" Elder Guo's eyes narrow as her words break off. The floor beneath our feet begins to shake. Her head swivels to the door. In the distance, there is the sound of drums.

Wenyi is the one who jumps forward first, throwing the windows open, revealing the courtyard below. Rows of soldiers march in time, sending tremors throughout the grounds of the palace. The air is suddenly filled with the sound of beating wings, the caged birds attempting to take flight, sensing danger.

Someone wails, the words ringing clearly across the rooftops, bringing everyone to their knees:

"The emperor has ascended! Long will he be remembered! The emperor has ascended! Long will he be remembered!"

Chapter Twenty-One

We are escorted out of the Hall of Reflection, directed to return to our residences. But we quickly enter into chaos, the gardens teeming with soldiers. I'm separated from the other competitors, trying to get my bearings, but I'm refused entry to a gate that appears familiar, then I'm funneled down another corridor until I am lost again. I'm gripped by the same panic as in the market, the drums beating a frantic beat in the distance, causing my own heartbeat to quicken.

"Clear a path!" Soldiers bark at a cluster of servants, many of whom are weeping.

My head turns and I see another group of people dressed in the finery of nobles, but one seems to have collapsed into a faint. I follow another group of servants, hurrying past, hoping they will lead me back to the servants' wing where I belong. But someone bumps into me, then I'm grabbed by an arm clasped in armor, pulling me in another direction.

"Wait!" I protest. "You've got the wrong person!"

The soldier who has ahold of me stops and bends down toward me, lifting his helmet up slightly to unveil the face beneath.

"Kang?" I half gasp, then, realizing my mistake in uttering that name in the open, I speak quickly, hoping no one else overheard. "You didn't come last night."

But I immediately regret those words. It sounds like too much wanting, too much of myself revealed.

"I wasn't sure if you wanted to see me again," he says. I catch a glimpse of a smile before it is once again hidden beneath the helmet.

Before I can say anything else, another shadow looms over us: a soldier with jutting wings of gold rising from his black helmet. The fine designs of his shoulders and the etchings of the grimacing demon on his chest plate indicate someone of a high rank. I freeze, certain he has seen through Kang's disguise.

"Servants are to return to their residences," he barks. "Upon order of the chancellor."

"Acknowledged, Marshal." Kang quickly clasps his hands into a salute, and his hand returns to my elbow. "Let's go."

We hurry together as fast as we can, my steps keeping time with his, until we are through the gardens and past another moon gate. We have returned to the Scholar's Garden, next to the black spire of the library pagoda.

"Down this way." He gestures, and we turn the corner onto the Path of Contemplation. With a jolt I recognize the stone lions, the black and white pebbles. The instructions of the princess loom before me: *Discover what he has planned.*

I suddenly feel like I am wandering through a maze of brambles, every turn a threat.

When he is certain there is no one to overhear us, Kang pulls off his helmet. "When I heard that the news about the emperor had been released, I knew it meant the window for her to make a choice about me was swiftly closing," he says, too close and too earnest. Ever so casual for a man who is speaking about his possible execution. "But I don't want to be remembered by you as a man who does not keep his word."

I'll see you again. A promise as soft as petals falling.

"What do you think she will decide?" I ask. "To lift the exile or . . ." I cannot even say it.

He inclines his head. "At least I will die having fought for my people."

It reminded me of his sincerity when he said he would ask for leniency, not for himself, but for everyone back home. Silver Needle has already told me the truth. If what I can find from him can ease the princess's suspicions, perhaps his life will be spared.

"Do you know a way out of the palace?" I ask.

There is a flurry of footsteps on the other side of the wall, and he pulls me into another alcove, this one housing a small bamboo grove and a wooden carving of flowers.

"Why do you ask?"

To spend more time with you. To find out more of your secrets. To save you . . . or expose you.

I know I need to choose the rest of my words carefully. "Our paths run parallel, in a way. Soon you will face the judgment of the princess, and my future will be decided in the next round of the competition." My finger runs over the smoothness of the bamboo, marveling at how nature still grows here, stifled in this small plot of dirt and limited circle of sky. "But you mentioned our day in Jia, and I'm reminded how happy I was that day as well. Freer than I've ever felt before. I wonder if we can return to that, even for an hour."

At first, I am hesitantly grasping at those fragile connections, but as I continue to speak, the words begin to grow stronger. I can taste the sweetness of pear candy on my tongue, igniting other memories—the warmth of the Golden Key as we touched, how we sank into one another, a closeness that I both feared and craved. Maybe I drew on the magic, pulling him to me, but the magic draws on me in turn, binding me closer to him.

"And if you could go into the city, where would you go?" he asks.

"I heard there are shops selling teacups carved from bone or ivory. Foods from the north that I've never seen before. All these things I have yet to experience. But if I fail the competition, I will have to return home and give up all my dreams of becoming a shénnóng-shī. I do not have the coin to complete the training and attend the exams." And of course, I will lose Shu if I fail this quest. The quaver in my voice is embarrassingly real.

Mother said there is power in words, in hopes we breathe into being. It dangles there before me, a dream once as far out of reach as the stars in the sky, my longing for a different life. A life that Mother had and then lost. She found her contentment later, but I still yearn for it.

"Before . . . it may have been possible," he says. "But now my face is known to all the city guards. I cannot travel in this disguise as easily, and I do not think I would be able to walk freely in the market without the helmet."

"It was a foolish thought." I shrug, in an attempt to hide how much I care. But I do care, much more than I thought I would.

A small part of me believed perhaps a shénnóng-shī would take interest in me during the competition, take me on as an apprentice based on my potential. But after the way I fumbled during the first round, I doubt anyone would want me now. With the competition now closed to the public, there is no other chance. If I don't win, I won't be able to save Shu.

Unless I get the promised help from the princess in return for my spying: the cure-all stone for my sister and enough coin to take care of my family.

"My mother told me of private gardens cultivated by scholar families, or even Jia's public gardens, where anyone may walk and admire the blooms," I say, grasping at any other possibility for us to spend time alone, uninterrupted. "Sometimes I feel suffocated by this place, where everyone is always watching, waiting for you to make a mistake..." My voice trails off.

"I understand," he says softly. "It's a place where you're not always sure if people wish you harm or mean well. That is one thing I did not expect to find in Lùzhou. Where people say what they mean and mean what they say."

"I would like to hear more about Lùzhou," I say. "If you are willing to tell me."

The walls shake again as more soldiers march past. He grabs my hand suddenly, pulling me close. I look up at him, feeling a flash of mortification. Does he think I'm hopeful for a tryst? Is that the price I'll have to pay to fulfill my task?

"I thought of another place I can take you to," he whispers. "Somewhere I won't be recognized. If you will trust me." He brings my hand up, opening our fingers to touch, and presses his palm to mine. *Trust.*

I feel the sharp stab of embarrassment in my gut. It is only me, dreaming of flirtations. I nod, not trusting my voice not to betray me. He gives me the same lightning-quick grin that still makes my pulse stutter. I hope the connection between us does not pull too tight, and he remains oblivious to the thoughts still warring inside my traitorous mind.

I follow Kang as he checks to make sure there are no soldiers nearby, and we scurry to another alcove. This one contains a plum tree, white petals scattered on the stones below. Another stone lion, paws raised, waits at the base.

He pulls at an iron ring on the wall, and the mechanism slides open to reveal a hidden tunnel, just like the one Ruyi led me through when she took me to speak with the princess. How many other tunnels run through this place?

"Stay close," he whispers to me when we are safely behind the door. "The tunnel gets tight in places, and sometimes we will pass right by the guards."

I follow close behind, mindful of his warning. We're able to walk comfortably side by side to start, but eventually have to walk one after another. After a time, the tunnel gradually begins to widen again before we emerge into a small chamber. There is a large iron brazier in the center, lit and emanating warmth. The light from the fire bounces off the plaques on the wall, making the inscriptions shine. There is no dust on the floor, no signs of insects or animals. It is obvious this room is well-cared for.

A bell rings somewhere above our heads. The sound of it is so close, it reverberates through my entire body. But the tone of it is familiar. It signifies the changing of the day, from morning to afternoon to the evening.

"We're close to the bell tower!" I exclaim. The tower is located at the southwest corner of the palace, and its sound can be heard from any corner of Jia.

"We are right underneath it," Kang explains, pulling an unlit torch from a stack in the corner. He uses the flames of the brazier to light it. "When the Ascended Emperor built the palace, he ordered these tunnels to be constructed, connecting the palace to various points in Jia as escape routes in case of attack. I spent a lot of my childhood memorizing these tunnels to hide from my tutors or my trainers."

He looks into the dancing light of the brazier, the fire reflected in his eyes. "One of the tunnels leads to the northern docks. Another to the teahouse district. That was built at Grandmother's request, so she could attend the performances without having to take an entourage of guards."

Grandmother. Dowager Empress Wuyang. It's strange to think about the fabled rulers of Dàxī's history as people with families. That Kang could know them as well as I know Shu and my father. The thought is disconcerting.

"We should keep moving," he tells me. We head into one of the tunnels, and as we walk I can feel the gradual slope of the ground beneath my feet. The air grows damper, like we are headed into the bowels of the earth.

"It's a peculiar feeling, coming back here," he murmurs when we reach a split in the path. He lifts up his torch to look in either direction.

"How long ago did you leave the palace?" I ask, hopeful that being in a place of his childhood will make him more susceptible to my questions.

"When I was nine," he says. "It's been ten years now. Everything is familiar, and yet..." I wait for him to finish his thought, but he does not continue.

I don't know how it feels to be expelled from a childhood home, to bear the physical brand of a traitor. But I do know what it feels like to be an outcast.

I place a hand on his arm, and he glances down at it in surprise, almost as if he forgot I was here for a moment.

"I remember now." He gives me a smile. "We're almost there."

CHAPTER TWENTY-TWO

WE DO NOT ADVANCE FAR DOWN THE TUNNEL BEFORE WE come to a wooden door, barred with a heavy beam on this side. It takes both of us to open it, covering our faces with our sleeves so we do not inhale the dust that fills the air around us; it's obvious the door has not been opened for quite some time. We ascend the steps, keeping low and quiet, cautious that we may be emerging into an occupied space.

The first thing I notice is the smell of incense, rich and cloying, as the rest of the room comes into view. The chamber has five walls, each holding a carved stone panel. I approach each with reverence, recognizing that they are depictions of the gods.

The Lady of the South has rippling robes and a flute in hand, her slippered feet on the back of a bird with great wings. Another panel features the Archer King, astride a great horse rearing, its massive hooves grazing the sky. Shénnóng is portrayed with a flowing beard, floating on a lily pad, flower in hand, while his reflection in the water shows a giant carp with matching long whiskers. Next to him is a man with bulging eyes and a ferocious, fanged grin, holding a drum in his hand. Lightning streaks the sky behind him, reflecting off the mirror held by the woman at his side. The Thunder Tiger God, clad in his usual black, and the Lightning Goddess, his wife.

The panel closest to the door features the Emerald Tortoise. All of them are stories familiar to any of Dàxī's children.

Above us soars a painted ceiling of the constellations, drawn in silver lines on a background of deep blue. Two figures fly across the sky, a dragon and a serpent entwined in eternal battle. Somewhere in the distance, there is the sound of chanting.

"What is this place?" I ask softly.

"Língyǎ Monastery, the tomb of the former emperors," Kang tells me. "They have one of the most beautiful gardens in all Jia."

"Gardens?" My heart leaps at the thought, even as my mind tells me I should maintain the ruse, that I shouldn't care so much. And yet, I miss strolling through the orchards and plucking fruit from the trees. I miss the work of harvesting the leaves from the tea trees. I miss the flowers, even though I disliked their prickly nature and the challenges of coaxing out full blooms. The palace gardens, though beautiful, are always under watch, and I've never been permitted to linger.

"They are currently performing the midday chant," he explains. "After they complete this session, they usually go to the dining hall. With the news of the emperor's passing, however, many of them will be called to the palace to assist. We should be able to go into the gardens and not be noticed, but we'll have to remain here until then."

I'm drawn back to the portraits again. This time I notice the shimmering iridescence of the details, inset into the stone. The beak of the bird, the mirror of the Lightning Goddess, the scales of Shénnóng's carp.

"These are beautiful." Even though I want to touch them, I know they should be preserved. "They must be quite old."

"Those were made by my mother's people, with stones taken

from the cliffs of the Emerald Isles," he says, with a hint of sadness to his voice. "They were part of the dowager empress's dowry when she married the Ascended Emperor. Lùzhou and Yún were in alliance . . . once."

I say without thinking, "But isn't that where—" I glance at him and notice the pain evident on his face, but it's too late to stop my brash words.

"Yes, a land where degenerates and bandits live in exile. But once it used to be a place known for carvings like these, where artisans lived in collectives and created marvelous things."

He brushes his fingertips reverently over the scales of the carp. "They were renowned for their work with the black pearls, which were used as jewelry or in headdresses and other adornments. The oysters' shells themselves were also used as inserts in carvings and sculptures. The pearls can also be ground into powder for medicinal use, to be ingested for vigor in battle or used in cosmetics to preserve youthfulness. The soil isn't rich there, and it's difficult to farm. We found other ways to live on that harsh peninsula of rock until . . ."

Kang's lips pull thin as his expression darkens. "Until the emperor decided to make an example of my father and anyone associated with him. He banned the sale of the pearls and made the salt farms and the stone quarries the only industries on the islands. Then he sent all those who opposed him there to die."

"How did they survive after all that?" I ask, feeling a rush of sympathy for all the innocents who have been affected by the emperor's wrath.

"Those who were physically able joined the army, while their families starved waiting for whatever meager wages they were able to send back. Some uprooted their lives and started anew elsewhere.

Those who couldn't took up arms and attacked the imperial ships transporting goods to our northern neighbors."

It is an awful sort of existence, watching everyone around you suffer. It is a familiar story—Sù was not without years when the harvest was slim due to pestilence or drought. When I accompanied my father to yet another house filled with the sounds of crying children, their cheeks hollowed out.

"I'm not saying the bandits are justified," Kang says quickly, misreading my silence for disgust. "But so many depended on the pearls. When their value fell, so did the hopes of—"

"You don't have to explain to me why." I shake my head, assuring him of my sympathies. "I understand. There were times in our village when the crops failed, but we were still taxed the same every season, even double if payments were so much as a week late. We all know of one or two people who retreated to the mountains to become bandits, so they wouldn't be a burden on their families."

No leniency when half a family was wiped out from poison. No reprieve from the demand for tribute offerings even while we buried our dead.

"My father continues to petition the governor for a season's reprieve, but mercy isn't a word in the man's vocabulary." I cannot help but tremble at the memory of seeing a man beaten in the market as punishment for his overdue taxes. Father and I had helped him bury his wife not even a month earlier, and his son a week before that.

It is Kang who places his hand on my arm this time, offering warmth and reassurance.

"It sounds like we grew up with the same injustices," he says gently. "This is why I noticed you in the market. When you helped the boy in trouble, it answered a few questions I was struggling with."

I look up at him, puzzled. "What questions?"

His gaze searches my face, as if he is still looking for answers there. "Ning, I—"

The sweet sound of chimes echoes in the chamber, disrupting the intimacy between us.

"That's the end of the midday chant," he murmurs, but he does not move.

"We should go," I tell him, even though a part of me imagines closing the distance between us and laying my head on his chest, offering him the same kind of comfort. Instead I turn and cross the room, forcing myself to clear my head. I need to get the information the princess is looking for, but I cannot grow to care for him in the meantime. I cannot have someone else I feel an obligation to, or else how could I betray him if I needed to?

How can I give another part of myself to someone else, when I already have so little to give?

We sneak through empty corridors until we step outside onto a landing, and the lush sight of the gardens spreads out before me, almost too much to take in. The just-opened buds I left behind in Sù have now erupted fully, some trees already flowering. Dragonflies buzz overhead, while other insects drone drowsily in the bushes. In the distance, the forest canopy sways to the breeze, but before the dense grove there are rows and rows of shrubs, waves of undulating green, dotted with blooms.

After descending the steps, we walk upon a covered pathway

that winds from the monastery to the gardens, lined with brick. Above our heads, red pillars hold up the intricately painted roof. A mural of birds flies overhead in dazzling rainbow hues.

"This was my grandfather's present to my grandmother when she accepted his offer of marriage," Kang tells me as we stroll under the birds, the beauty of our surroundings having uplifted our moods for the moment. "The mountains of Yún are famous for their rare birds and she missed them, so he commissioned this to be built and tended to by the monks."

"It's as if they could come to life." I marvel at the vibrancy of the colors. They must be retouched every year to retain such hues. But I am not one for covered paths—I need to be among the plants, soaking the sunlight into my skin.

I step off the walkway at the next corner and into the field of flowers, surrounding myself with peonies of all colors. I take a deep breath and inhale their scent, and underneath, the smell of the earth. I don't know if all shénnóng-shī have this natural affinity with plants, or if it's something unique to my mother's abilities, but it is here where I am certain some part of the old gods remains with us still.

I open my eyes to see Kang still watching me from the path, an odd expression on his face.

"I feel like I am finally able to breathe," I call out to him, unable to contain the joy I feel at being among the growing things, no longer closed off by stone walls.

Cautiously, he takes one step off the path and then hesitantly walks through the flowers, as if he is afraid he will hurt them.

"They're not as fragile as you think." I tease him by grabbing hold of a stalk and shaking the bloom in his direction, making him wince. "They bend but they don't yield easily. You can raze plants to the ground, burn them, but some will always return the next year, and the year after that."

I remember how much I cried when the orchards and the gardens burned, like I could feel the trees dying, and how Shu was at my side, even when I was sniffling in my bed at night. She would whisper what Mother told us, that they would come back, and it was easier to believe the words when they came from my sister's lips.

I clear my throat, trying to channel my father's stoicism instead. "Sometimes you have to break off the branches and remove the diseased limbs in order for the plant to be healthy again. Not so different from breaking bones to set them, or cutting a swollen limb to run an infection dry."

"I believe you," he says with a laugh, seemingly amused at my rambling.

"You two!" Shouts in the distance interrupt our moment, and we look toward the monastery to see two monks hurrying toward us.

We've been caught.

I look toward Kang, mouth agape, but he quickly reacts. His hand finds mine, and he pulls me after him as he yells over his shoulder, "Run!"

Chapter Twenty-Three

We crash through the flower sea, the branches parting for us as we rush by. The flowers bow their heads and whisper, *Hurry, hurry.* We burst through the shrubs onto a grassy slope. The sharp-eyed monks have called for reinforcements and they split in their pursuit, hoping to surround us and box us in.

Before us a canal runs past a grove of trees, leading to a lake dotted with lotus pads. A half-moon bridge curves over the water running through the canal. We fly over the bridge, ducking under the willow branches; they leave itchy remnants behind in my hair. The path curves here, around a small man-made mountain, carved out of yellow rock. I expect Kang to lead us over the path and into the other grove of trees, where it would be easier for us to circle around and lose our pursuers, but instead he races for the rocks.

"Wait—" I say as he begins to climb over the side of the decorative mountain.

"Trust me," he says, quirking the corner of his mouth upward, eyes sparkling as bright as the waters behind him.

I look over my shoulder and the monks are not visible any longer, but I'm certain they're not far behind. I can't risk getting caught with Kang outside the palace. I have to follow.

Instead of climbing upward, he skirts around the base of the rock, balanced on the narrow overhang. There is a sharp drop into the murky water below. We only have room to crouch side by side, maneuvering ourselves into a small cave at the side of the mountain. Except we are still visible to anyone who walks farther down the path and closer to the pond. I turn to Kang to see what we are supposed to do, but he tucks himself between two protrusions of rock, and then . . . disappears.

I hear the voices of those searching for us fast approaching, and there is no time to think. I'm on my hands and knees, scrambling after him, diving into the crevice in the rocks. My hands search for places to grip as the sun-warmed rock turns damp and slippery. Without much illumination in the cramped space, I fumble for sure footing, muddying my skirts in the process.

The narrow opening widens as my eyes adjust to the darkness, and I can make out steps carved into the stone. I squeeze myself between the two boulders after Kang, continuing to descend until we emerge in an underground cavern.

Looking up, I see a crack across the top of the cavern, a separation between the rocks that must have been moved here on top of this space, to hide what is contained below. A swath of sunlight cuts across the space, and it dances across the surface of the pool at the bottom of the cavern. The waters glow with a blue-green hue, like an impossible mirage.

"What is this place?" I whisper to Kang when we carefully make our way around the pool on a slim ledge, barely wide enough for me to place my feet side by side.

"It's an underground spring," he responds. "I spent a lot of time here after Grandmother died. The abbess at the time was willing to take care of me whenever things got . . . tumultuous in the palace."

Tumultuous. An interesting word choice.

"When I was smaller, it used to be a lot easier to make it through those rocks." He chuckles, but there's a nervous quality about his amusement. Like this place has stirred up something within his depths.

"We have to climb over this boulder and there's a beach on the other side. We can wait there until the monks give up." Kang pats the stone in front of him.

I look at the smooth surface, unsure. This is different from climbing onto a roof, where there are clear places I can put my hands and feet.

"Did you know these are sacred waters?" Kang tells me with a grin, as if he senses my nervousness. "When the First Emperor fought in the Battle of Red Rain, it was said the warlord Guan Yong chased him into the caves but did not pursue, because his clan believed these caverns to be haunted. When the First Emperor and his men walked out of the caves, Guan Yong and his followers laid down their swords, because their enemies had faced the spirits hidden in the caves and had come out victorious. His people knew no fish could live in these waters and no insects could thrive here, but the First Emperor drank from the pond and tasted only sweetness. He then triumphed over the southern clans with assistance from Guan Yong.

"Years later, the Ascended Emperor started construction on the capital, but when they wanted to build in this area, the earth collapsed. They found the underground spring and the cave system. When the Ascended Emperor heard that this had happened, he came to visit the site, and he saw a giant carp swimming in these waters. But when the Ascended Emperor's men jumped into the spring to find it, they could find no sign of the creature. It was said then that this place was blessed by Shénnóng, and Língyǎ was built to preserve this site."

"I've never heard that story." I'm enthralled by the idea of standing in a place once visited by the gods. I peer down at the water to see if there is any magic hidden in its depths, but I see only stillness.

"You can try the water for yourself," he says, teasing. "See if it tastes like the legend says."

I raise my eyebrow. "I'm guessing you sampled the sacred waters many times as a boy?"

He laughs, putting his hand to his chest in mock affront. "Your words draw blood. Will you shame me in front of the gods?"

"Show me the way, before we are struck down for our disrespect." I can't help but chuckle.

Kang quickly scales the side of the boulder without hesitation. He moves unencumbered by his armor, like someone who has worn it all his life.

"There's not enough room up here for both of us," he calls out from the top. "I'll wait for you on the other side."

I acknowledge him while my hands run over the stone, searching for fingerholds. I find dips and cracks, use my toes to find leverage, then pull myself up, discovering imperfections in the rock to hook on to in the process. I'm slower and more careful than Kang, but it doesn't take long before I pull myself over the top and onto the ledge above.

It's even more beautiful up here. On a stretch of pebbled beach down below, Kang looks up at me with a grin. Handsome and tousled and wild.

Until his expression changes.

"Ning . . . ," he tells me, quiet and fearful. "Beside you . . ."

"What?" I swallow whatever I was about to say and follow his gaze to my left.

A green-and-yellow snake lifts its head at me, hissing. Its small black eyes are focused on me, a threat.

Moving slowly, I get onto my hands and knees, sliding my foot back until I can find a place to hold my weight.

"I'm not going to harm you," I tell it, keeping my voice low. "I'm just going to—"

The snake darts forward, snapping at my arm, and I snatch my hand back, out of reach of its fangs. But the movement throws me too far in the other direction, and my foot slips.

I fall backward into emptiness.

The last thing I see is Kang's shocked face, his hand reaching out for me. Then I break the surface of the blessed waters and sink into their cold depths.

CHAPTER TWENTY-FOUR

THE WATER QUICKLY SOAKS INTO MY SLEEVES AND MY skirts, weighing them down. I struggle to take a breath, and the water rushes into my nose and open mouth, choking me. By the time I regain my senses enough to move my arms and kick my legs, I'm already hopelessly tangled in fabric.

Fire ignites in my chest, even as the cold grips my limbs and seeps into my bones. Pain, like nothing I have ever felt, burns through me.

The water is sweet on my lips and tongue as it drowns me, the lightest sense of bubbles on the back of the throat. So, I think, on the verge of hysterics, *The legend of the First Emperor is true.*

Bursts of light pop before me, one after another. A sea of stars, streaming through the night sky. The current calling me into the promise of warmth, into letting go. But then I see Shu's face through the dark, the way she said to me, *I believe in you*, and I know I cannot let the water take me.

Something grabs on to my arms through the warmth. I fight against the pleasant stream, allowing the pull to carry me away. We ascend, leaving the stars behind us, until I am thrown onto my back, the world in smears of color above me. My vision wavers, clears, and a face emerges.

I think I hear my name. Rough hands grab my shoulders and

roll me onto my side. Forceful strikes hit my back. I expel water onto the ground, suddenly able to breathe again, taking in great big gasps of air. I struggle to push myself up with one elbow, and a garment settles around my body. I didn't know how much I wanted the warmth until it's there, and my teeth chatter against one another.

I sit up with his help, still sputtering.

"Are you all right?" Kang hovers, attentive. Something flickers inside me, like tinder struggling to light.

"You saved my life," I manage to gasp out, my throat still hoarse from coughing.

"I waited," he says apologetically. "I waited and waited for you to surface, then when you didn't, I thought I went in too late."

"I don't know how to swim," I admit, drawing the garment tighter around me, then I realize what I'm wearing: his outer tunic. Pieces of his armor are scattered around us. Chest plate, helmet, leg pieces. Tossed aside in his haste to jump in after me.

I start to shake, remembering the pull of that current. How if it wasn't for Shu, my bond with my sister still waiting for me back home, it would have been so easy to give in. Strands of hair slide down in front of my eyes, making it difficult to see. I try to swipe them away, but my hands continue to tremble.

"I'm sorry," he says. He reaches up and gently brushes the hair out of my eyes, the movement slow and deliberate. His touch slides against the curve of my forehead and my cheek, brushing against the tip of my ear.

"What . . ." My breath catches. "What are you sorry for?"

"For not reaching you sooner," he whispers. His touch stops at the soft place under my jaw, where I am certain he can feel the frantic beat of my pulse. His eyes are pools of darkness, even deeper than the one I fell into. I can see myself reflected inside, a speck of light in the dark.

Kang's concern draws me in, his touch a promise. He's waiting for my answer, and I give in to the pull, leaning forward to close the distance between us. The lightest brush of my lips against his. He tips my head up and deepens the kiss, until it is a different sort of drowning, until we are forced to draw breath. The tunic falls from my shoulders as he pulls me closer, enveloping me in the warmth of his body.

We are both a little breathless when we let go of each other.

"Thank you," I murmur, and try to self-correct: "I mean . . . for saving my life."

"I'll rescue you ten times over if I will be kissed like that every time," he declares, making me laugh, chasing away my embarrassment.

"Ning . . ." His expression changes from amused to serious in an instant, and I know it is a practiced thing to have such control of his emotions. "You are the first girl who has ever greeted me with a swift kick to the shins. The first girl who has ever made me feel . . . normal."

"That is decidedly abnormal," I tell him after a pause, not knowing how else to respond.

"You asked me before . . . about Lùzhou." He touches his chest. "They marked us with a traitor's brand. When I first arrived, I tried to hide it, but it made me look odd, wearing a tunic when everyone else was bare-chested. Then I realized they all recognized me anyway, so it was easier to stop hiding. It was a long time before they accepted me."

I think he understands, as I do. How it feels not to belong.

Kang leans away from me, running pebbles through his fingers, not meeting my eyes. "They respected my father, because he fought against the raiders from the mountains. He defended their homeland, and my mother ... she was descended from their clans. She was to be betrothed to the emperor, did you know that? When my father stopped the raiders, he brought her to the capital to be wed to the emperor at my grandmother's request, but the marriage never happened."

"The general claimed her as his own," I say, repeating what was taught to me in the history lessons. One of the many crimes the Prince of Dài was accused of. Forcing a political marriage for his own gain, driving a wedge between brothers—

"No!" he says sharply. "They grew close on the journey from Lùzhou to Jia, and she refused to have another. The dowager empress acquiesced, in time ... but history will always remember my father as the one who stole another's intended."

I am beginning to understand that history is never so simple. Not the story of my parents, not the story of Kang's parents, or the two of us ... I quickly bury the thought, knowing it is something dangerous, something I do not dare to imagine.

I realize I can turn this into an opportunity to find out more of what the princess has asked me to uncover, even as the guilt gnaws at me in turn. "Do you hate him? The emperor?"

"I ... I don't know," he says hesitantly. "He did everything in his power to destroy my family, but he was also a capable ruler in some aspects. He could have executed us all, but instead he sent us into exile, against the recommendations of his own advisers."

I'm not sure I would have been able to say something so reasonable about someone who threatened the people I love.

"I wanted to meet him and see for myself the type of man my

uncle was after all these years." He shakes his head. "Now I will never get the chance."

"The people at court . . . the ones you said were still loyal to your father . . ." I venture forth with more questions. "Did they tell you how the emperor died?"

Kang's head swerves back to look at me, his gaze suddenly sharp. "Why does it matter?"

Careful, Ning . . .

"There have been rumors he was poisoned by the Shadow."

He waits expectantly, and I decide to tell him, in the hopes it will chase away his obvious suspicion. "My mother was one of the victims of the poisoned tea bricks," I explain. "That is why I am here. Why I need to win the favor of the princess."

He considers this, frowning deeply. Finally he says, "My sympathies. I know the sharpness of that pain. My birth mother passed giving birth to me. My birth father was a commander with the Kăiláng battalion, who died on the battlefield. My adopted mother took me in, ensured that I knew I was wanted. Protected me even when there were those in her own household who were offended at my presence. When I lost her . . . a part of me died as well."

He draws me closer again, this time offering only an embrace for warmth and comfort. I rest my head on his shoulder, even though I know I shouldn't be grateful for this fleeting moment.

"But . . . ," he says after a pause. "You say your mother's death is related to the favor you want to ask of the princess. Are you looking for vengeance?"

"I would ask for the head of the Shadow if I could," I snap, and the vehemence in my voice reminds me of the anger that continues to simmer under the surface. I close my eyes and turn my face away. He has seen too much of my frustrations and my failures.

195

To his credit, Kang does not react to my outburst. He only plays with my hair, running the strands through his fingers.

"Did you know," he says, his breath stirring my hair, "the women of the Emerald Isles are a fierce lot? They know how to fish with a spear and dive for pearls as well as the men. They are just as adept at spear-fighting. I doubt my father could have forced my mother into anything. It was said she challenged him to a duel for her hand in marriage."

"Really?" I'm grateful he's sharing a part of himself, offering a distraction from my sadness. I imagine a proud woman, one who is able to bear arms to defend her homeland from invaders. Who willingly uprooted her life to marry a man she had never met, but who found another instead. "She dared to challenge the general to combat?"

Laughter makes his shoulders shake. "She challenged him to see who could stay underwater the longest. He lost."

I laugh, too. "I think she would have gotten along with my mother."

"I know she would have." He waits a breath before saying, "If she was anything like you."

"Kang..." I straighten again, sitting in front of him so I can see his face. "I need you to tell me the truth. You once mentioned that the princess had a stone that can heal all illnesses... is there really such a thing?"

When he doesn't reply, I grab hold of his hands, so he can feel for himself, through the connection that quivers there between us. A pressure builds in my head, like water against a dam. All my hopes, balanced precariously on the answer.

"I have to know."

He seems taken aback at the force exerted through my grip.

"I've heard rumors," he says. "But . . ." He slowly extracts his hands from mine and places them on my shoulders instead. "If such a stone exists, don't you think the emperor would have used it to save his empress or the dowager empress? That my father would not have stolen it to save my mother's life? That the princess would not have used it to save her father? Do you think all those people would have died, if such a thing exists?"

I hear his words, but also do not. I cannot acknowledge such a terrible truth, that the foolish hope that keeps me in the palace—even through the mockery, the threats, the embarrassments—is a lie. That even if I won each round and finally emerged victorious, Shu may still die in spite of it.

"Who is it?" He regards me with those eyes that continue to see too much. "Who do you want to save?"

"My sister," I whisper. "My sister is dying."

My life with her has always been so entwined, waking and sleeping in the same room. One of my earliest memories was holding her after she was born, and now she may die at my hands.

Like our mother before her.

The pressure is too much, and it breaks me, unleashing the tears in a torrent. I sob in his arms. A broken, pathetic thing, ruining everything I touch.

Chapter Twenty-Five

KANG SAYS NOTHING AS HE GATHERS ME INTO HIS ARMS, holding me tight. More tears than I imagined I could contain leave me, spilling through my fingers.

"If my sister dies, I'll have nothing left," I tell him through sputtering sobs. "My father is already half gone to his grief, and I don't think I can save him if Shu dies, too."

He uses his thumbs to carefully brush the tears off my cheeks, but I push him away. I don't deserve to be comforted by him, and I don't want his pity.

"How can it be your fault," he asks, "if it was the tea that poisoned her? You didn't know."

"Because I was the one who poured the tea." I drag my sleeve furiously across my eyes. "I should have known to look for the poison. I should have seen the signs."

He scoffs at that, and I press my mouth into a thin, burning line.

"Ning . . ." He pulls me back, that earnest expression returning again. "Listen, how long does it take to become a shénnóng-shī? Ten years? How many years could you have been training? Two? Three?"

Not even. Here and there, when Mother forced me to sit down during our shared lessons. But I don't give him the satisfaction of knowing that.

"We trust the emperor to provide. We believe the Court of Officials will protect us."

"What are you talking about?" I choke out.

"I'm saying it's not your fault," he says. "The emperor, the ruler of Dàxī, surrounded by all his guards, could not prevent his own death at the hands of someone who wished him ill. You could not have known about the poison. Even your mother, a trained shénnóng-shī, did not detect it before she drank it."

"But . . . ," I say, uncertain. *I should have read the signs . . .*

"Someone is killing the people of Dàxī with the intent to spread unrest," he continues insistently. "If you want to blame someone, then blame those who distributed the poison. Blame the officials, blame the ministries. But don't blame yourself."

I regard this boy, with his assurances, shattering my excuses with the confidence with which he uttered those words. Words that border on treason. And he also revealed something else: He knows the emperor died from something other than illness. But did the Banished Prince arrange for his death? Or is someone else responsible?

I know the princess wants me to ask the delicate questions, to coax the truth out of him. But I've never been that sort of person, able to hide behind smiles and flirtations.

"Are you here to put your father on the throne?" I ask him. Dangerous questions and dangerous games.

Kang blinks, surprised. "Not even my father's loyal officials would dare to ask me that."

"I don't have any loyalties within the court." I shrug, keeping my voice light, even though inside, my heart hammers, desperate for an answer to bring back to the princess, mindful of her threat against my family.

He regards me for a moment, then gives me a wry smile. "No, you are not like them." With a set to his jaw, he continues, "There's a darkness descending on the empire. The poison, yes, but also floods and earthquakes. My father believes a new dawn is coming for the dragon throne, but I still remember the girl I grew up with in the palace. Our grandmother would not have raised a fool, and I wanted to see for myself if there is still a chance for peace with Zhen."

The sound of the bell reverberates through the cavern, signifying the change of day. I realize I have to return to the palace for the evening meal, or I will be missed.

"We should go," he says, but he looks out at the water, shadows under his eyes.

I do the only thing I can think of. I lean over and cup his face, kissing him with gratitude. For holding me while I cried, for saving me from drowning, and for chasing those shadows of guilt away. The bell rings above our heads again and when we finally separate, he looks dazed, but he is smiling.

We return to the palace, the taste of him still lingering on my lips. Yet his answers conjure more questions that worm their way through my mind.

Just like the palace itself, tunnels upon tunnels, leading nowhere, and no exit in sight.

I worry Lian may be waiting in our residence, wondering where I am, but there are only the two maidservants. They make no mention of my damp clothes as they assist me with drawing a bath. While I'm drying my hair, Lian strolls in with grass in her braid and her glowing skin a shade darker, grinning from ear to ear.

"The sun was bright today, perfect for riding," she declares through the wooden privacy screen while she changes, tossing her dirty clothes over the side. She seems to be in an excellent mood.

"Where were you?" she asks. I hear a splash of her entering the tub. "I tried to find you after the proclamation, but you were nowhere to be found."

"I hid in the library," I say, telling her the first place I can think of.

"We all have our distractions, I suppose," she responds.

"Do you think the competition will be postponed?" I ask.

"I would venture a guess and say the princess is meeting with her closest advisers tonight."

"What do you think will happen now that the emperor is..." I cannot even make myself say it; the words sound too much like sacrilege.

"The Court of Officials love their ceremony," Lian says, unperturbed. "The astronomers will be consulted, then an auspicious time will be chosen to prepare for the rise of the new empress. I am certain they will continue with the appointment of a court shénnóng-shī, as well as whatever other titles they can bestow."

How many of these officials and nobles will be forces moving against the princess, doubting her capability to rule?

That is all the other competitors discuss at the evening meal, speculating about how long the princess will wait before the ascension ceremony. How messengers have been dispatched to all corners of the empire to inform the regional officials of the news.

Even though the current political situation is dire, it means there is less attention on me after my confrontation with Shao last night. When we rise to retire for the evening, Lin Wenyi—the monk from Yěliǔ—and his companion, Hu Chengzhi, give me nods of acknowledgment, and I give them one in turn. It seems that I may have misinterpreted his words; perhaps he was defending me, not taking part in Shao's ridicule.

Small steps forward. That, at least, I am capable of.

When we return to our residence, my eye catches a glint of gold on the lion statue in front of the building. A complex embroidered knot, with a jade pendant in the center.

I have been summoned.

I already knew I was being watched, but the prickling feeling of discomfort still follows. I wish I could have all the rumored abilities of the shénnóng-shī, able to see through walls or reach into dreams, instead of blundering about, almost dying in the process.

A long, thin box sits on the table, my name written on it in an unfamiliar scrawl. I tuck it into my sleeve before Lian notices, afraid it relates to the princess and her impossible task.

Later I lie in bed, with only my thoughts for company, waiting until Lian's breathing slows to a familiar rhythm. I realize I have become accustomed to the sounds of the palace, the *tap-tap* of the tree branches hitting the rafters, the distant murmur of voices. I am now used to the silk covers that slide against my calluses without catching, being able to eat until I've had my fill without my stomach feeling uncomfortably full from the richness of the dishes. Just like Steward Yang said, it is too easy to live this pampered life, this fantasy.

I pull out the mysterious box, wanting to see what the princess has left for me. It is the length of my arm, made of nondescript wood. I slide open the top panel and find a small dagger waiting for me inside. I pick it up and feel its weight, noting the rippling design that appears like waves carved into the decorated sheath. I pull the dagger out, its sharp edge catching the light. At the base of the hilt, an inset black pearl glows with its own luster.

A note lies at the bottom of the box: *For you.*

Kang.

He had noticed the way I admired the chamber of the gods at Língyǎ. He had spoken about the artistry of his people and wanted to share a piece of it with me. My face warms at the thought. Even if I have no idea how to wield a weapon, I still tuck it into my tunic, enjoying its comforting weight.

I slide my legs out of the bed and carefully make my way to the receiving room. From the cabinet, I pull out the tray I hid earlier while Lian prepared for bed. I need the steadying effect of the tea tonight. I wait for the water to bubble, then scald the utensils and the pots. When the steam dissipates above the opening, I place the strands of tea leaves into the pot.

I believe in you. Shu sent me off with that assurance, and I have lost myself to my own self-pity and guilt.

The strands of Lion Green seep into the water, turning it the lightest tinge of its namesake color. I place a few pieces of goji berry upon the surface, vaguely remembering that Lian mentioned its properties for cultivating alertness. The red berries plump up and release their essence into the water. I allow myself a few more, needing the additional strength tonight, my first attempt at using something unfamiliar.

This is the only thing I will truly miss after leaving the palace:

the wide selection of teas, easily accessible, even with my lowly status.

I drink it without waiting for it to cool, letting it burn a path down my throat. The magic unfurls within me immediately, called forth as easily as a petal opening to the sun. The faint scent of camellia drifts by, and I know I am ready to face the princess.

CHAPTER TWENTY-SIX

HUDDLED UNDER THE HOOD OF MY CLOAK, I KEEP TO THE walls, trying to stay with the shadows. The criers follow a schedule, tracking the course of time, and any deviation is strictly punished. The palace guards are less predictable but prone to fall into routine as well.

I have always tracked the natural pattern of living things, having grown up depending on these signs for our food. Birds flying across the sky to signal an early winter, or marks of disturbance in the forest, hinting at the arrival of spring. What are the guards if not another pattern to notice?

I slip between buildings, counting steps under my breath as I cross the path to the pond and pass the kitchens. I pretend I know this as well as my family's small patch of earth.

The press of the mountains above us, their stone peaks unyielding and comforting against the sky. Not so different from the looming rooftops of the Hall of Eternal Light.

The dense tangle of the wildberry bushes, hiding the presence of small, darting birds. I crouch and walk through the rows of purple-leaf shrubs, covered with tiny pink blossoms.

I am through the central garden when I notice the bobbing light of the lanterns in the distance. I press myself against the wall and watch them make their way past the library. The tea sloshes about in my stomach, leaving a bitter aftertaste on my tongue—I let it steep for too long. My skin prickles with a strange sensation. My head swivels too fast, catching the beating of wings in the light, and I am suddenly the hawk swooping overhead in the dark. I am the spider making its way up the brick next to me, spinning its web. The noises of all living things around me swarm inside my head, demanding my attention.

The ring of the gong sends me to my knees, crushing the plant below me, releasing a pungent scent. I press my hand tightly to my mouth, so that I do not cry out.

"The third hour!" the criers call out. "The third hour!" *The Hour of the Ghost.* I will be late.

I make my way to my feet, head still spinning. The stars seem to hum mockingly above my head, whispering my name.

I stumble down the empty path to the library, away from the guards. My hands I keep on the contours of the wall, its roughness tethering me to the physical world even as I feel like I am about to burst from my body. I don't notice the slight slope in the ground until I twist my ankle, the sharp pain wrenching me back inside my body, clearing my head slightly.

I put in too much goji berry. Another mistake. There are some additives so strong they pull you outside your body entirely, until you're cast into the wind and too far away to return. Your physical body will wither away without your spirit to inhabit it.

I catch movement out of the corner of my eye, and I throw myself behind a statue. I watch as the figure slides against the wall, blending in with the shadows, using the shrubbery to their advantage. If it weren't for my drink, I'm not sure I would have noticed them. The outline of the body ripples, lit up from within. As they slip through a gap in the trees, the moonlight catches the face, and

I see it. The flatness of the features, the mask that has haunted my dreams.

The Shadow.

I should sound the alarm, but when I look around, the rest of the garden is still. The guards will not be passing through this place for a time.

The Shadow touches the wall and the hidden door slides open. The light from the lanterns catches the glint of a blade pressed against their side. Stepping into the tunnels means they will have direct access to the princess's inner garden. If I scream, perhaps the guards will be able to find me before they silence me forever, but that is only if they are able to hear me at all.

Father's voice rises unbidden in my mind: *We always have a choice.* A choice to stand up and do what is right. Even when I did not understand it in my childish ignorance, he still spoke up for the villagers, often at great cost to himself.

The panel is on the verge of closing. I balance on a precipice, the cliff of indecision. Forced to choose: stay or go, jump or cower.

I slip through the gap and pull the lever, shutting myself in with Dàxī's monster.

The Shadow moves ahead through the tunnel, and I keep my eyes on their back. The magic courses through my veins. I feel in and out of myself. The voice at the back of my head screams at me: *Rip the mask off! Demand the name of those responsible for the poison!* Whether they are the creator or merely the distributor, if they know of the blood on their hands.

They pull on the iron ring on the wall and the door slides open. They step through, intent on their deadly purpose.

"Stop!" I yell.

The figure up ahead falters but doesn't stop. The air ripples, the world folding in on itself, and suddenly I've cleared the space between us in a single breath. I run into them full tilt, and with a grunt, they fall, rolling, not expecting me to be so close.

It has to be something in the goji berries. The magic makes everything too bright, and my mind is one step behind, watching dimly as if from a distance, while my body moves. I land with my knee against their chest, but they are already trying to roll away. My attention is drawn to the patch of darkness under their left rib, the way they clutch at that side. I push my weight into that spot, just to hear a scream. A wild, ferocious sound of pain and anger.

Their other hand fumbles for the sword, but the dagger is unsheathed in my hand in an instant, pressed against their throat in another. When the metal slices the skin, they still, eyes looking up at me, breathing muffled by the mask.

"Tell me!" I demand. "Are you the one who poisoned the tea bricks?" I wish I had scalding Silver Needle to pour down their throat, to rip the truth out of them.

Another person is upon me in an instant, grabbing me from behind and pulling me away. I struggle, swinging the dagger wildly, but an iron grip grasps my wrist, striking a pressure point. The blade falls to the ground, useless.

I suck in a breath to scream, but I'm thrown to the ground easily, like a sack of rice. I want to roar at my weakness but scrabble backward in the dirt instead, turning to face whoever pulled me off the Shadow . . . and the scream dies in my throat.

Princess Zhen crouches beside the body of the would-be assassin.

I don't understand.

The sound of drums thunders in the distance. Someone has sounded the alarm.

The princess gestures at me wildly. I approach.

"Help me get her into my chambers," she demands.

"But . . . they came here to kill you," I sputter.

"No, you fool." She reaches down and rips the mask off the Shadow's face. It's Ruyi, eyes closed, mouth contorted into a grimace. A line of red seeps at her throat where I've cut her. "Grab her legs. Unless you want the guards to find you."

I force myself to bend down and help the princess lift Ruyi, still reeling from the revelation of Ruyi's identity. The princess is able to lift Ruyi's body easily with my assistance. She struck the pressure point without hesitation, knowing how to weaken my grasp. I commit this knowledge to memory—she is no cowering flower.

Once we reach the princess's quarters, we place Ruyi on the bed, then the princess directs me back to the garden to clear the rest of the evidence. I secure the dagger into my sash and then pick up the Shadow's sword. With my other hand, I pick up the mask that landed on the stones. The wood, smooth against my fingers, is still warm from Ruyi's face.

Returning to the inner chambers, I note the elaborate screens and beautiful watercolor portraits hanging in the residence. The princess lives in the middle of many treasures. A princess foretold to be both the light and the ruin of an empire.

She looks to be a portrait herself, cast in the golden light of the multiple braziers lit around the room. Her face is scrunched with worry as she paces. Ruyi's body convulses, and she rolls to her side, where she vomits a torrent of dark fluid. Princess Zhen is there immediately, without hesitation, pressing a cloth to her bodyguard's forehead.

"What did you do to her?" she snarls at me.

"No . . . ," Ruyi protests weakly. "Not her."

Then comes the sound of many feet striking the wood floors, followed by shouts of "Highness! Your Highness!"

The princess looks past the doorway, eyes wild. She points to the screen at the side of the room, and I duck behind it, still holding the sword and the mask. Scented robes and luxurious fabrics surround me; this is her dressing area. I pull myself farther into the silks, hiding myself as I listen to the raised voices beyond. Through the screen, all I can see are silhouettes, but I know these are armed men.

"Do you deem it appropriate to barge into my bedchamber at this hour?" The princess speaks in a restrained tone, showing no indication of the emotion she exhibited not even a moment before.

"My apologies, Highness." The guards nervously shuffle their feet. "We had a breach in the palace walls, and we are concerned for your safety."

"As you can see, there is no one here but myself. You should be out there, trying to find the intruder."

"Yes, Princess." One of the soldiers raises his weapon in a salute. "We will find the one who dared disrupt your rest and bring you his head."

"See to it that you do," she says, her voice cool and composed.

The stomp of boots leaves the area, and they are gone. I shove the spill of fabrics off me and hurry to the bedside. The princess tugs off the pile of covers she had thrown over Ruyi's body, and I gasp when her face is revealed.

Glassy, unblinking eyes. A trickle of black at the corner of her mouth.

"Ruyi!" the princess whispers through gritted teeth, shaking Ruyi's shoulders, all composure lost. "Wake up!"

For a moment I consider leaving her to die. Permit this course of perverse justice if she is truly the one who distributed the poison throughout the empire. But I shake the thought off easily. Saving Shu's life is more important than my desire for vengeance, and if I save Ruyi's life, it will bring me closer to the truth.

"Move," I demand of the princess, all courtesy gone. When she does not listen, I pull her away.

"What are you doing?" She looks at me, lost to panic, hands clawed and teeth bared, ready to tear me apart if I hurt Ruyi. This is beyond loyalty and care of her handmaiden, this is . . . something else.

"If you want her to live," I tell her, "get out of my way."

CHAPTER TWENTY-SEVEN

PRINCESS ZHEN MOVES ASIDE, BITING HER LIP.

"My father is a physician," I say to her, adopting the voice he uses when his patients' family members are in hysterics. "I will do her no harm."

No more than what has already been done, anyway, but I don't tell her that.

She nods then and gestures for me to continue.

This for me is a different kind of ritual. Steady hands, calm nerves. Not so different, I realize, from being a shénnóng-shī.

I pull the dagger out and, ignoring the gasp of protest next to me, cut away the layers of Ruyi's tunic until the wound is exposed. I hiss when I see the splintered shaft of an arrow buried in her side, the blood bubbling around it.

I touch the skin above the wound, and she writhes under me, coming in and out of delirium. She is still reactive, and that is a blessing at least, but I know this is not a regular arrowhead. It was coated in a poison designed to inflict pain.

I've seen it before. *Crow's head.*

The plant has beautiful purple flowers, but the entire plant, especially the root, is poisonous. If even a small piece of the root is ingested, it can kill someone in an hour. I've seen it used by the mountain bandits, soldiers dying from their poisoned arrows when they do not reach a physician in time.

I gingerly palpate her side. The flesh around the wound is hardening, black vessels spreading outward, the poison seeping into her body.

"Tell me," the princess asks, her face streaked with tears. "How bad is it?"

"She's been poisoned," I say. "I can pull out the arrowhead and stop the bleeding, but I also have to draw out and neutralize the poison before it kills her."

"Anything you need." She draws herself up. "Anything you need and it is yours."

Despite the urgent task at hand, a darker part of myself recognizes that this is my chance to get the answers I need. I told Kang I would ask for the head of the Shadow. And now I have not only her identity but her life in my hands.

"Why was Ruyi in Sù?" I ask.

Princess Zhen blinks, not understanding.

"Tell me why she was in Sù!" I demand. "Is she the one responsible for the poison? Is she distributing it at your behest?"

"How dare you!" she snaps, taking a step in my direction, fists clenched at her sides.

"The longer you wait," I remind her, "the deeper the poison will enter her body, and the harder it will be to save her." I gamble on the suspicion that she is willing to trust in an untrained physician's assistant rather than call for the aid of one of the royal physicians. It means she has something to hide.

The princess weighs this, then she sighs as she looks down at Ruyi. "I sent her to look into who is behind the poisonings, and whether they had a direct hand in what happened to my father."

"Why did you hide his death for so long?" I ask. "Did he disagree with your plot utilizing the tea bricks? Were you planning to cause the unrest yourself and come back with a pretty cure? Win the hearts of the people?"

Red blooms across her face. "I would be very careful with your next words. I could have you executed the moment you step out of this room."

Ruyi's body thrashes again underneath my palms. She lets out a guttural moan. I hold her down quickly, pulling her eyelids back. I can see only white.

"Look at her!" I yell at the princess. "Tell me. Why was she in Sù?"

"Stop! Yes!" The princess climbs onto the bed and kneels at the head of her handmaiden, speaking rapidly. "She was there investigating on my behalf, following the procession that delivered my invitations across the empire, seeing if anyone would interfere. But someone followed her at each turn, sowed seeds of distrust, until it became difficult for her to keep her disguise.

"But I swear to you." She reaches out and grips my arm. "I have nothing to do with the poisonings. I want Dàxī to be reunited and strong. I will not do it by killing commoners."

She could be lying to me still, but her eyes are only for Ruyi, her concern obvious.

"A life for a life," I say to her, ready to bargain. "If I heal her now, you will owe me a favor. Do you have the cure-all stone?"

Princess Zhen blinks at me, then dismisses me with an agitated wave of her hand. "That's just a folktale. It doesn't exist. Do you think I would not demand its use now if it were real?"

So Kang told me the truth, but something inside me still crumples at the thought.

"Then the use of your royal physicians," I tell her. "For treatment of the poison—"

She interrupts me with a growl, unable to hide her frustration. "Don't you understand? The poison is what killed my father. The royal physicians were unable to slow down its course. The only way to stop it is to discover the antidote."

My heart hammers in my chest. Someone dared to poison the emperor, and now . . . I have a new purpose. I have to find the antidote.

"You will grant me access to your storerooms then," I say quickly. "Access to the antidote, when it is discovered."

"Yes, done," she says without hesitation. "Now help her. Please."

"Where are your kitchens?"

I know from speaking with Steward Yang that there is a smaller kitchen for the inner palace. At this time of night, the ovens are quiet and the stoves dark, but I am still cautious.

I draw on both my mother's art and my father's practice as I rummage through the pots and drawers. Slices of licorice root and round, dried pieces of bitter buckwheat. Long strands of ginseng, like an old man's beard. I gather everything I need and hurry back to the princess.

The room is almost unbearably warm due to the instructions I left behind. The braziers have now been moved closer to the bed. The princess has torn garments into strips for bandaging and stoked the fire until it is hot enough to disinfect the blade.

"If this was a regular arrowhead, I would leave it, allow it to plug the wound," I explain to the princess, so she does not strike me down for cutting into her handmaiden. "But because of the poison, I have to pull it out. It will be bloody."

She nods.

After wiping Kang's blade clean on my tunic, I pass it through the fire a few times to cleanse the metal, before preparing myself for the task of extricating the arrow from the wound.

"Hold her," I command, and once I am sure she has a good grip, I place my hand on the broken shaft. Using the dagger, I make an incision to help loosen the head and slide the arrow out. Blood spurts, splattering the front of my tunic. Ruyi's body arcs and then she crumples again. The princess narrows her eyes, but her hands hold firm as she grits her teeth, bracing herself with one leg off the bed.

Even though I know it is due to the pain, I test Ruyi's pulse to be sure. Weak, fluttering, but still there. I have to work fast, against her body, which is slowing down. All blood will run to the heart, carrying the poison with it. I'm running out of time.

"I can draw the poison out, but I don't think she will survive without something to strengthen her body," I tell the princess when I scrutinize the extent of the wound. "I need help."

"What do you mean, help?" she asks.

"I need another shénnóng-shī, or at the very least, a shénnóng-tú," I say to her.

She shakes her head. "I can't . . . I can't involve anyone else. It's too dangerous. The poison . . ." She hesitates for a moment before continuing. "It leads to someone in the Ministry of Rites, perhaps even the council itself."

I could almost shake her, force it out of her, but the terror in her expression is real. The way she clutches Ruyi, smoothing the hair away from her face. I decide to go with the truth.

"You have to choose: your plan, or her life?"

She looks down at Ruyi, the conflict clear, but then her expression smooths, as impenetrable as the wooden mask the Shadow dons.

"Who would you suggest?" she says. Only the barest quiver of her cheek betrays her true emotions.

"Lian. The daughter of the Kallah ambassador."

The princess nods. "Only her. No one else."

I bring Lian back to the inner palace through the hidden tunnels as directed, making a brief stop at the kitchens along the way for more ingredients. Lian keeps glancing over at me during our trek through the tunnels, muttering to herself. It was easy to convince her of the urgency of the matter, with my disheveled hair and the blood on my tunic.

The only thing she says to me when we approach the princess's residence is: "All that time spent at the library, huh?"

"I promise you"—I usher her through the door—"I will explain everything after."

The princess looks up when we enter and greets Lian with a nod.

"I require your skills." I gesture toward the figure on the bed. "You say your mentor specialized in strength. Do you think you would be able to fortify her body and keep her alive while I draw out the poison?"

Lian chews on her lip, considering this. "Poison?"

"Yes. An arrow dipped in crow's head."

"Ah." She recognizes the name. "I've seen it done, but I haven't tried it myself."

"Yǐ lí cè hǎi," I mutter to myself. Our task is like trying to measure the sea with a single gourd. Nearly impossible with the limitations of my age, my lack of knowledge.

Lian snorts. "No wonder you need my help. All we can do is try."

At least one of us is optimistic about our chances of success.

Lian gets to work on her tonic, using the tray of ingredients we collected at the kitchens.

"I wouldn't call myself a healer," she says as she pinches this and pulls out slivers of that and places them into a pot. "But my teacher knows how to push the physical limits of the human body. Perhaps this will help hold her together."

I glance at her ingredients to make sure my choices will not counteract the effects of her tonic. Lian has chosen mugwort to improve circulation, crimson mushroom to strengthen the heart.

"Usually I would brew this overnight," she says, shaking the herbs. "But we don't have time."

Definitely not, with the dampness of Ruyi's skin, the black rings around her eyes, and the black veins creeping ever closer to her heart.

The herbs steep in the hot water, then Lian pulls the bag out of the pot and squeezes it over a bowl. Cupping the bowl in both hands, she takes a deep breath, then blows across the surface. I can feel the infusion of magic, the spicy scent of cinnamon, even though I know there was none in the mix.

"Sit her up," Lian says, a subtle shift in her voice. A commanding tone, like someone else speaks through her. The surface of the bowl ripples.

The princess adjusts her bodyguard's position so Ruyi is sitting between her legs, supported against her.

"Open her mouth."

The light in the room begins to flicker, even though there is no breeze. Princess Zhen looks like she is about to protest, but I give her a shake of the head. She nods in resignation and tips Ruyi's head back. The liquid goes in, but Ruyi coughs, and the tonic trickles out the corner of her mouth.

"Keep it in," Lian directs me as she holds the bowl above Ruyi's head again.

The princess pulls Ruyi's mouth open, and with my assistance, we close it once all the tonic enters, forcing her to swallow. The tension in the air eases, and the room once again smells faintly of incense.

Lian sinks back to her seat and blinks. "It's done," she whispers, sounding once again like herself.

I draw in a shaky breath as I approach. I can feel the weight of the princess's and Lian's gazes, expectant, waiting for me to fulfill my part of the bargain.

For Shu, I tell myself, and climb onto the bed, readying myself for the task ahead.

Chapter Twenty-Eight

MY DILEMMA IS EVIDENT BEFORE ME. I NEED TO EXPEL THE poison from Ruyi's body, but she cannot lose more blood in her weakened state. I sift through the tray with my fingers, hesitating over this ingredient and the next before settling on peelings of the umbrella tree, a common ingredient in any apothecary shop. I wish I had stronger ingredients, such as hú huáng lián or the bark of the silk flower tree, but those would be in a physician's storeroom and not as easily accessible.

I mash the concoction of bark and leaves between my fingers until it becomes something I can easily manipulate in my hands, a living poultice. Then I pack the paste into her wound, leaving dark smears against her skin. Rolling the remnants into a ball, I place it under my tongue. The taste of it is repulsive, but I force my lips to close. I've seen my mother perform this ritual before, when she worked alongside my father, the two of them practicing their respective arts side by side like an intricate dance.

I place my hands on either side of Ruyi's head and close my eyes.

Shénnóng is communion, a joining of your soul to theirs. Be vulnerable, be open…

I understand now. The magic is not in the ceremony of pouring the tea or the sharing of the cup. It is in the connection, the brief joining of souls. The tea leaves are a channel, the ingredients the signposts.

I can see Ruyi lying at the roots of a great tree, surrounded by a swirling darkness. Swallowing my fear, I approach her, the tendrils of smoke parting at my feet, but there is no telltale smell of fire.

Where the smoke dissipates, I can see past her skin and muscle. Her body is translucent, lit up by dazzling pathways of red and gold—blood and life essence moving through her. But there, spreading from the wound at her side, is a writhing, pulsating darkness. Its tendrils have already wrapped around her intestines and liver, tracing their way upward toward her beating heart.

Leaning forward, I place a hand on her shoulder. She looks up at me with dazed eyes.

"Who are you?" She is afraid, knowing something is not right.

I don't know what to do.

Above our heads, the tree rustles, then the head of a crane dips down through the leaves. It is a beautiful bird, with snow-white feathers and a head crowned with vivid red. The Lady of the South.

Her voice rings in my head: *The receiver must be willing.*

I think of how the princess carefully wiped the sweat from Ruyi's brow. How she threw herself into harm's way without hesitation to protect her handmaiden from harm. Each touch speaks of shared intimacies.

"Zhen sent me," I tell Ruyi now. "I only want to help."

"Zhen?" A bit of clarity returns to her as she turns her face toward me, then she gives me a slight nod. I don't know if she sees the bird above us, but I look up at the goddess, silently asking her what I must do next.

She inclines her head. *Reach in and grab it.*

When a goddess instructs, I know I must listen. Even though

every part of me is shrieking in protest at the thought of touching that . . . darkness, I reach in. It feels like my hand is sinking into warm water, like when I touched Kang with the assistance of the Golden Key. I force myself to contain my revulsion when I can feel a slippery chill glide through my fingers.

Ruyi screams when I try to pull it back, as if I am ripping her heart out of her body. The darkness grows barbs, sinking into her organs like nettles embedding themselves into flesh. Setting my jaw, I grasp the darkness with two hands, struggling to hold on to it with all my strength. It thrashes, attempting to burrow its way deeper, trying to make its way to her heart, but Lian's tonic shimmers like a silver cage, repelling its attempt to take hold.

"Stop!" Ruyi cries out. "You're killing me!"

The rustling grows louder above our heads, as if the tree is blown by a wild wind I cannot feel. The crane has disappeared.

With a sickening *pop*, the darkness comes free. In my hands, it feels like pulsating, muscular flesh, and it lashes at my arm, drawing red welts. Blood beads like rubies against my skin. Malevolence creeps into my mind, a fluttering of tongues brushing against the edges of my mind. It wants nothing more than to consume. It craves life, for it has no life itself, and I open myself to it.

It slithers up my chest. I can sense its hunger and eagerness as it forces itself into my mouth. I choke, tears filling my eyes, hands going to my throat. It tastes of spoiled meat and decay, the rot of betrayal, the resentment of being forgotten. It is going to take what it was promised. Blood and memories, flesh and life . . .

With a gasp, I return to my body. Throwing myself off the bed, landing on my hands and knees. I spit the medicinal ball out of my mouth. It splatters on the wood floor with a sickening sizzle, and smoke rises from the pulp. The smoke forms itself into a lithe, twisted form. Grotesque protrusions begin to sprout from the serpentine body, and three heads emerge, features shaping themselves before our eyes like a sculptor forming wet clay. Three heads with human faces, skin a gray pallor. Thin lips, pale eyes, and a sound like the grinding of teeth emanating from the gashes of their opened mouths.

I stare at this hideous apparition, my body frozen in terror. It lifts itself up on its coiled body and the mouths smile down at me, revealing sharp, daggerlike teeth.

With a cry, the princess lands before me, a curved half-sword in her hand. The blade sweeps in a deadly arc and the heads roll when they land, coming to a stop not far from my feet. The body wavers on itself before toppling onto its side. As quickly as it formed, the monster disappears into smoke, leaving the scent of putrid flesh and a black mark on the floor, like someone held a torch too close to the wood.

The sword lands on the floor with a clatter, and the princess crouches in front of me.

Her mouth moves, but I hear nothing.

The last thing I remember is slipping into blessed darkness, closing over my head like the waters of the sacred spring.

A gong sounds, reminding me there is something I must do, someone I have to meet. It's almost the Hour of the Thief. Panic grips my chest, making it hard to breathe. I fumble with the blankets, kicking.

"Ning! Ning!" Lian slowly comes into focus, her brows drawn together in worry. "You're awake," she sighs.

"Where..." I look around, and I see I'm in our room. I don't remember coming back here. There's a dull thud in my temple, and my throat is raw and burning.

Lian thrusts a cup into my hands. I drink it eagerly, and it washes a soothing path as it goes down. There are no additives, no magic. Only a good cup of tea, brewed to sweetness, as familiar as a mother's embrace.

"How did I get back here?" I ask.

She's sitting on a stool she has moved by my bed, looking as serious as I've ever seen her. "The princess had one of her guards carry you back," she says.

"Ah." I try to nod, but that sends a sharp twinge of pain skittering across my skull. I wince and press my fingers into my forehead, but it doesn't ease the pain.

"It'll take some time to get better," Lian says, then adds hastily, "You probably already know that. Being able to do what you . . . accomplished." She has an awed look in her eyes, like she's not certain of who I am anymore.

"I saw the goddess," I whisper, uncertain of who I am either. "She helped me."

"The goddess?" she echoes.

"A bird . . . the Lady of the South?"

She nods in understanding. "We know her as Bi-Fang, Goddess of Fire."

After a pause, Lian finally asks me the question I can tell has been circling in her mind. "What happened last night? Why were you in the inner palace?"

I'm seized by the same sort of hesitation I felt the day I returned from my encounter with Kang. I'm afraid of judgment, afraid she will accuse me of cheating. But Lian has always helped me without question. I've seen her kindness with the kitchen staff, the same respect extended to everyone, from the servants to the highest officials. She has offered friendship, and I have lied to her from the beginning. Now at the very least, she deserves the truth.

I begin, hesitant at first, with my mother's death and my sister's poisoning. How I grappled with the Shadow, then met Kang in the market. How it led to my encounter with the princess, and finally the events of last night. The only things I do not speak of are the intimate moments between me and Kang. Those I keep for myself.

"How did you hide it from everyone?" she sputters when I am done. She's pacing the length of our room, braid swinging, considering everything I've told her. "Secret meetings with the princess? Sneaking around with the emperor's nephew?"

"I would be happy to leave all this behind, if I could only secure the antidote for my sister," I say, determined.

"So then . . ." She looks at me. "What about after? Will you stay there?"

"My mother was able to do it," I say, as if there is no twinge inside me when I speak those words, as if I have not spent most of my life looking for escape from that village.

"It sounds like your mother made her choices for her family, but what about you? What do *you* want?"

I don't want to talk about my mother. I don't want to talk about my future, imaginary or not. "All I know is I need to focus on finding the antidote. If the poison that affected Ruyi is the same as the one that killed my mother . . . That snake creature . . . have you seen it before?"

Lian shudders. "Those faces were an abomination. Nothing like that should exist."

"I think the goddess tried to warn me before," I tell her. "When I first encountered the poisoned tea, I saw a snake, too. The two of them must be connected somehow."

Lian crosses her arms, considering this. "Someone tried to kill the closest person to the princess. Not to mention the multiple attempts on her own life."

"And someone has already killed her father, the most powerful and protected person in the empire." If I value my life, this is knowledge I should keep to myself. But I need someone with knowledge of the intricacies of the court. Lian would be able to tell me who I can speak with, and who I should avoid.

My friend does not appear surprised by this, only troubled. "You know this for certain?"

"The princess did not deny it."

"It's just as my father said." She shakes her head. "The Prince of Dài will return to reclaim what he believes to be his."

"After all this time . . . ?" Ten years is a long time. For an empire to change, for loyalties to shift.

"I was in the palace when the Prince of Dài attempted to overthrow the emperor." Her voice is soft, but the fear in her eyes betrays her. "I was young, but I still remember. How scared I was when Father sent me through the back gate. I watched the palace burn. The court splintered. Many were executed when the rebellion failed."

She pauses in her pacing to regard me with a severity that makes her appear older than her years. "But many innocents who played no part died, too. I don't want you to get hurt. Be careful, Ning."

I am reminded of the night I tiptoed out of the house in the dark, when a girl younger than me in age, but wiser in all other things, gave me a similar warning.

"I would like to think we are friends," I say, my way of apologizing for hiding things from her.

"We are." She gives me a smile, and the way ahead seems less daunting, if only for a moment.

CHAPTER TWENTY-NINE

THAT EVENING WE DON OUR COMPETITOR'S ROBES, OUR new outfits devoid of color or ornamentation. Only the royal family can be clothed in mourning white, but the rest of the palace residents show our respect by wearing black. White banners hang from the rafters and before every doorway to remind us of Dàxī's loss.

We do not resume the competition in the Hall of Reflection, but instead, as befitting the virtue of wisdom, we meet in the top room of the library pavilion. From here, the latticed windows are cut into the shape of flowers and reveal the lights of the palace grounds and the city beyond. Outside, a warm spring rain drizzles over the rooftops, casting everything in a misty hue.

This room appears to be one for meditation and practicing calligraphy, as there is only one scroll hanging from the wall, with three characters written in a flourish:

人之初

The eternal question and conflict posed by the philosophers: Is it human nature to be good, or evil?

How many emperors and empresses have stood here in this very room and looked up, pondering how they will answer that question in order to guide the people of Dàxī? Has Princess Zhen ever stood in the very place where I am standing now, thinking about the same question? What is her answer?

The birds are again present in their gold cages, their permanent residence not the Hall of Reflection like I initially believed. This time I take note of their feathers—a rich, deep purple, fading to green tips. Their eyes are dark spots with a bright sheen, the curve of their scarlet beaks ending in a sharp point.

"We return to the third round of the competition." Elder Guo looks particularly foreboding in black robes, like a fortune-teller about to pronounce a dire omen. She is the only judge present at this time, having already passed along her regards from the others this evening. They are preoccupied with the future of the empire for the moment.

"It is imperative that we continue with our efforts," she continues. "We will not allow dissidents to disrupt the course of the competition. For Dàxī is a mighty river, and they are only broken branches, to be carried away by the current."

Her words are meant to provide reassurance, but I've learned to see through the platitudes of court officials, how their actions sometimes conflict with their grandiose pronouncements. After all, with enough dissidents, one could build a dam that could divert the most powerful of rivers.

"Behind me are the Piya, the embodiment of the phrase 'attack poison with poison.' We train the birds from birth. They are continually fed a diet of poisonous creatures, until they are both immune to poison and are poisonous themselves." She smiles at our shared confusion and unfamiliarity with such creations.

"I thought they were birds of legend," Guoming says. "They aren't real."

"I assure you," Elder Guo says, "they are very real. You may recognize them by another name: the poisonfeather bird. Their bite, their claws, their tears, their excrement ... all contain poison. They are also excellent poison detectors, for they will not ingest what they cannot endure. Now, for your next task ..."

She gestures at the birds. "Only by working closely with your partner will you be able to succeed. One of you will transform a lethal poison so that the Piya will willingly ingest it against its nature. The other will counter the poison and save the bird's life. If the Piya refuses to ingest the poison, you will fail. If the bird dies, you will fail. Only if your team fulfills both tasks will you be able to move forward."

"What sort of poison will need to be transformed?" Wenyi asks, a question befitting one who has dedicated his life to the academy.

Elder Guo's eyes gleam, and she utters with doting affection, almost as one would say the name of a dear child, "Jīncán."

Gasps of revulsion, my own included, join the sounds of the birds.

"She's mad," Lian comments under her breath, and I agree.

The jīncán is a gold silkworm, an abomination of nature. Mother said it was folklore, an ancient ritual practiced by those who used to tamper with darker magics. It is a chaotic magic that will eventually devour anyone who delves too deeply into it.

The silkworm about to form its cocoon is harvested and sealed into a jar with poisonous creatures gathered under the darkest night of the new moon. The jar is buried, then opened one week later. The creatures will have slaughtered one another, and the pupa will turn gold, having subsisted on the blood of the ones that devoured each other beside it. The pupa never emerges from the cocoon, residing there in a suspended state. It is not alive, but neither is it truly dead.

Some say the spirit of the silkworm leaves the body entirely, and the spirit can only be satisfied with blood. One drop of the creator's blood binds the jīncán spirit to do its bidding, but you run the risk of being devoured if you do not keep it fed.

Once I might have laughed at the absurdity of such a horror. But then last night I pulled a snake wearing three human faces out of a woman's body. There are darker and stranger forces out in the vast, wide world than I could ever comprehend with my limited imagination.

"Tomorrow you will have access to the storeroom of the royal physicians. We will reconvene in the evening, after the summer rites have been performed." I had forgotten that tomorrow is the Call to Summer, a festival signifying the change between seasons. "Tonight you will choose one of these birds and tend to it in your residences.

"These birds are national treasures," Elder Guo says as we survey the Piya, considering the daunting challenge presented before us. "If they come to harm, it is not only your position in the competition you should worry about, but what sort of punishment you will receive."

Shao and Guoming elbow each other with confident smirks, not worried about the threat. They are the ones who rush to the pedestals first, swiftly ushering away their chosen bird. I look at Lian and she gives me a shrug. I know nothing about the care of animals, but the choice is made for us soon enough. I lift the one remaining bird from its pedestal, and it gives me an indignant squawk at being jostled.

"What about the jīncán?" Shao asks when we all return to our places, birds in hand.

I trust none of the other competitors apart from Lian, even though Wenyi and Chengzhi are amicable enough. But of the remaining shénnóng-tú, I trust Shao the least, after having seen him in the residence of the marquis.

"You will be permitted the use of a single dried pupa tomorrow evening," Elder Guo says, "upon which you will perform the transformation for us to review."

We bow as we leave the chamber. I can't help but glance back once more at the question on the calligraphy scroll hanging above our heads.

Good, or evil?

"How much do you know about these birds?" I ask Lian once we return to our rooms. I set the bird on one of the side tables. It swivels its head in an uncanny way, watching our every move.

"Not much," she admits, peering at it through the bars of the cage. "They are . . . unnatural creations. I cannot imagine how many birds have to die in order to create them."

"The same for the jīncán." I shudder. "So many had to die, and for what?"

Lian nods solemnly. "It is contrary to the art of Shénnóng, to what my people call the t'chi, for its sole purpose is the taking of a life. It is a weapon, nothing more, as much as Elder Guo likes to pretend it has a higher purpose. I'm surprised the ministry has approved its use."

"Perhaps it is a way for the princess to see who exhibits comfort with the use of poisons, and in turn, will lead her to the one responsible for the poisoned tea bricks," I speculate.

Desperate people resort to desperate things. It is a daunting task before the princess, to wade through the murky pool of the court, determining who is loyal and who is an enemy.

"She remembered me," Lian says, idly picking up a nut from the table and setting it on the edge of the cage. The Piya twitters and flies down to peck at it. When the bird deems it edible, the nut is tossed up in the air and eaten swiftly.

"Who?"

The bird ruffles its feathers and pecks at the floor, chirping. Lian pushes more nuts through, and the greedy creature swallows them one by one.

"Zhen," she says, sounding like she is lost to memory. "Older Sister, I used to call her. When we were children, we were permitted to play together. But then the fear of rebellion came, and she was kept apart for her own safety. My father saw this and cautioned me that someday someone may want to hurt my family and hurt him, through me. He said that was why I had to be watchful and useful, because that day could come sooner than expected."

My time spent in the palace, all the things I've learned, have begun to change my understanding of my childhood. How I used to view everything through a warped mirror, and how I am still searching for clarity.

"She does not know who to trust," I tell her. "How can she?"

Lian offers the bird a peanut, and it squawks, annoyed. "She may be right in one aspect. If she is able to determine the source of the poison and figure out an antidote, she can at least appease some of the people."

"Many of them are just tired and afraid." Lost, like me.

"My father has been preparing for this day. The stars have already foretold it. The empire will split, and change will come." She says it with confidence, as certain as the sun rising from the east, and I envy her staunch belief in the words of the astronomers.

"What do they see? Is her rule foretold?" I ask, curious. "Why can they not reassure the people who will be a good ruler and who will be a bad one?"

"Everyone is able to see the stars; it's the interpretation that is the dangerous part." Lian frowns. "The stars are not a straight road but a split stream, each breaking into smaller ones, infinite possibilities outlined across the sky. And it's a risky profession. You may say something that will anger a powerful person, and then . . ." She makes a slicing motion across her throat.

"Not everyone wants the future to be seen," I remark, and she acknowledges this with a nod.

Lian picks up the cage with the bird, ready to bring it into our sleeping area.

"You don't mean for us to sleep with the Piya?" I ask, skin already crawling with the thought of those eyes watching me while I'm dreaming.

"You heard the warning Elder Guo gave us. If the bird dies, we'll be removed from the competition, and worse."

I puzzle over this, not understanding, until the realization comes. Kill the bird, strike us from the competition. With the bird in our care, we're vulnerable to sabotage.

"Games within games," I mutter, sick of the intrigue. It reminds me again of my own ignorance.

"I told you before, Shao's family is deeply connected in the court," Lian says. "In both the department of the royal physicians and the Court of Officials, but he is the first of his family to have demonstrated an affinity with Shénnóng. Liu Guoming is a distant relative of the marquis, and his family has been in the tea business for generations. Their families know intimately how the tea and entertainment districts function with the officials. It is advantageous to them to have an ear in the court or influence in Hánxiá.

"The games will continue in the palace tonight. It is best we stay vigilant. Get some rest, Ning. We'll both need it."

Chapter Thirty

I WAKE TO THE SOUND OF SCREAMING, A HIGH-PITCHED keening that yanks me from the depths of dreaming and throws me roughly into the dark room. The noise seems to come from everywhere at once.

I throw off the covers, immediately looking for Lian to make sure she is not the one in anguish. Her eyes are two bright dots across the room as she clutches the blankets to her chest. She lifts her arm and shakily points to the corner. A breeze swirls around my legs as I notice light streaming from an opened window.

Above our heads, a shadow sweeps. We duck, and I realize that the source of the terrifying wail is the bird, heading for the window between our beds.

"Lian!" I yell. "Close the window!"

She leaps up and slams the window shut before the bird can find an escape. The Piya shrieks again, aggravated, then settles on top of one of the cabinets, preening itself with fervor.

I fumble for the matches and light the candles, and the room finally comes into view.

There is an overturned stool in the corner. Two legs are visible behind the screen, clad in black pants and black boots. I grab Kang's dagger and pull it from its sheath, holding it ahead of me with a shaking hand. As I approach, I smell a stench like emptied bowels, like sickness.

"What . . . what is it?" Lian asks.

Using my foot, I nudge the leg and it flops to the side. Dagger at the ready, I pull the screen aside to reveal the face of the man lying on the floor.

Lian's shriek is muffled, but I can still hear the terror contained behind her sleeve. The man had fallen to his side, one arm underneath him, the other hand clutching his throat. His tongue is swollen, purple, flopping out the side of his mouth like a slug. There is blood seeping out of every orifice. Trickling out his nose and ears and streaming out the corner of his eyes like tears.

It looks like he died painfully, brutally, with no peace in his final moments.

"I'm . . . I'm fairly certain he is dead," I say to Lian, trying to reassure her, but the quaver of my own voice betrays me.

With a loud crash, someone bursts through the doors of our residence, footsteps rapidly approaching. I quickly thrust the dagger up my sleeve and out of sight. We are suddenly surrounded by guards in our small room. They avert their eyes, raising their swords to their foreheads in a salute. One of them steps forward and bows to us.

"Apologies for our intrusion," he says. "We have been tasked to watch over your residence tonight, but it seems we have arrived too late to be of any assistance. I have sent for the chancellor—he requested to be informed if there was a disturbance in your residence."

"Chancellor Zhou?" Lian's brows crease. "Why would he be concerned for our safety?"

I hear the sound of footsteps in the courtyard, then the

chancellor himself strides into the room. He is in casual robes, which appear as if they have been hastily thrown on. His hair is tied back in a simple knot, instead of in the usual hairstyle of the court. His expression is somber.

"I had hoped it wouldn't come to this." He walks over to where one of the guards kneels beside the dead man, searching through his armor. "It looks like someone was determined to remove you both from the competition."

The guard stands and salutes. "Reporting, sir. There is no identification on him that I can see."

"We'll find out soon enough. Carry him out and strip him down." Chancellor Zhou dismisses the guard with a wave, then turns back to us. "Come join me when you are ready. Captain Wu will show you the way."

We wait for one of the soldiers to collect the bird with heavy gloves, coaxing it carefully back into the cage with food. The guard attempts to take the Piya, but Lian makes sure it stays close to us, reminding him that the bird must be left in our care until the next round. He eventually grumbles something but acquiesces, leaving us to make ourselves presentable for an audience with the chancellor.

Captain Wu leads us through the corridors while the palace is in slumber. There is no pronouncement from the criers to orient us to the hour, but I can feel the fatigue in my body and mind. The trees of the gardens and the statues appear to take on ominous shapes, shadows stretching into grotesque forms. I wish I had a fresh cup of summer tea with gingko to clear my thoughts.

We enter a side gate, and I recognize we are being admitted to the inner palace—properly this time, instead of sneaking around through the tunnels. We walk on stones where the empress herself used to tread, past painted murals on the walls, depictions of warriors and maidens and scholars. It feels like too many eyes are following our every step.

Stepping over the threshold, we enter a grand room where the braziers are lit, illuminating the rich tones of the redwood paneling. The center of the room is sunken, meant for entertainment. But instead of the chancellor, it is the princess who waits for us on one of the platforms, drinking from a cup. Lian and I drop to our knees before her.

"Leave us," the princess commands. Captain Wu and the rest of the guards disappear.

"Come." She waves us to our feet.

I am reminded that I had threatened the princess the night before, forced her hand. And regardless of the fortunate outcome, somehow I don't think she's the forgiving sort.

"I . . . I hope Ruyi is recovering, Your Highness," I say, clearing my throat.

She gives me a considering look before answering. "Spoken like a true physician's daughter," she says. "There is no need to be so formal with me. You have saved the life of my beloved, and for that I am grateful. You may refer to me as Zhen if there are only the three of us present."

"That is a great honor, Your—thank you." Lian bows, and I follow in turn.

"Sit," she instructs, and we kneel on cushions on the lower platform.

"She was restless most of the day, but able to take in some food," Zhen says. I can hear the undercurrent of worry in her voice.

Lian shakes her head. "I am horrified someone would do such a thing. Poison is a despicable weapon, but I commend you for keeping your composure. I heard from Father that you addressed the court earlier today and gave a speech that roused their spirits for the days to come."

"You remember Grandmother's ... lessons," the princess says, and there's a mirroring grimace on Lian's face.

My friend nods. "I only ever had to endure them for a few months of the year, but I used to have nightmares of her chewing me up and spitting out my bones if I ever spoke out of turn."

Zhen chuckles, then lets out a soft sigh. "How I wish she were here ... she would know what to do. How to navigate the court, how to ..."

"I agree," Lian says solemnly. "She would know what to do."

"Let us speak in confidence." Princess Zhen leans forward, intent. "Within this room, I promise you will have my attention. If you are honest with me, I will be forthright in turn."

She turns to address Lian first: "I appeal to you, one who was once my young companion. My grandmother gave me her word your family could be trusted. Can I rely on you to provide your counsel and your discretion?"

Lian touches her hand to her shoulder, an acknowledgment. "As my people once recognized your grandmother as the Princess of Peace, so too will I, if you are willing to recognize the pact between our families."

The princess nods, then her gaze falls heavily on me. "At first I disliked your brashness and saw it as offense," she says. "But I realize I need fewer flowery words and proclamations of loyalty. I need those who will be able to challenge me if I am failing my people.

"What say you, Ning of Sù?" She searches my face, as if looking for any hesitation. "When you quoted the revolutionary, were you signaling for change, as the marquis accused? Are you willing to be a voice for the people and help me continue my father's legacy, for the prosperity of Dàxī?"

For a moment, I despair at such a burden. How am I to know if she will be a good ruler? I have seen how people have suffered under greed and corruption, but if she is as unaware of the crimes committed by the officials as she claims, then perhaps she would be willing to do what must be done. Perhaps she would be willing to enact change.

"If you will address the plight of the people and demonstrate your ability to uphold your promises—" I choose my words carefully, feeling their weight. "Then you have my word, I will be honest with you."

"Good." Zhen leans back, satisfied with our oaths. "Now let us discuss what happened tonight and what is to come. There is much to be done."

Chapter Thirty-One

"I HAVE ATTEMPTED TO FOLLOW THE UNREST AT THE BOR-ders," Zhen tells us. "I know some of the officials have been using imperial authority for their own gain, but I have only learned how far the corruption has spread in the past few months."

It pains me to know that the princess was so unaware of the troubles of the empire. I can't help but wonder if, before he fell ill, the emperor had intentionally kept her in the dark.

"Illegal occupation of land, sale of tea and salt at exorbitant prices, bribery, threats, use of force . . . but nothing sickens me as much as the poisoned tea." She slaps the table before her, her frustration made clear. "I have used my resources to fund my investigations, but it has been difficult. The spies remain loyal to my father, and I am not sure how many of them also report to others in the court."

Now I understand why she would enlist us to her cause. We are relatively unknown in the capital, and it is easier to ensure our loyalty.

"You believe it is someone in the Court of Officials." Lian raises an eyebrow. "Perhaps even one of the ministers. Not another kingdom attempting to undermine the strength of Dàxī."

Zhen shakes her head. "Talum to the west is undergoing civil war, and its ruling family is occupied with their own concerns. The northern kingdoms have to make their way through the Pillars of Sky in order to present themselves as a threat. Their navies are too limited to be of consequence."

Lian quotes a familiar phrase, "The tree may stand strong, but the rot starts from within."

With a grimace, Zhen continues. "It is natural to speculate that it would be outside forces trying to cause unrest, but all my sources point to officials who are influential within the court. They have joined in their support of one who they believe has a better claim to the throne."

"The General of Kǎiláng." Even I can figure this out.

"Yes." She sighs. "My ambitious uncle. I know there are those in the court who believe he should have been the emperor years ago."

"You think he is involved then? In the poisonings?" I'm unable to hold in my emotion, so desperate is my need to know. "And you believe the poisoned tea bricks are the key to finding out who is exerting that influence?"

"Precisely," Zhen states. "It is a major strike against the heart of the people, but in doing so they revealed much of themselves, more so than with the previous assassination attempts. I'm attempting to analyze the provinces they targeted, whether there's a pattern. But our analysis of the tea bricks leads to but one conclusion—the poison was created with magical influence. The work of a particularly talented shénnóng-shī."

I should have known from the beginning. Its undetectable nature, the elusiveness of the antidote . . .

Lian frowns. "You had to find a way to gather the shénnóng-shī and the most promising shénnóng-tú to the palace to continue the investigation."

Zhen nods. "The induction of the court shénnóng-shī involves lengthy rituals. Without calling for this particular competition, I would have no other reason to summon all the shénnóng-shī of the realm to Jia."

She rises from her seat and walks to a wall scroll, pulling it aside. The scroll cleverly hides a doorway, and she calls out for whoever is in the next room, before returning to her cushion.

The chancellor enters, flanked by guards. It's confirmed then. He is in cooperation with the princess to unearth the mastermind behind the poison, and that is why he was watching our residences so carefully.

"Did you uncover the identity of the one who tried to attack the bird, Chancellor?" Zhen asks. Seeing his hesitation, she waves her hand. "You may speak freely in front of them."

The chancellor inclines his head and provides his report. "The thief gained entrance to the residence by the rooftop and the opened window. He had gloves and attempted to grab the bird, but it spat in his eyes, blinding him. When he let it go, it bit him at the wrist. When the saliva entered his blood, it took its course, and he perished." Resulting in the mess remaining on the floor of our residence.

"Those cursed birds can fetch a high price in the black market," Lian states. "I'm not surprised he tried to steal it instead of killing it."

"It would have accomplished two purposes: put coin in his pocket and eliminated both of you from the competition," the chancellor says.

The princess nods. "I suppose we will see who shows up with a bird tomorrow and who does not." After a pause, Zhen's attention returns again to me. "We should speak about Kang."

Ah yes, the discussion I've been dreading. I can feel the weight of all their gazes on me, just like the eyes of all those figures on the murals. Because she asked me in front of the chancellor, it must mean he is privy to our agreement.

I start, voice shaky, "He took me to Língyǎ Monastery."

Chancellor Zhou regards me as if seeing me with new eyes, painfully reminiscent of my father's disapproval. But I stare back, holding my head high.

The questions come, one after another.

"Língyǎ?" Zhen asks. "Why Língyǎ?"

"Did he take you to meet the abbess?" the chancellor asks. "Did she say anything about an alliance with his father, or give hints about their plans?"

"He took me there to see the gardens, and we were almost discovered by the monks, so we hid in an underground cave while they searched for us." Where I fell in, and he saved me, and he kissed me until we both lost our breath. "And we . . . talked."

"Talked?" The princess encourages me to continue.

"We talked about him growing up in the palace, with you."

"Do you think he harbors any ill will toward the princess? Is he a risk to her?" Chancellor Zhou presses on with his stream of questions. He seems to be unhappy with my answers, wanting something more.

"He says Lùzhou is suffering because its people are unable to find work," I reply. "They have limited ways to make a living and are forced to commit unlawful deeds to survive."

Zhen turns to the chancellor. "That is what I've told you as well. If you would allow me to leave the palace and enact the policies we discussed, we can alleviate some of their suffering."

"We must keep you safe, Your Highness," the chancellor says.

"How can I answer to your father's spirit, your grandmother's, if I do not?"

"I'm tired of being safe!" Zhen raises her voice, eyes flashing. "I am tired of being coddled and protected! It's time for me to learn how to rule. We have to draw out this faceless enemy before it is too late."

"We are getting closer to the truth. You are aware of the information we have on Kang," the chancellor says quickly, ready to soothe her temper. "You know he is not to be trusted."

"What information?" I ask, but Lian folds her arms and speaks over me. "Did you use Ning as bait?"

Zhen regards her steadily. "I don't believe I placed her in any harm."

Before I can consider the implications of this, the chancellor is already speaking again. "Our spies have seen Kang with the Marquis of Ānhé, spreading his father's influence to the southeastern regions. The marquis and the general have bribed officials of the ministry, conscripting more and more people to the salt marshes and setting up training camps for their own army in secret."

"Kang says he believes the poison to be dishonorable," I protest. "He only wishes to advocate for his people."

I don't know why I continue to defend him, only that I am certain the boy I spoke with beside the secret spring was sincere in his words. The Golden Key tells me so; it hums in my heart.

"We merely suspect," the princess acquiesces. "The evidence against my uncle is clear, but we cannot be certain of Kang's loyalty yet."

"Could it be he didn't know?" Lian ventures forth timidly. "Could it be his father kept him in the dark?"

"I've forgotten you knew him, too," Zhen says. "Before."

"Don't be naive," the chancellor snaps. "Both of you saw how he behaved at the ceremony. He swooped in to gain her trust, pretended to spare her the blade, but those assassins were probably sent by his father. It was an elaborate ruse. He has probably wielded a sword from the time he could walk, trained with outlaws of the empire into his youth. He is a weapon. That much is clear.

"I believe the evidence will surface in time," the chancellor finishes with a dour smile, then speaking to Zhen: "Will you tell her, or shall I?"

They exchange looks, and the princess turns back to me again. "We have communication—*trusted* communication—that a component of the poison hidden in the tea bricks is unique to Lùzhou. A type of yellow seaweed, kūnbù."

There is a sudden roaring in my ears. The truth crashing over me like waves, threatening to drown me under its weight.

"I am sorry," she says gently. "It is unlikely he is as unaware as he claims." I hate the look of pity on her face.

"Are you closer to a cure, then? An antidote to the poison?" I demand.

I should have focused on that all along, not allowed myself to become so distracted by a handsome boy from the market. Wasting time wondering whether he wanted me for some nefarious purpose because of my shénnóng-tú abilities, or if he truly wished to get to know me as he claimed.

Our paths should never have crossed.

"We are making progress," the chancellor tells me. "But we are only able to delay the course of the poison, not eliminate it entirely."

"Do not worry, Ning," the princess says to me. "I keep my promises. You will have the antidote if we discover it, access to the storerooms if we do not. But I need both of you to remain in the competition. Keep watch over your competitors, report to me any peculiar behavior, any strange interactions."

Lian and I nod in understanding.

"And I would very much like one of you to become my court shénnóng-shī," she says. "I need people close to me. People I can trust."

When we leave the chamber, I feel the ghost of a brand on my chest. I remember when Kang spoke of the loss of his mothers, the one who birthed him and the one who took him in, so much like the loss of my own. Could he have concealed his hate so well? His desire for revenge?

He lied to me, a quiet voice protests within, stinging from the betrayal.

I know better now.

Chapter Thirty-Two

Chancellor Zhou has us moved out of our residence, as it is now sealed off for further investigation. Due to the influx of ministers and officials called to the palace for the upcoming funeral rites and the remaining rounds of the competition, the servant residences are full. Lian and I now reside with the scholars in the upper levels of the library, on the fifth floor. It is a circular room with simple furnishings. I prefer the sparseness to our previous accommodations; I've grown tired of being surrounded by fragile, breakable things.

I fall asleep quickly, the fatigue of the past few days washing over me like a wave. When my eyes open again, the room is already filled with sunlight. The Piya is singing, looking for attention, the light filtering through the fabric over its cage. I pull the covering off and it greets me with more warbles, jumping off the stand. It pecks at the bottom of its cage, looking for food.

"I'm sorry," I tell it. "I have nothing to give you right now." It cocks its head, watching me again with its inquisitive eyes. I shudder. One bite from this bird and I will die a quick, painful death. I decide to stay as far away from it as possible.

Qing'er is the one who delivers our morning meal, exclaiming at the view from our window. I only feel safe speaking of what transpired last night after he is gone, not wanting to involve any-one else in these increasingly dangerous endeavors. The stranger slipped easily through our window, without the chancellor's guards noticing. Instead of trying to take the bird, he could have killed us in our beds.

We slurp fat noodles in light broth, layered with pieces of sweet green gourd and slivers of pork. Qing'er said this was a northern tradition, noodles for summer, especially as the solstice approaches, and dumplings are meant for winter. Although because of how much the emperor loved dumplings, they are usually eaten all year round in the palace. I can't help but wonder how the tastes of the kitchen will change when another ascends the throne.

Lian offers the bird a bite of the gourd, but it refuses the green flesh with a distasteful expression.

Once our bowls are empty, I finally tell Lian the details of my encounters with Kang. How I shared a cup of Golden Key with him, then the Silver Needle, to test his true intentions—and how I failed. But to my surprise, Lian does not chastise me. Instead she seems impressed.

"To be able to gain mastery of the Shift is a great gift," Lian says with awe in her voice. "You are talented, Ning."

The thought pleases me, but it reminds me of how much more I have to learn. The great tree in the darkness, where the goddess spoke . . .

"Is that what it's called, that in-between place? The Shift?"

"Yesterday I felt it, I think, for the first time." Her eyes gleam. "That feeling of stepping outside your body that you experienced. It was different from imbuing already strong men with strength, more than just adding wood to the fire. When I helped Ruyi . . . I held her connection to the world. I protected her. I spoke with her when you grappled with the dark creature, kept her from slipping into the beyond. In our legends, we refer to death as a cliff, an eternal fall. When I was there, I pulled Ruyi away from the edge, but I heard something else call my name."

She shudders, and I feel for her, this kind girl I dragged into my quest to save my sister. I reach out and take her hand.

"Thank you," I tell her. "For assisting me without hesitation when I needed you. Thank you for being a true friend."

All I can offer are my words. I have no riches, no rare ingredients, nothing to bargain or barter with except my friendship. And she accepts it, as regal as any princess in the history of Dàxī.

We descend the stairs to the main levels of the library in order to review the available texts regarding the mystery of the Piya. When one of the scholars notices the bird and asks for our names, he takes us down another set of stone steps into a small chamber below.

"What is this place?" I ask, noticing the cracked bamboo scrolls and the books wrapped in protective cloth.

The scholar bows. "This is the restricted section of the library. The chancellor has indicated that you are welcome to access any of the books here." Chancellor Zhou must have agreed to provide us with aid at the princess's behest.

Lian examines the shelves, selecting *A Treatise on Northern Poisons and Herbology* by a famous Ānhé physician, Qíbo. I select *Língshu*, a text penned by one of the great shénnóng-shī who visited the court of the Ascended Emperor, and a slim volume of poison interactions and toxin neutralization from Hánxiá. Even though I gaze longingly at works such as *Discussion of Tea Cultivars of the Yún Region* and *On the Selection of Tea Ware for the Enhancement of the Drinking Experience*, I select *Recipes for Fifty Ailments*, and on a whim, place *Wondrous Tales from the Celestial Palace* on top of it. I see Lian's eyes linger on the title, but she does not criticize my choice of such a fanciful text, one that even the most superstitious citizen of Dàxī would dismiss as mythology.

Back in our room, we debate over the old texts, recording notes from the treatises written by the masters of the art, who seem to be in conflict as well. I am desperate to retrieve all the knowledge from these volumes at my fingertips, hopeful that an obscure ingredient in here is an antidote to the poison I am seeking. We learn of the rhinoceros's horn, supposedly a counter to all poisons, but it is a rarity in itself, the beast found only in a distant kingdom. There is a mention of the black pearl of Lùzhou, reminding me of Kang, but it seems to be an enhancer of the properties of certain ingredients rather than being a poison counter itself.

We continue to ask and answer each other, always circling back to the key questions for this challenge: How do we transform the jīncán and use it as a lure? And then how do we rid the bird of it?

I doze off, jerking awake to the sound of Lian singing a pleasant tune to the Piya, and the bird trilling back. The two of them have seemingly developed an affection for one another while I rested.

"Can you even bear to poison it?" I tease, and she flutters her hand at me in dismissal.

"You can do the poisoning, and I will do the saving," she decides, and I am in agreement.

I read about how the Piya are fed their unique diet from birth, building up from seeds to insects, then to larger creatures, growing their awareness and their immunity. When they are old enough, they transition to human dishes, where they can begin to detect the poison present in food. I read about the five venoms—the scorpion, the snake, the moth, the toad, and the centipede. All of them condensed into the fabled jīncán, and something the bird should easily detect.

Later in the afternoon, Qing'er brings us our midday meal along with a platter of fruit and nuts. I experiment with a mild poison, a berry that irritates the stomach but is pleasing to the eye. The bird pecks at it until it opens, but then refuses to ingest it. Tricky creature.

While we eat our turnip cakes, dipping them in soy sauce and chilis, we continue to test what the Piya will eat. At home our turnip cakes are plain and steamed, but here in the palace there are bits of sausage and dried shrimp mixed in. The bird refuses the sausage but nibbles on the shrimp and bites of cake.

I glare at the bird in frustration as we continue to puzzle through this riddle.

"You shouldn't overfeed it," I say to Lian, who coaxes the bird with a grape. "If you do, it won't have the stomach for the poison tonight."

"Poor Peng-ge," she sighs.

"Peng-ge?"

Lian laughs. "It's a nickname given to boys in Kallah. I think it suits him."

I can't help but chuckle in turn, even as the daunting task looms ahead of us. We continue to debate while I stretch out on my bed and Lian continues to pace. Her muttering is now as familiar to me as the crackle of the fire and the ringing of the bells.

Another hour passes, the sun making its descent in the sky,

approaching the time of the third round. Until the uncertainty inside me continues to grow and fester, until I cannot stand it any longer, and I throw the scroll I'm holding to the ground. Peng-ge and Lian jump at the sound.

"There's nothing in these texts!" I grumble. "Nothing . . . nothing . . . nothing!" One by one, I toss the stack of books on my bed, until the last one knocks them all over with a satisfying crash.

"Feel better now?" Lian asks.

I grunt at her, arms crossed. We both stare at Peng-ge, preening himself.

"The bird will eventually develop a distaste for poison," I say out loud, returning to the puzzle before us, hoping that this time we can unravel the problem, "and will refuse to eat what may harm it."

"This is what I am struggling with," Lian says, folding her arms over her chest as well. "In order to counteract some poisons, you have to ingest another poison, but there is always the risk of countering the toxicity of one and then succumbing to the other."

"What did Elder Guo say to us that day before we found out about the emperor?" I ask, struggling to remember her words.

"The bird will only take in what it is able to endure," Lian recalls.

I stare at her, the solution revealing itself in my mind, like a hand brushing steam off a fogged mirror. "Fight poison with poison," I tell her excitedly. "That's it! That's the answer!"

Lian looks at me, still confused.

"We force the bird to ingest the poison somehow. It will do so, in order to save itself. If it believes there is an even greater threat than the jīncán." My mind is already going through the list of ingredients that will make someone more susceptible to influence. Mother uses them to calm those who are in mental distress, and I can use them to coax out a different reaction.

"I don't want to hurt him." The corners of Lian's mouth pull down into a genuine frown.

I place a reassuring hand on her shoulder. "We'll save him. I'm certain of it."

After a lengthy pause, Lian finally nods, acquiescing to my horrible, yet necessary plan.

Chapter Thirty-Three

The setting sun sends streaks of pink and orange across the sky, reflected in the water of the lily pond behind the pavilion. A beautiful backdrop to the third round of the competition, but I do not have the luxury to admire such views. Instead, I mentally rehearse the steps to the daunting challenge ahead of us. Deceive the Piya, save the Piya.

Our judges are seated on the stone chairs already built into the pavilion itself, speaking to one another while waiting for the competition to begin. Three of them are cloaked in black, bare of courtly ornamentation, adhering to the ritual of mourning. The princess sits clothed in an austere robe of white, hair adorned with silver flowers. The sweep of her skirt shows the faintest hint of embroidery, chrysanthemums in gold.

Mother never liked chrysanthemums, due to their association with funerals. When we laid her to rest, there was not a chrysanthemum in sight. It feels like a bad omen to see them now, even though I know that is a foolish thought.

Only six of us are present: The two shénnóng-tú who are companions of Shao and Guoming have not joined us. I note their absence as we stand before the judges. Only three pedestals, three birds. Something must have happened.

Elder Guo stands. "The minister has performed the summer

rites to appease the heavens, for the gods to bless us with fair weather and a bountiful harvest. It should be an auspicious time for Dàxī, but instead we have uncovered a plot to cheat in our competition."

Behind us, an official enters the pavilion and bows to the judges. The pendant swinging from his sash indicates he is from the Ministry of Justice. Even though his sword is sheathed in an ornamental scabbard, and we are far from Sù, I still feel a familiar chill at the sight.

"We have determined that the mercenary was hired by the Zhu family in an attempt to influence the competition in their son's favor," he reports. "They have provided their confessions and will be sequestered to their residences, awaiting judgment."

Beside me, I hear a chuckle. Glancing over, I see Shao and Guoming, barely able to contain their glee. It would not surprise me if these two had some hand in influencing the other competitors to attempt their subterfuge. A whispered suggestion, a nudge and wink. At least Wenyi's expression is stoic, and Chengzhi appears disgusted by the discovery.

"Greed continues to remain in the people of Dàxī," Elder Guo says with distaste. "We must remember that the path to wisdom is self-restraint. We must not give in to our primal selves." The princess looks perturbed by this comment but does not interrupt the elder's speech.

"First, we will see how you fare in this challenge." Elder Guo nods in the direction of Shao and Guoming. "The items you have requested are already present in the pavilion, marked with your names."

After greeting the judges with courteous bows, the two of them separate—Guoming to the table where the ingredients are laid out, and Shao to collect their Piya from the pedestal.

An enclosure is moved into the middle of the pavilion by the servants: a wooden frame with wire-mesh walls placed on a waist-high table for optimal viewing. Shao releases the Piya into the enclosure, where it tests out its new space by flying from one side to the other. The stage is set.

Shao nods at Elder Guo, who gestures a monk forward. He hands Shao a covered pot the size of his palm, the corners sealed with red wax. A warning of the dangers contained within.

"I am honored to be standing before the judges today, and to set eyes upon these rare creatures." Shao bows with a flourish. Guoming stands next to him, holding a tray with one cup in the center, filled with something steaming. Shao carefully breaks the wax seal and sets the pot on the table before him. With steady hands, he uses a pair of chopsticks to lift the jīncán out for all to see.

It's such a small thing, the silkworm pupa. Only the size of a thumb. The color is pale gold, almost translucent, as if the poison has leached all the color out of it. Shao places it carefully on the plate, then covers it with another bowl.

Selecting the cup from Guoming's tray, he salutes the judges and then drains it in one mouthful. I smell the scent of rain, perceive the same peculiar feeling prickling my brow. Shao uncovers the plate with a flourish, and in the center, gleaming, is a plump red date. The jīncán has disappeared.

"An illusion," Lian breathes beside me.

Shao laughs, turning toward her, the rush of the magic making him amicable for once. "Not an illusion. A transformation. To the Piya, it will taste like a date."

"Marvelous!" Marquis Kuang approaches, face taking on a calculating expression. "How long does this transformation hold?"

Shao shrugs. "Depends on the skill of the shénnóng-tú. A

257

competent apprentice should be able to maintain it for the span of one incense stick." The arrogance returns swiftly with Shao's declaration: "In my class, I hold the record. A breath over two hours."

That's more than double the expected time.

"Impressive." The marquis nods and returns to his seat.

"It is not sufficient for the jīncán to merely appear as something else," Elder Guo calls out. "The bird has to ingest it."

"Of course." Shao bows and slides the plate into the enclosure.

The Piya settles beside the plate and regards it. Deeming it good to eat, it plucks the date off the plate and swallows it whole. Only a moment passes before it begins to convulse. The nature of the jīncán is such that ingesting a few small flakes of it over time results in a slow death, but to partake in such a large amount at once?

The bird makes a high, keening noise of pain and despair. The other two Piya in the pavilion screech in concern. Guoming is there immediately, reaching into the cage. He pries open the Piya's mouth with gloved hands and pours a tonic down its throat. It's too weak to fight him, but it feebly attempts to fend him off with a flap or two of its wings.

It jerks, once, twice, then the date is expelled successfully from its body, covered in a slick fluid. The bird lies there, dazed, chest heaving, but still alive. The monk, waiting to the side of the pavilion, quickly approaches and returns the transformed jīncán back into the pot. The bird is ushered away as well, having endured its purpose.

"Well done," Elder Guo pronounces. "A worthy resolution to the dilemma presented. Now, our next pair of shénnóng-tú will demonstrate their abilities."

She turns to me and Lian expectantly.

Something churns inside me as we approach the dais. Mother

told me that if anyone is found to have died at the hands of a shénnóng-shī, the murderer's name will be stricken from the *Book of Tea*. She died of a poison created by one of us, someone who walked in pretense along the path of Shénnóng. And someone in the palace knows who it is.

That cold thought is the only thing that steadies my hands as I prepare to do this cruel deed.

"I'm sorry, Peng-ge," I whisper to the bird as I carry its cage to the enclosure. It chirps at me, oblivious to the fate that awaits it. I close the door and watch it tentatively hop out of the cage.

The pot is placed into my hands, heavy and cool. My fingernails sink into the softness of the seal, releasing the lid. I regard the jīncán sitting at the bottom. Such a small, unnatural thing. I lift it out and set it into a bowl. Lian passes me a jar of water, which I pour on top of the jīncán in a thin stream. The gold silkworm rises, then sinks as it absorbs the water, releasing its essence.

I slide the bowl into the enclosure with Peng-ge. It is accustomed to my presence now and hops forward to explore the bowl's contents. Its trust makes this worse, as I watch it test the water. For a moment I hoped it wasn't as smart as the elder had promised, that it would see the water and drink. But it seems to recognize the danger contained within and flits away, uninterested.

The tray on my table has only three items. A knife. A block of tea. A bowl.

Picking up the tea brick, I inhale its scent. Tea leaves packed together and formed into a block the size of my hand, left in the dark to ferment and age. Easy to transport, easy to store.

Using the flat blade, I slice off a chunk of tea and place it into the waiting bowl, strands of asarum sitting at the bottom. Lian walks forward with the heavy kettle, the water already awakened.

When she pours it into the bowl, it releases a fierce sizzle. I need it strong and I need it potent, to wield it as a weapon.

Just like the shénnóng-shī who murdered my mother.

Closing my eyes, I lift the bowl with both hands and bring it to my lips.

CHAPTER THIRTY-FOUR

SHAO MADE THE JĪNCÁN APPEAR AS SOMETHING ELSE, PER-formed a trick of the senses. I will use my magic directly on the Piya instead.

The taste of the tea is thick, heavy, leaving a bitter coating on my tongue. The magic awakens quickly, drawn to its promised purpose. Father uses the asarum to clear the throat and nasal passages, circulating warmth. But to the shénnóng-shī, it is used for another purpose. To reach out to the mind of another, providing the power of subtle persuasion. In my palm, I hold a single feather belonging to Peng-ge that I collected from the base of its cage.

Please, I send a plea up to the goddess. *You helped me before. Do so again, even though I know I am exerting a terrible influence contrary to your tenets.*

Following the strands of magic, I step out of myself, imagining my hands reaching for the Piya, calling its name affectionately. The bird lifts its head, as if it can see me approaching, though I am aware the judges will only see me with my eyes closed, lips moving slightly.

Peng-ge cocks its head, its mind simple and not comprehending. It knows only the basic things, having been raised in the confines of Hánxiá, in its enclosure covered with trailing begonias and ivy, never knowing the freedom of the open sky. It knows hunger, it knows thirst, and it recognizes what will make it sick.

"You're thirsty," I whisper to the Piya, gaining hold of that ill feeling. "You've been thirsty for a long time. For days, without water."

The bird squawks as the discomfort creeps into its mind, tendrils of my magic snaking in to take hold. It feels wrong at every step, and bringing forth the bird's thirst causes the feeling to also be reflected in myself; my lips crack and my mouth runs dry.

Inside me, I find the tender spot, the twisted nettles of every resentful feeling, every bitter thought I've had since the chancellor unveiled one of the components of the poison and revealed that Kang had lied to me at each and every step. This magic, a dark and seductive pull, calls on me to use it against another, to make them feel the pain I felt.

My throat stretches itself painfully, needle thin, desperate for moisture. The Piya tries to lift itself and flee from the influence of the magic, but it manages only a few weak flaps of its wings before falling.

"Drink," I coax, leading it to the poison.

Taking hesitant, tottering steps, it swerves toward the bowl of water. It is torn between survival and sickness, between living and dying. It fights against everything it has been taught, and finally succumbs.

It dips its head and drinks its fill.

I stumble backward, Lian catching me as the connection between me and Peng-ge is severed when the bird loses consciousness.

"All right?" she asks quietly, and I nod, draining the flask she passes me, eager to wash the filth of that taste out of my mouth.

It tastes of cruelty and power, not so different a flavor from the crow's head. But my stomach turns before I have a chance to consider it further.

Lian works to rid the poison from Peng-ge, using what we learned from expelling the poison from Ruyi. The crimson mushroom for strength, then the umbrella-tree bark to wrestle with the toxin. The effects of the poison are weakened, as the bird only drank the infused water and did not eat the jīncán itself.

I empty my stomach into a pot in the pavilion corner, understanding intimately now what Mother meant about Shénnóng's price. The magic turns on the wielder tenfold if using it for harm. But I've never gone against her teachings before, and it feels like a slight against her memory.

A fleeting thought occurs to me while I am sick: How powerful the shénnóng-shī who is responsible for the tea bricks must be, to be able to direct the poison at so many, with seemingly no effect against themselves.

"Here." I look up to see Wenyi offering me a handkerchief, averting his eyes. I accept it with a mumbled thanks, aware of my disheveled appearance. I use it to wipe the spittle from my lips and face, making myself presentable again. He acknowledges me with a nod, before returning to his spot beside Chengzhi.

By the time I return to stand beside Lian, the servants have already cleaned the enclosure. She gives me a small nod, indicating she has completed her task successfully, and we face the judges, ready to hear if we have passed their test.

Elder Guo stands with drawn brows, appearing conflicted. The marquis regards me with a scowl while Minister Song shakes his head slowly. The chancellor whispers something to the princess, who nods in response.

"The judges have deliberated and have determined you acted in accordance with the rules of the competition," the elder announces. "While we do not condone this type of . . . influence upon such helpless creatures, we recognize that you did bid the Piya to drink the contaminated water, and purged the poison from it. You will continue on to the final round of the competition."

It was not the pretty resolution they had hoped for, not the sort of demonstration they can magnanimously present to dignitaries and officials, but we have solved the riddle. I know now their preferences for the type of pretty magic common in the capital, and it makes me seethe. This much is clear: They know nothing of life outside these beautiful walls. I ball the handkerchief tight into the palm of my hand, reminded yet again how I do not fit into their expectations of courtly behavior.

Lian places her hand on my shoulder, as if she can sense my dark thoughts. I know the ugliness of the emotions I had to draw on in order to hurt that bird, and I am ashamed of them.

"We did it," she whispers. I wish I felt elation at our accomplishment, and not a sense of approaching dread.

There is a short break as the servants approach to hang lanterns from the roof of the pavilion, providing illumination for the final pair. Crickets sound in the distance. Somewhere in the dark, a frog croaks.

Wenyi and Chengzhi approach the platform and bow to the judges. Chengzhi is the one who releases the bird, while it is Wenyi who takes charge of the poison. He shields the lower part of his face with a covering and grinds the jīncán into powder—the traditional approach, as it is odorless and tasteless, perfect for slipping into any waiting food or drink.

Chengzhi brings over a large pot and sets it on the ground before

Wenyi, who pours in the powder. We all watch expectantly as the pot begins to shake, the sound of something moving within. With held breath, we hear the noise grow louder as something thrashes within. And then ... stillness. Whatever is inside has succumbed to the jīncán's poison.

Using two long sticks, Chengzhi pulls out a dripping snake from the pot. I recognize the slender form of a water snake, brown body with black speckled patterns. It hangs limply as Chengzhi maneuvers it to the enclosure, shutting it within the same space as their Piya. The bird retreats to the back of the cage, regarding the intruder with caution.

Lian and I look at each other, not understanding how the Piya is to ingest the poison if it is already contained within the snake. Wenyi draws out a piece of something black and crumbling from a pouch on his tray and places it under his tongue.

A strange, cool wind sweeps through the pavilion, stirring our hair and our sleeves. The lanterns sway above our heads, their shadows jumping across the stone floor. The scent of frost, with a hint of pine, hangs in the air. Like stepping into the forest in winter, when we ascend the narrow paths into the mountains to harvest wild mushrooms. When I tip my face up to the sky, I am almost certain snow is beginning to fall—

"It's moving!" someone gasps.

Returning my attention to the enclosure, I see the body of the snake twitch. It moves in an odd manner, as if it is constructed from segments like a wooden toy. It pulls itself together in an approximation of life, yet it should be dead. The snake rises and its head bobs jerkily, tongue darting out, tasting the air.

There is something wrong with its eyes, covered with a pale film. It turns, still bobbing in that unnatural way, bumping its head against the mesh. Swaying, it veers and then—it meets my eyes. For a moment, the two of us regard each other in stillness, until its head swivels away, and it returns to its search.

I only imagined it, I'm sure.

The snake notices the bird then and raises itself up in a challenge. Its shadow lengthens on the stone floor. The Piya extends its wings, seeking an escape route, screeching a warning, but there is nowhere for it to go. The snake hisses, baring its fangs. The snake is the first to attack, darting forward. With a furious squawk, the bird takes hold of it in its talons, even as the snake fights to break free. The bird bites the snake again and again, sending bloody splatters against the floor of the enclosure. Until at last, the snake seemingly succumbs to its wounds and lies still. The bird, also bloodied, begins to tremble and then shake, the poison taking hold.

On the floor, their shadows quiver, forming mysterious shapes, clawed creatures approaching our feet. I step back, even though I am almost certain they are just shadows . . . almost. The scent of frost grows stronger, and our breath can be seen in the air, an impossibility in summer.

Chengzhi strides forward, a small dish in hand. He places it in front of the bird, and I recognize what's on it as feverberry, the same berry I offered to Peng-ge in the library earlier, the one that induces mild vomiting. The bird pecks at it and eats the clump of berries rapidly, then throws up a mess of black liquid. The poison expelled, death averted.

Wenyi lets out a sigh, and the shadows in the pavilion ease, retreating back into their normal shapes. He wipes his brow and takes a sip of water, his complexion paler than normal.

The judges clap politely. The marquis frowns, covering his face with a handkerchief, his distaste clear. Minister Song appears slightly pale, taking a quick sip of his water as well.

"That was certainly a sight to behold." Elder Guo strides forth with a raised brow. "Use the poison to create a threat, forcing the bird to be on the defensive, and in doing so, ingest a small amount of jīncán in the snake's blood. One that can easily be expelled by purging."

"Can the snake be revived?" the princess asks, appearing troubled.

"No, Highness." Wenyi bows his head. "It is animation, approximating movement, nothing more." A puppet, dancing from a string. It is a clever solution, but one unappreciated by the judges.

"Pity," the chancellor comments. "It would have been preferable if the snake could have lived."

Their Piya is carried out of the enclosure, making pitiful noises, but my attention remains on the snake, remembering the one that attacked me on the rock. It does not move, its one visible pale eye staring into nothing. The servant slides it back into the pot, where it lands in the water with a heavy squelch. Blood drips down the side of the table.

It's dead, I repeat to myself. *And the shadows are only shadows.* As if repeating it often enough will make it true.

Chapter Thirty-Five

We stand before Elder Guo, waiting to be dismissed, the round concluded.

"Only six remain." She clasps her hands together. "Six competitors, but room for only three in the final round."

"Three?" Guoming yelps, his confidence slipping in an instant. The four young men regard each other uneasily, assessing who is the biggest threat—notably ignoring Lian and me.

"Legend says that when the world was first created, there were six gods. The Bird of the South, the Tiger of the North, the Carp of the East, and the Tortoise of the West. The Twin Gods ruled over them all—the Jade Dragon of the river and the Gold Serpent of the cloud sea. But the Gold Serpent became jealous of how our ancestors worshipped the Jade Dragon for bringing water to their fertile lands and offered up great treasures that filled his underwater palace."

Even if it is a story I have heard many times before, her words ring hypnotic in the air, drawing us in.

"He deceived his brother by luring him into his mountain domain, and trapped him under the granite peaks of Kūnmíng. To demonstrate his displeasure at the pitiful humans, the Gold Serpent flooded the Purple Valley with storms, and many perished.

"The four remaining gods attempted to overthrow the Gold

Serpent, but he proved too powerful for even the other gods. They banded together and broke the Jade Dragon from his prison, and the skies thundered from the fierce battle. Brother against brother. God against god."

The ancient story spoken into the night seems to gain power on its own, and the wind stills. Even the frogs have stopped croaking. There is only silence as we listen to the conclusion of the creation tale.

"When the Gold Serpent finally fell from the sky, his blood dotted the lakes and ponds of Dàxī like rain. Where his blood touched water, water lilies bloomed. But the Jade Dragon also perished, and the four gods lifted him up into the heavens. They were never seen to walk among humans again."

Elder Guo's voice softens. "When the water lily flowers, we remember how the gods once roamed the earth. In the pond behind me there are three water lilies with treasure hidden inside their blooms. The first three of you to find one and bring it back to us will continue forward in the competition. May the gods guide you in your search."

She bows, and the challenge is on.

A loud splash sounds as Guoming has already raced down the stone steps and is in the water, shoving aside floating leaves. Chengzhi is not far behind him, taking just as little care with the plants. Shao carefully steps into the water, reaching down to tentatively touch a closed bud. Wenyi stands at the edge of the pond, considering the stretch of water lilies before him with a pensive look. The fragile alliances have already broken, each of them now fending for themselves.

"Treasure." Lian joins me at the water's edge. "What do you think it means?"

"I'm not sure." I frown, kneeling by the trampled path through the lilies that Guoming and Chengzhi made with their bodies. Touching my finger to a leaf, I can sense the plants screaming, their roots having been disturbed. Even without tea as a bridge, the plants have always spoken to me. I can hear their pleasure in sunny days or when they murmur excitedly, *Rain is coming,* like small children.

But the magic makes it easier to sense them, hear them whispering to each other. *The people came. The people came into the water, but they were careful. Not like these brutes. They will not find what they are looking for.*

What they remember: fingers carefully prying open a bloom, holding it apart. Something being placed inside, small in size. Round, with a pungent scent. I ask them if they will show me where these secrets are.

I open my eyes and Lian is watching me, a small smile on her lips.

"I know where they are," I say to her, voice low so the others do not hear. "I'll get you one. Come, we can go to the final round together."

Lian's smile wavers when I expect her to exclaim with her typical enthusiasm and delight, and I do not understand why.

"Remember when we first met?" I gesture at the men splashing, stumbling about in the dark. "We wanted to show them there are shénnóng-tú outside Jia. To prove them wrong. Here is our chance!"

It could be her attempt at kindness, to make sure she will not be my competitor in the final round, but I want to be there with her together. A worthy friend and opponent.

"I'm sorry, Ning." She shakes her head. "I can't go ahead in this competition. I wanted to tell you tonight, after the end of this round. My family is returning to Kallah."

Even though I know the nature of the competition means we will have to part eventually, I had hoped she would still remain in the palace because of her father's position. That I would still have a friend and wouldn't have to be alone.

Seeing the look on my face, she leans closer and whispers, "The princess has sent me away for another purpose. Do not worry about me." She pokes me in the shoulder, hard. "Go!"

I return to the water lilies, still reluctant. It doesn't seem fair. But the plants whisper eagerly, directing me to where the prize is hidden. *There . . . there . . .*

Following their encouragements, I find one not far away, a flower that whispers about the secret tucked inside it. The wet seeps into my shoes and the bottom of my skirt as I bend down and cup my hand around the bloom, asking for permission to reach within.

The poets call them "Sleeping Beauties," because they open with the midday heat and then close at night when the air cools. But under my fingers, the petals slowly unfurl, revealing a small black ball at the center. I pick it up, and it pulses with a peculiar warmth against my skin. I give the water lilies my silent thanks, and the surrounding blooms wave in acknowledgment.

Stepping out of the pond, I am the first to return to the pavilion, and offer the ball for Elder Guo's inspection. She sniffs it and nods, proclaiming that it is good. Someone else gives a shout as another competitor discovers the next hidden treasure. I wince at the number of water lilies that were disturbed for them to find their prize, and hope the gardeners will be able to tend to them.

We all return to the pavilion after a time. I stand with Wenyi and Shao as the ones who emerge victorious. Guoming's dark expression does not hide his displeasure at losing so close to the end, and

Chengzhi looks resigned, arms crossed. Lian is the only one who still looks pleased, as if a weight has been lifted off her shoulders.

"For the three of you who will not be moving forward, I commend you all for reaching this point of the competition," Minister Song says, resuming his role as the Minister of Rites. "You will return to your households with recognition, commendations sent to your shénnóng-shī, and treasures for your families. You will be reunited with them tomorrow. Rest well tonight."

The three of them bow and leave the pavilion. Lian gives me a wink of encouragement and a wave, then she's gone. Even though I should be glad I am moving on to the next round, I still feel a sense of loss.

"Now . . ." Minister Song returns to us, regarding us intensely. "The final round of the competition. The future court shénnóng-shī stands before me." He meets our eyes in turn, as if he is able to see our weaknesses, our doubts and hesitations.

"The astronomers have spoken," he announces. "A ruler will ascend, and the court shénnóng-shī will provide wisdom and guidance, like those who have advised before you. Your final trial will be presented before the court. They will witness the marvels of Shénnóng and deem one of you worthy.

"Keep the medicine ball you found inside the water lilies. You will need it for the next round." We all look down at the inconspicuous shape in our hands, wondering what clue it might provide us about what awaits us in the final round. "Your belongings will be moved into the Residence of Harmonious Spring tonight. And tomorrow . . . we shall see which one of your stars will shine the brightest over Jia."

CHAPTER THIRTY-SIX

THE WEAK MORNING LIGHT ILLUMINATES MY UNFAMILIAR, luxurious surroundings. Without Lian's morning greeting or even Peng-ge's chirpy serenade, the room feels cold.

I've made it to the final round. My goal is within reach, yet I remain restless.

I try to distract myself by reading through *Wondrous Tales*, but it does not have the same pull as those stories usually do.

Walking through our garden courtyard, I see Shao and Wenyi playing a game of strategy through the open doors of Shao's quarters. The two mirror each other, focus intent on the board before them, elbows on their knees. Directing their horses and chariots across the board. There is no invitation extended to me, and I do not intrude. I am well aware of where I fit in these perfumed corridors.

I attempt to leave the residence to at least stroll in the gardens, but there are soldiers positioned at the door by decree of the chancellor, for our own protection. But I've seen how easy it is to enter and leave the palace, the number of tunnels that run through the walls. How safe can any of us ever be in the palace?

"Wait!" one of the soldiers calls out to me. "A letter came for you." He bows and passes me a bamboo scroll, secured with twine.

I sit on the redwood stool in my receiving room and examine

the scroll, expecting it to be a letter of farewell from Lian. Except when I open it, I realize it does not unfurl. Instead it is a tube meant for transport, something sealed within—a rolled-up sheet of paper and a soft scrap of embroidered fabric.

A peony, the empress of flowers, blooms from the center of the fabric, a vibrant red. Each petal is lined with gold thread, stitched with painstaking detail. But it is growing in a bed of rippling grasses of a peculiar color, deep red to dark purple. In the background are spotted branches like trees, in various shades of pink. The moon glows in the sky like a watchful eye.

In the corner are characters in red thread, depicting a phrase from one of my mother's favorite poems, one she made us recite frequently, learn by heart. It is the poem that tells me this is Shu's handiwork.

海底有明月
圓於天上輪
A bright moon mirrored in the sea.
As round as the wheel in the sky.

With shaking hands, I unfurl the sheet of paper, dreading the message in black ink, written by my father's hand.

Ning-er,

I hope this letter reaches you in time.
I know you have left us in search of a different life, and I do not begrudge you of that. I admit I thought you would fail, entertain this foolishness for a few days

and return to the safety of home. It isn't until these weeks have gone by that I recognize I have chosen my pride rather than my daughters.

I should not have devoted all my time to the villagers, believing you capable of looking after yourself. I did not imagine you would take on such a burden on behalf of your sister. That should have been my role.

But now I have uncovered more ways in which I have failed you both. Shu has been experimenting with tea bricks, testing an antidote on herself. I should have seen the hubris of her youth and tried to stop her. She has tried to prevent me from reaching out to you, but now she is too weak to protest. She only asked that I include her embroidery to let you know she is thinking of you. She believes you will return successful.

I do not think she has much time left.

Please, I ask you, come back and say goodbye to your sister.

— Father

A teardrop splatters on the page, smearing the ink. I retreat to my bedchamber before anyone can see me weeping. My fingers grope for the prayer bead necklace, hidden in my sleeve. But the comfort I seek eludes me.

My sister has never forsaken me, even when she was beloved by all and could have easily left me behind. She was the one who remembered my dreams, pushed me and said, *Go*. I thought I wanted to bring home all the riches a palanquin could carry, show them that the pregnant girl they scorned has a daughter who is adviser to a princess, prove to my mother's family that we are worthy of their recognition. But in the end, it is always the thought of Shu, the certainty she is waiting for me at the end that propels me.

I read my father's words again and again.

As I am here in the palace working toward an antidote, Shu has been doing the same even from her sickbed. Why would she do something so reckless? I want to return to Sù and demand an answer. But another part of me laughs, knowing only she would have the sheer stubbornness to come up with such a gamble. She has been risking her life to find a cure, even as she entrusted me to fight for her in the trials. And now, what do I have to show for my escape to the capital?

A meager clue from the chancellor. A kiss from a boy I shouldn't have kissed on a beach beside a hidden lake.

I know I should keep my promise to myself, for him to remain a beautiful memory, a foolish tryst. But I am too far tangled with him. I have to pull that loose thread, even knowing everything will unravel.

Mingwen arrives at my residence to deliver the midday meal, disrupting me from my dark thoughts. Cold noodles, continuing the summer tradition, tossed with peanut oil and sesame sauce, releasing a mouthwatering scent. Other small dishes accompany the noodles: thin sliced stewed pig's ear and shredded cucumber mixed with chunks of garlic. But when she sets the dishes on the table, her presence reminds me that servants can travel freely around the palace.

I will have my answer. It may be the only way I can find the cure before my time—Shu's time—runs out.

I will rip it out of him if I have to.

I stand up and close the door, gesturing at Mingwen.

"I need to borrow your uniform for an hour," I tell her as she is setting the utensils down on the table. She turns to me, a frown already forming, ready to deny my request. But then I'm clutching at her arm, begging her.

"Just an hour," I plead, piecing together a plan with what little I have. "All you have to do is stay in my residence, tell them you are resting and require privacy for quiet reflection if they come to find you."

Her frown deepens. "Where are you going? You will be disobeying a direct order from the chancellor. They will never allow you to continue if you are caught."

I race to my bedroom and fumble among my belongings to find my mother's hairpin.

"Please." I hold it out to Mingwen, the jewels sparkling in the light. Many of the beautiful things my mother had had from the capital she sold for coin, but she had kept this one. Cherry blossoms dotted with pearls on gold branches, a reminder of her life in the palace. A representation of all the happy memories she fed me, and much more she never shared.

Mingwen takes the pin and examines it, appearing conflicted. "You are willing to part with this?" she asks.

"Lend me your clothes and keep my secret, and it is yours," I tell her.

She looks down at the pin again, before closing her hand over it and nodding. "One hour."

Adjusting the basket on my arm, I nod at the guards at the door. The hair Mingwen piled up on my head and secured with her own pin feels heavy, lopsided. I keep my breath held as I walk away from the residence, expecting one of them to call out my name, expose my ruse, but no one stops me.

I recognize the marquis's residence, with its red pillars and brown walls, in the distance. Walking down the other path, I keep my gaze to my feet when passing the other servants, hoping to appear inconspicuous. I stop at the gate to the Residence of Winter's Dreaming, which I confirmed with Mingwen is where the son of the Banished Prince resides. High white walls hold up a black roof, stone wolves guard the door. *Is it an honor, or is it a prison?*

The guards at the door let me pass, seeing me as a faceless kitchen servant. I note the red helmets and armor, indicating they're members of the elite palace guard. Aware of Kang's skills, they have assigned highly trained men to guard him.

This courtyard is small, much smaller than the other residences, but still elegantly maintained. White and black stones form curved patterns, encircling small bonsai trees on raised platforms. The door up ahead is open, revealing a small receiving room with a pair of carved wood chairs and a table between them. A scroll hangs on the back wall, a brush painting depicting the rooftops of a city.

Hesitant, I make my way up the steps and over the threshold. To my right and left there are arched doorways, marked by carved filigree. A wooden screen of birds hides the room to the right from view. The left doorway opens to a larger room, from which drifts the calming scent of benzoin.

Benzoin is meant to ease stress and soothe a restless mind. I wonder what thoughts Kang is trying to chase away.

I take another step closer. The room before me appears to be a study, but the shelves are mostly empty. There are only a few scrolls, some unrolled, and others haphazardly stacked on top of one another. A discarded robe hangs on the back of a vase.

Kang stands at a round table, leaning on the surface with his arms outstretched, hair tied neatly, and collar smoothed. He is dressed in light blue befitting the younger members of the court, not the mourning white meant for the emperor's family or the black of bereavement donned by the ministers. Lian would question whether the princess thought it an insult, a mark of his preferred distance from the royal family. But all I can think about is how the blue suits him.

"You can set the tray over by the door," he says, not looking up from what he is studying intently.

"I . . ." I try to find my voice, my rehearsed speech. I want to hurl my verbal barbs at him. I want to hurt him as much as he's hurt me, but I can't seem to form the words.

He turns to look at me, and it takes a moment, but he straightens when he recognizes me. A stack of scrolls falls to the floor with a clatter, knocked over by the startled sweep of his arm.

"Ning," he breathes, and my heart falls to my feet to join the scrolls.

Chapter Thirty-Seven

We kneel at the same time. I place my basket to the side in order to help him. He gathers the scrolls into his arms, while I pick up two that had rolled to my feet, all the while taking him in. Gone is the reckless son of a wealthy merchant, hair down to his shoulders, leading me through the streets of Jia. He looks like a scholar waiting for the exams instead, reputable. He sets the scrolls onto the table, while I place the ones I have on a shelf.

"I didn't know it was you," he starts hesitantly. "Or else I would have..."

I interrupt him by turning and fumbling for what I hid in the basket instead, thrusting the wooden box in his direction when I face him again. Trying to prevent my emotions from showing up on my face, trying to prevent him from saying something we will both regret. The Golden Key hums, recognizing him, trying to pull us closer.

Confusion spreads across his face as he slides the lid off. The beautiful dagger is there, cleaned of Ruyi's blood. I liked the feel of it in my hands when my senses were heightened by magic, but I don't want any memory of him to remain with me when I leave this place.

"It was a gift," he says, not understanding.

I envision sealing myself in a fortress, surrounded by ferocious beasts, in order to say what I must. To sever the ties between us so irreparably that there is nothing left to mend. The truth is what I wield, as sharp as any dagger.

"I spoke with Zhen," I say to him. "She told me your father was behind the poisoned tea bricks, that the main ingredient was yellow kūnbù, a seaweed grown only in the Emerald Isles."

Surprise flickers across his face, then his mouth draws into a thin line. "If I swear to you right now, on the old gods, that I didn't know about this, would you believe me?"

I remind myself that he is an adept performer, able to wear his expression as smoothly as any mask.

"Does it matter?" I ask, and he flinches like I've struck him. "From the first moment I met you, you have lied to me. Every time you've offered a glimpse of yourself, with the Golden Key, the Silver Needle, but still continue to twist the words so you can hide your true intentions."

"And those are?" His words prickle, sharp as nettles.

"To get close to the princess," I say to him. "To earn her trust, promise her no harm, draw on her sympathies using your friendship as children. Once you are safely established, then you will find a way to assist your father onto the throne."

As I continue to speak, his outrage changes to sadness, then finally eases into resignation.

"Everyone knows about my father's ambitions, his desire for vengeance, and they would not be wrong if they see him as a threat," he says, voice flat.

"You're going to tell me you are not like your father? Because you are his *adopted* son?" I retort. But when the words leave my mouth, they spin in the air like leaves in the wind, taking on new intentions. Mocking. Meant to hurt.

"There are many things I thought you could be," he tells me, clenching his jaw. "But I didn't think you would be so purposely cruel." He turns away so I cannot see his face.

I realize then how much I hurt him with a single comment, knowing what I know about his past. About how he felt like an outsider twice over, first in the general's household, then when they were banished to the Emerald Isles.

Even though I want desperately for him to look at me again like he used to, when he held me close, I need to make sure this knife goes in as deep as possible—to protect myself and everything I could lose if I fail.

"You don't know anything about me, either," I say quietly. "I lied when I begged you to take me out of the palace, I lied about my loneliness. I had to get close to you, at the bidding of the princess, and that was the only way I could think of."

His shoulders hunch and I can see color flooding into his face. I know he is thinking of all our shared words and intimacies, wondering what was real and what was a lie. Now I feel a nasty twinge of vindication. Let him be as uncertain as me.

He turns back to me again, voice cracking. "And did you find what you were looking for?"

"Not enough. I would have done things differently."

He blinks, looking at me hesitantly, waiting to hear something kinder, and I shatter that hope. "I should have pretended to care about your cause, encouraged you to get the antidote from your father."

"So everything out of your mouth was a lie?" he says, shaking. "Just two liars, telling each other words we thought the other wanted to hear?"

I say nothing, but he suddenly laughs. He bends forward, hands on his knees, laughing until he sounds like he will be sick.

"Are you quite finished?" I ask him when he pauses to wheeze a little, drawing in a hurried breath.

"I . . ." He makes a sound between a chuckle and a choke, rubbing his arms as if they pain him. "I meant everything I said. Every word. If I had the antidote for your sister, I would have given it to you."

"You can stop trying to convince me of your lies," I say, even though I hate that some part of me still trembles, wanting to believe him.

Kang reaches out and touches my cheek. Even though I should slap him away, scream and call him traitor, a part of me still longs to lean into that touch. Into the insistent tug between us that I do not know if I can blame on the Golden Key any longer. We are two people who are trying to find a place to belong, to live a life without pretending, without the complicated histories of our families. But the distance between us is too far, as vast as the divide between brothers who fought for a throne, or gods who tore apart a continent.

"My people have a blessing," he whispers, eyes as deep as sacred pools and mountain lakes. "*May the sea be willing.* May it bring you what you are looking for. I will never begrudge you that."

His hand falls back to his side, and it takes all my effort, all my strength, not to grab it, not to pull him close and kiss him senseless until all the words fall away, until none of it matters anymore.

But I don't.

Mingwen opens her mouth when I step through the door, but I shake my head and she does not ask any questions.

I read Father's letter again. This time, I'm able to decipher the worry behind the lines of careful restraint, the effort it must have taken for him to admit he was wrong.

I do not think she has much time left.

I resist the urge to rip the letter to pieces, and instead I throw the book of *Wondrous Tales* against the wall, where it hits with a satisfying crack.

Foolish stories for foolish children, Father once called them.

He was right.

Chapter Thirty-Eight

EVERYTHING HAS LED TO THIS POINT. ALL MY CAREFUL deceptions, all the things I never thought I was capable of. I am dressed and powdered, hair brushed and pinned to appear presentable. I miss Lian's bad jokes about banquets and wish again she was still here with me.

Third in line in the procession, I trail behind Shao and Wenyi. I pat my sash again, for the tenth time, to make sure the medicine ball is still there. We enter the Courtyard of Promising Future, where we once performed in front of the citizens of Jia. It is empty now, except for a scattering of soldiers along the walls.

We ascend the grand stairwell, for the first time permitted to walk the path many honored guests have walked before us, an acknowledgment that one of us will soon become the next shénnóng-shī to serve the court.

I grit my teeth. The choices I made have gotten me here, and I will see it through.

We enter the Hall of Eternal Light. The windows are opened again, and the view of Jia's vastness is awe-inspiring, meant for visiting dignitaries and foreign powers to witness the glories of the Emperor of Dàxī.

The room is filled with members of the Court of Officials, the nobility and the scholars. Two sides of the court: Influence and Knowledge. All of them have donned the black mourning sash.

My eyes sweep over the officials, most involved in casual conversation before the formal gathering is to proceed. Who among them betrayed the emperor? Which of them has pledged fealty to the Banished Prince? And who distributed the poison through Dàxī?

The gong announces the start of the proceedings. The officials settle with a rustle of robes, while the ministers stand on the dais to receive the princess. The competitors are also given cushions near the back of the hall, and we kneel. The empty throne presides over us all.

The herald announces her arrival, and we bow.

Princess Zhen strides across the room, a vision in her robes. Peonies cascade from her shoulders, dark purple blooms outlined with gold, striking against the white background. She wears a small formal headdress, jeweled birds glinting in the light when she turns her head. But instead of Ruyi, there is another familiar figure following her, dressed in deep purple robes, matching the color of the peonies, a black sash around his waist.

Kang, son of the Banished Prince. Clad in a color permitted only to royalty.

The officials buzz, uncertain, while I wish I could fade into the wooden screen behind me and become one with the wall, remembering the harsh words we uttered to one another in his residence. But he does not glance in my direction. My contrary heart should be thankful for this, yet a part of me still aches at this disregard.

Zhen sits at the seat to the right of the empty throne, as befitting the regent and soon-to-be ruler of Dàxī, while Kang stands behind her.

The herald steps forward again, and with a nod from the

princess, he unfurls his scroll. "Rise to hear the royal proclamation, people of Dàxī!"

The court murmurs, the officials getting to their feet. Their expressions contain only bewilderment, as if this is not a common occurrence, but I do not have Lian beside me to interpret.

"By decree of Princess Ying-Zhen, regent of the gloriously Ascended Emperor, recognized from this point forth as the Emperor of Benevolence. Acting on behalf of the consulted ancestors, with respect to the period of mourning and her duty to foster peace across the whole of the kingdom. To remember and recognize how the dowager empress was once known as the Princess of Peace. In honor of Empress Wuyang's betrothal to the Ascended Emperor, uniting two kingdoms and bringing an end to war . . ."

The herald pauses and clears his throat. The princess stares above all the heads of the officials, expression distant, eyes unseeing.

"The princess of Dàxī will be betrothed to Xu Kang, formally recognized as the adopted son of the Prince of Dài—"

The room erupts like a hornets' nest. But all I hear are three words repeated endlessly in my mind: *Princess. Betrothed. Kang.*

Kang, who jumped from the rooftop into my courtyard to wish me luck in the second round of the competition. Who gave me a beautiful gift from his homeland, showed me the secret parts of his childhood, told me of his dreams for his people. Who I was sent to spy on, who I hurt and betrayed.

My face burns as we drop, foreheads to the floor, receiving the proclamation. I close my eyes, recognizing how the chancellor was right: I am naive, thinking myself capable, but I am only a pawn sliding alongside the cannon on the board.

The two of them played me against each other, and I had wanted so desperately to believe them both.

The officials begin to shout, trying to speak over one another. Their words all run together in an incomprehensible rush.

"Quiet." The princess silences them with a single word.

I open my eyes to see her with her hand raised. The two figures on the dais blur into smudges, as distant as the stars.

"Your Highness," a voice thunders across the room. I pinch myself, letting the pain return me to focus. The man who strides into view is clad in ceremonial armor, gleaming red. "The Ministry of War has felt the effects of the coup, years later, even after the initial rebellion was quelled. Is it wise to resume those ties?"

A river of assent flows throughout the room, heads bobbing in agreement.

"The loss of the Prince of Dài has always been a blight on our history." Minister Song steps forward, a book open in his hand. "Consulting the *Book of Rites*, I believe Xu Kang is an appropriate bridge between the two. He was the adopted son of the prince, but his birth father had obtained the rank of commander in the army, fought in the War of Two Rivers. His name was inscribed into the family texts by the dowager empress herself. He would be granted the rank of the Prince of Dài, mending our history."

Other officials now speak in support, dividing the room.

Another steps forward, introducing himself as the official for the management of Lùzhou. "We have kept a close eye on him all these years. He has never been involved with the rumored uprising. He grew up working on the salt farms and trained in another battalion, even though he could have easily joined the general's former troops. It is well-known that he began his first post as a scout and worked his way up to captain."

Minister Song flips to a new page in his book. "Before the emperor ascended, he expressed his desire for his daughter to find a suitable match. At this point of transition, when the throne remains empty, we should all aim to spread a hopeful message. To quell the voices of the dissenters. This union may well turn the tide."

The mood in the hall seems to shift as Chancellor Zhou rises, his sharp gaze sweeping the room. "The princess herself has acquiesced, speaking for his character, having known him from childhood. Did we also forget he saved her from the assassins on the first night of the competition?"

The grumblings of the officials settles to a quiet rumble.

At this point, the princess rises from her seat, her voice like a bell, clear and authoritative. "I welcome the counsel of the court, as you have guided my father and my father's father. I rely on your help to maintain order in these dark times. The astronomers have been consulted, and they have determined that three is the auspicious number for my reign. My ascension, my betrothal, and the appointment of a new shénnóng-shī."

With a sweep of her robe, she sits, concluding the matter.

"Let the final test begin."

CHAPTER THIRTY-NINE

WE HAVE NOT HAD AN AUDIENCE OF THIS SIZE SINCE THE first round, and the feeling of eyes on me is like the unwelcome sensation of ants crawling over my skin. I keep my head down as I walk past the waiting officials to join the judges at the front of the room.

Chancellor Zhou is the one who steps forward in welcome. "The judges have been blessed to witness the various abilities demonstrated by these three shénnóng-tú during the course of the competition. They have conjured up memories and dazzled our senses. They have countered poisons and coaxed truths from lies. We have given tribute to the virtues which provide guidance to our earthly existence.

"Harmony," he calls out—demonstrating yet again how he is able to control a crowd, commanding the attention of the court. "In pairing of food with tea, recognizing the regional variations that contribute to the composition of our great empire.

"Honesty and humility," he continues. "A shénnóng-shī has a duty to provide the truth, even when the truth can harm. For only in receiving and accepting truth can a ruler confidently lead.

"Wisdom and compassion. A reminder that Shénnóng is a teacher and physician, a farmer and philosopher. A shénnóng-shī knows, as well as any physician, the balance between the internal and the external. We are humbled by death, but we will not bow to it.

"Finally, tonight we honor the virtue of dedication, the sacred connection of the shénnóng-shī to their patrons."

He claps his hands three times. Servants begin to stream in, carrying cabinets and tables between them. The officials part for them as a circular stage is created in the center of the room. Three chests. Three tables. We three competitors are sent to stand beside them, regarding each other from around the circle. My hands clutch the edge of my table, etching the curve into my palm.

Minister Song approaches us with a bamboo holder, red fortune sticks protruding from the top, like ones that can be requested from a temple for a blessing from the gods. "You shall draw lots."

Shao shakes out the first stick and places it on his table. Wenyi does the same, appearing somber. Finally, it comes to me. I close my eyes, tip the holder, and slide the stick out.

Shao's lot reveals the Emerald Tortoise, and Wenyi, the Black Tiger. Mine, unfurled with trembling hands, is the White Crane. I pray this is a good omen, hoping the goddess has continued to guide me.

The herald calls out for the champions to enter. Two men and one woman enter the hall, each dressed in their respective colors. The representative of the Tortoise is a solidly built man, with dark brows and a mass of unruly black curls. He's dressed in a loose, sack-like shirt and shorts that reach the knee. His legs are massive tree trunks, rippling with muscle, ending in bare feet. He salutes the princess with both hands, a massive redwood staff in his fists.

The Black Tiger champion is a muscular woman, arms bare

except for red wraps wound around her wrists. Her flowing pants narrow around the ankles, and gold rings sparkle from her fingers. A single gold hoop is fastened to one ear. Strapped to her back are a pair of crossed swords.

The final representative, the champion of the White Crane, is a slender man dressed in a white robe. His hair is tied up in a sleek topknot and fastened with a single silver hairpin. If it weren't for the sword at his side, sheathed in a blue scabbard, I would have thought he was a scholar. He salutes the princess with clasped hands to his forehead, bowing from the waist.

With their perfect posture, the grace of their movements, there is no doubt these are skilled martial artists.

"Throughout Dàxī's history, cities would rise or fall following the ancient tradition of the duel. The prowess of two champions, willing to sacrifice their lives for the honor of claiming a city, or defending it," the chancellor intones. Then he turns to regard the room. "Who will stand for Jia?"

"I will."

Heads turn to Kang as he descends the dais and walks into the circle. I can see the soldier's son in the set of his shoulders.

My hand flies to my mouth, muffling a gasp. At once I feel a rush of fear that I've given myself away, but all attention is on Kang as he bows to the chancellor.

"The betrothed of the princess." Chancellor Zhou smiles. "You will put yourself in harm's way and stand for Jia and Dàxī? You will prove you are worthy of the hand of the princess?"

"I am eager to demonstrate my loyalty to the throne of Dàxī," Kang says, confident and unafraid.

The servants unveil the covered chests beside each of us with a coordinated flourish, forcing my attention away. They are each a chest of drawers, familiar in appearance—one could be found in any apothecary. Each of the drawers is labeled with a small plaque.

"You will have the length of one incense stick to pick the drink you will make for our champion," Chancellor Zhou says, "using the dān you harvested from the water lily yesterday to strengthen your connection and your bond to Shénnóng."

I fish out the ball from my sash, recognizing now its intended purpose. It is a more potent form of the mash I created from ground-up herbs to remove the poison from Ruyi, meant to assist us in achieving the Shift. What little I know of it has always been that the process of developing dān was lost, the methods having been too carefully guarded and relegated to history. It was said to be a magic amplifier, like a voice carried between narrow cliffs, until you could be heard from one side of the mountain to the other.

Shao is already confident, heading for his chest of drawers with intention. Wenyi regards the champions with careful consideration, gaze lingering on Kang with a frown as if he finds him lacking. I take a hesitant step toward the chest, my hand skimming over the ebony surface. I can almost sense the pulse of the tree from which it was carved. My mother would have loved this cabinet—the wood lacks any strong fragrance that could taint the components inside, and its hardness ensures that the ingredients will not absorb into it over time.

There are different varieties of tea leaves in the top drawers, all rare teas, worthy of tribute to the emperor. Two of them speak to me in particular: Heaven's Stream is one that is barely treated, only the youngest buds permitted to be gathered, and Hidden Autumn is an older tea, permitted to grow fully into the fall, then sunbaked until its inner sweetness is released. Opposing properties, depending on how I wish to approach the challenge. I skim over the other additives. Goldenflower, jasmine, honeywood, and dried safflower. Huáng qí is also an interesting possibility, its strengthening properties already known to me from previous uses.

Lian and I discussed how she had imbued her tonic with strengthening magic, so although it is not my specialty, I know the basics. Kang could do with increased awareness as well—but not so strong as to lose himself in his surroundings, like I personally experienced with the Lion Green. Or perhaps I need to give him something to dull the pain of fighting. But the problem is that my knowledge of fighting styles is woefully lacking, because I have never attended a tournament. I can only hazard a guess as to the specifics of the champions' skills.

I make my choice of three ingredients: goji berry for awareness, the bitter yù jīn to improve circulation and relieve pain, and purple mushroom to increase endurance. A cup of tea worthy of challenging the representatives of the gods.

The first round begins as soon as the stick turns to ash, and the chancellor provides the next set of instructions. "You will have the length of a spiral incense to prepare and offer your selection, then for your champion to defeat the challenger. *Defeat.* There will be no ties, no second chances. The challenger must yield. To leave the circle is a failure. To be the first to have blood drawn, failure."

So many unknowns. I look down at my ingredients, already questioning my choices.

"The judges have ranked the remaining competitors by their performances so far. First to begin, Chen Shao of Jia." The chancellor nods at the herald, who lights the spiral incense, and the competition begins.

Shao moves forward to brew his cup, and the herbs soak in the water, releasing their aromas. The underlying scent of magic prickles at the back of my throat. Kang accepts the tea with a bow, downs it without hesitation, then steps onto the competition floor.

The servants have covered the ground with woven mats. The Tortoise moves languidly, sweeping the staff like an extension of his body. Kang moves with speed, dodging his blows. Whenever the staff hits the floor, it's enough to shake the ground beneath us. Eventually, the staff meets the sword with a thunderous crack, and Kang slides back with the force of it, almost falling out of the circle. He rights himself again, and the battle resumes. The wood bends, then snaps back, the sword meeting and returning blows as the opponents clash, separate, and meet again. Kang twists and sidesteps, curving his body like a bow to avoid being crushed by the sweep of the staff.

Shao sits on his chair, beads of sweat forming on his brow from the exertion. His lips move silently, communing with the gods, just like when Mother would wrestle with a particularly difficult ailment. I wonder if Kang can hear Shao's voice in his head, whispering.

Ten moves later, Kang's sword is at the throat of the Tortoise, and the large man bows, conceding defeat.

The hall fills with applause. The audience is enraptured, despite their initial hesitation toward their champion.

"Well done!" they call out. Shao wipes his face with a handkerchief, his usual smirk gone. He stands on shaky legs and bows, leaning on the armrest for support.

"Lin Wenyi, acolyte of Yěliǔ," the herald announces. Chancellor Zhou gestures for Wenyi to proceed. The tall figure moves with an elegance that speaks to his training. Clean, concise movements. No exaggerated efforts to entertain the audience. I'm pulled into his ritual even with my own trial approaching.

He uses a stone bowl instead of a cup, with higher sides than a typical one used for eating. Tipping the bowl to one side, hot water is poured down the side and leaps up the curve, creating the illusion of jumping waves. Using his hand to gently rock the bowl, he ensures that the water covers all his ingredients, taking on the golden hue required of a good brew.

He places the dān under his tongue, then he hands the bowl to Kang, who accepts it with a nod and tips the tea into his mouth. As he swallows, he grimaces at the taste. It must have been strong. He enters the arena with the Black Tiger, and with the strike of a match, the next round begins.

The Tiger moves her feet in sweeping motions, circling back and forth without a clear sense of direction. Kang pulls back, observing her movements, trying to determine where she will place her foot next. There is only the slightest bend in her knees, then she jumps, easily clearing the space between them. Using her fists, quick as lightning, she beats him back, putting him on the defense. Kang blocks and uses his sheathed sword to sweep her back, but doesn't yet draw it. She regains her balance, then rocks back on her heels, eyes glimmering in the light.

A raucous yell erupts from her throat as she leaps again, this time drawing the swords from her back in twin silver arcs. I already noted the unique hilts, which have a guard for the hand that finishes in a sharp point, but the blades are also like nothing I've seen before. The steel is a thin curve, with wicked-looking hooks at the end. Kang uses his scabbard to block the attack, shoving her back with force, then draws his sword in one smooth motion, metal ringing against metal.

The attack is on. The Tiger crosses her swords and then advances with whirling movements, the swords appearing as if they are spinning in circles. At times her right hand turns in one direction as her left dips instead of rises, attempting to break his guard. He blocks them all, but her speed puts her at an advantage. His feet slip and falter as he tries to withstand the force of her strikes, but she continues to push him closer and closer to the edge of the circle.

It takes me too long to notice there is something wrong with Kang's movements. The tip of his sword seems to move too slowly, and each time he tries to adjust his movements to match the intensity of her attacks, he stumbles slightly. He does not exhibit the strength with which he responded to the Tortoise. In fact, he looks to be barely defending himself against the onslaught of the dual blades.

With the crescent sweeps of her blades forming two circles, the hooks catch his sword and she pulls. His sword is flung into the crowd of officials, and they scatter like fish in a pond.

The point of the sword sinks into the ground, the hilt quivering in the air.

There is silence in the hall. Kang clutches his shoulder, blood seeping from between his fingers, dripping onto the mat below his feet.

He bows to the Tiger, acknowledging his defeat.

CHAPTER FORTY

"IT APPEARS YOU HAVE FAILED THE CHALLENGE," CHANCEL-
lor Zhou says to Wenyi, though his voice is not unkind.

But Wenyi does not address him. Instead he looks up to the
princess and salutes her with his closed fist tucked into an open
palm. A salute of deference, accompanied by a deep bow.

"Although I am not worthy, I ask to address you, Your Highness." There is a roughness to his tone, and from my perspective,
I can see his legs trembling. I have never seen him lose his composure in the time we've spent together in the palace. I should
have paid more attention to what he was doing, rather than being
entranced by Kang's fight against the Black Tiger.

Zhen gestures. "Speak."

"I have sullied the competition, Princess," Wenyi says, but without contrition, without apology. Instead of lowering his head in deference, he looks up at her directly instead, as if in challenge.

"What have you done?" The chancellor's words slice through
the air.

Wenyi drops to one knee in a swift motion, his robe flying
behind him. "I prepared for your champion a concoction of tea
that saps away his strength and disrupts his inner balance. I had
hoped the Tiger would cut him in half. I could not bring myself to
assist this . . . traitor to the empire."

It takes all my effort not to look in Kang's direction.

"Are you saying you put something in his drink?" The princess leans forward, frowning, the worry for her betrothed evident. Their connection must be stronger than I initially believed, forged from childhood.

"I do not stoop to poison." Wenyi's mouth curls with disdain, and he points a shaking finger at Kang. "That is the weapon of *his* family."

His accusation hangs in the air, a storm cloud waiting to devastate the land below. Hatred twists his handsome features into a scowl.

Princess Zhen settles back in her seat. "The matter of who the poisoners are has not been resolved by the Ministry of Justice," she drawls, then turns to the officials, who are still watching this scene unfold with uncertainty. "Unless, Minister Hu...there is something else you have not reported to me?"

One of the ministers hurries forward and bows low, his hat dipping to one side in his rush to stand before her.

"Has the Ministry of Justice determined it is my uncle who is behind the poisonings? Is there something I should be aware of?" Zhen's voice grows silky, dangerous. It is evident that her temper is rising, whether at the insolence of Wenyi's behavior or at the continued display of dissension in the court.

Nothing remains of her uncertainty—this is an empress in the making.

Minister Hu drops to his knees, touching his forehead to the ground. "No, no, Your Highness. We have not yet determined who is responsible for the poisoned tea."

"My family is from a town close to Lùzhou." Wenyi raises his voice, not willing to bend. "There has been a rash of disappearances from our town. People forcibly conscripted to the army, torn from their families. Those who refuse end up poisoned instead. Please, I beg you look into this, Highness—"

A blur of movement and a flash of metal. Wenyi falls to the floor, gasping, struck down where he stood. The Minister of War stands with his sword unsheathed, pointed at the back of Wenyi's head.

"You dare demand anything from the princess?" he snarls. Two of the palace guards step forward, flanking him. "Take him away."

The guards lift Wenyi under his arms, dragging him backward.

Wenyi looks toward the judges and the officials, but no sympathetic face looks back at him, only ones full of fear and uncertainty. It feels eerily similar to the times my village observed the governor's cruelty. Everyone was too afraid to challenge his might, fearing for their families. Is this sort of tyranny what I am supporting? Is this the change the princess promised?

Realizing there is no rapport to be found in the crowd, no sympathy for his cause, Wenyi suddenly begins to struggle in the arms of the guards, yelling, "Beware! All of you! Shadows will soon follow!"

He is pulled out the doors, screaming all the way.

When the doors are shut behind him, the ominous lines of the prophecy still linger, weighing on all in the room. The relaxed, festive air has disappeared.

"The competition must continue." Minister Song stands up again in front of the officials, attempting to maintain his composure. But his fingers smooth down his robe, betraying his nervousness.

Princess Zhen stands to face the court, her expression severe. "We will not permit the actions of one dissident to disrupt this event, and we will continue despite his attempt to cause unrest. The enemies of Dàxī will not see us cower."

When she returns to her seat, the rest of the officials mumble among themselves but also find their own chairs, appeased for the moment.

"Are you well enough to proceed?" Chancellor Zhou asks Kang, who gives a stiff nod.

Then the chancellor turns to me. "And you?"

Even though I want to hide instead of speak, I have to ensure that I have not been placed at a disadvantage. "Chancellor, will you permit me to read the pulse of the champion? To know if the negative effects of the tea from Wen—I mean, Competitor Lin—will affect his performance?"

Chancellor Zhou looks toward Princess Zhen, and she inclines her head in agreement. She exhibits no sign of recognition, no acknowledgment of familiarity. As if I have not held her hand while she wept over her handmaiden, or argued passionately with her over the divisions within the empire. The chancellor nods, permitting me to approach.

Kang regards me warily, with lowered lashes, looking somewhere at my shoulder instead of meeting my eyes directly. A royal physician has already bandaged his arm, and he does not sway when he stands. But I have to be sure.

"How do you—" "Can you—" We attempt to speak over one another, then return to awkward silence. I fumble to pull my sleeves back, while he clears his throat and still averts his gaze.

I gesture for him to sit on one of the stools behind him, and he obeys, the picture of discomfort. I ask him to place his elbow on the table, and extend his arm for me to reach.

Closing my eyes, I allow the murmurs of the court officials to fade into the background, focusing only on the feeling of his skin below my fingers, pretending he is just another faceless patron. I must navigate by feel alone. My father's voice continues to chastise me across the empire. *Use all your senses. Focus, Ning!*

I listen to Kang's sluggish pulse, still affected by whatever Wenyi gave him. But he feels warm to the touch. A stinging scent emanates from him, almost like pepper. Finally, I look up to meet his eyes, taking in his flushed face, his decidedly unhappy expression, and note the expansion of his pupils. All signs point toward too much heat emanating from his body.

Wenyi used his ingredients to overly invigorate Kang's blood, making him dizzy and unsteady, impulsive and easy to anger. I drop his hand, and he pulls away immediately, standing up as if he can't bear to be in my presence a moment longer.

I retreat to stand beside the chest of ingredients, waiting for instructions.

"Are you ready, Competitor Zhang?" Chancellor Zhou asks. "Because you had to counter the sabotage of the previous competitor, you are permitted to exchange one ingredient you have selected. Choose wisely."

When I have completed my exchange, I say, "I'm ready."

The match is struck, the incense lit, and I proceed to my final trial.

CHAPTER FORTY-ONE

I KNOW TIME IS AGAINST ME, SO I MOVE QUICKLY. USING the mellow Hidden Autumn tea, I steep it with my replaced ingredient—water-lily buds, a nod to the humble flower that spoke to me and gave up the dān at its heart. I ask it to grant me its cleansing properties, to counter Wenyi's brew and strengthen the lingering effects of Shao's invigorating tea.

I place the cup in Kang's hands. Meeting my eyes, he raises the cup with both hands. His eyes are dark pools, beckoning me closer, and I must resist their pull.

Trust me, he asked of me once. Now it is his turn to believe in me.

I place the dān in my mouth. As the sweet and bitter flavors soak into my tongue, the magic unravels within me in response. It leaps easily from me to him, remembering him with an almost audible sigh. Once again, we are wrapped in the scent of camellia, like we stand surrounded by my beloved tea trees.

We return to that hidden place revealed only by the Shift. I see him, with the golden outline around his body, the brand burning above his heart. But I can also see myself in his eyes, a girl with black hair and wheat-colored skin, dark eyes regarding him with sadness. The magic ripples between us, strands like malt candy, drawing the heat generated from him and spilling it into me, until I can feel the weight of it on my body like a heavy cloak.

He opens his mouth to say something, but I force myself to turn and sit in the competitor's chair. He watches me turn away, and I feel the regret emanating from him in waves. It's only a moment, a mere breath in reality, but in this place of magic and dreaming, the connection is prolonged agony. A reminder of all we shared and the little that remains.

Go, I tell him, even as he hesitates, and he finally turns to join the champion in the circle. His steps are lighter, his thoughts flowing with greater clarity. I feel the dampness of sweat already forming under my arms, the heaviness taking hold of my limbs.

The man in white stands still, his sword held behind his back, while Kang acknowledges him with a bow. Almost as if an invisible bell was struck, the two of them move in unison. They circle the ring, mirroring each other with careful, deliberate steps.

Until the Crane draws his sword in one swift movement, and the graceful curve of it is revealed. He wields the single-edged dao, different from Kang's slender, double-edged blade. The White Crane raises one arm, holding his sword above his head, lifting the opposite leg, until he is birdlike in appearance. He holds that form only for a moment, gathering his inner strength, then explodes forward with a flurry of slashes.

The weapon must be heavy, but in his hands it appears feather-light, twisting in the air with the ease of an arrow. I sense the twitch of Kang's muscles echoing within my own as he moves to block, his sword rising up to meet the other weapon, the impact ringing in our ears. The two of them are then joined in a frenzied dance of blades.

Sweat begins to drip down from my hairline into my eyes, from the exertion of pulling the negative energies away from him. The remnants of Wenyi's magic are the swiftly moving feet of hundreds of crawling spiders, trying to find purchase. They want to bite, to feast on the gold essence flowing through Kang's body, their intended target. But because they cannot have him, they devour me instead, leaching my energy, until my eyes threaten to flutter closed.

I pinch myself at the tender points between my fingers, forcing myself to stay awake. The drumbeat of Kang's heart pulses with my own, beating in my ears. My body continues to burn, begging for a reprieve from the relentless heat.

The fight continues in front of me in a whirlwind. I encourage the powers of the purple mushroom, giving him the ability to withstand the Crane's repeated strikes. The yù jīn eases the ache in his limbs. My hand clutches at the table, even as I can feel the sword in his hand, how his body moves through the memory of the forms he learned from a young age. He practiced in rain and the dark of night, in bitter cold winds on the side of a cliff, or blindfolded in the snow, when the slippery stones under his feet threatened to throw his weight off-balance.

All his training is unleashed in this single moment, heightened by the effects of the water-lily bud. A break in the pattern of the Crane, changing the grip of his hand to move to another form. Kang turns in a flash, whipping the edge of his sword in an opposing motion, catching his opponent's blade out of alignment. The man stumbles, caught unaware. With another thrust, Kang slashes the air, and a piece of white fabric flutters down to the ground.

The White Crane stops, lifts his sword in front of him, and bows. The tattered remains of his sleeve slide down his arm, revealing a clear line of blood. Defeat.

I spit the medicine ball out of my mouth into the waiting bowl, breaking our connection. I cannot stand to be in his mind a moment longer, the burden on my body unbearable. Finally, the waves relent, the heat easing until I can draw a breath, until I am a little more myself again and less of him.

It's done. The final round, and I am still here.

The officials are slow to clap, but once they begin, it is a thunderous sound in the hall. They have recognized the feat I have completed, and for once, I can acknowledge the power I am growing into. That I will become worthy of my mother's legacy.

"Wait!" a voice calls out, disrupting the glow of my success. The Esteemed Qian, the former court shénnóng-shī, steps forward. "Your Highness, it is with great regret that I must report there is something amiss."

I stare at him, not understanding. I have completed the task at hand. What could I have done wrong?

"Speak," Princess Zhen commands, even as she appears reluctant to hear his next words.

After a hurried bow, he straightens and clasps his hands behind his back. "As an experienced shénnóng-shī, I have witnessed many trials, many ceremonies. I had my suspicions, but today, after viewing the final round, it confirms everything I suspected."

The Esteemed Qian stops in front of my table, too close for comfort. I want to move away, but my legs still feel too weak to hold me, and I fear falling for the entire court to see.

"The girl from Sù." He turns to glare down at me, his hatred as apparent as Wenyi's disdain for Kang. He raises his arm and points one finger at my face, and the other in Kang's direction. "And the son of the Banished Prince. They had a connection prior to this final round of the competition. A traitorous alliance."

Sputtering sounds emerge from my mouth, nonsensical. It is the princess who recovers first, quickly speaking. "I was made aware of a previous meeting between Xu Kang and some of the previous

306

competitors. Zhang Ning had also come forth of her own accord and relayed her concerns privately. However, she did not know the identity of the champion in the final round; that was decided only hours ago. I do not believe they intended to deceive the court."

She is a much better liar than me—presenting it as a misunderstanding, nothing more, while explaining very little of our association. She raises her chin, almost daring the older man to disagree.

The shénnóng-shī bows again, to a level that is almost mocking in its attempt at deference. "I do not disagree, Highness, if the encounter is as superficial as you say. A chance meeting. But my suspicions were deepened when I conducted my own investigations, and I found the conspiracy even greater than I could ever have imagined."

A prickling feeling crawls up my arms and behind my ears, like the crawling creatures of Wenyi's magic.

The Esteemed Qian continues, "This girl dared to consort with your betrothed in public, sharing a cup at a teahouse."

"How is this relevant?" Minister Song demands. "Perhaps he bought her a cup of tea out of curiosity about her abilities, and she was unaware of his role in the final round. Only the judges knew he would be present, and none of us would share that information, I assure you."

I glance at him in surprise, not having expected any of them to speak up on my behalf.

"To those who are uneducated in the art of Shénnóng, this may be an innocent meeting. But to a shénnóng-shī, it holds greater meaning," the Esteemed Qian counters, gesturing in emphasis. "A shénnóng-shī's bond is greatly strengthened from previous encounters, as any shénnóng-tú who has been training for a time would know.

"I was already made aware of Competitor Zhang's . . . behaviors in the previous round, some of her unconventional choices. It is why I looked deeper into her history. The results of the investigation were only made known to me earlier today."

A tendril of fear creeps down my back. He must have sent inquiries back to my family. Did his messenger speak with my uncle, who resented my mother? Or to the villagers, who remembered how she returned to the village in shame?

"I inquired in Xīnyì village about her mentor. All the responses were the same: Her sister, Zhang Shu, was the apprentice under their mother's tutelage. Zhang Ning has lied about her training. She was not worthy of bringing the scroll to attend this competition." His words are like hammer blows, beating me down. "In truth, she was studying under the guidance of an imperial physician . . . a *disgraced* imperial physician, who fled the palace years ago in shame, after impregnating one of the maidservants."

"Is this true?" Princess Zhen regards me with an inscrutable expression.

All the lies I've told, the choices I've made, all the things I did to get to this point, and in the end, *this* is what ruins me. The shame of the family. A girl, born to an unwed mother.

I want to shout at her, tell her the truth of my past. About how my mother loved my father, and they risked their lives, left everything behind to start over together.

But all I can bear to do is nod. The marquis gives a snort of satisfaction beside her. He will finally be rid of me.

"Then it is with regret that I have to say, although you have excelled and demonstrated your abilities . . ." I feel Zhen's next words, as painful as a knife to the gut. "You are disqualified from the competition."

After all of this. After all this time.

I have failed.

"The judges hereby proclaim Chen Shao of Jia the victor!" Minister Song announces, his words calling forth thunderous applause from the court. "Tonight we will celebrate with a banquet held in his honor as the Court of Officials recognize our new shénnóng-shī."

Shao is surrounded by ministers and officials offering their congratulations. I am brushed aside, already forgotten. I suppose I should be grateful I have not been thrown into the dungeons, yet I still feel like a hollowed husk. I have given everything I possibly could, and still it wasn't enough. The Esteemed Qian gives me a final contemptuous smile, before turning on his heel to stand beside his apprentice, to share in the adoration. Such courtly games I will never get to play.

The princess had given me her word that she would help me with Shu, but I have no means to force her to keep her promise. I realize it now—how laughable my attempts were at trying to force the hand of the future ruler of Dàxī. She dangled it in front of me, knowing how eager I would be to jump at her every whim, then discarded me just as easily.

I make my way to the back of the room, remembering Father's letter. I must return home to face his disappointment. And then with dawning horror I realize that I have drawn the attention of the palace to what happened years ago. It would be easy for the Ministry of Justice to resume the investigation into his disappearance. I may have doomed my family as well.

The room is suddenly stifling. I brush by one of the officials, mumbling an apology. I can see Kang trying to make his way toward me, a set to his jaw, while others attempt to talk to him, to recognize his new elevated position in the court. There is nothing left for us to say to one another, and every time I remember he is intended for another, I find it difficult to breathe. The guards pull open the doors, and I run through them and into the night.

I don't remember how I make my way back to the Residence of Harmonious Spring, only that my hands find and fold my clothes, shoving them without care into a cloth sack. I need to find my mother's shénnóng-shī chest... but perhaps they will return that to me if I can pen a carefully worded letter to the princess once I am back in Sù and can ensure that my family is safe.

When I am done, I see for myself how precious little I have obtained during my time in Jia. All the finery that surrounds me seems to mock me now. I had dared to covet all this, believing that one day I could live in a grand residence. It's an illusion, as fake as the dragon Shao once created out of steam. A reminder of my conceit.

I allow myself to let a dark thought unwind from the deepest recesses of my mind: What if I took everything and paid for a voyage far from Sù and from Jia? I could disappear into the mountainous gorges of Yún or become another wanderer seeking a new beginning in the City of Jasmine. Pick a new name, find an aging physician to finish my apprenticeship. Grow a small garden and practice the art of Shénnóng in secret. Without the burden of my parents' history... and carry with me the guilt of my sister's death for eternity.

I pull out Shu's embroidery and hold it with shaky hands. The moon watching over a strange scene, dipping into the sea, something born of my sister's vivid dreams. It reminds me how I will return home empty-handed, reopening old wounds from my parents' past. I stuff the cloth back into my sash.

Tears spill out, hot on my cheeks. My hands fumble to remove the jeweled pins from my hair. When they do not give, I rip them out, pulling strands from my scalp in my carelessness. I unwind the sash around my stomach, shedding the fine clothes until once again I am back in my homespun tunic, returning to my former self.

I can never forsake my sister.

This is who I am.

The girl from Sù.

Chapter Forty-Two

THERE IS A TENTATIVE KNOCK AT THE DOOR TO MY RESIdence, then a quiet creak as it opens. I drag my sleeve across my eyes, embarrassed to be seen in such a haggard state. To my surprise, the person standing there is Mingwen. She regards me with sympathy.

"The maids are waiting outside your door," she says softly. "They will assist you into the clothes for the banquet when you are ready."

The once dour Mingwen has become someone familiar to me, and I realize there are those in the palace who I will miss once I am home again.

"I'm leaving," I inform her. "There is no reason for me to remain in the palace."

Mingwen nods. "Steward Yang was worried; she sent me to find you. If you will not go to the banquet, then at least come to the kitchens to say goodbye."

Seeing my reluctance, she adds, "The capital is not a safe place for a young girl to be wandering about in the evening."

It is a familiar warning, like the ones Father used to give me about the capital. With a heaviness in my heart, I realize I should have listened to him. But it is too late now.

"We'll make sure you find your way to the ferry safely in the morning." She rests a reassuring hand on my shoulder. "Now come. We'll get you fed."

I'm lured by the temptation of one final meal in the palace, and the reluctant acknowledgment that she's right—I should say good-bye to the people who have been kind to me.

I'm given a tunic to pull on in the kitchens. While I wash up, my mind returns again and again to the Esteemed Qian's revelations, my destined failures. Doubt circles me like a fish swimming in a too-small pot.

"Ning!" Qing'er exclaims when I enter the kitchen next to Ming-wen. The boy wraps his arms around my waist. I force myself to give him a smile so he will not be subjected to my misery.

"You haven't come to see us in a while." The boy grins up at me. "I thought you and Lian forgot about us."

I hesitate, remembering my promise to Steward Yang to stay away from her staff. But now that I am done with the competition, there is no reason for the officials to accuse me of subterfuge. I glance over at Mingwen, who gestures toward the kitchen with encouragement.

I give the small boy's hand a squeeze. "Show me where I can help."

Qing'er leads me to one of the large tables, and the bakery staff welcomes me with a chorus of greetings. Standing shoulder to shoulder with them, I assist with assembling large platters meant for the banquet. I find it easier to pretend that the food is meant for some faceless court official, and I'm just another servant perform-ing my usual duties.

I help with extracting small crabs from molds, the shapes previ-ously formed last night out of crabmeat and roe mixed with rice. After they are fried golden, we scatter them across a nest of crispy noodles, sprinkled with sesame. At the next station, one of the chefs uses chopsticks to carefully place delicate dumplings shaped into fish among the crabs, to give the appearance of darting in and out among them.

The next course is another platter I would call a display of art rather than a plate of food meant to be devoured. Bamboo lids are lifted to reveal steamed pink gao shaped like flowers, their petals dotted with red beans to indicate the flavor of the filling within. The gao are configured into blooming bouquets around a phoenix sculpture carved out of a daikon, with carrot slivers for decoration.

There is no time to think, no time to fret or worry about my eventual fate. My hands are busy with placing each portion just so, artfully arranging the creations so as not to destroy someone else's hard work. I take in the frantic energy of the space, inhale the sweet aromas that surround us like a cloud, settling into our hands and onto our skin.

Until finally, our tasks are done. The last platter is sent out and the kitchen fires are banked. We pull up benches and push the tables together, many of us sighing when we sit and rest our aching legs. Bowls are passed around, piled high with fluffy rice. Before us there are remnants of the evening's banquet that did not pass Small Wu's inspection: collapsed dumplings and misshapen pastries. The staff from the Meat Department join us, bringing their own stools and contributions to the dinner. They add slices of plump red and dried black sausage, glistening slabs of roasted pork, and pieces of crispy-skinned chicken.

As I'm surrounded by laughter and conversation, this kitchen feels like a home. Like another type of family.

I am only a few bites into my bowl when we hear the pattering of feet running down the stone path outside the kitchens. A young man appears first, dressed in a similar uniform to the kitchen staff. He leans over, panting, out of breath. Chair legs scrape against the floor as Small Wu and others stand up from their seats, the conversation coming to a swift stop.

The young man gulps in a breath and then shouts, "Something... Something's happened! At the banquet... Something's wrong with the food!"

At first, the words run in an incomprehensible jumble, then the implication of what he has uttered strikes us all at once.

Steward Yang appears at the entrance, strands of hair loose from her usually tight bun, collar askew from her run, and her mouth pinched. Her eyes settle on me before she closes the distance between us in an instant.

"What are you still doing here?" she says to me sharply.

I look back at her, not understanding. "You told me to come. You sent Mingwen."

Steward Yang's expression twists, shifting from uncertainty to fury. She looks over my shoulder. I follow her gaze to Mingwen, who is trembling.

"I told her to get you *out*," Steward Yang says, voice low. "I told her you should get as far away from the palace as possible."

Pieces begin to fall together, aligning on the game board. Someone wanted me in the kitchens during the banquet.

The older woman shakes her head. "I should have suspected when she so eagerly volunteered."

"Please, you have to understand!" Mingwen clutches at the servant next to her, but they all give her a wide berth, leaving her standing alone. She pleads, with her hands extended in front of her, "They threatened my family! They said we would all be executed for theft, because of her!" Her voice rises, hysterical, gesturing in my direction. "*She* gave me the hairpin! It was hers!"

"Steward Yang," I whisper. "What's happened at the banquet?"

She doesn't respond for a moment, biting her lip. I can almost hear the abacus in her head again, calculating possibilities and numbers, trying to figure out a solution.

"Listen very carefully. We may only have a few minutes to save our hides," she calls out to everyone in the room. "None of you will admit to seeing Ning here, do you hear me?"

Heads nod as Steward Yang sends out orders rapidly, sending staff scattering in different directions. She pulls me through another set of moon doors, deeper into the kitchens. We hurry past shelves stacked high with ingredients, pots and pans ready for tomorrow morning. Past darkened ovens with smoldering embers within their openings.

It is near the women's quarters where we see movement up ahead, and Steward Yang pushes me in another direction, down a side corridor, but other footsteps rush in behind us. There are shouts in the distance, then a line of armored bodies and spears cuts off the end of the corridor, trapping us in.

"What is the meaning of this?" Steward Yang still maintains her composure, but the guards remain silent. "I demand to speak to Captain Liang!"

They ignore us but refuse to part when we approach, keeping us back. We do not have to wait long before a few of them part at the entrance to the courtyard, letting a man through. The familiar figure stops before me, greeting me with a brilliant smile.

"Hello, Ning," he says, in his rich, deep voice.

It's a voice I dread, one that reminds me of being ten years old, cowering and afraid.

Wang Li, the governor of Sù.

He's broad-shouldered with a slim waist, hair in a tight top-knot, his uniform tailored to emphasize his height. He wears a black cloak lined with green, a jade pendant swinging from the hem. My aunt always called his imposing figure handsome and striking, but I think those who hold that opinion are fools. They do not see the way he savors the fear of his victims when he is on the hunt.

Now, I recognize I am his prey.

"This is a governor of Dàxī!" one of the soldiers at his side barks. "Do you not know your place?"

Steward Yang's hand still grips my arm, and I can feel her shaking next to me. Slowly, she kneels before the governor, and I follow. My mind spins, my two lives colliding at this very moment.

I know what it means when the governor dons the colors of the ministry, when he brings his pack of dogs to accompany him. When he strokes the hilt of his sword like he is begging for a reason to draw it.

Governor Wang speaks, voice carrying over the heads of all the guards, for everyone to hear and bear witness. "Zhang Ning of Sù, you are in suspicion of conspiring with rebels who are enemies of the empire, the murder of the princess's personal handmaiden, involvement in the plot to poison the court officials at the banquet tonight, and fleeing the scene of the celebratory banquet. You will be taken by the Ministry of Justice for questioning, as you have been deemed a danger to the public."

Ruyi ... Ruyi is dead?

The last time Zhen spoke of her, she spoke of Ruyi's recovery. But she has not been seen at any of the subsequent rounds, even though she is usually at the side of the princess. My heart burns at the thought of the loss of so many lives, one of them my own patient who I believed I had saved.

All their eyes are upon me, and I can only force out a few words in a whisper: "That's not true."

"No matter." Governor Wang drinks in my suffering with obvious delight and gestures for the guards behind him to approach. "Make sure to gather the rest of the rats from the kitchens."

Chapter Forty-Three

My arms are wrenched behind me and tied with rope, then I'm yanked to my feet by one of the armored men. The governor's personal guard are few, clad in similar cloaks, the same jade pendant swinging from their sword hilts. They flank him as he strides ahead of us, leading our procession. The others who carry out his orders are dressed in the black of the city guard, different from the striking red armor of the palace guards I have grown accustomed to.

We march back through the kitchens, joined by other soldiers who have caught more kitchen staff, who struggle in their grasp. I am forced to walk quickly to keep up, and it isn't long after we leave the servants' wing when I am separated from the others, pushed to follow behind the governor while the others are led elsewhere.

"Where are you taking her?" I hear Small Wu's and Steward Yang's voices calling out in protest. My throat tightens at the thought: They cared about me, even at the risk of endangering themselves. I can spare only a quick glance at the commotion behind me, three men struggling to pull Small Wu back, before I'm shoved forward. We move west toward the center of the palace.

Hot tears threaten to spill over, but I blink them away and swallow them down. Mingwen may have given me up, but even in my bitterness I cannot fault her. Knowing she has small children, knowing what I know now about all of them. They're all people with families, in and out of the palace—now implicated in this wicked scheme that I'm not sure I can possibly dig myself out of.

Think, Ning! I tell myself, drawing on the lessons of both my mother and father. One who taught me to clear my head and use my mind, the other who showed me how to observe and remember.

How much time passed after the final dishes for the banquet were sent out? The bakery was in charge of desserts, so that would have signaled the last course. The banquet did not commence until later into the evening, as I had already passed the criers calling out the second hour when I left the residence with Mingwen. I spent at least an hour in the kitchen, if not longer, and now, with the sliver of moon hanging high and slightly off center, we must be into the Hour of the Ghost.

The governor leads us through corridors I do not recognize, and I notice the change in our ranks. We appear to be growing in number—joined by more city guards, dressed in black ... which is peculiar. When they greet the palace guards at the gates, I notice yet another peculiarity: Instead of Shao's particular way of biting off phrases, typical of the capital, these guards sound like Wenyi, with his northern lilt. Details I would never have recognized before, living in Sù.

We stop before another gate, one that is grander and more imposing, our entrance blocked by guards. The gate is brightly lit by torches on either side.

"Kneel," one of the guards demands. Before I am even able to respond, he pushes me to my knees. The ropes that contorted my arms behind my back are cut, and I bite back a cry of pain at the blood rushing back into my fingers. They force my hands in front of me instead, securing my wrists and ankles with chains.

"Where do you think I'm going to run to?" I comment humorlessly.

"Quiet!" the guard watching barks at me, brandishing his sword.

It's here in the light of the torches that the glint in the hilt catches my attention. I stare at the silver sheen inset into the wood—just like the shimmer of the rock carvings on the walls of the temple. Just like the design etched into the dagger Kang gifted me.

The black pearl that has fallen out of fashion, declared worthless by a jealous emperor.

The one still revered and cherished, defiantly, by the inhabitants of Lùzhou.

I bite my lip to remain silent, to hide the shock of what I've noticed. We continue to wait for admittance into the courtyard, and with furtive glances, I pay attention to the soldiers around me, and I realize . . . I see it everywhere. There's a flash off a pendant, a glint catching the edge of a brooch.

I'm surrounded by soldiers adorned with black pearls, and they are all dressed in the armor of the city guard, following the orders of the governor of Sù.

My heart is suddenly too loud inside my chest, beating a steady warning. Something is horribly wrong.

"Enter!" an official calls out from beyond the gate, and I am ushered through.

The small courtyard is surrounded by high walls. In the middle sits a raised platform, braziers lit with dancing flames at each corner. The path to the platform is lined with guards, and I'm oddly reminded of the first round—I was ignorant and hopeful, instead of anxious and afraid.

Chancellor Zhou waits for me behind the table in black robes, wearing the winged hat of a judge. A jade brooch in the center stares at me like a reproachful eye, representing the always watchful heavens. Behind him is the flag of Dàxī, representing the reach of the emperor. Two other officials in full court regalia are present as well, witnesses to my judgment.

I'm pushed forward by rough hands to ascend the platform by myself, the wood creaking under my feet.

"Zhang Ning." The chancellor's face in shadow reminds me of the statue in the temple to the God of Hell, presiding over the denizens of the underworld and their punishments. He is far more imposing than our county magistrate, a simpering man who always cowered under Governor Wang's instructions, who was more interested in saving himself than ensuring that justice was achieved.

"Bow before your betters."

The guard waiting on the platform shoves me to my knees, bruising them. No cushions here. The taste of blood floods my mouth from where my tooth has grazed the inside of my cheek. Still, I slowly raise my body up to a more dignified kneeling position, even as I can feel myself trembling.

"You stand on trial before us, representatives of the court of Dàxī, a role given to us by the divine, to face your crimes. There is evidence that you have conspired against the empire. You have collaborated with those who seek to create unrest."

There is no familiarity in those dark eyes.

"Your list of accusations . . ." He pulls open a black scroll. The dragon still snarls from the back, but instead of its usual ferocity, it looks more like a disappointed grimace. "Lying to a court official about your training as a shénnóng-tú. Obscuring your family ties with enemies of the state. Continuing your deception even as you progressed in the competition. Infiltrating the kitchens and recruiting for your revolutionary cause, resulting in the death of the princess's loyal handmaiden when she discovered your plans. Poisoning members the Court of Officials when you did not gain your desired position, and attempting to flee the scene of your crime."

Shock gives way to disbelief at this list of accusations. I stare at the man who had seemed kind, warning me away from the marquis. He stood beside the princess and assisted me with advancing in the competition.

He sets the scroll down, regarding me with a grave expression. "You appeared to be a simple girl from Sù, who made the honest mistake of reciting a poem written by a revolutionary. You claimed innocence, but we should have sent you to the dungeons for your insolence. I should have listened to the marquis instead of permitting you to continue. Now he rests with his ancestors, and we are bereft of his wisdom. I have failed in my duty to protect the empire."

So, the marquis is dead. One of my supposed victims.

"You have destroyed the lives of many, Ning of Sù," he says. "I am loath to imagine the havoc you would have brought upon the empire had you been appointed as the court shénnóng-shī. If all your scheming came to fruition."

He picks up another scroll and continues my list of crimes: "Fang Mingwen, a senior maidservant. Found with a stolen jeweled hairpin in her possession, assisted you with leaving the competitors' residence and entering the kitchens. Sentenced to sixty strikes with a cane."

I choke. Twenty strikes are enough to break a man's leg. Forty strikes are sufficient to cause internal bleeding. Sixty strikes... sixty strikes would kill her. When I placed that hairpin in her hand, I might as well have sentenced her to death myself. But who was it that instructed her to bring me to the kitchens? Who threatened her with the lives of her family?

"Yang Rouzi, head steward of the Kitchen Department. Found to have concealed her knowledge of your past. Conspired with you to obtain and distribute the poison at the celebratory banquet. Sentenced to death by hanging. Her family members will be stripped of their roles and banished to spend the rest of their lives in service to Dàxī in the stone quarries."

My heart drops, words utterly failing me. *Chunhua, Qing'er ...*

I struggle to my feet. A heavy hand falls on my shoulder to push me back down, but the chancellor shakes his head, gesturing for him to step back. The guard obeys.

I spit the blood from my mouth onto the platform, leaving red splatters on the wood, and look up at him. Seated so high above me, to remind me of my commoner status. How easily they can fabricate their lies.

"I want to speak with the princess," I call out, glad my voice holds steady.

The two officials behind him glance at each other and whisper, but Chancellor Zhou's face remains impassive. "What could you possibly have to say to her?"

"I have information for her ears only."

He dismisses me with a wave. "She has given me the authority to lead this proceeding, to judge you as we see fit. She is not interested in what you have to say."

My ears thunder with rage, as if the spirit of the Black Tiger is roaring inside me. I thought she could be trusted. I held her lover's beating heart in my hands and extracted her promise. A single favor. I believed myself a keen negotiator, but all I learned was my capability for cruelty.

Liars, thieves, traitors all. Everyone in this place. Including me.

"I am not the only one who touched the food in the kitchens," I argue, even though I am aware it would mean little to those who have already determined my guilt. "You should be searching for the real murderer."

Chancellor Zhou's lips draw into a thin, mirthless line. "Do you think I would be so foolish as to bring you to trial without evidence?"

A servant approaches and empties the contents of the sack he is carrying on the floor. But instead of the clothes I had stuffed it with when I attempted to leave the palace, out slides an assortment of jewelry and coins. Books on poison follow, from the restricted section of the library, the ones I had left behind in my room. And then ... the broken pieces of my mother's shénnóng-shī box. All the powders and herbs and dried flowers she so painstakingly collected ... ruined.

I let out a strangled cry and attempt to step forward, to salvage what I am able to, but the guard yanks me back.

"Keep her away from those ingredients," the chancellor warns as the strong arms of the guard restrains me. "Who knows what she could bring forth with her magic."

Returning to my trial, he continues with each piece of evidence, walling me in brick by brick. "Smuggling stolen treasures out of the palace. Books on poison. Have you no shame?"

I remember how Wenyi kept talking, even though no one listened as he was dragged away from the Hall of Eternal Light. He wanted to save Dàxī, to save Jia. I remember what Lian said about how the capital burned. The darkness within me rages—*Let them burn.*

But still, I continue to fight. For Shu.

I have to get myself out of this place and get back to her.

"If you've already questioned Steward Yang," I tell him, "then you'll know she wanted me to leave the capital immediately after I failed the final round. Someone told Fang Mingwen to keep me in the palace."

Chancellor Zhou looks incredulous that I am still speaking. "You—"

I raise my voice to speak over him. "The soldiers of Lùzhou are in the palace. They stand with the governor of Sù."

"You're mad!" he calls out, but he glances over his shoulder and assesses the worried expressions of the other officials. His gaze darts to the soldiers behind me, and even as he attempts to pull together the cracks in his mask, I realize too late what I should have seen all along.

He already knows.

I have not been paraded in front of the citizens of Jia and given the humiliation of a public trial. I thought it was because he wanted to make a quick example of me, but now I see his true goal: A corpse can no longer speak.

I yell, as loud as I am able, "Call for help! Traitors are in the palace! Traitors loyal to the Prince of Dài!"

"Silence her," the chancellor hisses.

"I want to speak to—"

A gloved hand covers my mouth, and I am jerked upward.

"Throw her into the dungeons," Chancellor Zhou proclaims. "She is sentenced to death by three hundred lashes, to be carried out at first light. The astronomers have consulted the stars and have seen that her blood will appease the gods. I hope the gods will be kind to her soul."

Spears are thrust in the air and the chorus of voices calls out, "Long live the memory of the emperor!"

As I'm dragged down the steps, I can't help the laughter that bubbles out of my throat.

An auspicious time for an execution. An auspicious time for murder.

Tomorrow I will die.

Chapter Forty-Four

The palace dungeons are underground, down a series of steps, enclosed by stone walls. The air is musty and damp, as if this place has not been in use for quite some time. Fleetingly, I remember the comment of the official who initially deemed me worthy of entering the palace, that those who were found to be impersonating shénnóng-tú were sent away. I had thought my worst fate was to be turned away from the palace, but now I know there are far worse things that await me.

The brazier on one side of the room is relit with the guard's sputtering torch. The cells are in the back—there are fewer of them than I expected. It's obvious that a few of the cells are being used for storage, and contain only cobwebs and broken pieces of furniture.

The chains are released from my arms and legs with a clatter, then I'm shoved into an empty cell. The door shuts behind me as I'm left rubbing the red lines on my skin, surveying my surroundings. There's a woven straw mat and a few questionable cushions in the corner, along with a pot for relieving myself. The guards return to their space around the corner, and I retreat to the far side of the cell, glad to be left alone.

After that first surge of hysterical laughter, my mind is now eerily calm.

My final night on this earth, leaving behind empty promises and too many mistakes.

I hear men's voices and the clinking of dice hitting a bowl. To the guards, I'm just someone who is passing through their lives for one brief moment, gone the next. I lean my head back against the wall and sigh.

"Ning?" I hear the rasp of a voice.

One I recognize.

"Wenyi!" I leap over to the bars that separate our cells. His body, which I had mistaken for a bundle of rags, lies crumpled in the corner.

He rouses himself to a half sitting position and I gasp, unable to contain my horror. He's been severely beaten to the point that his features are almost unrecognizable—except for his shorn head, a rarity in the capital. Half his face is purple and swollen. He tries to drag himself toward me but only manages to move forward a little before lying down again, wheezing. The blanket slides off his legs, and they are misshapen, broken so badly he will never walk properly again.

"What happened to you?" I whisper.

"They..." He swallows. "They threw me down here. Accused me of staging what I did in the final round as a protest, a slight against the empire's authority." Every few words are accompanied by a wheeze. I fear his lung may be punctured. He needs the swift attention of a physician, and instead they discarded him like trash.

"They tried... tried to see if I would turn against those who sent me. And then, when that failed, they beat me to find out who I was working for." He smiles, showing bloody, broken teeth. "I disappointed them."

"Who tortured you?" I ask.

"Men working for the chancellor," he says, closing his eyes.

I lean my forehead against the iron bars, letting the coldness sink into my skin, a painful point of focus. Of course it was the chancellor; he must be the one behind the scenes, feigning loyalty to the princess, while working against her alongside the Banished Prince.

"I heard him speaking about his plans, about the *general*. Admitting that he was the one who poisoned the emperor. I guess he figured I was not a risk any longer." Wenyi tries to laugh but ends up coughing instead. Blood blooms against his sleeve, leaving smears against the fabric.

His eyes glint in the dim light, catching my own. "The princess . . . You have to get word to her, a warning."

Wenyi fumbles in his clothes, pulling out two folded squares of paper. He crawls toward me again, this time reaching just far enough so they touch my fingertips. I tuck them carefully into the pouch in my sash, making sure they're secure.

"One letter is from my family. It outlines all the atrocities the General of Kǎiláng has committed in Lùzhou in order to gain power. My mother owns the teahouse in the town of Ràohé on the border between Lùzhou and Yún . . . the second letter is for her." He hesitates. "Let her know what happened to me . . . please?"

"I'll . . . I'll try to reach them. Teahouse. Town of Ràohé," I repeat back. "If you are the one who survives, I am Dr. Zhang's daughter, of Xīnyì village. Get word to my family that I am not a traitor."

Wenyi nods. "Dr. Zhang. Xīnyì village."

And then his expression changes to one of burning intensity. He clears his throat before asking, "Did you poison the court? I heard the guards say the marquis and the Esteemed Qian were among those who were killed."

My throat constricts. Even if the Esteemed Qian was an arrogant fool who had me thrown out of the competition, I would not have wished for him such a painful end.

"No," I respond wryly. "It is contrary to the art of Shénnóng and to the physician's path ... 'I do not stoop to poison.'"

Wenyi gives me a weak grin, recognizing his own words. "There are a few things I have to tell you," he continues, speaking through his pain, even though he must be in agony. I wish I had something to ease it even slightly. "I suspect that with Shao soon to be instated as the court shénnóng-shī, his loyalty will shift to support the chancellor. His family is too enmeshed in the court for him to risk going against Chancellor Zhou. Do not trust him.

"And beware of Hánxiá Academy," he warns me. "When I left Yěliŭ, it was rumored their loyalties were changing, that they were unhappy with the recent restrictions imposed by the emperor regarding their access to the tribute teas. But the monks at Yěliŭ may still assist you, if you bring them my letter and my name—"

I shake my head. "Don't say that. I will beg the princess to find you a physician. I will convince her to see you for herself. Same with your family, your hometown. You will see them again."

He stares at me for a long while, before giving me a small nod. "He tried to speak on my behalf ...," Wenyi murmurs quietly, almost as if to himself.

"Who?"

"The son of the Banished Prince," he says. "I thought I may have heard his voice ..."

His words trail off as his eyes flutter closed.

"Wenyi?" I whisper urgently. "Wenyi!"

I try to reach through the bars in order to touch him, but he's too far away. I stare at his body until I can see the rise and fall of his chest, to ensure that he is still breathing, before my fingers slowly let go of the bars.

I jerk awake, realizing I slipped into sleep. Exhaustion still tugs at my eyelids, trying to coax them shut, but the scent of something familiar tingles my nose.

The sound of dice and the guards' conversation has stilled. I strain to hear something, anything, but there is no sign of another presence in the next room. But then I notice, in the flickering light cast by the torches, that there is movement.

A long, dark shadow, cast along the wall. Coming closer.

My mind stills. Perhaps the chancellor has decided that leaving me alive even through to morning is too much of a risk. I grab the pot, the only thing I can use to defend myself, even as a foul smell emanates from the open spout.

The figure that steps into view is dressed in black, moving so fast I'm uncertain if perhaps I'm still dreaming. They smell of incense and burnt wood. The cell door opens, the lock dropping to the ground with a clatter. I retreat back, the pot still held in front of me. I wonder if I should swing at the body or dump the contents on the head.

The figure in black pauses, and fingers reach under the wooden mask, pulling it away. Dark eyes, long-lashed, stare back at me wearily. The scar down her throat, half-healed . . . the one I gave her.

Ruyi. Handmaiden to the princess, presumed dead. Standing before me, reeking of magic.

"I owe you my life," she says. "You can put that down. I mean you no harm."

I hesitate, then slowly place it at my feet.

"I was told you were dead." I thought it explained Zhen's absence tonight, thought she was lost to her grief. I don't believe in ghosts, but she stands here before me.

"She lied, sent me away to heal and make preparations." She steps forward, frowning. "But before we continue, I have to ask you this. Where do your loyalties lie?" Her hand rests on the hilt of her sword. A promise, and a threat.

I stare back at her. I suppose I could lie, say something pretty and useless that she wants to hear. But I've always been a terrible liar, and I'm tired of lying now.

"My loyalty rests with the ruler who will protect their people from harm," I tell her. "With someone who does not use human lives as pawns."

Ruyi stares back at me for a moment, then smirks, her hand dropping away from her sword. "She was right. You do not shy away from the truth. Even though you should have been dead ten times over by now, for some reason the stars shine upon you."

I would disagree, considering my current predicament. "Where is the princess?" I ask instead.

"Confined to her rooms," Ruyi says. "Chancellor Zhou says it's to keep her safe, but most likely it's to keep her unaware of your swift execution at dawn."

If Zhen is not on the side of the chancellor, then it means she is unprepared for what is coming.

"You have to get her out of the palace," I say urgently. "The soldiers from the Emerald Isles are inside the capital."

The magic ripples around her. "You saw this?"

"They came with the governor of Sù. He found me not long after the officials were poisoned."

"You have to come with me," Ruyi tells me, eyes brilliant even in the dark.

"I can't. You have to get him out." I shake my head and gesture to Wenyi's form in the other cell. "Get him help and then return for me later."

Ruyi's face twists, her annoyance apparent.

"We have no time for this," she snarls, but she turns on her heel and heads to the other cell, crouching before Wenyi's unconscious form. She puts her hand on his shoulder, and I wait for him to move, to recognize that I kept my promise.

But Ruyi narrows her eyes. Her fingers go to his neck, checking for a pulse.

She looks up and tells me everything I need to know with a gentle shake of her head.

I am too numb to scream, but I commit him to memory. Another name to add to the list, another innocent life lost to these courtly games.

Someday, I will avenge them all.

Chapter Forty-Five

I TRY TO EMPTY WHATEVER REMAINS IN MY STOMACH INTO that pot, but end up dry-retching instead. Ruyi returns to my side and places her hand on my shoulder, a reassuring presence. I can feel the magic thrumming off her, from the heat of her hand through even the layers of my tunic. She feels like she's vibrating from within, a string pulled too taut.

I stand up and press my hand to her forehead. She tries to flinch away, but I've already felt how her skin burns. Someone filled her with too much magic, and it's tearing her apart from the inside. There is something familiar, though, about that scent . . . and how the magic inside me acknowledges it in response.

"Lian sent you," I say, and she nods.

"Come with me. There's nothing left for you here." She offers me her cloak and I accept it, wrapping it around myself. I take one last look at Wenyi's body and mumble a phrase of the funeral rites, hoping a part of his soul will find its way back to Ràohé, and back to his family.

I try not to look at the bodies of the guards, the blood pooling beneath them. But still the twinge of guilt remains. More blood, more death. I brought Ruyi back to life, only to have her empty out the souls of others.

Whose life? Whose death?

I concentrate on putting one foot ahead of the other through the tunnels of the palace. The farther we walk, the heavier her weight leans on me, trying to keep herself upright. Deep in the twists and turns of the tunnels, we trudge on, but she stumbles more often than she should, and I know she doesn't have much time left.

She seems to know it herself, hurrying forward until we stop before another series of rings on the wall. She pulls them in a sequence, then a small door slides into view. We tumble back into a familiar residence, the Dowager Empress Wuyang gazing at us with reproach from the wall.

Princess Zhen leaps to her feet when she sees us stagger inside. She's dressed in plain clothes, prepared for travel.

"Everything is ready?" she asks, already at Ruyi's side.

Ruyi nods.

The princess touches her hand to her bodyguard's forehead, concern evident. "You're burning up," she scolds.

The way Ruyi looks back at her is too intimate, and I turn away, not wanting to intrude on their privacy. They exchange a few more words in low voices before Zhen calls me over.

"Can you do something for her? I'm not sure she can travel in this state."

"I'm fine." Ruyi brushes her away, but then struggles to right herself. "We should have just left."

"She saved your life. I made her a promise." Zhen's eyes meet mine. "I don't forget my debts."

I'm already rummaging in her drawers and shelves. "She's pushed it too far. I need something to expel the magic from her."

Zhen nods. "Anything you need. You'll find an assortment of tea leaves in there."

Sweeping aside the fabric and the papers, I pull out as many jars and pots as I am able to. I open each pot, sniffing what's contained within, returning what I do not need.

"Ning!" I turn to see Ruyi sway, Zhen struggling to hold her up. I quickly assist the princess in lowering her down to a chair. Ruyi groans and drags her hand across her mouth; it comes away smeared with blood.

It's disconcerting to see a fearless woman appear so uncertain, and with a pang in my chest, I think about Lian somewhere in the distance, anchoring the magic. I hope she's safe.

"What's wrong with her?" the princess demands.

"Lian's ability," I explain quickly, continuing to set up the ritual. "It always has a cost. It's dependent on the ability of the shénnóng-shi who casts it, as well as distance and duration. If the receiver pushes the limits too far, the magic turns on them, too."

"She ran a horse to death getting from Kallah to the palace after she regained enough strength to move . . ." Zhen smooths the hair around Ruyi's face. "She showed up right before the banquet. She wanted me to leave, but when I found out about the order for your execution, I asked her to get you."

I tell her of my discoveries while waiting for the tea to steep. About the governor and his companions from Lùzhou. The infiltration of the city guards. But Zhen's reaction is not as I expected. She looks resigned.

"It's sooner than I expected, but I knew they were coming. I knew the chancellor was involved when Ruyi was attacked while performing an investigation on my behalf, struck by the poisoned arrow. He was the only other person who was aware of her mission. I sent her away in order for him to think I was unprotected, easier to manipulate. Now is their time to strike, to finish what my uncle started."

I pour the tea, brewed strong, the fragrance wafting from the cup. Osmanthus flowers and tangerine peels, stiff with sugar, begin to soften in the water. When it is done, I tip it into Ruyi's mouth, and this time she takes it without hesitation. They trust me, even with all those accusations against me, and I am thankful for it.

The Shift happens easily now, strengthened by my previous contact and Ruyi's willingness. An echo of Lian's magic, contained within her, answers my own. As if trimming an unruly shrub, I take some of the magic into myself—transferring a fraction of that potent power into me, the speed and the strength, easing the burden on Ruyi's body.

Her eyes grow unfocused, but she breathes easier.

"Can you stand?" I ask her. She nods and gets to her feet unsteadily. "You're going to feel weak until you get a full night's rest. You cannot exert yourself again, not even to defend *her* life from an assassin." I tilt my head toward the princess, and Ruyi manages a small smile.

"The magic could burrow even deeper, somewhere I may not be able to reach," I add, but I doubt she will heed my warnings if Zhen's life is at stake.

"I'll help her." Zhen ducks under Ruyi's arm and holds up the taller girl, and I hook my elbow against her other arm to steady her on the opposite side.

The princess sweeps aside a silk hanging on the wall and presses the hidden panels until the mechanisms groan behind the wall. She lights a torch using the brazier and passes it to me to hold. We support Ruyi through the tunnels, making slow but steady progress. We make turn after turn, until Zhen holds up her hand, bringing us to a stop. On the other side of the wall, we hear movement—boots against the ground, metal brushing against metal as they march. I suspect they may be able to hear my heart beating so violently in my chest. But in time, their steps soon pass without cries of alarm, and we continue until we reach a doorway that leads to a grove of bamboo. The servants' quarters. I discard the torch into a rain barrel, not wanting the light to attract attention out in the open.

A cart waits for us at the gate, filled with large pots, a sleepy-looking donkey tied to it. Zhen heaves Ruyi onto the cart, and I pull myself up next to her. Sniffing the air, I smell wine.

A head pops out from under the blanket. I barely manage to stifle a surprised shriek, and even Zhen pulls a dagger and points it at the figure in the dark.

"It's me, it's me!" Qing'er whispers, waving his arm above his head.

I pull him to me in a crushing hug, refusing to acknowledge his protests. "How did the guards not find you?" I grab hold of him by the shoulders, surveying him from head to toe, to make sure he's not hurt in any way.

"Small Wu made me hide in the chicken coop and made a big ruckus to lead the guards away," Qing'er says, sniffling. "There was only enough room to hide me, no one else. I stayed very quiet and then ... I ran into Guard Hu.

"Grandmother always says I can trust Guard Hu," he states with the confidence of young children. "He told me to hide here, and the princess would come and find me. And now here you are." He tries to smile at Zhen but doesn't quite succeed.

I give the princess a look over his head, and she nods, confirming that Guard Hu is the one who made the arrangements for leaving the palace.

"You did very well," I tell him.

His lower lip quivers, and I can see he is trying his very best to hold himself together.

"Will Grandmother be safe?" he whispers.

Zhen steps closer and kneels until she is at his eye level. "We have to leave the palace right now. Your safety depends on it. But I promise I will make every effort to make sure your grandmother is safe as well."

"Thank you." Qing'er gulps, wiping away tears, trying to look as dignified as possible.

I squeeze him again, just to be sure he knows he is not alone.

We set off for the teahouse district, with only the clopping of the donkey's hooves to accompany us. The cart carries us past shuttered businesses and quiet residences. But even now, somewhere around the Hour of the Thief, the teahouses are still ablaze with light. Pulling into an alley, we tie the donkey up to a post behind Peony House and ascend the back stairwell. I know the four of us are a conspicuous group, and I cannot help but continually check over my shoulder.

Zhen knocks at a set of doors on the second level, and we are admitted to a private room. Looking around, I can see it's an understated but tastefully decorated receiving room. A man and a woman are the only occupants, and they bow to greet us.

The man is not much older than my father, with lines around his eyes, showing he has led a life full of smiles. The anxious-looking woman next to him, probably his wife, reminds me of the way Mother would hover around Father when she believed he was doing something unwise. With our ragged appearance, Ruyi appearing as if she is on the verge of collapse, I can see we are a reasonable cause for alarm.

Zhen quickly gestures for them to rise, dismissing the need for court niceties. Qing'er and I maneuver Ruyi to sit heavily on a stool. "Official Qiu," she acknowledges with a nod. "Madam Sun."

The official's attention swings to me. "And this is?"

"She will become my shénnóng-shī when I reclaim my court," Zhen says. Even though I know she may not have an empire to rule if everything unravels in the coming weeks, it shows me she still remembers her promise.

"I understand." He nods, then returns to the business at hand. "The person you have requested to meet is waiting for you in the next room."

"One more thing," Zhen says. "I know I have asked more of you than you are obliged to give, but our efforts have put this boy in danger. We have to move him away from the palace for his own safety. Can you place him under your protection?"

Qing'er looks up at Official Qiu, trying to maintain his composure—he manages, except for his quivering lower lip.

"Yes, of course!" The wife swats her husband's arm, not even waiting for his response. "We will take him. A child should always have a home. Come with me. Auntie will get you some treats."

She puts her hand on his shoulder, and Qing'er looks to me for permission. I give him a nod. Even though I wish I could keep him with me, I know there are more dangerous roads ahead.

"Go on," I encourage him. "I'll see you again."

He follows her, and I am happy that at least he will be well taken care of.

"Now if you will follow me." Official Qiu pulls aside the heavy tapestry, revealing a doorway. "We will speak to the astronomer."

CHAPTER FORTY-SIX

THE MAN WHO WAITS FOR US ON THE OTHER SIDE HAS A thin beard and is dressed in plain white robes. A white jade pendant swings from his sash when he stands and bows to us.

"Astronomer Wu." Zhen clasps his hands with warm familiarity, and he returns her greeting with a fond smile.

"Please, sit." He gestures to a round table, surrounded by stools.

I take my leave toward the next room to assist Ruyi, but the astronomer calls out to me. "You should hear this as well, Daughter of Shénnóng."

With hesitation, I perch myself on the edge of a stool, not sure why I have been asked to stay. The number of astronomers in the empire is fewer than the shénnóng-shī listed in the *Book of Tea*, but no one is certain how many are in their ranks. I never thought I would be permitted to be in the presence of one, much less attend one of their readings.

"I am thankful you made the effort to meet me at risk to yourself," Zhen says. "It will not be forgotten."

"You have a hard path ahead, child," Astronomer Wu says with great solemnity. "I'm not sure it will be a kindness for you to know what the stars have intended for you. I admit, I have considered encouraging you to walk an easier path."

Zhen scoffs at the thought. "I am a daughter of the Li family. I will not turn to the easier path just to save my own life."

"Although we are not like the shénnóng-shī, able to see the threads of a person's possible future from a single cup"—he spares me a glance—"we can see the courses of kingdoms and empires. We see the paths of multitudes, each life affecting another, and to pull out one star is impossible. But there are moments within the stream where the paths divert toward uncertainty. You stand at the precipice, one of a cluster that gleams in the midst of it all.

"There's a darkness coming for the empire. A darkness, rising from the heart of Dàxī."

With each word uttered, I can perceive the threads being unwound, stars coursing through the night sky. A different magic from the one I am used to, but magic all the same.

"How do we stop it?" Zhen leans forward then, intent on finding the answers.

"There is light from the north, but it can easily be smothered by the darkness." The words are cryptic, difficult to understand. "But your path will stop here if you do not leave the city tonight. The stars are clear enough: Stay in Jia, and you will be extinguished."

The princess rubs her temple with obvious frustration. "Where do I go? Where do the stars lead me?"

"The way is never clear," Astronomer Wu says apologetically, stroking his beard. "Individual destinies are too entwined with one another. A combination of hundreds, thousands of choices. We can only provide guidance, suggest the best course possible, and hope. Hope for the future of the empire. Hope for peace."

"And the guidance for me is to . . . leave. Leave my home. Leave my people behind." Zhen turns away, expression darkening. "Run."

She suddenly looks in my direction. "What would you do in my position, Ning? Would you stay and fight for what you have, even though you may fail? Or would you go?"

I consider the various interpretations of the astronomer's riddles, before offering my thoughts. "If you stay, your name will be recorded in the history books as a princess who fought for her throne and died. You told me your uncle is a master strategist, and you are currently unprepared. He waited for his opportunity; I would do the same. Regroup and return, when the time is right."

She ponders this for a moment, then nods.

Astronomer Wu seems satisfied by this, and for a moment I feel as if I am standing on the precipice of change he spoke of. The stars diverting, rearranging the course of the empire, with this one decision.

Shadows will follow.

Is Zhen the target of the darkness, or the origin?

"Will you do us the honor of pouring us tea?" Astronomer Wu asks me, pointing to the tea ware set out on a table to his right. The water is already warmed on a brazier, ready to pour.

The tea leaves smell like smoke and pine, especially pungent. The water releases even more flavors, a faint sweetness reminding me of longan flesh and earthy spice. A mind in turmoil brews bitter drink, so I permit myself to become lost in the process again.

I still mourn for my mother's beautiful redwood chest, and someday I will have the ability to re-create it, build a collection I can call my own. But in the meantime, I slip some tea leaves into the pouch in my sash, joining the other pieces I have collected these past days. I don't know what is waiting for us in the journey away from the capital, but I know I will inevitably have to reach for my magic on the road.

I bring the cups over to the table. With murmured thanks, they drink the tea, and I can feel the magic already sensing what they need most. Easing tension from their necks and shoulders, smoothing out the lines on their faces.

"Thank you." The astronomer sets his cup down with a sigh. "For you, I would suggest the opposite."

I stare at him, not understanding.

"You should stop running. Return to where it all began. You may find the answers you are looking for."

Before I can ask for clarification, there is a knock on the door. Official Qiu steps through, worry lines etched on his brow. "Pardon my interruption, but there are soldiers gathering in the teahouse below. I do not believe they are aware of your presence, Highness, but it is best you leave before someone recognizes you."

Zhen nods and stands to face Astronomer Wu, bowing deeply. "We are grateful for your guidance." He stands as well, acknowledging her in turn.

When we return to the other room, we are given uniforms. Changing behind the screen, we shed the clothing of the palace servants and pull on the soldiers' uniforms instead. I manage a sloppy imitation of a topknot.

"Your companion . . ." I overhear Official Qiu's wife speaking to Zhen. "I had her rest on the bed while you spoke with the esteemed astronomer. Do you want us to take her in as well? We can dress her in our maidservant's uniforms. She . . . does not seem well enough to travel."

Zhen pulls her hair tight and tucks the helmet under her arm. "No," she states brusquely. "She will be coming with us."

"Are you certain, Princess?" Official Qiu says. "You must move swiftly to the docks. The ferry will not wait."

Zhen turns on him, eyes flashing fire. "She is my family, and they tried to hurt me through her. I've tried to send her away for her own protection, and she crossed the entire empire to save me. I will never leave her again."

It is difficult to maneuver a barely responsive body down the stairs, but Zhen and I somehow manage to balance Ruyi between us and get her back into the cart. I pull the blanket over her while Zhen sees to the donkey, readying it for travel.

"You there!" a gruff voice sounds behind us.

I start, turning around, hastily making sure all of Ruyi is covered. A man steps out from the lit interior of the teahouse. A soldier. "What are you doing with that cart?"

I blurt out the first thing I can think of: "Grabbing another jar of wine like I was asked."

He frowns. "Wine?"

I pull one of the heavy jars from the back, taking the weight on my thighs. "Yes, we were sent on an errand to find more wine. Nothing but the best!"

I hope the jars from the palace are not marked in a unique manner or this entire ruse will collapse. He still regards me with suspicion, checking the label to be sure. My legs quiver as if they are made of water, ready to give out at any moment.

"Fine," he finally growls. He gestures to Zhen, who ducks her head, hiding her face in the shadows. "You there, grab another jar. We'll make sure our honored guest is served the best."

"Who is coming?" I whisper to Zhen, who carries the other jar next to me as we ascend the back steps.

She shakes her head and stares ahead. "I don't know. Let's set these down somewhere and take our leave."

We are led through the kitchens, where people run back and forth between towers of steaming baskets. A man wields two woks, tossing vegetables expertly over a roaring fire, while a boy squats beside him, feeding the flames.

We continue through to the dining area. There are dozens of bodies crowded into the main level of the teahouse, some in the black of the city guard, others in brown army uniforms.

"More wine!" the soldier who led us inside roars, throwing his arms around our shoulders.

The soldiers cheer. We are forced to take off our helmets so as not to appear inconspicuous. The possibility of us slipping away quietly lessens with each step. The heavy pots are taken from us, their seals broken swiftly. The wine is poured into round bowls, much of it spilling out the sides. Somewhere in the room, a group of men break into raucous song.

"There's more where it came from!" The soldier releases us, laughing. He tips the bowl into his mouth, dribbling wine down his chin.

"Cheers!" They raise their bowls toward us, and before we can protest, we're pulled to sit down on stools at a table. Zhen and I exchange uncomfortable looks but continue to play the part. The wine flows freely as the conversation grows louder and the jokes increasingly vulgar. One of the soldiers tells war stories to an attentive audience, while to our left, a drinking game involving rapid hand gestures and curses is in progress.

I hold a fake smile on my face as I speak to Zhen from the corner of my mouth. "What do we do?"

"Play along," Zhen says, and scoops up a bowl from the table, downing it in one gulp. The man next to her guffaws and slaps her on the back.

A city guard raises her bowl to the sky. "Things are changing, my friends! No more patrols. No more chasing after petty thieves. We'll soon be making a decent living!"

"I'll drink to that!" her companion shouts, and they guzzle down more wine.

Another soldier stands unsteadily, patchy stubble barely growing on his lip. "I'll make a name for myself!" He slams his foot onto a stool. "They'll call me the Conqueror!"

"You're drunk, you fool!" A soldier with a grizzled beard roars with laughter, throwing a cup at his head. The young soldier ducks, and the cup hits a man behind him. He turns and glares at our table, which erupts into uproarious laughter.

I feel it before I see it, a sudden shift in the air.

Around us, the soldiers pull themselves to attention. At first, it's the thud of a single fist on a table, then it's a steady rhythm, everyone pounding their fists in sync.

Zhen puts her hand on my arm, bracing herself. "No," she whispers, so close her breath brushes the back of my neck.

I turn to see a man with a commanding presence standing at the entrance to the teahouse.

"General!" someone calls out, and others echo the title with reverence.

He strides in as if the crowds are expected to part before him, as if he knows he will be obeyed.

I realize with horror who this must be.

The Banished Prince. The General of Kǎiláng.

Chapter Forty-Seven

WHEN HE TURNS HIS HEAD, I CAN SEE THE BLUE-BLACK pattern on his face. At the center is the word for exile. The tattoo is meant as an imperial punishment, for everyone to see your traitor's mark. But from that word, a defiant pattern emerges, lines curving around his brow and under the jaw. The guards beside him bear similar tattoos, and they wear them with pride, honored to be marked with the same art as their general.

"He will recognize me," Zhen whispers to me, gripping my arm, as everyone begins to applaud and call out their welcomes. "If he sees me, I'm dead."

We slide off our stools to stand with the rest of them. Behind me there is no clear path to the kitchens, the press of bodies too thick for us to slip away.

"Companions!" the general calls out. His voice is warm, resonant over the heads of the crowd. "Ten years ago, I was banished from the capital by my own kin. I have despaired at the fall of the Li name, at the struggles of the people. But now it is time for us, my true family, to return and restore Dàxī to its former glory!"

I am shocked at his impudence. He dares to walk into one of the most prominent teahouses in the capital, showing his face in the city streets without concern.

The astronomer was right. Darkness is descending.

Something cold touches my arm, and I look down to see that Zhen has drawn a dagger, the flat blade pressing against my skin.

"Stop," I hiss at her, while the general begins to make his way through his soldiers, greeting many of them by name. With sinking dread, I realize he is pouring each person a drink, adding something from the flask at his side. The stories always said he commanded the loyalties of his battalions easily, and it's apparent in how he treats his soldiers with respect and acknowledgment.

"You can't possibly think you would be able to walk out of here alive if you try to kill him," I whisper to Zhen, placing my hand over the blade.

"He's the one who orchestrated my father's poisoning," she snarls. "I will watch him bleed with my knife in his chest."

I for one, want to live. I want to find the antidote for my sister. I want to see the plateaus of Kallah with Lian. I want to stand on the peaks of Heaven's Gate and peer into a different kingdom.

The general is getting closer, and I reach for the only thing I have: my magic. I pull the pouch from my sash. With a twist of my hand I drop my bowl on the table, spilling most of my drink. I pick up the neglected pot of tea, and it's still half-full. Not many are interested in tea with the wine so abundant. Better for me.

I break the pieces of tangerine peel and also use my fingernail to grate slivers of golden root into the tea. The general is twenty paces away, and fast approaching. I thrust my elbow into Zhen's side, forcing her to lower the knife. I pour half my bowl of tea into hers, placing my hand around her own. The bowls begin to warm under my hands, and Zhen jumps beside me, assuring me she feels it as well.

"Follow. My. Lead," I tell her through clenched teeth, praying she will obey.

The general stands in front of us. I stare down at my hands.

"Friends." He nods, pouring something from a flask into our bowls. A sprinkling of unfamiliar fine powder. I do not know what it is, if it will interfere with my magic, but there is no other choice.

We drink.

I taste the powder first, gliding against my tongue. There's a nuttiness to it, quickly washed away by the flavor of the tea. The magic flares to life, pulsing strongly inside me, more powerful than I have ever experienced. I think about animals, crouched behind leaves. I think about mist, obscuring our features. *We look familiar, but no one you can name.*

"You . . ." The general's eyes narrow; his attention is drawn to Zhen's face. "I recognize you."

"We are honored to meet you," I say, the magic changing my voice, lowering the tone. I sound ten years older. Pressing my arm against Zhen's body, I can feel the magic humming through us. Changing our features, forming the ones he wants to see.

The General of Kǎiláng meets my eyes, and I can see myself reflected in them. A girl. A woman. Terrified. Calm. The liquid in my bowl begins to move, although the general does not notice. It winds itself into the figure of a three-headed snake, rippling on the surface. Ghostly whispers join the hideous omen. I struggle to compose my face, to hold my head still and not look for the source of the noise.

"May the sea be willing." I manage to force out the words of Kang's blessing, even as the whispers grow louder, and my unease deepens. Something whistles in the distance. A long, malevolent note.

The general blinks. My reflection disappears from his eyes, and he smiles. "May the sea be willing," he echoes, and turns away.

I almost collapse onto my stool as the drunken revelry around us resumes. A man stumbles into me, a vial of the same powder the general had given us rolling out of his pocket. It comes to a stop near my foot. I pick it up, noticing the gray tinge. This must be the pearl powder Kang spoke of, revered among his people.

"Wine? More wine?" someone else calls out.

"We'll get more." Zhen stands, the magic still changing her voice so that she sounds like a hardened soldier. Her features waver, the illusion melding to her face. I pray that it holds long enough for us to leave, and I shove the vial into the pouch with my other things.

We pass through the heat of the kitchens, and I gulp in the cold night air when we exit the back door; I know how narrowly we've just escaped death.

"We have to get to the ferry," Zhen says, maintaining her composure much better than me. "There's no more time. Our transport will leave at the Hour of the Rooster."

"Help me sit her up." While Zhen pulls Ruyi to a seated position, I pop the seal from one of the wine jugs and splash the wine over her still body. Before the princess can protest, I reassure her: "We'll pretend to be drunkards."

Taking hold of her, we stagger toward the port, moving as quickly as we dare. Emerging from the market district, we pass a procession of palace guards on horseback. At the center, a young man sits astride his horse, posture tall and clad in armor that is a striking pattern of black and gold. When we walk by, I cannot help but lift my head to look at him, only to see him watching me in return.

No ... It couldn't be ...

I quickly drop my head. I recognize those eyes, that mouth. The son of the Banished Prince, soon to be reunited with his father.

We are so close, and Kang could easily rouse the attention of his guards, send them chasing after us.

I can feel his gaze, burning through the back of my head. But no hoofbeats follow us to the pier, and no one else stops three soldiers, stinking of wine, slurring nonsense.

We arrive at the boat just as the criers call out the Hour of the Rooster, and after flashing Official Qiu's seal, the captain allows us to board.

"We'll set off at once," Zhen instructs. "Move south along the Jade River, until given other directions."

The captain nods, and soon after we set sail away from the port. Away from Jia.

Away from Kang.

CHAPTER FORTY-EIGHT

WE'RE SHOWN TO OUR QUARTERS ON THE LOWER LEVEL OF the ship, and we heave Ruyi onto the narrow bed. Zhen sinks to the bench, all the strength gone from her.

"Where do we go?" she whispers. "What do I do?"

She looks less like a princess and more like a scared girl. Not much older than me. I'd forgotten she's only nineteen.

Sitting down as well, I try to find encouraging words to speak to her, but find none. All I have to offer is more bad news, more warnings. In our haste to leave the city, I had one remaining piece of information I realize now I have yet to pass on to her, and I hope at least it will help her retain her focus.

"I spoke with Wenyi in the dungeons," I inform her, pulling out the pouch from my sash. "He said Yěliǔ is still loyal to the emperor, but Hánxiá may have gone to the rebellion."

I place the items on the small table between us. The vial. Shu's embroidery. Father's letter. Mother's knot. A few petals of osmanthus and strands of tea leaves. I pick up the two squares of paper from Wenyi and unfold one of them. Quickly reading the words, I confirm that this is the letter with reference to the disappearances Wenyi spoke of, and pass it to her.

"Wenyi? Why did you not bring him with you?" Zhen reads the

words with renewed interest. "He could have been a benefit to our cause."

"I'm sure he would have liked to be able to tell you himself, but he... passed in the night."

Zhen glances at me, expression softening. "You have risked it all, Ning, and for that, I am grateful."

While she reads, I pick up Shu's embroidery again, running my finger over the stitches. The beauty of the peony reminds me of the teahouse we escaped from, and also that entertainer who assisted me in the second round of the competition. I never managed to get her name. The moon represents me, I am certain, her love stitched into this fabric.

"We must go to Yěliǔ," Zhen says to me, worry drawing down the corners of her eyes, after taking in what was revealed in Wenyi's letter. "If we speak to the monks there, they may provide more information on what Wenyi has shared with us. If what he says is true, then the poison must have originated from Hánxiá."

I still have more questions than answers, but Zhen instructs me to get some rest instead. She lies down next to Ruyi, while I curl up on the bench. The candle sputters next to me and casts long, leaping shadows on the wall as restless thoughts run through my mind.

My heart is torn, knowing the decision I must make tomorrow, when the ship will continue south, then turn west at Nánjiāng. We will be passing through Sù, and close to my village.

Do I follow the princess, knowing the brilliant minds at Yěliǔ may have the answers that will lead me to the antidote? Or do I listen to my father's pleas and return home?

The chancellor had said he was certain a shénnóng-shī was the culprit behind the tea bricks, but was that a lie? And how did he get the magic arrow that poisoned Ruyi? I saw the three-headed snake again when I shared the tea with the general. What is Shénnóng trying to tell me? If the poison is from Hánxiá, then why would a component of the poison be seaweed from Lùzhou?

Sleep continues to elude me, and I sit up again, quietly growling in frustration. I look down at my hand, realizing I've crumpled Shu's embroidery in my fist, holding it close to my heart like a talisman. Smoothing out the fabric, my eyes catch on the peculiar color of the grass again. Rippling strangely, as if . . . moving in water. Then the spots on the stunted branches of the trees. Holes.

Not trees . . . Coral.

I recognize it now. Seaweed. The moon reflected. The poem. I've been looking at it all wrong. The moon is in the water. This is not my sister, reminding me of home. She knew Father would not allow her to continue her experiments for the antidote, so she sent me an outline of her discoveries.

This is a recipe.

Sweeping the scrolls off the small table, I find ink and paper, and I begin to write.

I wake to quiet voices, my face resting against my notes on the table. I wipe the drool from the corner of my mouth with my sleeve as the words swim in front of my eyes.

As sleep retreats, panic sets in, shooting through me as I hurry to the porthole, clutching the paper to my chest, afraid we have traveled too far. I see the busy port where we are currently docked. I've slept all day while we traveled down the river. The tower in the distance, brilliantly lit against the night, is one I recognize: Nánjiāng. I feel something sag inside me with relief, and I steady myself against the wall. It's not too late.

"Ning?" I turn to see Zhen and Ruyi looking at me with worry.

I show them everything I've found. Shu's discoveries, and how I believe I may be in possession of the missing piece of the antidote. They look at each other, silent communication passing between them, then Zhen turns to me with a nod. "We will help you in any way we are able."

I had thought Zhen would insist upon traveling to Yěliŭ first, in order to act on the knowledge from Wenyi's letter, or Ruyi would be the one to doubt my abilities, but they continue to surprise me.

"Thank you," I tell them, voice hoarse with emotion.

I'm returning to Sù. I'm ready to go home.

On the road back home, I ponder the strangeness of the direction my life has taken. Sitting astride a horse behind the fearsome Shadow, who I thought was my enemy, following a princess who may soon be heir to nothing.

My agitation grows as we approach the village. What waits for me at home terrifies me more than waiting for my death in the dungeons. I must reach Shu before it's too late, and the antidote must work against the poison. I cannot imagine any other possibility.

We take the road around the village, avoiding as many people as possible. I leave Zhen and Ruyi in my mother's grove of pomelo trees, knowing her spirit will protect them.

Picking up my skirts, I run down the familiar road, climbing up Philosopher's Hill, the moon lighting my way home. As I cut through the tea garden, the trees welcome me. Hearing them now, I know it's not my childish imagination.

Hurry, hurry. Their whispers chase me down the next hill, until I see the rise of our roof. My hand clenches tightly around the curve of the vial containing the pearl powder.

The door flies open beneath my hand, thudding against the table. My footsteps thunder through our front room. I brush aside the bead curtain to see Father looking up from dabbing Shu's face with a damp cloth, and my breath catches. It's just enough hesitation to see the emotions that flit across my father's face—relief, sadness, regret.

In the pale moonlight trailing through our windows, my father looks much older than when I left him. Haggard lines are worn deep into the crevices of his face. He looks worse than after we buried Mother, as if he hasn't slept since I've been gone.

"Ning?" he asks, and his voice is as rough as his appearance. "Are you a ghost?"

I kneel at his side, taking Shu's hand in mine. Her head is turned away from me, but she seems to sense I am near. She turns to face me, eyes glassy and unseeing.

"Mother?" she rasps out. I can smell the sickness on her breath. Her lips are cracked and bleeding.

"It's me," I tell her. "It's Ning. I've come back."

"Mother." She begins to cry. "You're back... I missed you so much."

I look up at Father, alarmed. "How long has she been like this?"

"A few days now," he says, shaking his head. "On and off. I try to get the fever down, but it returns. There have been a few nights I've found her wandering outside. I've had to tie her down, to keep her from leaving..." He chokes back a sob.

That's when I look at her wrists and see the red marks there. A swell of anger rises inside me, then I notice his red-rimmed eyes, the stains on his tunic from blood, vomit, and who knows what else.

I force myself to channel my fury at the poison. My father did not cause this, and all the angry words in the world will not bring my mother back. But I might yet be able to save my sister.

"I think I have the antidote," I say to him. "I can purge the poison from her."

"Tell me." He grips my arm, some clarity returning to his gaze. "Tell me what to do. I will help you." He doesn't question me like he usually does. He stands, awaiting instruction.

"I need lí lú and licorice root," I tell him. "As well as Mother's spring tea leaves." I know we have tea leaves from more recent harvests, but there is nothing that would compare to the leaves she prepped with her own hands.

My tea ware still remains on the shelf in the main room, covered in a layer of dust. Returning back to our room, I look around our home with new eyes. Compared to the luxuries of the palace, the surroundings are worn and tired. No delicately carved screens, no incense emanating from braziers that can be lit day and night.

But the woven knot I made for luck still dangles by the window, bleached pale from the sun. There's the crack in our mirror, from the time Shu and I were chasing each other and I fell against it, knocking it over. The worn pattern on the doorway where the bead curtain rubs against the frame, the one Shu always imagined looked like a dragon, calling it our door guardian. Something squeezes in my chest.

A hand sweeps the bead curtain aside again as my father steps in, bringing over everything I've asked for from the storeroom.

I touch my own tools. The bamboo, the wood, the pot with my fingerprints on the curve and the misshapen lid that never quite fit right. But it's all mine. This is where I'm from. I had to come back before I could move forward, the astronomer said.

I place the ingredients into the bowl. *The moon reflected in the sea.* Each component of the poison has its own mirror in the antidote.

Dried lí lú, thin strands, smelling of soil. Slowing down the heart, opposing the invigorating properties of the white peony root, weakening the grip of the poison.

Licorice, sliced into thin pieces. Mitigating the toxicity of the yellow kūnbù.

Pearl powder, the missing component. Shu had thought it was coral, balancing and stabilizing the antidote, difficult to obtain so far inland. But it was something even more rare and unexpected. For the pearls have fallen out of favor, and the General of Kǎiláng designed a poison that would not harm his own people. I tasted it in the shared cup, recognized its power in strengthening hidden magics.

Allowing it to steep, I turn instead to the tea leaves brewing, lifting the lid off the pot. It smells like spring, like sprouts emerging from the soil, reaching for the next sprinkle of rain. I pour it over the medicinal ingredients. When I bring the bowl to my lips, I can almost feel the brush of white wings against my cheek.

The soothing warmth runs down my throat, spreads through my entire body.

The Shift comes easily, without need of the dān, even while Shu is lost in her dreaming. Because she is my sister—I was there on the day she was born, our connection built upon our intertwined lives. I can see her these past few weeks, poring over Father's books, with her chin cradled in her hand. Pulling herbs from the garden in secret, watching for me and Father to appear over the hill. Furtive scribblings on slips of paper, shoved into a drawer or tucked underneath a basket. *Not jasmine, not ginseng. The poison does not respond to bleeding…*

But she found something that resonated with the small bit of lí lú she ingested, and she suspected the white peony root to be the culprit. There was no way of getting word to me without Father becoming suspicious, so she stitched the hidden message into the embroidery.

The poison made her confused, made it difficult to focus. She saw strange images sometimes, heard whispers in an empty room. Figures emerged from the mist, dreams crossing into reality: birds with human legs, butterflies with blinking eyes on their wings. A giant serpent with golden scales, hissing her name.

The pearl powder courses through my body like lightning, sending me through her memories and into the present, where I find her wandering through a grove of trees.

"Shu!" I call, but she does not seem to hear me. I follow her into the mist, running after her through the forest, like I've done so many times before. The trees are shadows, rustling beside us as I give chase.

She stops at the bottom of our favorite tree and turns back, beckoning me to come closer. She's already climbing when I reach her, ascending quickly. We used to play this game as children, daring the other to climb higher. I can see her feet dangling above me.

Shu waves. "I'm up here!"

My hands touch the bark. It feels real against my palms. I start to climb, finding the next branch, pulling myself higher and higher. But still she remains one step ahead, just out of reach. I know, with an awareness of the goddess whispering to me, that if she breaks through the canopy, she will be lost to me forever. I climb faster.

I hear a whistle, like the winds of an approaching storm. That discordant, piercing note I heard when I saw myself reflected in the eyes of a general.

Above us, a dark shadow descends. As it comes closer, it draws itself together into a dark, undulating form. A serpent with a long, forked tongue and fangs curving from the corner of its mouth. The red points of its eyes bleed hunger.

Shu perches on a branch to my right, frozen in fear before this creature that has haunted her since I left.

I should have been here to protect her.

Branches and leaves fall around us like rain.

I feel the brush of the serpent's hunger against my mind, like that of the three-headed snake I tore out of Ruyi. It looms overhead, red eyes appearing like polished orbs; I can see my reflection within them. It sees me and wonders what I am.

You..., it hisses in recognition. It does not speak aloud, but instead its voice rings through my head. *I've seen you before. In the palace.* Every word it utters is like a sharp pinprick of ice, driving itself into my skull.

But when it speaks, it gives me glimpses of what *it* is as well. It attached a piece of itself to the arrow that pierced Ruyi's side, creating the three-headed monster that feasted on her essence.

I see the answers to the questions I've been asking all along—why the poison was undetectable even by the most experienced shénnóng-shī, why the royal physicians could not find the antidote.

It's because this poison was created by something else entirely. Something ancient and waiting, biding its time.

Shénnóng..., it snarls, revealing its sharp fangs. It hates Shénnóng and all his followers. It despises the old gods and all humankind, everything they represent.

It lunges toward Shu, wanting to swallow her whole, to satisfy the hunger it feels after she eluded it time and time again.

I don't hesitate. I throw myself in the serpent's path. Its fangs sink into my skin, and I scream.

"Ning!" Shu cries out, and catches my hand. Our fingers reach each other, take hold, and she pulls me toward her. My arm is wrenched out of the grasp of the serpent, and we fall through the tree, the branches snapping under our weight, whipping and lashing at our exposed skin. I hang on to her tightly, protecting her with my own body.

The serpent slithers down the tree, following.

I close my eyes, both of us tensing, waiting for the inevitable impact . . . and return to my own body, my face wet with tears.

"Ning?" Shu struggles to sit up. Beside us, our father cries, too, sobbing like I've never seen him before.

I hurry to her bedside, holding the bowl up to her lips. She drinks it with eyes still on me, disbelieving.

"I dreamed . . . ," she says with awe. "I dreamed you came to find me."

I smile through my tears. "I promised you I would come back, didn't I?"

There's a shadow enveloping Dàxī, and a princess waiting for me in a grove of pomelo trees. But in this moment, nothing else matters. My sister is alive.

Then Father is suddenly there, holding my arm up.

Two trails of blood mark where my skin was broken by the serpent's fangs. Black tendrils slither across my skin like poisonous, choking vines.

The bowl slips out of my hand and lands on the floor with a clatter.

Shu's face is the last thing I remember as the darkness sweeps me away.

ACKNOWLEDGMENTS

As I CONTINUE ON MY WRITING JOURNEY, THERE ARE MANY people I have to send my appreciation and thanks for helping me reach this point.

Thank you to my editor, Emily Settle. For your insightful edits and your help with finding the heart of my story. This book wouldn't have become the story I wanted to tell without your guidance.

Thank you to my copyeditor, Valerie Shea, and production editors, Kathy Wielgosz and Avia Perez, for your attention to detail and for dealing with my waffling regarding tone marks.

Thank you to the rest of the Feiwel and Friends team for believing in this book and assisting with its publication. Many thanks as well to the marketing and publicity team for championing *A Magic Steeped in Poison*: Gabriella Salpeter, Leigh Ann Higgins, Morgan Rath, and Cynthia Lliguichuzhca. Thank you also to my Canadian publicist, Fernanda Viveiros.

Thank you to my cover designer, Rich Deas, and cover artist, Sija Hong, for bringing Ning to life so beautifully.

Thank you to my agent, Rachel Brooks, who never gave up on me and is endlessly patient with all of my random thoughts and emails. For always being available and enthusiastic about my work.

To the 2016 Pitch Wars mentee group, thanks for your continued support, especially my dear friends Suzanne Park, Rebecca Schaeffer, and Sasha Nanua. I'm excited for all of your books and your upcoming projects. Thank you to my mentors Axie Oh and Janella Angeles, who introduced me to the writing community and provided me with so much guidance in navigating the publishing world.

To Nafiza Azad and Roselle Lim, I'm so happy that we connected. I very much appreciate the safe space for our candid talks and our shared love of good food.

Many thanks to the authors who paved the way before me. Seeing your books on the bookstore shelves made me believe it was possible to write my own Asian/Chinese-inspired fantasy: Cindy Pon, Julie C. Dao, Ellen Oh, and Joan He.

To Kat Cho and Deeba Zargarpur, thanks for your early reads and your support of my writing. Many thanks to Zhui Ning Chang for your thoughtful feedback.

Thank you to my sister, Mimi Lin, who read my beginning drafts and put up with my late-night texts and cheered me on.

Finally, thank you to my husband and partner, Aaron, for your continued encouragement and love.

GLOSSARY

Term	Chinese	Pronunciation	Meaning
dān	丹	dān	Medicine contained in pill or powder form, usually associated with enhancement of magical properties
jīncán	金蠶	jīn cán	A gold silkworm pupa developed from venomous creatures, resulting in potent poison
Piya	埤雅	pí yǎ	A poisonfeather bird referenced in mythology
shénnóng-shī	神農師	shén nóng shī	Master of Shénnóng magic
shénnóng-tú	神農徒	shén nóng tú	Apprentice of Shénnóng magic

Character Name Pronunciation Guide

Name	Chinese Name	Pronunciation
A'bing	阿炳	Ā Bǐng
Chen Shao	陳邵	Chén Shào
Fang Mingwen	方明雯	Fāng Míng Wén
Gao Ruyi	高如意	Gāo Rú Yì
Hu Chengzhi	胡承志	Hú Chéng Zhì
Li Ying-Zhen	李瑩貞	Lǐ Yíng Zhēn
Li (Xu) Kang	李(許)康	Lǐ (Xǔ) Kāng
Lin Wenyi	林文義	Lin Wén Yì
Liu Guoming	劉國銘	Liú Guó Míng
Luo Lian	羅蓮	Ľuó Lián
Qing'er	青兒	Qīng ér
Small Wu	小吳	Xiǎo Wú
Wu Yiting	吳依霆	Wú Yī Tíng
Yang Rouzi (Steward Yang)	楊柔紫	Yáng Róu Zǐ
Zhang Ning	張寧	Zhāng Níng
Zhang Shu	張舒	Zhāng Shū

Place Names of Note

Place Name	Chinese Name	Pronunciation	Location
Ānhé (Province)	安和(省)	an hé (shěng)	Southeastern agricultural and coastal province
Dàxī	大熙	dà xī	The Great and Brilliant Empire
Hánxiá (Academy)	函霞(寺)	hán xiá (sì)	Academy dedicated to the Blue Carp (studies of agriculture, animal husbandry, and tea)
Huá (Prefecture)	華(州)	huá (zhōu)	Prefecture to the west of the capital city
Jia (City)	佳(都)	Jiā (dū)	The capital city
Kallah (Province)	佧垃(省)	kǎ lā (shěng)	Northwestern grassland province
Língyǎ (Monastery)	陵雅(寺)	líng yǎ (sì)	Monastery, tomb of former emperors. Located within Jia.
Lùzhou (Prefecture)	綠(洲)	lù (zhōu)	Northeastern prefecture composed of a peninsula and a group of islands, also known as the Emerald Isles
Nánjiāng (Town)	南江(鎮)	nán jiāng (zhèn)	Town on southern bend of Jade River

Sù (Province)	溯(省)	sù (shěng)	Southwestern agricultural province
Wǔlín (Academy)	武林(寺)	wǔ lín (sì)	Academy dedicated to the Black Tiger (studies of military strategy and martial arts)
Xīnyì (Village)	辛藝(村)	xīn yì (cūn)	Ning's home village
Yěliǔ (Academy)	野柳(寺)	yě liǔ (sì)	Academy dedicated to the Emerald Tortoise (studies of justice and rites)
Yún (Province)	雲(省)	yún (shěng)	Northern mountainous province

Chinese Medicinal Ingredients Mentioned (Listed Alphabetically)

Name of Ingredient	Chinese Name	Chinese Pronunciation	Scientific or Common Name
asarum	細辛	xì xīn	Root of *Asarum sieboldii* (wild ginger)
benzoin	安息香	ān xí xiāng	A resin obtained from bark and used as incense and perfume
crow's head	烏頭	wū tóu	Root of *Aconitum carmichaelii*

dānggūi	當歸	dāng gūi	Root of *Angelica sinensis*
fù pén zǐ	覆盆子	fù pén zǐ	Leaf of *Rubus idaeus* (raspberry)
golden root	紅景天	hóng jǐng tiān	Root of *Rhodiola rosea* (also known as roseroot)
huáng qí	黃耆	huáng qí	Root of *Astragalus propinquus*
hú huáng lián	胡黃連	hú huáng lián	Root of *Picrorhiza scrophulariiflora*
kūnbù	昆布	kūn bù	Seaweed
licorice root	甘草	gān cǎo	Root of *Glycyrrhiza uralensis*
lí lú	藜蘆	lí lú	Root of *Veratrum nigrum*
mugwort	艾草	ài cǎo	Leaf of *Artemisia argyi*
pearl powder	珍珠粉	zhēn zhū fěn	Ground from pearl or shell of *Pteria martensii* (oyster)
purple and crimson mushroom	紫/赤芝	zǐ/chì zhī	Various fungi of the *Ganoderma* genus, such as *Ganoderma sinense* and *Ganoderma lingzhi*

silk flower tree	絨花樹	róng huā shù	Bark of *Albizia julibrissin*
tea leaves / camellia flower	茶葉/花	chá yè/huā	Leaves and flowers of the *Camellia sinensis* tree
umbrella tree	傘樹	sǎn shù	Bark of *Schefflera actinophylla*
white peony root	白芍	bái sháo	Root of *Paeonia sterniana*
yù jīn	郁金	yù jīn	Root of *Curcuma aromatica* (turmeric tuber)

Author's Note

Chinese medicinal ingredients used in this book are inspired by traditional Chinese medicine in both modern and ancient texts. I have taken liberties with the use of these ingredients for the story, and there are no links with the current practices of TCM practitioners today.

The philosopher's question (人之初, rén zhī chū) is the beginning of the *Three Character Classic* (三字經), a classic Chinese text from the Song dynasty. The subsequent answer in the actual *Three Character Classic* is that people are born fundamentally good, but in the Dàyī empire it is a question instead.

The lines written in Shu's embroidery were penned by the poet 賈島 (Jiǎ Dǎo, 779–843), a Tang dynasty poet. The full poem is as follows:

> 海底有明月，圓於天上輪。
> 得之一寸光，可買千里春。
> A bright moon mirrored in the sea,
> as round as the wheel in the sky.
> Capture that bit of light,
> to afford eternal spring.

Thank you for reading this Feiwel & Friends book. The friends
who made *A Magic Steeped in Poison* possible are:

Jean Feiwel, Publisher

Liz Szabla, Associate Publisher

Rich Deas, Senior Creative Director

Holly West, Senior Editor

Anna Roberto, Senior Editor

Kat Brzozowski, Senior Editor

Dawn Ryan, Executive Managing Editor

Kim Waymer, Senior Production Manager

Emily Settle, Associate Editor

Erin Siu, Associate Editor

Foyinsi Adegbonmire, Associate Editor

Rachel Diebel, Assistant Editor

Kathy Wielgosz, Production Editor

Avia Perez, Production Editor

Follow us on Facebook or visit us online at mackids.com.
Our books are friends for life.

THE STORY CONTINUES…

A VENOM DARK AND SWEET

COMING AUGUST 2022

31901067963431